IN THE CLOSET, UNDER THE BED

Lee Thomas

Smith Point, New York
2009
www.DarkScribePress.com

ADDITIONAL BOOKS BY LEE THOMAS:

Stained
Damage
Parish Damned
The Dust of Wonderland

Printed in the United States of America
First Dark Scribe Press Printing, December 2009
ISBN-13: 978-0981863214
ISBN-10: 0981863213

ADVANCE PRAISE FOR
IN THE CLOSET, UNDER THE BED...

"From lyrical to poignant to funny to beautifully grotesque and back again, this smart, gleefully original collection showcases Lee Thomas' Herculean talent. What I love most though, is that Thomas gets the purpose of horror: to cast light on the darkness, so that we readers recognize what is good, what is obscene, and what our society has confused between the two."
– Sarah Langan, Award-Winning Author of *The Missing* and *Audrey's Door*

"Lee Thomas' stories always start as a come-on, with silky smooth prose that draws you into a comfortable world so effortlessly you fail to see the razor-sharp teeth before it's too late. This is horror at its best, guaranteed to leave you with the shivers, whether you wanted them or not."
– David Wellington, author of *Monster Island* and *23 Hours*

"There are plenty of truly frightening and horrific moments in *In the Closet, Under the Bed*, but these stories go beyond the scare. Lee Thomas explores sexual and personal identity; the everyday confusions and complications of being human. His stories are always emotionally authentic, and the answers to the questions he poses never come easy. This is smart, contemporary horror with a compelling conscience."
– Paul G. Tremblay, author of *The Little Sleep*

"With this superlative collection of stories, Lee Thomas cements his reputation as one of the most powerful and most original voices in horror fiction today. If you're not reading Thomas, you're missing out on a bold and unparalleled experience."
– Nicholas Kaufmann, Bram Stoker Award-nominated author of *General Slocum's Gold* and *Chasing the Dragon*

"Like every master craftsman of horror, Lee Thomas is weirdly inventive, with an arsenal of tricks and techniques up his sleeves and a universe of creatures, ghouls, ghosts, spirits, and body shifters to unleash on his characters, and readers of his new collection of short stories, *In the Closet, Under the Bed* will reap the rewards of this explosively talented writer. These stories are monstrous and thrilling and sexy and disturbing. But what makes them truly remarkable and fantastic is their distinctive milieu — gay men battling supernatural forces with dizzying results. Lee Thomas is not only defining the genre of 'queer horror' with his new collection, he is setting its gold standard."

— Jameson Currier, author of *The Haunted Heart and Other Tales*

"Lee Thomas brings to the writing of queer horror fiction a versatile sense of genre and a fierce emotional agenda. Here is a man with issues, as well as back issues. This intense and dynamic collection includes dark psychological narratives, grim physical horror, visionary fantasy, crime and science fiction. You will find fifteen stories in which the multicolored threads of horror and queer sexuality are woven together – but which are, first and foremost, stories about human nature."

— Joel Lane, British Fantasy Award-winning author of *The Lost District* and *The Terrible Changes*

MORE PRAISE FOR LEE THOMAS...

"Offers further promise that Thomas could emerge as a leading voice in modern horror fiction." – *Publishers Weekly* on *The Dust of Wonderland*

"A worthy successor to Clive Barker, Lee Thomas has a firm grasp of both the epic and intimate aspects of horror fiction. Simultaneously touching and scary, emotionally real and grotesquely fantastic, *The Dust of Wonderland* is a wonder." – Bentley Little, author of *The Academy*

"The prose is vivid, the pacing right on the money and I was guessing straight on through to the end. Ready and waiting for the next one, Mr. Thomas!" – Jack Ketchum, author of *Old Flames* and *Off Season* on *Stained*

"Thomas' rich prose harkens back to the moodier works of Straub's *Shadowland* or King's *Dolores Claiborne* ... In *The Dust of Wonderland*, Thomas explores that totality of the human experience like a master painter, first with broad strokes to color the palate then with a fine-point brush to bring forth the depth and detail." – *Dark Scribe Magazine*

"*Stained* begins where most novels end, with an act so terrible it will make your skin crawl. A master of the 'New Southern Gothic' Lee Thomas shows that there are things lurking beneath the surface of us all that are better left alone." – P. D. Cacek, author of *Canyons*

"Almost certainly the most compelling book I've read in the past year, with an engaging story, characters that are what characters are all about, and a handful of very creepy scenes... Thomas is a dynamic storyteller, putting all the dramatic elements in place right from page one... A novel well worth seeking out." – Stephen Mark Rainey, author of *The Nightmare Frontier* and *Blue Devil Island* on *Damage*

"*The Dust of Wonderland* is a haunting, heartbreaking novel, part supernatural thriller and part coming-home drama. Lee Thomas is a fantastic writer with a gift for invoking our most intimate fears—and preying on them mercilessly. Bravo." – Christopher Golden, Bram Stoker Award winner and bestselling author of *The Myth Hunters*

IN THE CLOSET, UNDER THE BED
Compilation copyright © 2009 by Lee Thomas

All rights reserved. No part of this book may be used or reproduced in any manner whatsoever without written permission except in the case of brief quotations embodied in critical articles or reviews.

This book contains works of fiction. All characters depicted in this book are fictitious, and any resemblance to real persons – living or dead – is purely coincidental.

Copyright for Individual Stories and Publication History:

"All the Faces Change" © 2009 by Lee Thomas
"An Apiary of White Bees" © 2007 by Lee Thomas
  Originally appeared in Inferno, *edited by Ellen Datlow*
"Healer" © 2002 by Lee Thomas
  Originally appeared in Stillwaters Journal
"Dislocation" © 2009 by Lee Thomas
"They Would Say She Danced" © 2007 by Lee Thomas
  Originally appeared in Horror World
"Shelter" © 2009 by Lee Thomas
"The Good and Gone" © 2008 by Lee Thomas
  Originally appeared in Killers, *edited by Colin Harvey*
"Appetite of the Cyber Tribes" © 2009 by Lee Thomas
"Crack Smokin' Grandpa" © 2009 by Lee Thomas
"Anthem of the Estranged" © 2004 by Lee Thomas
  Originally appeared in A Walk on the Darkside, *edited by John Pelan*
"I Know You're There" © 2009 by Lee Thomas
"Down to Sleep" © 2009 by Lee Thomas
"I'm Your Violence" © 2008 by Lee Thomas
  Originally appeared in Unspeakable Horror: From the Shadows of the Closet, *edited by Vince Liaguno and Chad Helder*
"Tears to Rust" © 2009 by Lee Thomas
"The Tattered Boy" © 2009 by Lee Thomas

Cover Design copyright © 2009 by Deena Warner Design LLC
Interior Layout by Deena Warner Design LLC

Acknowledgements:

By necessity this is a significantly abbreviated list. Thanks to David Thomas Lord and Michael Rowe for taking the time to read these stories and offer their thoughts in the Foreword and Afterword of this volume. I send much appreciation to Steve Berman and Greg Herren, both of whom were instrumental in bringing this collection about. Additional thanks to Ellen Datlow, Vince Liaguno, and the members of NYC's finest writing group, Who Wants Cake, all of whom burn bright and shining — blinding even at such a great distance.

DEDICATED TO:
Mongo Betina for your humor, brilliance, insight,
and the occasional cruelty.
Thank you.

And as always,
To John Perry

Table of Contents

Foreword – David Thomas Lord 15

All the Faces Change 19

An Apiary of White Bees 33

Healer 55

Dislocation 67

They Would Say She Danced 81

Shelter 89

The Good and Gone 107

Appetite of the Cyber Tribes 121

Crack Smokin' Grandpa 137

Anthem of the Estranged 157

I Know You're There 177

Down to Sleep 189

I'm Your Violence 203

Tears to Rust 225

The Tattered Boy 243

Afterword – Michael Rowe 263

Foreword

David Thomas Lord

Shhh, quiet down, everything will be all right ... eventually.

Eventually, the dawn will push back the darkness and sunshine will keep the monsters at bay. Yes, eventually. Eventually, the terrors of these pages will subside. You'll be able to breathe again. You'll be able to associate in genteel company. You'll regain hope. But not just yet. The sun is still set, darkness pervades, and that thing is inside the closet. It is under the bed.

As readers, we are compelled to wonder why books are titled as they are. *The Great Gatsby* is not "The Good Gatsby," or "The Fine Gatsby," or even plain "Jay Gatsby." *Moby Dick* isn't "Captain Ahab." *Jane Eyre* is not "Rochester." And we are just as compelled to conclude that the title is a key of sorts, a clue toward understanding or an indication of what it is we are about to read. And so, with "In the Closet, Under the Bed," we view the stories through the lens of the title. Not just through childhood fears, but also adult invective.

It seems that in horror literature, as in life, that our greatest fears are imbued on a thing only while it is *in* the closet. That thing, while inside the closet, is a form of pent-up energy, coalesced from loneliness and isolation, from denial and repression. It is a thing we ourselves give its greatest power. We feed it our fear. Well, that thing is bursting to be free. Once out, the fear becomes the reality. Once a horror is freed, it is a thing to be dealt with, an obstacle, a struggle, reconciliation perhaps. But it is there and tangible and only has the power we instill in it.

Lee Thomas has used the phrase "in the closet" in a duality of meanings. The "monster in the closet"—that boogeyman we use to keep restless children in their beds at night—is the horrific meaning. That theme is the fear of the unknown, of that edgy, murderous entity that lies in wait at the corners of sleep. And yet, Thomas, also and simultaneously, uses the phrase in its more contemporary form, wherein what we keep in the closet is our secrets, those personal personality patches we seek to keep segmented from general society. And to what avail? Read on, for Thomas manages to explore all the "closet themes" in the fifteen stories in this collection. So the question is: Do you want to know what's under the bed, dare to open the closet door?

In "Anthem of the Estranged," TV tabloid producer, Michael Donnelley, finds a "closet door" ajar and views an alternate dimension of wraith-like beings. And while he is used to forcing open the closet doors of his subjects on his show, "Picking up the Rock," never before has he stumbled upon his own secrets that way.

Lee Thomas engages the most contemporary usage of "in the closet" in his opening story, "All the Faces Change." He uses the theme of hidden, repressed sexuality and homophobia in other stories as well: "Healer," "Dislocation, "I Know You're There," and "The Tattered Boy."

Tim Elliot encounters his high school friend, Robbie, after many years. A single kiss reminds Tim of their former relationship—one Tim has locked in the closet through denial and fear, and by marriage and children. But Robbie remembered, remembered the hurt, both physical and emotional, at Tim's hands. And he uses what he's learned over the years to terrify Tim into seeing why "All the Faces Change."

Down on his luck, Gus Howe is trying to care for his sickly son as best as a homeless man can. The lore of the disenfranchised says there is a Healer who can cure any illness—for a price. And the price for death is flesh. Gus begins the ritual and The Healer comes, but leaves without extracting any form of payment except Gus' promise that he will get out of his situation. And even though Gus kept to his promise and created a good life for himself, his new partner, and his now-grown and happy son, death costs flesh. And "The Healer" must get paid.

Breath play, or sexual asphyxia, is how Eric achieves "Dislocation" at the hands of Jake, a sex partner he keeps hidden from his wife and family. Although this was to be a one-time encounter, Jake must get Eric back in order to remove another life he installed into Eric's consciousness. The other personality, Marcus, is not happy living Eric's closeted, wife-and-kids lifestyle, so Eric must get both Jake and Marcus, literally, out of his life. How much sacrifice is Eric willing to make?

In "I Know You're There," Lynch uses his employee, Michael, as one of his "birds," those who can astral project to spy on his clients. But

Foreword

Michael's activities aren't as controllable as Lynch would like, and Michael's interests don't end merely at Lynch's clients. Lynch discovers, first-hand, that there are worse things than being watched. But when he attempts to put an end to Michael's astral intrusion into his life, he discovers how bad life can get when your stalker is always there.

When Willem meets "The Tattered Boy," he is fascinated by the filthy urchin dressed in rags. Willem finds Bastiaan far more intriguing than his own mentally crippled son at home. Willem visits him daily in his hovel, until Bastiaan makes an advance that Willem finds both abhorrent and desirous. He both wants the boy and wants to rid himself of that want.

We rarely share all the myriad facets of our personality and interests with all we meet and know. There are closets for certain secret parts of ourselves; retreats we share with only select others. Then there are closets within those closets. And trunks within them, and boxes in the trunks. Each separate and segmented and ciphered. Those things we cannot, will not share will all. But that is by intent. We determine. We create. The closet is ours and we own the key. But we do not have power over all the things we keep shut up in the closet. One is beyond our control. He is the boogeyman. It is a being born of irrational fear. We feed it by the attention we give to hiding it. We feed it our fear. This boogeyman has no fixed appearance; it changes with our wants and our worries. For even if there was no parent, no older sibling to formulate the monster in our childish heads, we would create the thing on our own. And that is the very creature of shadow Lee Thomas releases in his stories, "Shelter," "The Good and Gone," "Appetite of the Cyber Tribes," "Crack Smokin' Grandpa," and "Down to Sleep."

In "Shelter," Randall Banks attends the showing of his friend Bea's huge acrylic sculptures, creatures part-human, part cruel god. After having sex with him in the gallery's bathroom, Randall's young boyfriend, Chad, wipes his semen-stained finger on the "tattoo" of one of Bea's most disturbing creations. Randall imagines that creation, Serphim, coming to his apartment while he slept and raping him. He searches for the model the image was based upon, convinced that he was the intruder. But when he finds him, the truth is far worse, and Randall discovers what it really means to give shelter.

Max Evans fills his bored, bed-ridden hours in the hospital by playing a game his grandmother taught him—"The Good and Gone." By concentrating, he releases his astral form and wanders the room, the building, the world. In his attempt to project himself to the home of a trick, Max is distracted by a Mr. Gohling, who is followed by a host of orange spirits. Still in his astral state, Max follows Gohling to his strange apartment, with its heavy and impenetrable metal shutters and doors. Max discovers the horrors in Gohling's secret room. He also discovers who, indeed, is good and gone.

In "Appetite of the Cyber Tribes," Walter embraces the cyber-age in trying to date via the Internet. But Walter is about to discover that the worldwide web is a series of rooms, each room hidden behind a closed and closeted door. And that the boogeyman doesn't always wear the face you hoped.

Lee Thomas again uses the Internet, this time as the metaphor for our new closets, in "Crack Smokin' Grandpa." The unnamed first-person narrator finds the man of his—and everyone's—dreams. Or are they remembered nightmares? In this story, the boogeyman hides behind a face that isn't his, but is mostly a projection of what is wanted and needed from him—a mythic superman. But, as all worship requires sacrifice, what will be surrendered—the man or the myth?

"Down to Sleep" opens the closet door of the Internet a final time, when the narrator finds his newest trick online. When he goes to Vern's home, he notices a photo of Vern and his lover, Tom. He knows Tom and met him the same way he's met Vern. An open relationship, he decides. And sex next. But a fleeting shadow, a noise in another room, means Tom is here, too. Tom breaks into the room. He's monstrous, huge, but still beautiful in his monstrosity. Our narrator longs to know what it's like to lie down to sleep in Vern's place.

From ancient walled-cities, to a world wide web, Lee Thomas explores the shadows you suspect are in the closet, the beasts under the bed. And in each dim corner, he finds a horror he gladly places inside and under yours.

All the Faces Change

When Tim was a boy, he knew where the monsters hid; they were in the closet and under the bed. At night, horrible beasts with wide red eyes and spit-dripping fangs lurked in the dark places of his bedroom. Tentacles slid over the floor, waiting to tickle his foot and grab tightly to his ankle before pulling him into some fearsome dimension. A man with no face stood beyond the closet threshold with his sharpened razors just waiting for little Timmy's mother and father to drift off to sleep so he could engage his brutal entertainments without interruption. With a child's unchained imagination, Tim believed in the beasts that lived in the shadows, even when the opening of the closet door and the lifting of the bedclothes proved time and again such things didn't exist.

As Tim grew he forgot about the monsters; they faded with his imagination. But the monsters never truly left him. They simply changed their location and their intent. They changed their faces and waited.

The man lay in the bed, and Tim Elliot tried to see his father in the withered face. He wasn't there. The sallow cheeks and ashen skin covered in white beard stubble bore no resemblance to the man Tim remembered. Even the eyes were those of a stranger. Sunken behind purple lids. Watery. Dreamy with morphine. Two years since he'd last seen the man, and the damage was all but complete. A doctor diagnosed the cancer nine months ago. Tim found out about it three days ago.

For god's sake, mom, why didn't you tell me?

Your father thought it best to wait.

Of course he did. Don't let anyone see your weakness: that was his father's philosophy. Hide it. Bury it as deep as you can. Dig all the way to hell and plant it there if you have to, but don't bother the world with your problems.

Here lies the vault of pain and joy, of fear and love.

Tim didn't know what to do. The last time he'd seen his father, the man was chopping wood in the back of the house. He was strong and striking. Now, he couldn't lift his head from the pillow. He couldn't focus his eyes, and Tim didn't know what to do, because he felt like a child in the man's presence. His father had seen to that. They'd never once had an adult conversation. Never once spoken man to man. When Tim announced his marriage, the coming of his first child, the buying of his house, there was no congratulatory conversation, rather he received lectures and warnings. Tim's opinions and ideas brought censure or at best amusement from the old man, his every action and word translating to: *stupid kid*.

"Can I get you anything?" Tim whispered to the dying man.

"I don't know you," his father mumbled.

The crisp afternoon air bit at nose, cheek and neck. He walked from the hospital, hands shoved deep in his pockets, arms tight to his sides. Dead leaves the colors of dried blood and gold crackled under his shoes. A gray foam of clouds hung above threatening rain – maybe snow. Was it cold enough for snow? It felt plenty cold to Tim. As he made his way toward his father's house, he replaced the ravaged face in his thoughts with practical concerns. He needed to call Ella and see how Tracy was doing – his youngest daughter had a cold. Lily, his eldest, had competed in her first skating competition that morning. Tim should call his mother and see if she needed anything from the grocery. He could stop on the way home. It was the least he could do for the harried woman.

His mother seemed totally lost without her husband. She was a soldier without a commanding officer – a servant with no master. Tim knew she wasn't weak or ignorant; she'd simply accepted her role as Mrs. Elliot, just as he'd accepted his role as the son of Mr. Elliot.

The tears hit him so fast Tim was sobbing before he felt the first sting of moisture in his eyes. He stopped on the sidewalk, lowered his head. He looked at an unwholesome-yellow leaf the shape of a valentine heart. Bugs had gnawed its edges; bore holes through its tissue. Emotions seared a path to his chest, bringing an ache behind his ribs and nausea to his stomach.

Stop it, he thought. *Quit acting like a child*.

All the Faces Change

It was his father's voice, speaking words Tim had heard innumerable times – in his father's den, on the baseball diamond, over the dining table. He hated that voice. Hated himself for conjuring it.

I don't know you.

Tim crushed the heart-shaped leaf under his shoe and continued down the sidewalk. He scrubbed the tears from his cheeks, sniffed loudly and put the painful feelings away.

Snow fell.

Tim walked out of the stuffy bar into freezing night air. Behind him the door closed, cutting off loud voices, struggling to be heard above the bar's sound system. The rhythm of a song still beat at his back. White flakes drifted to the ground. They whirled in the halo cast by the streetlight ahead. He saw a figure in the parking lot, not far from his car, and Tim paused.

The man was short but broad of build, looking like a movie mobster in his black overcoat and crimson silk scarf. The cigarette burning between his fingers added to the impression. But the face lacked the weathered veneer of a man familiar with violence. It was a boy's face. Soft and expectant. The man didn't take his eyes from Tim. Gazing beneath his lashes with a palpable lust, he drew from his cigarette. His tongue darted out to touch his upper lip before he exhaled a cloud into the freezing night. Tim was familiar with this look; he'd seen it dozens of times at the park across town from his house. He'd spent more than one evening there, sitting in his car after work, waiting for such approving eyes.

Slowly the man turned, but he kept his gaze on Tim as his body pivoted. He set off across the parking lot, away from the bar.

And Tim followed.

He climbed out of the passenger seat of the silver sedan and checked the parking lot, wondering if anyone from the bar loitered between the cars. Relief at finding the lot void of curious souls dripped over him like the moisture cooling on his thigh. Tim adjusted his coat and started toward his car.

"And that's it," the man behind him said.

Tim turned. "Thanks," he offered awkwardly, but something about the guy's position against the car struck him. The body was nearly covered by the chassis and Tim only saw the man's face. He'd barely looked at the man when they were in the car, but he'd certainly noticed the features before getting in the vehicle. Now, though, he *recognized* them. This was a different context or the light had changed. Something had changed, because he knew this face. It belonged to a dead boy.

He squinted, imagined that his grief had conjured the face from the past, or perhaps it was the whiskey drawing this death mask. "Robbie?" Tim asked.

"You do remember," he said, lighting another cigarette.

Tim had known Robin Hope in high school. They had been friends for a time. Senior year, Robin, who insisted on being called Robbie, disappeared. He was thought dead. For years, Tim had sought out news of his lost friend but heard nothing. After so much time, he assumed the boy was dead – everyone did.

A thick cloud, part steam and part smoke wafted around Robbie's head. Snow salted his short hair and the shoulders of his black coat.

"I can't believe this," Tim said, feeling all the more uncomfortable for the familiarity of the man.

Robbie shrugged. He took another draw from his smoke and walked forward. "Stranger things have happened."

"We all thought... "

"Thought or *hoped*?"

Tim didn't immediately register this last comment. Robbie came up to him, only a step away, and Tim found himself fascinated with the man's face. The hair was clipped short and neat, almost buzzed to the scalp, and there was a healthy amount of gray for a man his age, but the face was as youthful as it had been when they'd sat in Robbie's basement drinking stolen beer. It was a round face, solid, and if it weren't for the eyes, Tim might have considered it kind. But Robbie regarded him coldly through half closed lids, as if Tim had recently slandered him.

"What?" Tim asked.

"Never mind," Robbie said. "I'm glad we got to see each other again."

"Me too." He didn't mean it though.

"Nice of you to say," Robbie replied, sounding bored. "I heard about your dad. Wondered if you'd be coming to town."

"Just for a few days. I've got to get back to the family."

"The wife. The kids," Robbie said as if naming diseases.

"Yes." The tone in Robbie's voice made it clear there would be no happy small talk between them, and Tim started running excuses through his head, wanting to be anywhere but in the cold parking lot under the snow with his former high school buddy. He had enough sorrow in his life.

"Playing that game, huh?"

"Excuse me?" The question startled him, though it shouldn't have. "Look, Robbie, we were just kids messing around."

Robbie nodded his head, stepping away from the car and crossing to Tim. He took a final drag from the cigarette and dropped it onto the lace of snow at their feet. "And five minutes ago?"

"I'm under a lot of stress," Tim said quickly. He looked over his shoulder to make sure no one had come out of the bar. "I have to go."

"Calm down, Stud."

"Look, it's late," Tim said, thoroughly uncomfortable with the conversation.

"Yeah, it is." Robbie said. He reached into his coat pocket and for the slightest of moments Tim thought he might pull out a gun or a knife. Instead he pulled out a business card. "You'll want to call me."

"I don't think so," Tim replied. "I'm glad you're okay, but I have to get home."

"You'll want to call," Robbie insisted.

Robbie slid forward and wrapped his hand around the back of Tim's head. He couldn't break the grip. It felt like his head was clamped in a vice. Then Robbie was kissing him hard on the mouth. Tim resisted, but the warm lips demanded reciprocation. Robbie's tongue slid between his teeth, brushed through his mouth.

It ended then. Tim yanked backward, only to find he was no longer being restrained. Robbie stood several feet from him, wearing a look of disgust.

Tim imagined his expression was similar. "Don't ever do that again."

"I won't have to."

"I'm not like you."
"Irrefutable."
"I'm not that way."
"Then you have nothing to worry about."

All the following day, Tim found his disquiet growing. Thoughts of his father and thoughts of Robbie hung on opposite ends of a pendulum blade's arc. Each time he invested consideration in either man, the blade swept back, closer to slicing. The morning was spent with his mother in the hospital room, gazing at the wasting man. Nonsense phrases dominated his father's speech. When he did surface to moments of clarity, he addressed his wife only, reminding her that their lawyer had all of the necessary papers – telling her to have the car winterized or the engine block might crack. Tim found himself jealous of these exchanges. When he tried to get his father's attention, the man stared at him with dull eyes. *I don't know you.* Invariably these glazed gazes ended with non-sequiturs ranging from baseball stats for long retired players to "I don't like cabbage, bring me some corn."

Frustrated that these meaningless phrases might be the last his father offered – no chance for a conversation of substance – Tim's mind escaped the room, but this defense was no more comforting. He thought about Robbie, whom he'd assumed dead. The kiss – its insistent anger burning his lips. Then back into history his mind traveled. Robbie's basement. The rec room. There, the kisses were also insistent but gentler, exciting. The sensation of skin on skin was overwhelming, and Tim fled these memories, back to the hospital room, his cheeks flushed and his breath short. The pendulum ratcheted down a notch. The blade swung closer.

Over lunch he reminded his mother that he needed to get home.

"It's an eight hour drive."

"You should be with Ella and the girls," his mother agreed. "You can bring them back for the services."

"Don't talk that way. There's still a chance he'll…" But Tim didn't believe the lie enough to finish it.

He was worried about his mother, but how did you comfort someone who was so damned practical?

He shouldn't leave he knew. So much stress showed on her face that Tim found it hard to look at her. Dark smudges stained the skin beneath her eyes, and her cheeks were drawn. He even thought he saw veins, like the root system of a dying plant, covering her face. The closer he looked, the more dreadful she appeared, so he kept his eyes on the foul tasting hamburger sitting on his tray.

"Your Uncle Len is coming to stay for a couple of weeks," his mother said. "He's just closing up the shop. He'll be here this evening."

"Good," Tim replied. At least she wouldn't be alone.

"I'll be fine," she assured. "Ella and the girls need you. You should be home with them."

Selfless as always, his mother was right. The thought of going home made him uneasy, though. The prospect of seeing his wife and daughters should have warmed him. It didn't. In fact, he inexplicably dreaded it.

He pulled into the diner. The snow had stopped but he couldn't help but think of Robbie, remembering the man standing in a parking lot, white flakes accumulating on his shoulders. Why had he sought Tim out? A quickie for old times sake? Tim hardly thought so. There was something malevolent in Robbie's eyes last night. The kiss harbored a different meaning. No intimacy there. No warmth.

He opened the glass doors and walked up to the hostess stand. A long counter ran behind the podium. An elderly man with a trucker's cap sat at the end farthest from Tim. The rest of the stools were empty. Behind the counter was the obligatory pie case with its assortment of cream pies. He looked into the main dining room and noticed that only two of the tables were occupied. The weather was keeping people home, but the dearth of customers didn't seem to be improving service. He waited another minute and then wandered into the dining room to take a booth by the window.

Gazing at the window, his face ghosted on the glass, he sought some comforting preoccupation for his mind. None came. His father was in his head. Robbie was in there. His house was there, too, though he was still unable to identify the source of his fear for the place. It was ridiculous. Why should he fear seeing Ella? She was a wonderful woman. Tracy and Lily were exceptional children. Tim figured his nerves were just fried from too much anxiety. Seeing his father reduced to a babbling cadaver on a hospital bed was more than enough shock for one week. Add to that Robbie's appearance – with all of the memories that conjured – and Tim was bound to be on edge.

"Get'cha?" the waitress said from over his shoulder, startling Tim out of his reverie.

He left his transparent face on the glass and turned to the woman. "I'll need a men... " The sight of the waitress locked the final syllable in his throat. He reared back in shock.

Her appearance frightened him. Yellow-gray hair swept back over the waitresses ears, but its texture was like fired clay – dry and unyielding – flaring out around her face and neck like the hood of a cobra. Her brow was triangular, ending in a blunt knob over the bridge of her nose. The nose itself was narrow and turned upward to a sharp point at the end. Veins like plant roots – the kind he'd noticed more subtly on his mother's face – ran in ridges over the cheeks and forehead. The harelip was so pronounced; he saw the waitress's teeth through the gap of skin running in a jagged line beneath her nose.

Tim knew he shouldn't stare, knew he should have sympathetic feelings toward this unfortunate woman. Though he was able to look away, his eyes focusing on a chip in the table's surface, he felt nothing but revulsion. He didn't want her touching his food.

"Coffee," Tim said.

"Still need that menu?" the waitress asked, not fazed by his uncomplimentary reaction.

She must be used to it, Tim thought.

"No. Coffee is fine," he said.

In three hours, he'd be home. Ella always kept something for quick meals in the freezer. Tim's late nights at work made such provisions a necessity. *Playing that game, huh?* The coffee would keep him awake for the drive. That would be enough.

He drove over the wet highway, stretching before him like a diseased tongue in the mouth of night. He sipped coffee from the tall Styrofoam cup his waitress had delivered with his bill. The snow had already melted from the blacktop, leaving it wet and shiny. A light frosting of white still covered the ditches on either side of the road.

His mind wandered back to Robbie, to the green and white striped sofa in his family's rec room. It had been snowing that day too – almost a blizzard. That's why they were home in the middle of the day, drinking beer from Robbie's mother's fridge instead of sitting in class.

He couldn't remember how it started. Did Robbie kiss him first? Tim imagined it must have happened that way. His clearest memory was of Robbie lying beneath him. The boy's smooth body was so warm. His erection rubbed against Tim's, ran solid and teasing beneath Tim's stomach. And the look in Robbie's eyes... That look. It was complete adoration, something Tim had never seen directed at himself before. For a time, that expression erased all of Tim's fears, made him forget that what he was doing was wrong.

Slogging home through snow that was deep enough to cover his boots, Tim lost hold of Robbie's adoration. In the biting cold, he felt only shame and confusion. When he reached the house, stomping his boots on the back porch to remove the wet clots of snow, he felt a sick anticipation, as if the expression on his face would reveal what he'd done – show it as clearly as a photograph to his mother... to his father.

That night over dinner, he was certain his father knew. But of course, the man didn't. Tim's fear made it difficult for him to separate his father's customary disdain from disgust at the acts he'd performed. Still, he felt certain that his father would at any time return his spoon to the bowl of stew and condemn Tim for his aberrant behavior. All that night, Tim ached in his room, waiting for the door to open, expecting his father to appear with hateful phrases and harsh wisdom.

Tim's fear toughened like a callous. He ended his friendship with Robbie the next day; at that point, he couldn't even look at the kid. Robbie had been persistent, demanding explanation, and their last encounter ended with Tim punching the boy in the mouth.

Two weeks later, Robbie vanished.

Tim sipped from his coffee again and looked into the night ahead.

Where'd you go, Robbie? And why did you choose now to come back?

He sat in his car, parked in the driveway. The lights in the living room were on. Tim saw a shadow pass by the curtains. Ella. The kids would be in bed by now. Lily had to get up early for skating practice, and

Tracy just liked to sleep. She said dreams were like television without commercials. Tim smiled.

Still, he didn't get out of the car. Not yet. He'd pulled into the driveway fifteen minutes ago, but he couldn't work up the courage to go inside. If Ella pulled back the curtains and saw him, he'd have to move, but she hadn't done that yet.

Dread kept him in the seat. The feeling had grown more pronounced with every mile of the drive. Surely it was little more than grief for his father, creating some anomalous emotional manifestation. He'd sat in that hospital room for three days, reviewing painful memories, lamenting a respect the dying man could never express – if he'd ever felt it at all. Tim hoped his own daughters wouldn't be faced with such turmoil should they find him similarly stricken.

Tim checked his pockets to make sure he had his cell phone, his keys, his wallet. Ella called this ritual his idiot check. He was always forgetting something in the car. He felt the wallet under his butt, jingled the keys in the deep front pocket of his overcoat; patted the chest of his overcoat, felt the bump of his phone beneath the fabric. In doing so, his fingers grazed over the stiff edge of a business card, tucked imperfectly in the breast pocket of the coat. He pulled the card out and read the front.

Robin Hope.

A phone number was printed below the name.

You'll want to call.

Robbie must have slipped it into the pocket during that last kiss. Tim thought he should have noticed it before now, but over the last few days his mind was in a constant state of distraction, so perhaps it wasn't such a surprise that he'd overlooked the presence of the card.

He tucked it deeper into the pocket. He would throw it out inside.

After checking the glove box and the console for anything else he might have forgotten, Tim left the car and walked to the trunk to retrieve his bag. The air was still bitter cold, and he wouldn't be surprised if the region was in store for another round of flurries. He hefted the bag and closed the trunk.

At the front door, he flipped through his keys until he found the right one and shoved it in the lock. His disquiet grew momentarily intense, causing him to grip the doorknob so tightly his fingers ached. Knowing he was being ridiculous, Tim released the knob. He breathed deeply and then reached out again. He opened the door to a blast of hot air and set his bag down in the entryway. This was home. This was safety.

He dropped his keys on the table to the left of the door. He would have called out to announce his return, but Tim worried about waking the girls. Likely, Ella was in the kitchen on the family computer or making herself a cup of tea, her latest nightly ritual.

Soon enough, he heard footsteps on the hardwood floor of the dining room. Tim walked into the living room to greet his wife, already smiling with the anticipation of seeing her.

What came through the opening from the dining room was not his wife. The head was smooth, vaguely reptilian, with a small puckered mouth harboring rows of needle-like teeth. The skin covering the creature was blue-gray like the flesh of a corpse. Pronounced veins lined the exposed dermis. Some were so thick they pushed through the skin, leaving cracked edges like torn paper.

Tim cried out and stumbled backward. He ran to the front door, ignoring the strange noises coming from the creature's wrinkled mouth. Yanking open the door, Tim slipped on the wet tiles and nearly fell on his ass.

As he righted himself, he remembered his family. What had this thing done to Ella? To the girls?

Tim looked up the staircase. His daughters. Jesus, his little girls.

"Tracy? Lily?" he called. "Ella!"

He raced across to the stairs and flew up them two at a time. On the landing, he pivoted and tore down the hall toward the door of the bedroom Tracy and Lily shared. As he approached the door cracked open and a dreadful head appeared. It resembled the creature downstairs but it was smaller, and faster. The thing charged from the room, leaping toward him. Tim spun away but the creature latched itself to his leg. He shoved it off of him, and the thing wailed a mournful cry.

He stumbled and hit the wall in time to see the larger creature appear in the stairway. It flew onto the landing, shrieking inhuman noise into the hall. At the smaller creature, it paused and bent down, throwing a vicious look at Tim.

He sprinted to the end of the hall toward the door of the master bedroom. Let them be there, he thought. Let them be locked inside.

The door opened. His family was nowhere to be seen.

Where are they?

Tim slammed the door and threw the lock on the handle. He backed away from the door, tears burning his eyes.

"Where are you?" he whimpered.

Hands on the door startled him. He jumped back, listening to the pounding on the wood, the jiggling of the knob.

"What did you do to them!" he bellowed.

He fled to the bathroom, needing a second locked door between himself and the creatures that had invaded his house. He flipped on the light and went to the sink. Looking at himself in the mirror, his face a mask of desperation, Tim noticed the white edge of the business card.

Robbie, he thought. *Robbie did this*. That twisted fuck had sent these things to Tim's home.

You'll want to call.

Tim freed his cell phone from the pocket of his overcoat. Instead of dialing Robbie Hope, he dialed nine-one-one, but the call didn't go through. No soothing operator's voice told him he'd reached the emergency dispatch, in its place was a scratching sound like fingernails on stone. Tim tried three more times but each effort was greeted by the dreadful scraping.

Robbie doesn't want you to call them, he thought.

Tim pulled the card from his coat pocket.

"What did you do to them?" Tim cried into the phone.

"I see you made it home in one piece," Robbie Hope replied.

"What did you do?"

"Relax, Stud," Robbie said. "The wife and kids are fine. At least they were."

"What is this?"

"Justice. Judgment. Just a giggle."

Muffled by the two doors, Tim heard the creatures pounding wildly on the bedroom door. How long would it hold?

"Where is my family?"

"They're in the house, Stud."

"Quit calling me that."

Robbie Hope chuckled. "They're in the house and they're perfectly safe, unless you do something stupid."

Tim ground his teeth together. He paced the narrow space between the toilet and the linen closet, the phone pressed tightly to his ear. The pounding on the bedroom door had stopped, and he found the canceled racket far too disturbing. They were already through the other door, he knew.

"How do I stop them?"

"You don't," Robbie replied. "I'm calling the shots."

"Then tell me what you want, asshole."

"Do you really think calling me names is the way to go right now?"

"What do you *want*?"

"I want you to listen."

Voices rose outside the bathroom door. The pounding returned in a violent tattoo, echoes of the beating filled the bathroom. The door rattled at Tim' back. The creatures shouted his name with high-pitched, raspy voices, demanding to be let in.

"After that afternoon in my basement, both of our lives changed. What we did terrified you. I get that. I got scared, too. But I didn't blame you for what happened. I didn't punish you for it."

"You started it," Tim blurted before he could stop himself.

"And last night, did I start that too? Did I put a gun to your head?"

Tim didn't know what to say. He felt the concussion of fists against the door at his back and his mind scattered.

"What ever happened that day happened because we both wanted it. But you freaked. You made it something disgusting and you held me responsible. It was my fault so you figured you'd make little Robbie pay. You told your dad, told everyone at school, but you didn't tell them the truth, did you Tim?"

"I don't remember."

"Convenient amnesia, Stud, but I don't buy it. You told your dad about the queer guy, told him all about the freak that put the moves on you. Then he got on the phone to my dad, who decided to beat me within an inch of hell. And at school you told anyone who would listen why you decked me, but you deleted your complicity. You left out all of the parts that made you hard. Before I knew it, my whole life was an avalanche and it was your fucking voice that brought the mountainside down. There was no place I could go where they didn't glare at me, where they didn't laugh. School and home were the worst. I was a target. The places a kid is supposed to feel the safest became nightmares for me.

"Like a lot of kids, I figured the only way out was to open my wrists and let all of the nasty life pour out of me." Robbie paused. "But I don't blame you for that. I was stupid. That was my decision. Fight or flight, you know? I didn't believe I could fight back then so I walked into the woods with a nice new utility knife, made myself a little seat on a pile of snow and opened my arms from wrist to elbow. And that should have been that."

"But it wasn't."

"A man found me," Robbie continued. "A very special man. He took me away and nursed me back to health. Then he showed me things. Oh, he taught me some amazing things."

"I'm losing my mind," Tim cried into the phone.

"You didn't lose it," Robbie replied. "I borrowed it for a while."

"Where's my family? What have you done to them?"

"Nothing," Robbie said. "My interest lies solely with you. One day, you'll see your life for what it was: a rather clichéd fairy tale with no happy ending. All of the resentment and loathing and fear and emptiness you endured to please a fucked up old man? Maybe you can live with that, but I shouldn't have had to suffer for it. You turned the world against me, Tim. Friends and family became monstrous. No comfort. No love. Just hate and disgust and disappointment. I've given those feelings a face, and I'm making you see it."

"You sent these things into my house."

"Wrong, Stud," Robbie replied.

"Quit calling me that!"

"They were always there. I just helped you see them."

"Where's my family?" Tim repeated, his voice wet with crying.

"They're outside the door, Tim. They want you to let them in."

An Apiary of White Bees

Oliver Bennett walked across the lobby of the Cortland Hotel, nodding to his employees and guests. The floor, a lake of travertine marble, swirling with veins of cream and beige-colored stone, absorbed the dull light of a stormy afternoon. Behind the concierge desk and sitting area, French doors ran the length of the west wall; their white slats parceled the concrete promenade, the grounds, and the cloud-veiled mountain range beyond the glass into a precise grid.

Oliver didn't care much for the Cortland. It was a landmark, decorated with extravagance and taste, but without a single concession to warmth. His wife Amanda wanted it, so he bought it, and they lived here because she wanted that too, but it was hardly a home. A home should be filled with personal belongings and intimate, happy memories. And at least one person in that place should love you.

The Cortland was an adequate shelter, Oliver supposed, pausing at the French doors, clasping a chilled silver handle in his palm. He looked over his shoulder at the lobby, observed the patrons, dressed in elegant wools, silks, and furs, moving gracefully amid the stiff-backed employees in their crisp black uniforms. Above, a Lalique chandelier hung like an immense pellucid beehive.

Oliver never noticed the similarity of shape before. The swollen center. The tapered extremes. *It really is a beautiful fixture*, he thought.

Outside on the veranda, he zipped his jacket against the chill and looked north over the lawn toward the swimming pool, now covered in a sky blue tarp. The swimming season had ended over a month ago, making the destruction around the pool less of an inconvenience, though no less of an eyesore.

The earth beyond the broken pool was wounded and raw. Ridges of dirt rose in a ring behind a run of yellow warning tape. A bulldozer squatted on the lawn. Oliver checked over his shoulder to make sure that Amanda wasn't watching him – a reflex only. His wife never watched him, never followed. He knew she couldn't be bothered to keep track of a man she felt, on kinder days, was simply an obstacle on the way to a bank account. That didn't stop her from complaining about his behavior, however. If she caught him lighting up, she would use it as an excuse to berate him for the rest of the day. But since she was nowhere to be seen, Oliver pulled a pack of cigarettes from his jacket and lit one. With his lungs warmed by the smoke, he crossed the lawn toward the hole in his property and the wonderful thing it held.

Two weeks ago, while digging a trench in an attempt to repair the pool's broken plumbing, a work crew was interrupted by the discovery of a brick barrier. As the excavation continued, the barrier revealed itself to be a wall – one of four creating a vault buried deep in the ground. Oliver was there that day, standing on the lip of the gouged earth when the door was revealed. His anticipation of its opening had been wonderful, the only good thing he'd felt in years.

Despite the protests of Joe Hopkins, the crew's foreman, Oliver insisted on being among the first group of men to examine the contents of the strange brick building. After all, it was unearthed on Oliver's property. It was his, and he had every right to be part of the discovery.

And what a find it was. Inside were crates of alcohol, stacked floor to ceiling. Narrow passages cut between them, so that Oliver, Hopkins, and two of his workmen could navigate the length and depth of the chamber.

They must have hidden it here during prohibition, Hopkins said.

And nobody remembered it was here?

Apparently not.

Amazing.

Oliver stepped forward, out of the memory, and drew deeply on his cigarette. He ducked under the cordon of warning tape and stepped over the thick cable feeding electricity to the lights Hopkins had strung in the vault. He looked into the hole. Scabs of dirt marred the brick wall and filled the creases in the door's planks.

Though he knew this was his property, and he had every right to be here, Oliver hesitated before stepping onto the steep grade that would take him down to the door. He wasn't doing anything wrong, but he felt wrong, and the sensation brought a distant memory, which made the afternoon chill several degrees colder.

I want to show you something.

Where are we going, Kyle?

Come on. It's okay. Your dad showed me this.

Oliver drew away from the hole, just one step, a minor concession to fear. Then he thought, *No, this is mine*. He dropped his cigarette on a mound of upturned sod and walked toward the door.

Square-faced lights glowed high on the walls, catching the grain of the crates in their cast. Walking through the narrow paths, Oliver imagined he looked much like a giant passing through a city of wooden skyscrapers. The air was thick with dust and the scent of rotted pine and oak. He paused and read the labels stenciled on the sides of the crates; some were still legible, others had faded to little more than stains. Of course, the names meant little to him. He had neither the mind nor the tongue of a connoisseur. Still, he wondered what these aged liquors might taste like after so long. Was time generous, giving the spirits some special properties, or had it sapped them of essence as it did so many other things?

He searched, looking for some indication on the wall of crates for the case that most deserved his attention. Among the labels he could read, he found some self explanatory – *Gin, Scotch Whiskey, Bordeaux*, and *English Rum* – and others told him nothing – *Belle of Anderson, Crown Prince*, and *Old Cabin Still*.

The more he explored, the more intriguing he found the vault, and Oliver believed he was working out a pattern in the room's organization. The pedestrian liquors – the whiskeys, the gins and rums – were at the front, while the middle of the room was filled with more exotic beverages – brandies, liqueurs and aperitifs. Further back, deeper in the maze of crates, the wines took hold. When he reached the back wall, he recognized the Dom Perignon crest on two stacks, though the letters were ghosted to indecipherability. Finally, he came to two crates set aside in a corner, not touching any of the other containers. These made him all the more curious for their total lack of identification.

Every other box in the chamber carried some blemish of ink but not these. To Oliver's mind, this was the trove he sought – its value corroborated by its anonymity. Using the knife on his key ring, he pried the lid. Aged wood and nails whined against his efforts. The edge he worked splintered. He dug in again and cracked the wood enough to glimpse the contents.

The bottles appeared yellow, but it was too gloomy to tell. They were uniquely shaped – six sided and nestled together like glass honeycombs. Each bottle was capped in wax that ran in clumped rivulets down the neck. They would do fine, he decided, and set to completing the task of opening the crate's lid.

Once the boards were torn back, he gazed inside. The case was designed to hold eight of the hexagonal bottles – three to a side, nestling two in the middle. But the two central bottles were missing, and a profound disappointment settled on him. Though, certainly, the culprit had absconded with the bottles nearly three-quarters of a century ago, he couldn't help but feel somehow violated.

Oliver carried a bottle of the mysterious liquor to the front of the vault and sat on a crate. He scraped the wax away with his knife, then brushed cream-colored flakes from the thighs of his trousers. Beneath this, a simple cork sealed the bottle, and it pulled free easily. He sniffed, and a sweet yet bitter odor, climbed into his nose. Oliver swirled the liquid around in the bottle, and yes, the glass was yellow. Then, he drank. The liqueur cooled his throat instead of burning like so many spirits burned; it numbed his tongue, his stomach, his muscles.

He prepared himself to feel sick, perhaps poisoned, but the drink enlivened his system. Taking another sip, he leaned back on the crate and observed the vault and found it much to his liking.

Unlike Amanda, Oliver didn't need everything in his world to be polished and precious. Whenever he could sneak away for a week or two on his own, earthier places beckoned him. Dockside bars where the men and women were calloused and broken; musk-reeking video arcades with black-walled mazes, leading from one erotic shadow to the next; sweating alleys, running like veins through terminal neighborhoods – these were his places. They tarnished the silver of him and the secret of their visiting made him feel alive.

Where are you taking me, Kyle?

It's a special place. A secret.

Lifting the bottle to his lips again, Oliver closed his eyes. The childhood recollection was back, and instead of fighting it, he entertained the memory, remembering a fine young man that he once admired, even worshipped.

Kyle was the son of the gardener who kept the grounds of the Bennett Estate. Two years Oliver's senior, Kyle was strong and tanned and confident, with a mop of blond hair and sinewy arms corded with veins. He was everything that Oliver was not, and as a boy, Oliver spent hours at windows or pretending to read by the pool to watch his hero work in the yard.

Succumbing to intoxication, Oliver remembered one day in particular. He was twelve years old and following his hero through the wooded area running at the back of his father's estate. Kyle's back muscles flexed as the boy pushed aside tree branches and leafy shrubs, leading Oliver away from the house. After hiking across the property, Kyle stopped at a large shed and opened the door.

Come on. It's okay. Your dad showed me this.

A ringing came up in Oliver's head. The sound grew shrill and then flattened out into a massaging resonance. With the monotonous hum buzzing behind his eyes, the memory skipped, turned sharp and painful.

Kyle was angry with him, shouting. Oliver ran away, confused and hurt and needing to be in his comfortable, familiar room. Desperate to be there. Panicked. He raced through the shrubs and low tree branches. Then he tripped on a root. Fell.

A thousand bees surrounded Oliver's head. The world shattered into a dozen dislocated images, stacked in a trembling array before his eyes, and the horrible words, words spat at him by the gardener's son, took on the drone of the swarming bees, grinding terrible accusations into his brain.

Oliver opened his eyes and waved a hand in the air to rid himself of the daydream bees. He couldn't remember why he was running, couldn't recall why Kyle was so angry with him when Oliver did nothing more or less than what his hero asked, but he remembered running. In his panic he'd tripped and fallen, crashing through a low hanging beehive.

Over thirty years lived and worn since that afternoon, but now, in this place he felt where each of those vicious creatures had stung him. A spot just below his left ear sang a particular ache now.

Despite the chill in the shadowed chamber, Oliver was sweating, and his breath hitched rapidly. The memories he indulged fueled an irrational yet intense erotic response in him, an aching heat that demanded release. Oliver put the bottle down on the crate beside him. He went to the thick wooden door and pushed it closed, cutting off the gray afternoon light. With his back to the door, he unsnapped his pants and stepped out wide to keep them from dropping to the dirty concrete.

He felt like a boy again, locked in his bedroom, his bathroom, a small wooden shack. The stinging at his neck aroused like a kiss, and the hive in his mind dove, tracing along the back of his throat, abrading his esophagus and gathering in his belly before working further into his system and down. The palm on his cock felt rougher than his own, more experienced. The shaft filling his hand was unfamiliar; it was too thick, too ridged with veins.

He squeezed his eyes closed to more perfectly feel the sensations.

The hive in his groin crawled frantically, seeking some means of escape. He inhaled and the bouquet of the liquor, the honeyed bitter scent, filled his head and triggered a painful yet perfect climax.

The thrumming ache of the fleeing swarm tore through his shaft as the imagined bees escaped into the black room. His ragged breath coaxed them out; tears wet his eyes.

In his ear, a single insect buzzed. A moment later, sharp pain flared on his cheek. He made a sound – almost a chuckle, more nearly a pant. Oliver's eyes sprang open. Before them, tiny pale dots like those following a particularly bright camera flash, dotted the gloomy air. He touched the wound on his cheek, already feeling the welt of a sting rising there. Covering this blossoming bump was a bit of fluid, thick and sticky to the touch. He searched his clothing and the floor for the body of the attacking bee, but found nothing. When he returned his attention to the vault's gloom, the pale dots were gone.

He shook his head in wonderment. Then, Oliver pulled the handkerchief from his pocket.

Go wash your hands, boy.

In the suite he shared with his wife, Oliver stared at the red welt just below his right eye and wondered on the coincidence that he should have been thinking about bees moments before being stung. The notion amused him. Indeed, he felt so good that he didn't care about the sour looks Amanda cast at him, as she dressed for dinner.

"What did you do to your face?" she asked, suddenly beside him at the mirror. She held a diamond teardrop to her ear and jiggled it to catch the light.

"Bee sting."

"There are no bees this time of year," Amanda said, dismissing his claim outright. She shoved against him to get a better look at herself, and Oliver walked away.

"Let's just hope that thing heals before Friday," she said.

"Friday?" he asked.

"Idiot," Amanda whispered just loud enough for Oliver to hear. "We're celebrating our find. I'm expecting everyone to attend. It'll be the usual crowd, and some new faces. I've invited that Joe Hopkins because he found the place, and I want the auction director to attend."

"What auction?"

"Well, we're not keeping those crates for posterity, Oliver. The auction house is having them removed and appraised. We'll find out exactly what they're worth, and I don't want you out there drinking all of the good stuff before they come, so you'll have to find another place to sulk until they're done."

The gardener's son led him through the trees and the shrubs. Sweat painted Kyle's back in a glistening sheen that Oliver wanted to touch. A trickle of perspiration ran along the boy's spine as he pushed aside branches and stomped forward; it pooled at the elastic band of his shorts, absorbed, turning the fabric at his waist from powder blue to navy. Oliver followed obediently. Something was different about Kyle that day; he seemed on edge, as if having Oliver along was an annoyance, even though he had extended the invitation. At the tool shed, far to the back of the property, the gardener's son stopped and put his hands on his hips.

In here.

The shed smelled of old grass and gasoline, dirt and paint. The fan of a willow branch curtained a small window high on the east wall.

A hand touched Oliver's face, and his breath came in tight, painful gasps. The gardener's son unfastened Oliver's belt and unsnapped his trousers. A rough hand slid over his belly, under the waistband of his boxers…

Breathing deeply against a wave of emotion, Oliver lifted the oddly shaped bottle, stared at the amber glass. Something about the drink. Some incredible element of the alcohol. It sharpened his fantasies, gave them a life, made them tangible and teasing.

All but lost in this consideration, Oliver was startled by the sound of someone calling his name. He corked the bottle, set it on the crate and stepped outside, where he met Abe, the grounds-man.

"You needed me, sir?" Abe asked.

Oliver told him about the crates he wanted moved. As he spoke the instructions, Abe's wrinkled old face clouded with worry.

"Mrs. Bennet said... "

"She doesn't pay you," Oliver said. "There are two crates. I'll show you the ones I want. Take them up to the second floor. Room 206."

He would be moving into that room for a few days. Amanda wouldn't mind; she never did.

Likely, she was courting a new lover. Amanda's mood toward him always soured when someone else was fucking her. Probably because her parade of men served to remind her that she'd settled for too little in marriage. They both had, and though Oliver considered leaving many times, the idea of being so completely alone was disturbing. Amanda took care of things – finances, social engagements, what clothes he should buy and when he should wear them. Such distractions were a burden, and he was content to leave them in her hands. Of greater importance, a companion, even one so incongruous to his needs, defined his place in the world and gave him a sense of belonging.

Why he should, in that moment, realize that being needed was wholly different from being necessary, he couldn't say.

Oliver closed the door to Room 206 and walked along the crimson carpet to the staircase. He paused on the landing, peering over the lobby's expanse. The crystal chandelier caught his eye. More than ever it looked to him like a giant beehive, made of gleaming clear gems rather than the fragile gray parchment of traditional nests. What wonderful creatures might create such a place? he wondered. This fanciful thought took hold in his mind, and his imagination filled the lobby with a swarm. Like soaring shards of glass, the bees flitted and danced in the air, climbed over the crystals of the fixture, disappeared inside to be warmed by two dozen low-watt bulbs.

The fantasy was all very beautiful to Oliver, who reached out a hand to grasp the carved banister. The people below, oblivious to his imagined swarm, chatted and wandered, read tourism pamphlets, while the air around them lit with a thousand specks of twinkling light.

"Mr. Bennett?"

Oliver started, and his magnificent swarm vanished. He turned away from the lobby and found Joe Hopkins smiling at him.

The foreman was a fit man in his mid-thirties with a brush of black hair framing strong and handsome features. Today he was not in his customary jeans and chambray shirt, instead wearing khakis and a black knit shirt beneath his leather jacket. Oliver returned the man's smile and nodded his head.

"Mr. Hopkins," he said.

"Surveying the kingdom?"

"Just gathering a bit of wool," Oliver replied. "What can I do for you?"

"Well, I thought you might be interested in the history of that wine cellar we dug up in your back yard."

Truth be told, his interest in the chamber had declined considerably. Amanda saw to that by having the hotel's publicist push the story to every reporter in town, making a spectacle of the place. It wasn't his anymore, not in any sense that mattered. Now that the crates of liqueur he wanted were stacked in his room, the speak easy cellar was merely a curiosity. Still, he didn't want to seem impolite, and he found Hopkins pleasant enough. He leaned back against the banister and said, "What did you find?"

"We were right about the whole prohibition thing. It was a hooch hut, sure enough," Hopkins said, grinning at his turn of a phrase. Oliver couldn't help but notice the thick muscles in the foreman's neck, pronounced and corded when he smiled. "Davis Cortland had the place built so his guests wouldn't have to go dry, had it buried deep."

"Are you saying they had to dig their way down every time they wanted a cocktail?"

"Didn't have to dig. There was a tunnel connecting that vault to the basement of the hotel. If we'd excavated the east side of the thing, we would've found it. Anyway, Cortland had the whole place sealed up before he went to sell the hotel. Bricked up the basement and the vault. Apparently, he didn't mention it to the buyer, and the place was forgotten."

"And how did you find out about this?"

"They keep the Cortland family genealogy at the library. It's all on their computer system, so I just plugged in a couple of key words and Davis Cortland's journal popped up." Hopkins paused and ran a hand through his hair. "Near the end there, old man Cortland was in pretty bad shape."

"How so?" Oliver asked.

"Well, both his sons died within about a month of one another. Both accidents. Cortland snapped. He found God in his own way, and he became convinced that his cellar, that's what he called the place, was cursed. Actually, he called it damned, but I guess it's about the same thing. Just craziness. He said that the boys were corrupted, led into sin by a low woman. That's what he called her anyway."

"Interesting," Oliver said. But he already projected the fallout of this discovery, and disappointment pushed in. Surely local journalists would dig up the same information, maybe more. As such, it was just something else to lament, another precious cache forcibly shared with the world and therefore meaningless.

Though he didn't exactly wish to remove himself from Hopkins's presence, he grew agitated with the conversation. But the foreman kept talking, telling Oliver about the Cortland family, and the patriarch's burgeoning madness – selling the hotel and starting a fundamentalist church in the family home, denouncing the decadent and opulent lifestyle his hotel once represented. Only when the conversation returned to the matter of Cortland's sons, Reginald and Michael, did Oliver's interest pique.

"I guess I can see how the old guy saw divine punishment in it. I mean, it's a pretty bizarre coincidence ... for it to happen twice, in two different parts of the hotel."

"Both boys died the same way?" Oliver asked.

Hopkins nodded his head. "They were stung to death."

A tingle of excitement flared in Oliver's midsection. "They must have been delicate boys to die that way," he said. "Were they allergic?"

"Couldn't say. Cortland gave the impression that both were stung numerous times. They probably upset a couple of hives."

"Remarkable," Oliver said.

"It's all really fascinating," Hopkins continued. "When Mrs. Bennett asked me to check into the property history I was dreading it. I'm not much of a book worm, but I got so damned curious, I kept digging."

Of course Amanda was behind this. "I see."

"Uh oh," Hopkins replied quickly. "The look on your face is telling me I should have kept my mouth shut."

"Not at all," Oliver said. He reached out and patted the foreman's shoulder. "Just a difference of opinion between my wife and I. I find her outlook unfortunate and a little sad. Amanda doesn't see a thing's value until she's envied for having it."

"And you like to keep things quieter?"

"Simply put... I like my secrets."

The day of his wife's party, Oliver sat at the window in his room and watched movers, under the vigilant eye of a slender man in tweed, remove the crates from the brick vault. The man in tweed, Amanda's assessor, made notes on a clipboard, and pointed and shouted. He read the labels on the crates, made more notes, pointed again.

Oliver closed the curtains, then drew the heavy shades as well. He went to the cases in the corner and pulled a bottle free. It was half empty. The last in the crate. He still had the second crate, though. Eight more bottles. They could last him another week, maybe two if he was conservative. Nonetheless, a flash of desperation, as if his supply had already run dry, tightened his chest. He fought to shake off this panic and studied the yellowish contents inside the glass.

Soon the ballroom below would fill with a miserable throng of the city's privileged. Oliver would have to smile and make small talk, pretend to care about exotic vacations and the tax benefits of buying bigger, more opulent homes.

Remembering what Joe told him about the Cortland family, he imagined little had changed over the years. They, too, probably held these kinds of affairs and likely spoke the same conversations. Oh, inflation changed the numbers being bandied about and trends changed the fashions, but Oliver couldn't imagine those long-ago conversations being any more interesting.

He opened the bottle and took a deep drink from the sweet fluid, immediately feeling its affects on his tongue. Oliver put the bottle on the nightstand and removed his clothes before stretching out on the bed.

He hoped to enjoy a brief period of bliss before putting on the host's mantle and indulging Amanda's need to be celebrated. He traveled through his memories, looking for a salacious moment on which to focus his attention, but his mind refused him. It kept coming back to the name Cortland. Oliver took another drink and stared at the ceiling, which was already shifting ever so slightly with his burgeoning intoxication.

Cortland had two sons. Both died from bee stings. The loss drove him mad. Joe had told him these things, but Oliver didn't want to remember them. He wanted to feel something good before being submerged in Amanda's fete.

But already he felt himself slipping away. He reached out and nearly knocked the bottle over. Once he had it firmly in hand, he brought it to his lips and sipped.

The room around him shifted, dissolved. Oliver replaced the bottle, struggled against the fantasy blossoming in his head, but failed. Instead of flesh and sweat and passion, he imagined...

A small dirty room, the walls and ceiling stained by cigarette smoke and dust. Water marks from faulty pipes spread over the plaster like monstrous amoebas. A bed was pushed against the far wall, the only surface in the room to be properly finished with a delicate, floral-print paper. And on the bed, two boys in their late teens, tanned and lightly muscled, lay naked. One smoked a cigarette. The other looked toward the door. There, just crossing the threshold, a petite woman, naked and lovely, with short-cropped hair – a flapper's bob – cast a glance over her smooth white shoulder. Around her, a swarm of pearl-colored bees swarmed, filling the room with their buzz.

Oliver pictured all of this easily, the details painted in washed out colors. He was disappointed to have entered the scene in the post-coital moments, having the heat of sex denied him, but something about this room, this place, felt so comforting he managed his displeasure and allowed himself to sink deeper into the fantasy.

Her name was Evelyn, he knew. Her small body moved gracefully amid her swarm, which cast a scrim of vague shadows, making the skin on her back and the supple curve of her buttocks appear to writhe and slide. Oliver followed her over the threshold and into another gloomy room, dominated by a single fixture.

It hung from the ceiling like a plump child, wrapped in a dirty shroud. The hive was enormous and the color of pastry dough. Opalescent bees by the hundreds crawled over its surface. Others flitted around the orifice at its base. On the floor beneath the nest, one of the oddly shaped bottles rested. A large metal funnel jutted from its neck. Honey dripped from the hole above, hit the funnel with a dull plunk and slid down.

Evelyn slowly lifted her arms, disturbing the bees around her. With a gentle wave, she sent them to join their kin at the hive. In these few moments, Oliver felt the woman's control, her absolute command of the insects. He also felt her joy at adding numbers to their ranks. She walked to the hive, touched its surface with her fingertips, then bent low to retrieve the bottle. Evelyn pulled the funnel from its mouth, set it gently on the ground, before taking the bottle away. At an unmarked crate, previously unnoticed by Oliver (how could he notice anything but the wonderful hive?) she again bent down, lifted a cork and popped it into the neck, driving it deep with a blow from her palm. She placed the bottle, which would later receive its cap of wax, in the crate and lifted an empty one from the floor beside it. This she placed beneath the dripping cavity and plugged it with the funnel.

Evelyn turned, a gentle smile pushing up the corners of her mouth. She ran her hands over her breasts and down her torso before lifting them to her hair, which she patted down.

Back in the room, the young man had finished his cigarette. He lay on his side, spooned by his companion, eyes filled with pleasure and dream. The second man's arm draped over the first, his palm gently caressing the belly of his brother.

For just as he knew the woman's identity, Oliver understood these two attractive boys were named Cortland. Reginald Cortland, the younger brother, looked content in the arms of his older sibling, Michael. Together, they tried to coax Evelyn back into the bed, but she was happy to stand apart, gazing at them.

A moment later, the dream changed. It happened so quickly, Oliver felt like he was dropping from a window.

Two broad men with flat features and stubble on their chins stomped into the room. They held short metal pipes in their gloved hands. The thugs observed the boys with disgust while the naked brothers yelped, then rolled away. They leapt from the bed, seeking their clothing. Another man entered the room. He was tall and straight-backed, wearing a fine woolen overcoat. His mustache was waxed neatly above his lips. He too looked with disgust at the young men scrabbling to dress, but fury was also in his features.

Evelyn protested, demanding the men leave her home, refusing to cover herself, even when one of the thugs slapped her harshly with the back of his hand and called her "whore."

Was Oliver the only one aware of the buzzing, growing louder in the next room? How could these thick men not hear it? It was nearly as loud as an approaching motorcycle.

The dignified man, (Davis Cortland, he knew), ushered his sons out of the room and through the house. Behind him, his men cried out.

Cortland looked back and saw the air filled with what appeared to be snow, but his men cowered under it, slapped at it with fat palms. They screamed when any of the flakes touched them. And Evelyn, the beautiful Evelyn, stood at the center of this storm, looking serene as the men dropped at her feet.

The scene tripped again. The sensation of falling was worse this time, and Oliver nearly fell out of his dream.

He sat in the back of a great sedan, looking through the window at a house being consumed by flame. Oliver felt despair and horror, knowing Evelyn was still inside, trapped with her swarm between walls of fire. Davis Cortland stood outside the car, hands crossed over his crotch, watching the house burn.

Oliver shook himself from the fantasy.

Emotions – hate, fear, anger, sadness in mourning the magnificent Evelyn's death – covered him like a thick syrup (*like honey*). He looked at the bottle on the bed table next to him, thought about the sweet liqueur held within and its origin.

He scratched his fingernails over his scalp, digging in deep until his neck tingled. He wanted the Cortland family out of his head, but they weren't quite ready to leave.

Though he did not return to the all-consuming fugue, Oliver caught glimpses, like memory, of the boys and their father: Reginald Cortland sitting in a corner on the floor of a hotel room, very much like the one Oliver currently occupied; he drank from one of the hexagonal bottles, his face streaming with tears, his hand masturbating furiously; the senior Cortland entered the room some time later to find his son dead on the carpet, the boy's body riddled with red welts, the bottle lying next to him; Michael Cortland, the older boy, sneaked through the hidden cellar, opening one of the crates Evelyn offered him and his brother as gifts; he sat in the tunnel that connected the hooch hut to the hotel, also crying, surrounded by the pale bees; he too was discovered with his skin destroyed and cold to the touch.

They couldn't control them, Oliver thought. Without Evelyn's command, the insects proved vicious and lethal.

He looked to the shadowy corner of his room. The bare wooden crates, holding the hexagonal bottles sat there. Above them, movement like sliding wax caught his eye. He traced his gaze up the wall, saw similar movement against the ceiling. With a shaking hand, he reached for the bottle. Paused.

As for the father, Cortland believed his boys were corrupted by the beautiful Evelyn (though Oliver considered the act a generous seduction); the patriarch saw his sons' corpses, saw the bottles of sweet liqueur accompanying them, and with the shattered mind of one truly despondent, he cast his judgment against all vice and had the chamber of spirits sealed. He would no longer break the laws of man, nor sin against the laws of his God. He turned his back on capital and embraced an extreme and unforgiving faith.

Davis Cortland didn't understand. He was a conservative man with a shallow mind and no capacity for wonder. Oliver knew the type well.

Downstairs, Amanda was busy with caterers and florists. He needed to shower and dress and play the fine host. They were throwing a party to celebrate the opening of Cortland's vault.

He lifted the bottle from the nightstand, held it to his lips and again peered into the corner, at the motion along the walls' surface. *Cortland just couldn't understand.*

Oliver corked the bottle and returned it to the crate.

The swing band played a mid-tempo tune. Ball gowns twirled and men in tuxedos smiled. Oliver stood away from the crowd, in a corner by the bar where he watched Amanda flirting with Joe Hopkins. With her arm on his shoulder, his wife laughed too loudly at something the foreman said and tossed her head to the side. She saw Oliver and her joyful expression switched off until she was again looking at Hopkins.

Oliver sipped from his martini, but the drink burned his tongue, tasted foul and poisoned. Throughout the evening, he had sampled the canapés and skewered delicacies circulated by the waiters, but they scalded and scraped his mouth, abrading his palate like bits of hot coal.

He put the martini glass on the bar, wishing he had smuggled one of his bottles down to the ballroom. Nothing else would taste right to him tonight.

Amanda ran her palm down Hopkins' cheek. The man threw a nervous glance at Oliver, and Amanda laughed again. She slid her arm through Hopkins's and led him deeper into the party, out of Oliver's view. The music clanged in his ears, and the bustle of people now felt threatening, as if they were just amusing themselves until it was time to turn on him and attack. To add to his unease, his eyes were playing tricks on him, or they were failing completely. The room began melting into a single oozing image. Details blurred then bleached out. The ornate moldings dripped, and the far wall shrank as if collapsing. Around him, the smiling faces were little more than threatening smudges.

He had to escape. With the shrill banging of the music in his head, he fled back to his room.

Once the door was locked, he ran to the crates stacked in the corner. Desperate to have the music out of his head and the sick-making panic made numb, he pulled the bottle free and removed the cork. What remained wasn't enough to calm him. The final drops of fluid trickled over his tongue, a mere tease. Oliver corked the bottle and replaced it in the top crate. He set the wooden case on the floor and frantically opened the second. Once the covering boards were removed he snatched a fresh bottle and chewed away the wax seal. He yanked the cork from the neck. Then, he poured the liquid into his mouth until the disturbance in his system calmed.

He reached a hand out to steady himself and felt the wall shift and tickle under his palm. Oliver snatched his hand away.

"Sorry," he whispered, turning away.

Soothed but still uncomfortable, he removed his jacket and ruffled shirt. He slid out of his trousers and socks and stood in his underwear, already feeling the need for another sip.

He ran a hand over his belly and rubbed small circles, coaxing the swarm in his head to again fill his sex. Thoughts of Amanda and Joe Hopkins engulfed him.

They were together, he thought. Somewhere in that damned hotel, his wife lay beneath Hopkins. Her lips were on his chest, tasting his sweat and pushing into the muscle and hair. She'd encourage him with sounds Oliver hadn't heard in over a decade, voicing passion she had never shown her husband, and the workman, driving deep into

Oliver's wife, filling her in a way Oliver never could, strained and flexed, showing her what a real man could offer.

Oliver poured a substantial slug of the liquid over these thoughts. It filled his head with a humming pulse, and his skin alit with friction.

The image of his wife laid back and wide open to the workman crystallized and a mouth fell on his. Hopkins' mouth. The weight of the workman's chest pressed down on him but he also felt the rise of Amanda's breasts under him. The duality of the sensations intensified until he felt hot sweat dripping from him and over him.

His fantasy, sparked by supposition and fueled by the numbing liqueur, did not position him between the two lovers; it fed him the sensations of both.

His cock grew warm, encased in wet skin as he thrust into Amanda's writhing body, and he felt the penetration between his legs, a thick shaft driving deep into his body, entering him through a channel he didn't possess. The smell of perfume filled his nose and was then replaced with a pedestrian aftershave. Hands stroked his ass and his chest and his back and his hips, and through it all, his sex burned with the gathering bees.

A solid rapping on his door snapped him from his fantasy, canceling the pleasure that tickled and stung the base of his cock, made it retreat. Instead of erupting from him, the buzzing ejaculate fled into his body. The bees were furious. Their furred bodies, their filament thin legs, their beating wings prickled his gut, his stomach and his sex. They clung to the membranes and jostled for space. The discomfort and frantic movement aroused him anew, and Oliver reached for the bottle on the nightstand.

The insistent knocking paused his hand. Oliver tried ignoring the summons, but it seemed the visitor would not be ignored. Oliver rolled off of the bed. He pulled his robe from the back of a chair and crossed the room.

Hopkins stood in the doorway. He greeted Oliver with a hello, rich in tone and salted with unease.

With the hive burrowing into his belly and the liqueur having numbed his mouth, Oliver said nothing, simply stepped back to allow Hopkins entrance.

Apparently uncomfortable and eager to hide it, Hopkins made a show of crossing his arms. Oliver noted the bulk of the workman's thickly veined forearms, and the hive ignited with frantic buzzing. Then,

Hopkins unfolded the arms and shoved his hands deep into the pockets of his trousers.

"Mr. Bennett," he said. "I know what you must be thinking, but I want you to know I'm not the sort to get mixed up with a married woman."

Oliver stared at the handsome man and thought about the gardener's son. They were similar, he thought. Both shared a strength, a power that emanated from their skin in hot waves. The association further stirred the hive, sent it flying low in his belly and high into his throat.

"I just want you to know that," Hopkins said. "The last thing I need in my life is a jealous husband." The workman laughed haltingly, forcing the sound through his lips in an awkward attempt to lighten the mood.

Oliver stepped forward. "I've never been jealous of her," he said. The foreman seemed perplexed, but this simple man would never understand the importance of such a statement.

When Oliver imagined his wife and her lovers, he took her place in the fantasies, feeling the strength and the rough hands on his body. Her men became his hero, every one of them was the gardener's son – his Kyle reimagined. He wrapped an arm around Hopkins' shoulder, locking the man's neck in the crook of his elbow. "Never of her."

He leaned forward and put his lips on Hopkins's. The hive swarming at the back of his throat and deep within his belly grew to frenzy. Hopkins' lips were warm but rigid. Strong hands pushed, and then they shoved. Oliver stumbled back, nearly fell and then regained his balance.

"What's wrong with you fucking people?" Hopkins yelled. He stepped forward and landed a fist on Oliver's jaw. The pain and concussion of the blow startled him but it was also exciting.

You liked that? You fucking freak? You rich boy piece of shit?

Kyle had struck him all of those years ago. Shouting obscenities and condemnations, the older boy punched and kicked and spat.

After their beautiful time together, while the resonating pleasure of their encounter still sang in his body, Oliver could make no sense of the abuse. Confused, Oliver fled the shack. He raced through the trees and the shrubs and into the waiting hive of bees.

Oliver tested his jaw, ran a hand over its pained arch. And the first of the white bees flew free of his mouth. It tested the air, bobbing and dipping with wings all but invisible from the speed of their beating.

Another followed. Hopkins shouted a curse and turned to run, but he was too close to the door and clipped his brow on the jamb. The blow sent him back a step.

Oliver's mouth ached from Hopkins' fist and from the abrading wings and bodies of the emerging swarm. Dozens of the white bees flew from his mouth to fill the gloom. Across the room, Hopkins cradled his forehead, gazing in fearful wonder at the buzzing squadron. One of the white creatures landed on his cheek.

It stung.

The workman's eyes grew wide; he choked out a plea, and then slapped at the insect, crushing it to a smear of liquid on his already swelling cheek. Oliver watched calmly, his system and mind soothed by the rhythmic beating of thousands of wings. Hopkins backed to the wall, hands up, covering his face, as a vague mumble of panic tripped over his lips.

Oliver lifted his arms and threw a look over his shoulder to the corner by the crates, suddenly alive with activity. A thunderous buzzing filled the room, and Oliver beckoned his swarm.

Oliver walked back to the bed, but in his mind he was running through brush and speckled sunlight.

His face burned with bee sting and throbbed with the beating he'd taken from his former hero. Nearly blind, he stumbled across his backyard to the kitchen door and tripped over the threshold. He cried, then screamed.

A fresh pain shot along his palm, and Oliver looked down to find a stray bee squirming in a gout of pearl-colored fluid. The trapped insect jabbed its barb into the meat at the base of his thumb, protesting its capture.

His father appeared, hovering over him, shouting about Oliver's stupidity. Oliver held his hand out to show his father the monster that still clung to him, and his father fell silent...

Your dad showed me this you fucking freak. And you like it? You rich boy piece of shit. I oughtta kill you and your faggot father.

The old man looked out the kitchen window, over the backyard and perhaps all the way to the back of the property where the tool shed stood. Seeming dazed, red with flush, he told Oliver to wash his hands.

Wash your hands, Boy.

Ignoring his son's tears and pleas, Oliver's father walked out the back door. A housekeeper appeared moments later, drawn by Oliver's cries. She wasted no time in helping him to his feet and to her car. She drove Oliver to the hospital where he spent the night in pain, hallucinating about his father and Kyle and bees.

By the time he was released the following morning, the gardener had packed his family up and left the estate. Oliver never saw Kyle again.

In the dark room, Oliver reclined on the bed. Naked, aching and swollen, he let the roar of wings clear the thoughts from his head. Painful lumps covered his chest and his belly; his cock was raw and misshapen by a dozen stings. A tear of semen dripped from the welted head and upon touching his stomach came to life with fierce movement, wings flapping and tickling his skin before pulling away to join the droning swarm above him. The small white bees speckled the air, crawled over the walls and dove from ceiling to floor. Their scent — bitter honey — filled his nose. On the nightstand next to him, the amber bottle stood empty.

He rolled his head, his swollen ear stinging when it touched the soft cotton pillowcase. Above the cases of liquor in the corner of the room, the ceiling already puckered with the foundation of a glorious shelter. The combed base of the hive was as big around as a serving platter and as white as snow. Drones scurried over the delicate construction, furiously adding material to the nest.

Somewhere below, the party continued. Amanda would be flirting with some new man, seducing him with Oliver's wealth, while degrading her husband with words of dissatisfaction. Here, though, none of that mattered, because, finally, he possessed something of his own, something his father's trespass could not taint, something Amanda could not imagine or covet or take. It was wholly his. The Cortland boys proved too weak for this responsibility. But not Oliver.

Like the lovely Evelyn, he would harbor and tend to his hive. He would be their master, their mother and their shelter.

His swarm would grow in number and strength, and by winter, the walls of the room would run with pearls of honey to be collected and stored. The two cases of bottles would never be enough to hold all of the magnificent liqueur.

"Oh please," he whispered to the room.

Six of his drones dropped from the platinum cloud to circle above him. Each beating of their wings brought the promise of pleasure and creation. "Please," he said again, and the white drones descended to penetrate his skin with their barbs. Agony erupted and was quickly numbed. Euphoria followed like an echo of the pain.

Beneath his hand, his anxious shaft, thick with knots, was already close to release. A sharp pain flared behind his ear. Oliver cried out, and the swarm's number increased.

Healer

The day disappeared over the horizon, casting amber through a window scarred with cracks. Inside a basement, littered and filthy, a man stood shaking as he drew the life from a cigarette snatched off the street outside the condemned building he called home. Smoke drifted like lost waves through the sickly illumination, and Gus Howe shivered because his shirt and jacket lay on the dying child at his feet. The boy had pneumonia. Pneumonia was serious. The price for pneumonia was flesh.

The coming night would be cold, perhaps freezing. That morning, he'd seen the frosting of dew on the window. A mild chill followed him through the afternoon as he scavenged and panhandled for the can of soup hanging over the open fire in the hall. Troy would never make it until dawn if he didn't get some help.

Maybe that would be better, better for them both.

After their one bedroom Subaru was towed away, they'd begun a nomadic existence in the streets of Seattle. The summers were fine; he and Troy could find a place along Green Lake or on the University campus. But the winter would be difficult.

Maybe it would be better if Troy slipped away in his sleep if only so the boy would never again wake up to pain and further evidence of his father's failure.

But he couldn't give up on the boy. They'd tried to steal him before, carry him off to some "half-way house." That's why he couldn't go to a hospital. If he went to a hospital, they'd separate them. The boy would be an orphan left to fend for himself with few if any memories of his father. Gus couldn't bear the destiny he imagined for his child, couldn't bear the thought of losing the only gift he'd ever been given.

The broken chair he used for wood popped, and the chemical reek of burning lacquer filled the room. Troy coughed weakly. The boy had no energy left to support the violent attacks, which had punctuated the early stages of his illness. Now he merely wheezed, occasionally emphasizing his condition with a sound that might have been a low chuckle. Aching, Gus listened as his son gasped for the stale oxygen filling the basement.

When he'd lost the job at Boeing, because the little jade vial of powder in his pocket meant more than the specifics of a jet engine, he wrote it off as bad luck. When his wife wrapped her Toyota around a light pole fleeing the house one rainy night because he'd been unfaithful to her, he played the mourning husband and blamed fate for his tragedy. Even as he led Troy down the slow, irreversible journey into the streets, Gus felt certain that his luck would change, and he could pull them up to where they'd once been. But four years later, with his son dying at his feet, Gus found his confidence eroding with every tremor that ran through his child's body.

It's the boy or flesh.

He couldn't remember exactly when he'd heard about The Healer. He'd thought of the name so often in the last few days that it almost seemed like a dream he'd had once. No longer the label of a mythical being, The Healer had taken on the credibility of a desperate hope.

"Tell me about him," he'd said that morning to Sig, the vet who worked the corner of Fourth and Pine.

"All I know is..." Sig looked over his shoulder then, as if checking the street for malicious listeners. "All I know is you call him and he comes. You write his name in blood, your own blood, and then call him. But he ain't free. You know Helen, the bag broad in the Market? Well, she got Syph' from some guy she was blowin' for breakfast money. This was years ago before her girlish figure went south. Anyhow, she called him and he cured her all right."

Helen. She was a round package, padded night and day in a dirty black coat with a fake fox collar. She worked the Pike Place Market, scraping change out of the tourist trade with her colorful personality. Helen told everyone that she lost her eye to pirates trying to steal her virtue. Sig claimed The Healer took it to clean out her throat.

"What does it cost?"

"What do you need?"

"Troy's sick. I think it's pneumonia."

Sig clicked his tongue several times and shook his head. "That's gonna cost ya'."

"How much?"

"Death costs flesh," Sig whispered.

Healer

Troy moaned loudly from the pile of scraps at Gus' feet. The boy already looked dead, dead and frozen. The tiny droplets of moisture clinging to his brow resembled iced condensation.

Gus retrieved the hot can of soup from the hall and poured a little into the old wine cap he used to feed his boy. Lowering the white lid to the boy's mouth, his hands began to shake. Troy's lips were the color of dusty grapes. The breath that crept from them barely reached Gus' cheek though he was almost nose-to-nose with his son.

When he poured the soup over his boy's lips, Troy gagged, pushing the thin liquid out the corners of his mouth. Gus wiped the boy's cheek and put the cap on the ground. He cradled the boy in his arms and whispered the Healer's name.

Gus returned Troy to the heap of trash and began searching the dirty chamber. He found what he needed in the form of a penny nail discarded in the corner. He wiped the filth from the metal and walked into the hall. He held the tack over the exposed flames of the fire until the head burned his fingers. Gus rushed back to Troy's side. Staring at his child, Gus drove the nail point into his index finger and cried out before coaxing fluid from the wound.

Gus pushed the bangs from Troy's brow and applied his finger to the smooth flesh of the boy's forehead. When the word *Healer* was fashioned over Troy's closed eyes, Gus again called for the spirit, searching the dingy basement for the creature's miraculous appearance. In the corners, where the refuse was stacked, he looked for the being. Squinting his eyes against the glare of the dirty windowpane, Gus scanned the street above for any sign of assistance.

He shouted. His voice ran through the other rooms beneath the building. The fire in the hall popped and snapped. Traffic eased by the window. But there was no sound of the Healer's approach.

And what sound did you expect, he asked himself. *Did you really think that you'd say that word and suddenly a magnificent vision would appear, offering ministrations for your son?*

He'd believed the perverse ramblings of the gutter society, bought into their myths and fables in order to avoid reality, while awaiting some crone or wizard dreamt up by Night Train soused minds.

No thunder was coming, no trembling building, no mystic flashes of light announcing the coming of their savior. In the end, Troy would slip away quietly, and Gus would have to leave his child's body beneath this dismal building in the hopes that the city might spring for a decent burial.

Lowering his son's head to the wadded paper pillow, Gus grew angry. He retreated to the hall and beat his hands against the concrete blocks until the pain became too great for him.

Death costs flesh.

The hospital was his only chance. If he were lucky, he'd stumble by a cop and get a ride to the emergency room. They could lock him up if they wanted to, could take Troy to their orphanage or halfway house or wherever. It didn't matter. Maybe, Troy still had a chance out there.

A chill breeze blew over his bare chest, and Gus shivered uncontrollably. His neck tingled. A raw scent, like the odor of rotting meat, assaulted his nose. Fear coursed along his spine, resonated through every nerve in his body. Gus stepped toward the room.

The Healer had come; it crouched over his son. Though its size was hard to determine because of its position, The Healer's content was easily discerned.

A thick haze of dirt and filth, roughly the shape of a human being, hovered over Troy's prone body. Refuse floated amid the grains of dust. A shattered soda bottle hung in place of a neck and torn papers floated in the torso like litter on the surface of an abused lake. The eyes were uneven shards of glass and the nose was made from the wine cap he'd used to feed his son.

And the mouth, the horrible mouth...

Gus turned away for a moment, only holding his stomach down with an immense strength of will. When he turned back, the Healer stood before him.

"Your need?" it asked.

The voice was soft with a hint of pleasure. The timbre startled Gus as he had expected an otherworldly roar or rasp. Still more startling was the mouth from which the voice emanated.

A rat, long dead and rotten, lay across the lower half of The Healer's face. It's legs stuck forward like the whiskers of a catfish. Its belly had been slit, and the edges of the wound moved like lips, exposing the visceral content. The rodent's tail curved around the side of the Healer's head, wrapping over the bubble of filth that made its ear.

Gus couldn't speak, he just pointed at the child in the heap.

"Terrible," the Healer said. "So young," it continued. "Often I come across the diseased; rarely do I come across victims." The Healer turned and began to kneel over Troy's trembling form, then it regarded Gus. "Someone once tried to welch on my fee," It explained in an amiable tone. "I tore his bicep off and shoved it in his mouth, so no one could hear him scream while I ate his belly."

Gus nodded.

"Now go in the hallway while I work."

Gus moved towards the hall and stopped in the threshold. "Be careful," he choked, casting another look at his son who lay in the shadow of the Healer. Gus drew another crushed cigarette butt from his pants. He lit it on a dying ember from his fire; the taste of turpentine pulled through the filter with the smoke, and Gus leaned against the wall, listening to the thunder of his pulse.

As he smoked, he began shaking again, from the cold, from fear. His son would live, but what was the payment? Would the Healer take his eye? A hand? A foot? Did it matter?

From the next room, Troy cried out; his distress was quickly followed by rounds of wet coughing. A moment later, Troy called for his father in a voice so weak Gus could not be certain he had heard it until the summons was repeated.

The Healer stepped into the hall. Gus looked up expectantly and then turned his head away, unable to look at the destroyed rodent working as the creature's mouth.

"Can you make it back?" The Healer asked.

Tears filled Gus' eyes. His shoulders trembled. "Back to where?" he asked, wanting only to run to console his son.

"Back to something grander than survival?"

Gus could not understand what this creature wanted, but he understood that it might save him a wounding. He nodded his head.

"Then begin," The Healer whispered. "This is not a place for you."

A moment later, a mound of refuse, crowned by the slaughtered rat lay at Gus' feet. From the next room, Troy called for his father.

"Dad?"

Gus woke from a light doze. Again, his son's voice peeled through the house. "Dad," he called with more urgency.

"In here," Gus said, throwing the newspaper off of his lap before quitting the crimson recliner and standing. He'd been dreaming of a dark place, a long ago place of shadows and filth and was now grateful to be awake surrounded by his comfortable furniture.

Troy burst into the den with a blinding smile and a sheet of paper gripped tightly in his hand.

Gus only needed a moment to realize what the sheet of paper in Troy's hand meant. "You got in," he said.

His son struck a cocky pose, head back, hands on hips. "Of course," Troy said. "But the full scholarship was a surprise."

Gus couldn't speak as pride filled his throat. He walked forward and threw his arms around his son, squeezing tightly until Troy said, "Hey, don't break me. My hands aren't insured yet."

Dear Dad,

How are the sticks treating you? I don't suppose you'd consider giving up the lake for a few days for something as silly as your son's graduation? (Just kidding, you'd damned well better be here. You worked hard enough to make it happen.)

Julie says hi. She's doing great. Her thesis is finished and we're going to jet off to exotic Baltimore for a few days with her family before I go into residency. But first, the big day.

You and a guest (how is Jack?) will be flown via commercial airlines in luxurious coach class to the City of Angels where you will be pampered in the lavish setting of my studio apartment overlooking scenic Ventura Boulevard.

And as if that weren't enough, you will receive red carpet treatment as you attend the premier of the graduating class of UCLA Medical. AND! I love you. Thanks for everything.

Troy

Healer

Death costs flesh.

Gus Howe woke suddenly, his head still swimming from the bottles of wine they'd consumed over a celebratory dinner before returning to Troy's apartment. Next to him, Jack snored lightly. He looked at the man's smooth shoulder and felt a twinge of guilt fed by a distant memory.

"You Goddamned freak," his long-passed wife cried, reaching for the keys to her Honda. "You've got a four year old son in the next room. How am I supposed to explain this to him?"

"Teri wait," Gus pleaded. "I didn't plan for this to happen."

The last words Terri ever spoke to him were, "I hope you get sick like all of those boys you read about. I hope you catch it and it kills you."

"Hey?" Jack mumbled.

"Nothing," Gus said. He slipped out of the sleeping bag and walked across the cramped apartment. He stopped beside the bed and looked down at the man Troy had become and wished Teri had survived to see that everything had somehow worked out.

Those first few years were tough, working entry level for one company or another and bartending in the evenings. But at least he'd been able to afford a small home, not much different than this box of Troy's. He'd focused his myriad addictions into a single dependency, the care of the young man who breathed lightly before him. And now his boy was going to be a doctor.

Gus left the bedside and walked to the window. Traffic raced below; headlights streaked the black band of road like comets racing through the heavens. On the side of the road, a newspaper rose up from the gusting current of passing vehicles. The sheet danced in the air for a few moments and then froze.

Around the paper, litter coalesced into a form that was vaguely human. A moment later, the shape took a step forward, up the grassy rise towards the apartment, and then it collapsed into a heap.

Gus stepped away from the window.

The Healer had come for its fee.

He always knew this day would come, even after the creature spared him in the miserable basement; Gus knew the debt was still owed.

There would be pain. But as he considered the last two decades, it seemed like a small price for such a tremendous blessing.

Gus knelt beside the sleeping bag and kissed Jack's neck. He stopped at the bed and kissed Troy's forehead. His son rolled over and made a warm sound before the quiet, even respiration of slumber returned.

Then Gus walked into the hallway.

A dervish of dust and bits of carpet fiber rolled like a dirty cloud under the cone of light at the hall's end. Gus closed the door quietly behind him.

"Something grander than survival," Healer said, gliding forward to meet Gus in the middle of the corridor. "Up from the dust."

Gus trembled in the face of the creature. Though a willing participant in this exchange, Gus could not alleviate his fear because he remembered the stories he'd heard all of those years ago, the stories of the street people.

"Please," he whispered, his voice an echoing rattle in his throat, "not my eyes."

Healer reached out a dusty appendage and stroked Gus' cheek. "Death costs flesh," it said with that soft, pleasant voice.

The corridor grew very hot. Gus closed his eyes, grinding his teeth as he waited for the Healer to take payment. He felt the cloud of fiber and dirt fall over him and Gus muffled a panicked sob. After what felt like several minutes, the caress of filth on his skin withdrew and Gus jerked back.

He opened his eyes and began searching his body for wounds. But his flesh remained intact.

And the door to Troy's apartment stood open.

Gus ran his hands over his arms and torso in a panic, praying to find some gap in his skin, all the while realizing that the flesh the Healer demanded was not his. Troy had been healed; the payment would come from him.

"Don't," Gus cried, racing for the door.

Inside the dark apartment, he struggled to make out the shapes, which seemed to be in endless motion. Jack rolled from the sleeping bag, or was thrown from it. The quilted fabric danced for a moment and then fell to the carpet. A lamp rose up on shoulders made from half a dozen medical texts. The lampshade burst into light, casting illumination behind a face made of melted-candle eyes and a mouth of ragged teeth created from broken glass. Gus charged the creature as it continued to take shape. An arm, the joining of a candlestick and a television remote, struck Gus along the temple, sending him to the floor of the apartment.

Troy and Jack rushed to either side of him as the Healer reared up on legs made of coiled fabric. Gus struggled to sit up. As he did, Healer stepped forward.

"I called you," Gus shouted to halt the creature's progress. "The debt is mine, not his."

"But you didn't call," The Healer said, broken glass gnashing through the fabric of the lampshade as it formed the words. "The child called, in your name, for your benefit. His illness was only a symptom of your disease."

"It was my blood," Gus said. "It was my voice."

The glass teeth parted as if to sigh. "The boy would have lived. You would have taken him for treatment; you'd already made the decision. In your hospitals he would have survived, but you would have returned to the colony of refuse, and it would have buried you in a handful of months. Even the innocent knew this. To him I came, and through him you were healed."

"Then take your payment from me," Gus demanded.

"You cannot provide what I need."

Troy stood. Gus reached out to stop his son, but the young man moved too quickly. "Troy."

"It's okay dad," Troy said. Something like curiosity, something like understanding flashed in Troy's eyes. Gus watched as his son approached the aggregation towering above them. The young man reached out to touch the lampshade face; he nodded his head and turned to cast a warm look at his father. "Be well."

The glass from The Healer's mouth took flight, circling Troy's head, shattering into a pellucid swarm of glimmering shards. The fragments dove at Troy, tearing the skin from his face and body, chipping at bone and carrying the young man's blood on jagged edges.

Gus cried into the storm that was destroying his boy. The glass continued to swarm, puncturing organs and whittling away at the material of Troy. The lamp crashed to the ground amid a clutter of textbooks. The candlestick and remote control similarly fell atop the pile as the glass persisted in the unknitting of Gus's son.

At his side, Jack trembled. Gus tried to stand but lacked the strength. Neighbors gathered in the hall, only to have the brief vision of the room's contents denied them by a slamming door.

Then the glass doubled its efforts, moving so quickly around the dripping skeletal debris that it appeared as little more than an occasional flicker of light.

But something was happening to the remains. Instead of being reduced even further, the glass was reconstructing Troy from the bits of him it had torn away.

Gus's chest flared with pain, a sharp anguish like nails in his heart. The cramp came again and again. The glass spun in ever broadening circles. Troy's face was nearly whole again.

And distantly he heard Jack calling his name.

"Gus."

The barely audible whisper cut through the clouds in Gus's mind. "Honey," Jack said as a warm hand ran over his cheek.

Gus opened his eyes to a room of blaring white. The light hurt his eyes, and he squinted quickly to filter the glare through his lashes.

"Thank God," Jack whispered, placing his head on Gus's shoulder.

The hospital room buzzed with activity, nurses squeezing I.V. bags and playing with machines, doctors nodding their heads and pointing before leaving the room. Wires ran from discs attached to his torso. The scent of Jack's cologne filled his nose.

Gus looked around, searched for the one face he needed to see. "Troy?" he asked.

Jack pulled away. Gus saw sadness in his eyes. What had happened to his boy?

His throat was sore and dry as if gone at with sandpaper. He tried to speak but the words caught on the arid plain of his tongue and withered.

Jack just shook his head solemnly.

Healer

Dear Dad,

Sorry it's taken me so long to write, but I've been having a hard time getting used to this. Sometimes, I think I've finally got it, and then I fall apart completely.

I just wanted to thank you and let you know that I am well, despite what you might think. You worked so hard to make me who I am, and I wanted to be sure you knew that none of your work was wasted. Though I can't see you now, try to find solace in the knowledge that I'm doing what I was meant to do.

Also, the day may come when you see a man wearing my face. Don't speak to him, dad. His time here, healing the unfortunate, took its toll. He deserves his own life now.

For now, give my love to Jack. And know that wherever I go, you are with me.

I've got to run. Someone's calling.

Troy

Dislocation

He can't breathe. Thumbs press beneath his Adam's apple; hands tighten around his throat. The face hovers over him, and it is handsome, intense. His lungs ache; his body convulses. "Fuck me," are the words lodged in his constricted windpipe. The ceiling burns white at the edges. Panic. His body bucks, needing air. Needing. The man's face, the light fixture above it, the ceiling above that, bleach out and lose distinction.

His climax stuns him. A cord of semen lashes his belly. Someone groans from far away.

White.

His name is Eric, and on this cold January afternoon, he comes to in a hotel room. At first, he can't lift his head; it weighs too much. The room tilts before his eyes. It rises then falls like the stateroom of a ship on choppy water. The gold *fleur-de-lis* pattern of the wallpaper expands and contracts in a slow respiration. Across the room, the intense man (whom he calls Jake, knowing it's not his real name) sits in a cream-colored chair with burgundy-striped cushions. He has the face of a high school quarterback, pretty and confident, though years beyond graduation. Already wearing his jeans, Jake drapes his socks over a thigh and looks at Eric.

"You okay?" Jake asks, though he doesn't look concerned. If anything he appears bored and eager to leave.

"Good," Eric croaks. He clears his throat. It is raw, painful, exhilarating. "Fine."

Jake nods and slips his foot into a sock.

In the chat room, they agreed on discretion and anonymity. Uninhibited. Hidden behind fabricated selves they discussed cock and ass, sucking and fucking. Friendship, work, hobbies, family: the burdens they left out.

Eric watches Jake slide on the other sock and leap to his feet. In his haste, he knocks the table next to him. The lamp there teeters and settles. Jake lifts his shirt off the back of the chair and punches his arms into the sleeves. Eric wonders if the man is ashamed. Scared? Or is he simply done?

The room drops to the left. Eric imagines the desk, the chair, the armoire sliding over the canted beige carpet. They crash into the wall, pile against the door.

But they haven't moved. The floor isn't tilted; the wallpaper isn't breathing. Eric just needs a moment to get his head together.

Breath play does this to him.

He discovered the practice in his youth, the erotic sensation of suffocation more intense than simple friction. Just a boy, Eric knelt in his closet, a shirt wrapped around his neck, the other end knotted to the clothes rod. Two times a day. Three. Four. He jacked his cock as the world evaporated. The walls around him grew thin, transparent, burned through by light.

White.

Eric blinks and his childhood is gone. The hotel room continues to rise. Still falls. The pattern on the wallpaper ripples, melts, slides. Eric rides the waves.

"Thanks," Jake says, throwing his coat over his shoulders like a cape. He flips the security latch. Opens the door. Leaves.

Eric makes another attempt to move; this time he succeeds. With his legs draped over the edge of the bed, he smiles, wipes his palm through the cold fluid painting his stomach and walks to the bathroom.

After showering, he calls his wife.

As always, dinner will be ready at eight.

The dining table is too big for them. It is made of glass, a thick transparent sheet, ten feet long. At parties, silver trays of canapés cover the surface, but for day-to-day it is too large. They huddle at one end of it. Eric sits at the head of the table. His wife, Shelly, is to his

Dislocation

immediate left, and his children, Nicole and Robert, sit on his right. Both teenagers slump over their plates and have messy hair but expensive clothes. Through the tabletop, he sees Robert's bare foot, tapping the rug.

Conversation is brief, perfunctory. The proximity of his family is stifling and hot. He has long since stopped noticing the fine furniture and detailed décor of his home, the accessories of his success. He considers his children and wonders why they sulk. He has given them everything children could want, and yet they still act deprived. They never speak to him. They make demands, but conversation goes no further. Eric spears a piece of salmon with his fork, looks at the pink meat, drops it back to his plate.

"It really is dry," Shelly says. She lifts her wineglass, drinks deeply.

Shelly is Eric's second wife. He married his first wife for prestige and a position with her father's company. She had been a plain woman, and his closest confidante. His best friend. Dead for years, now. No trace of her left, save the children slumped over the too-large table.

Robert taps his bare toe on the carpet. Eric excuses himself and pushes away from the table. He tents his napkin over the barely sampled meal and retreats to his study. At his desk, he travels through chat rooms. His vision blurs momentarily, and the computer screen drops to the left. Eric closes his eyes, concerned.

Eric thinks he should call his doctor and then doubts it. Maybe it's just the flu coming on. Everybody was getting it.

Against the black screen of his eyelids, he sees a woman's face; it is freckled with blood. In her hands, she holds a wad of cloth, drenched red. She is screaming and crying, clasping the bloody rags to her chest and hunching over them in a gesture of protection. Squinting in pain, as if stricken by a cramp, she turns her face away.

Eric opens his eyes and the room tilts. Then it levels off.

He has an instant message window on his screen; it's Jake.

The message reads: *Who is this?*

Eric wakes to the sound of Shelly's screams. At first, he is confused and startled. He is on top of her; her nails are in his back; her thighs are clamped at his hips. Breathy gasps fill Eric's ear. He drives into her, a violent collision; she screams again, then the panting gasps. And again. And again. At the back of his mind and deep within his belly, desperation burns.

He has never wanted her this badly.

He has never wanted her at all.

Eric rides the elevator to the top floor of the corporate tower. He says hello to familiar yet nameless faces. These are the associates; they have not earned their way into his memory. They are little more than children to his eyes; lustful brats with hard-ons for success who beat off to the pages of Fortune Magazine. They all wear blue suits, faces suspended over yellow ties. Eric imagines their heads, torn away at the neck, lanced on golden spears. A room of them. A field of them.

Eric is disturbed by the thought. As he walks to his office, he can't imagine what fissure of his imagination it crawled from.

Who is this?

Jake's message from the previous night. Eric didn't know if the man was trying to be funny; he imagined so, even if he didn't get the joke.

For Eric, it didn't matter. Jake had agreed with the terms, including the one about a single encounter only. No lasting communication. No involvement. Just sex and then memory.

Eric made his position very clear in his reply: *Please observe our agreement and cease contacting me.*

Jake signed out of the room a second later.

Eric had a family to protect, a career, a life. He had no intention of jeopardizing them by encouraging men that might turn possessive, cruel, dangerous. Most of his tricks accepted the rules; they wanted nothing but release themselves, but some …

Some expected more.

He knew their motivation. He had power, had money; men liked to look at a face like his when they were fucking. Their egos drank from him and swelled.

Gilt by association.

Coffee in hand, Eric sits at his desk. After signing his name on a dozen letters, returning e-mails and a single phone call, he is back in the chat room.

Dislocation

The names sharing the chat room are familiar; Eric has already fucked or discouraged all of them. Small world, breath play. All of them were after the same coin, and defined themselves by its sides. Not heads or tails. Hands or throats.

He meets a colleague at lunch and while they are laughing about Gordie Michaels' hair plugs, the room blurs. Eric rubs his eyes. Again, the room slants and rolls. His colleague's face melts like heated wax. Eric feels clammy.

The flu? Definitely not the flu.

Eric rushes through lunch. On the sidewalk outside of the restaurant, he laughs at something his colleague says. Over the man's shoulder, he sees Jake standing far down the block. Eric's laughter halts, and fear, cold and electric, surges. Not a coincidence, he knows. Jake has followed him, watched him.

His colleague climbs in the back of a black Lincoln. The driver closes the door. Eric waves at his own driver and points at his watch. He holds up his index finger: *One minute.*

Eric stomps down the sidewalk. As he approaches Jake, he again thinks the man wears the face of a high school quarterback, ten years removed from glory.

"What do you think you're doing?" Eric demands.

"I wanted to see you again," Jake says. Despite his words, he appears bored.

"We had an agreement."

"I make a lot of agreements. I keep most of them."

"I suggest you keep this one. I'm not interested in pursuing this dialogue."

"A dialogue? Is that what we're having, Eric?"

Eric is startled to hear his real name spoken by the aging quarterback. The syllables collide at his temples and knit his gut into knots.

"That put some color in your cheeks," Jake tells him. "I know a lot about you. Your wife. Your family. Your business. I do my research; it's my job."

Blackmail, Eric thinks; in seconds, he sees the entirety of his life crumbling like a palace of rotted wood. "How much do you want?"

"This isn't about money, Eric. Meet me later at the hotel."

"I will not."

Once the words leave his lips, the street, the pedestrians, the buildings and the cars, flip. He stands in absolute darkness as if the tilting world pitched him into a tar-filled chasm. He is hot and claustrophobic. His entire body pulses with the strain of his heart. He has to get out of this place. Struggling. Clawing.

Light strikes his eyes and cold air washes over his face. Eric is standing on the sidewalk again. Jake is before him, angry and rigid – whispering but furious.

"... calm down, Marcus. This happens sometimes. It's a minor setback."

Eric throws a look over his shoulder, looking for the man Jake had called Marcus. For a moment, he is convinced that he stands in the middle of an ambush, but the walk is empty except for lunch crowds making their way back to offices.

"You're fucking nuts," Eric says.

Jake's face burns red; it tightens. His jaw muscles bulge.

Around them, pedestrians cast nervous glances on the exchange; they walk in an arc around the two men. Afraid now, Eric backs up a step. He does not know how much of the conversation he missed while in that dark place, but he is certain that Jake is insane.

Eric hurries down the sidewalk away from the raving man. He throws a look over his shoulder. Jake is not following. Eric slides into the back of the Mercedes and tells his driver, "Take me home."

Eric spends the afternoon in bed. His wife is at a meeting of the Symphony Board; his children are at school. Soon, they will come home and the house will fill with the booming and shrieking of their TVs and stereos. For now, the only disturbance is the housekeeper, vacuuming the upstairs hall. On two separate occasions, the bedroom sways and dips. He dozes to escape his anxiety. Not awake. Not asleep. Eric is revisited by the image of a woman speckled with blood, desperately trying to protect the glistening, red package in her arms.

When she turns away from him, he looks up and sees the bloody bulb of a hammer poised above his head.

Eric is startled out of his doze. He is followed by a low voice, "Shhhhhhh."

Dislocation

Eric shakes the dreadful image out of his head. He is sickened by the violence; it frightens him that he has conceived it.

Jake has done this to him. The strain of the man's pursuit has broken something in Eric's mind. Something would have to be done.

But what?

Jake refused his money; his only demand was a second meeting, but Eric didn't believe it was about the sex. Sex was too easy – as available as bread. Emotion didn't play into this; Jake did not love him. Yet, Jake did need him. Why?

Eric considers hiring someone to make the man disappear. Surely, someone he knows can orchestrate Jake's absence. But such extreme thoughts are foolish; he is not a gangster or a movie thug.

So, what was to be done?

Seeking inspiration, Eric climbs out of bed and carries his questions to the bedroom window. He gazes down on his estate, the hedges, the fountain circled by the cobbled drive. And when the world begins to spin out of alignment in a dislocating drop, Eric fights the sensation. The struggle makes him nauseous, but he holds on.

He throws his hands against the window casement to steady his body. And he fights.

A flood of voices crashes over him. The name, Marcus, peels through his head. Images roll like foam on the crests of the tide. Again he sees the frightened woman dotted with blood. He sees a baby in its crib, crying and fussing. He sees the hammer in his hand, watches himself use it until the squirming infant is still and silent.

Shhhhhhh.

He sees a factory and knows that his days are spent there, making plastic toys. A fat man with a greasy mustache yells, spitting tiny flecks of saliva as he bellows his rage in Eric's face – only the name he's screaming is different: Marcus. He remembers a childhood – not his – and a round, red face hovering over him. The face just floats. No body. No limbs. But still able to inflict pain.

And all of the noise: machines birthing ugly wads of plastic; children crying; his wife bitching about their cheap furniture; his boss shouting; his mother sobbing; his father grunting like a pig.

The name: Marcus.

Still holding the edges of the capsizing world before him, Eric begins to understand. The extent of his violation is grotesque. He trembles, his knuckles white on the window frame.

If he can just keep himself from being turned inside out and shoved into the furnace-hot chasm behind his eyes, he will find Jake. If…

Surrounded by paneling, bookshelves, rich black leather furniture, Eric sits at the desk in his study. Steel-blue light paints his face and neck. He flies from one chat room to the next, seeking Jake's handle. But Jake is absent, leaving Eric desperate and sickened.

When his wife pokes her head in the door and asks about dinner, he snaps at her. He is busy. "Leave me alone."

Eric is in bed. Another man's memories mingle with his. The man's name is Marcus, and his history is bruised and abraded; it is misshapen by violence. Eric believes that Marcus is real.

And then he doesn't.

"Eric?"

He looks up from the quilted duvet to see who has spoken his name.

Shelly undresses by the window. Her body doesn't interest him. Only a decade ago, she was a beauty queen. She had big tits and looked good on his arm; she was what was expected of him. Eric hears the muffled blare of a movie pounding from his daughter's room and winces at the noise.

"You didn't have to bark at me," Shelly tells him, pulling a robe over her shoulders.

"I'm sorry," he says, because he knows it's what he's supposed to say.

Shelly stands at the end of the bed with her arms crossed. "I take a lot of shit from you, Eric, and I've never complained about it. You keep this family a mile away. You barely notice us. That's fine. That's you. But if I have to turn my head away and pretend I don't know about your trips and your afternoon meetings, the least you could do is show me some courtesy."

The way she emphasizes the words "afternoon meetings" unnerves him. He wonders how much she knows and how she knows it. Did she hire a detective to follow him or was it simply a guess, a suspicion?

"Yes, Eric, I know you fuck around. I don't know who she is, and I don't want to know. But if I have to play the good wife, then you'd damned well better *play* the good husband."

The word "she" frees him. Shelly knows nothing; she merely suspects.

"You're wrong," Eric says, managing to sound wounded. "And that's the end of this discussion. I'm sorry if I've been distant. The company has taken some bad hits this quarter, and it's running me down. Your other claims are simply ridiculous."

"This quarter?" Shelly asks. "Jesus, Eric, when weren't you like this?"

He throws the covers back and climbs from the bed. Shelly is shouting at him; her voice is loud, painful. Her hand grasps his shoulder. He slaps it away. Then, he leaves the room.

In the hall outside of his daughter's bedroom, he listens to the grinding soundtrack of the movie she is watching. He knocks on the door and enters.

"It's almost over," she says. She assumes he is only there to complain.

But Eric doesn't speak; he looks at his daughter, the arch of her brow, the curve of her nose. For her third birthday, he hired a pony for her to ride. The animal had terrified her. It is the only clear memory he has of her childhood.

"What?" she insists, as if he has been badgering her for hours.

Her face is pinched in exasperation; it is unfamiliar in every way.

Eric steps out of his daughter's room and closes the door. Downstairs he passes his son in the hall. The boy grunts, "hey," and hurries away.

Throughout his house, he finds strangers, and the regret lodges in his throat like a chicken bone.

At the computer in his study, he enters a chat room. It is just after midnight before Jake appears. They are in the same room in which they first met. Before Eric can send a message, a window opens on his screen.

Does your wife know how to fuck you? Jake writes. A smiley-faced symbol appears below the taunt. *Does she strangle the cum out of you?*

Eric's anger and disgust knot low in his throat. He feels foolish for having wanted the man, but then reminds himself that it is the act that seduces him, not the players. Jake's only significance was his willingness, his presence.

But Jake is different than the others. He is dangerous.

Why are you harassing me? he writes.

No time for games, Eric.

The screen tilts, falls and capsizes.

Before he can stop the pitching room, Eric is thrown back into darkness.

Blind. Burning. Confined.

He pulls out of the chasm and finds himself on the staircase in the middle of the night. In his hand he holds a stainless steel tenderizing mallet.

From his position on the stairs he cannot tell if he was climbing them or descending. He studies the ridges of the mallet; rows of tiny silver pyramids run over the beating head.

Upstairs, in the hallway, he is afraid to open any of the bedroom doors. He stares at the door of the room he shares with Shelly, looks at the knob; it is made of crystal; its facets are dark and sharply edged. A flash of memory reminds him of a woman and the child she could not protect.

Marcus's wife.

Marcus's child.

Eric returns to his study and places the mallet next to his keyboard. He jabs a button and the computer screen wakes. The message window still floats on the upper left corner of his screen. The window is full though he had exchanged only a few lines of text with Jake before blacking out. Eric scrolls up through the text. He stops at a random point and reads.

I thought it would be different.

You wanted his life, and you're damned well going to pay for it.

It's still so loud. Everything is so fucking loud. Why won't they shut up?

Eric looks over his shoulder at the door to his study and imagines the other doors further down the hall; the door to his daughter's room;

the door to his son's room; the door separating his bedroom from the corridor. He looks at the silver mallet.

Just keep it together, Marcus, Jake's next line reads.
I can't think.
Marcus?
Marcus! Reply you stupid fuck.

Eric scrolls down two lines: More of Jake's demands for a reply, more obscenities. Jake's last line of type is directed at him.
Eric. Hotel. Tomorrow.

Harsh afternoon light ignites the gold spears of the wallpaper pattern. Eric stands next to the bed; Jake sits in the cream and burgundy striped chair. It is a different room but very much the same as the one that witnessed their first encounter.

Jake speaks first; he looks at Eric but sees something else, something very far away.

"They locked me up when I was a child. They thought I was crazy because I heard voices. All of these fucked up screaming voices demanding that I hear them and help them. To me they were ghosts; to my parents they were a defect in my brain. So, I spent my childhood terrified, medicated and institutionalized. I was fifteen when I figured it out and twenty before I learned how profitable it could be."

"It?" Eric asks, the word making no sense.

"Finding skin for the voices."

"I'd say it's time to up the dosage on that medication."

"Stop the shit, Eric. You know what's going on, and you and Marcus can't coexist. So, I need to put him someplace else."

Eric doesn't believe him. He's captured too many remnant thoughts from Jake's client. This is a trap, a lie.

He still asks, "How?"

"Same as before. I cut off the air, take you to the edge, and then just a bit further. There is a point, a moment when the spirit separates from the body and can be smuggled out."

"Or in," Eric says. He steps away from the bed toward Jake.

"Not this time. The procedure either works or it doesn't. I have no choice but to make other arrangements for Marcus."

"You know he's a murderer. He beat his family to death with a hammer. He killed his own baby."

"Not my problem or my business."

"Business," Eric scoffs. He takes another step forward. Another. "How much of my money was he going to give you?"

"Irrelevant, Eric. It didn't happen."

"Obviously, it was more than you thought I'd pay to get my life back."

Eric stops in front of the chair and stares down on Jake, who makes a show of checking his watch; the prick is so arrogant.

The lamp on the table next to Jake has a metal base. It's thick and square and tapers beneath a creamy, pleated shade.

"He hit them at the temple first," Eric says. "He didn't want them to scream like his boss did. He just wanted them quiet."

Jake's lips draw into a sneer. "Don't even think about it, Eric. You try it, and you're stuck with him."

Eric shrugs. "He's not so bad," he says.

Then, he grabs the lamp, and with a smooth backhanded motion, buries a corner of the square base in Jake's temple.

None of them will leave the room. Eric knows this; he planned it that way.

Not Jake. Not himself. Not Marcus.

The damaged lamp rests on the floor; so does Jake. Eric sits on the edge of the bed and looks at the dented pieces of both. He reaches into the pocket of his overcoat and pulls out a length of nylon cord. Pale blue shadows run through the white cable, a trick of the light.

Eric asks himself how this happened; it seems impossible, and for a moment, he accepts the fact that it is impossible. In life, Jake had no more power than the average lunatic; Eric harbors nothing but ambiguity. He is alone in his body and his mind.

Jake's body, the broken lamp, they tilt and become liquid before Eric's eyes. He blinks, grasps the cord in both hands and pulls tightly as if the nylon were his tether on reality.

When the disorientation passes, Eric stands and strips off his clothes. He folds his trousers and jacket neatly and lays them over the bed. He even folds his socks and underwear.

Dislocation

While knotting one end of the cord around the clothes bar in the narrow closet, his cock grows hard. Memories of childhood anticipation rush through him. Fear. Excitement. He runs his palm up the tether and then down.

He thinks that in these last moments he will have some revelation, a flash of wisdom that will add a fraction of meaning to his life. But he is simply naked, stroking a length of rope.

His wife – a token, a trophy, a prop – is shopping less than a mile from the hotel. His children are at school; they are unhappy. They have always been unhappy. His home, a well-appointed museum of twenty-first century consumption, is empty. Even his arrogance abandons him.

Why live, he wonders, stroking the rope.

"Why die?" he asks himself.

Even with the question in the air, he ties a loop in the end of the cord, but as he cinches the knot, his legs take him away from the closet and the clothes rod. The makeshift noose drops from his hand, though he still reaches for it.

"You'll go to jail," he tells himself. "Even if you managed to escape and get out of the country, they'd find you."

He says, "Jake paid for the room. No one has to know we were here."

"They'd know."

"Give it some thought."

"But ... "

"Shhhhhh," he says. "Just give it some thought."

They Would Say She Danced

The clock read eleven forty-five, and Deidre's heart beat a little faster. She sat in her kitchen with the lights out, the curtains drawn. The scent of fried catfish still hung in the air hours after the supper dishes had been washed. In the drainer by the sink a single plate and glass dried next to the black skillet. She was alone now, had been since a heart attack took her husband T. Roy two years back. He died on the linoleum over by the Frigidaire a week shy of Christmas. Deidre's gaze fell on the spot. She noticed the flooring curling away from the baseboard, and then turned away. The radio sat on the table next to her, its volume tuned so low she had to lean in close to hear what was being said.

"...outside of this maximum security prison... "

Her phone rang, startling her. Though why it should she couldn't say. The thing had been ringing all night. One call after another, clanging and scraping over her ears – the chains of a ghost struggling to emerge from her wall.

Deidre sipped her coffee, cold now, and hugged herself until the caller gave up. In a minute, maybe two, the phone would ring again. She'd thought about turning off the ringer or taking the headset from the cradle, but she endured the racket. Only fifteen more minutes.

"As a society we should practice mercy and forgiveness," an impassioned voice cried through the radio.

"Did he show mercy to his victims?" another voice asked moments later.

"I say kill the bastard. It's a hell of a lot more humane than what he did to those women."

Deidre nodded her hear. "Yes," she whispered, "Yes." Quickly she swiped at the back of her neck with a palm. She clutched the nape and held tightly, leaning toward the speaker to hear what else the people on the radio would say.

"Sean Michael Walters is a human being who needs... "

"Sean Michael Walters is an animal who should be... "

Sean Michael Walters. He was a sadist and a murderer, killing sixteen young women before justice found him.

My poor girl, Deidre thought. Florence – dear Florence with an entire life to look forward to – gone.

Walters was a monster who'd spent ten years humiliating, torturing and butchering his victims in a trailer only three towns over. Then he'd spent another two years awaiting trial and twelve more on death row, using up his appeals. Deidre wished the police had shot him on sight. It wasn't a Christian thought, and she regretted that, but ever since her daughter's death she'd carried loneliness and misery, twin emotions that weighed on her back and shoulders like a concrete shawl.

Someone knocked loudly on Deidre's front door. Reporters. They wanted a statement, wanted to know how she felt now that Sean Michael Walters was about to pay for his crimes. Why couldn't they leave her alone? There were so many other families to console, and she'd told them everything she had to say years ago at the trial. She no longer needed to expose her broken heart to the media. In a dozen minutes it would be over. The weight would fall from her stooped shoulders, and she'd be free, and maybe then – maybe then she'd speak to the reporters. Deidre could just imagine it. Unburdened. She'd turn the lights on and smile – smile for the first time in decades – and she'd throw open the door to the eager faces of the journalists. They would report that she was grateful this terrible time had passed. They would say she was in good spirits. They would say she danced.

She'd loved her baby girl so much, how could she not rejoice once that monster was punished?

Deidre stood from the table, leaving the whispers of the radio behind for a moment. At the stove she poured more coffee into her cup and checked the clock. Eleven fifty-one. Ten minutes left.

Back at the table, she thought about Florence, wondered what her life might have been like if she'd lived. It was a familiar and painful consideration, one that dated back decades. Things were tough back then. They hadn't been a rich family: T. Roy's job at the lumber yard kept the bills paid, and Deidre's hours as a clerk at the Hobby Hutch brought in a bit for niceties, but there had never been a lot of money around. Still, Deidre knew that Florence would have become something special. Something wonderful.

The Seer Man had told her so.

Thinking about him made her shiver, but it was right that Deidre thought of him now at the end of it all, since he was there at the beginning.

Even before T. Roy forced her to visit him the Seer Man had scared Deidre.

His name was Xavier Crolt, and he practiced his hoodoo in a big house out on the Old Loggers Road. Crolt had looked to be in his seventies at the time. His face was as dark and wrinkled and spoiled looking as a peeled apple left on the sill. With eyes that barely showed through his drooping lids, he might have been thought wearied with age, but only if you stood back a good twenty feet. Any closer and you saw the cold twinkle of those eyes, the fox-sharp calculation. His white hair was unnaturally lush. It swept back from his tanned brow in a thick snowy wave, and upon meeting the man Deidre imagined he might have been handsome once.

T. Roy took her to Crolt only a week after she announced her pregnancy. She'd been so excited about the child. If it turned out to be a girl Deidre would name her Florence after her mawmaw. She couldn't wait to be a mother, but she didn't want to see Crolt. She'd heard awful things about him – whispers at the beauty parlor – but her husband insisted, and T. Roy was not accustomed to being questioned, especially by his woman. So they'd driven north to the Old Logger's Road.

Crolt answered the door wearing a proper suit with a crimson vest fastened over his rounded belly. His thick white hair was brushed back neatly, and he was courteous in tone. But his eyes traced over Deidre like a weasel eyeing an egg.

The Seer Man led them into the foyer. The house was as cold as Christmas in Vermont, though the temperature outside soared. Crolt asked T. Roy to take a seat in the parlor, sweeping his arm toward the room and leading Deidre away down an unlit hall. Her stomach clenched in fear, being alone with this man. The ache was so bad, she worried her terror might actually hurt the baby she carried.

They entered a small room, the windows covered by thick cypress shutters. A single light burned from a lily shaped fixture attached to the far wall. Foul herbs and old blood scented this room. Layered with these odors was the fragrance of wax, coming from the dozens of candles situated on a sideboard to her left. Black wicks poked from craters of scarlet, cream and plum. The place was dark and cold and moist like a cave.

Crolt asked Deidre to remove her clothes and lie on a desk that occupied the center of the room. A down comforter, blemished by innumerable unwholesome looking stains, covered the desk and a pillow was situated at one end.

The frigid air and growing dread made her tremble. This wasn't right, she thought. How could T. Roy think this was right?

"You best hurry up, Girl," Crolt told her, removing his jacket. "Sometimes it takes all day for a vision to impress itself on me."

"All day?" Deidre asked, her voice a dry whisper.

Crolt rolled up a sleeve and squinted his small eyes at her. "You got nothing to be worried of," he said. "Hundreds of women been on my table. Some like it so much they leave their men at home and come on back for a private visit or two."

The words, delivered with a wink, repulsed her. She wanted to run out of this dark room, wanted to flee the house and never come back. But T. Roy would be angry if she didn't let Crolt do his work. And for as much as Crolt frightened her, T. Roy's anger scared her more.

"Now, you just get them clothes off and let Crolt do his work."

"Would you please turn around?"

Finishing the roll of his second sleeve, Crolt let out a coughing chuckle. "No need for the shy, Girl. I'm gonna see it all soon enough. Would you feel more to home if I stripped down too?"

Appalled, but trying to hide it, Deidre said, "No, Sir. That won't be necessary."

It took her almost three minutes to get undressed. Her trembling fingers were clumsy with the buttons on her dress and the hook of her bra. When she draped the undergarment over a chair, she noticed how the cold had teased her nipples, and she clamped her hands over her breasts, feeling ashamed. Tears welled in her eyes, spilled down her cheeks, but she kept her sobs deep inside.

How much humiliation did T. Roy expect her to endure? This wasn't right.

"Now, you see there," Crolt announced, once Deidre was bare and shaking before him. "You got nothing to be ashamed of. A beauty, you are. Now, you climb up on my table there."

She did as she was told and though she was only going under the Seer Man's hands, she felt as if she were going under a scalpel. Once situated on the table, Deidre looked away from Crolt. She gazed at the floral wallpaper beneath the lily-shaped lamp and picked a leaf out with her eyes, a small golden leaf. She stared at the shape and forced her thoughts to it, even when the dry rough hands touched her belly.

The coarse palms ran over her navel and up to the lowest of her ribs. A finger brushed her breast, and she gritted her teeth. Through the glaze of tears, she looked at the leaf on the wall and tried to think about something nice... a warm forest pond, a picnic.

Crolt's thick fingers gently kneaded her belly, and he hissed out a trembling breath. "Oh my," he said.

The concern in his voice made it through Deidre's distracting daydream. She snapped her head around to look at the awful old man and asked what was wrong.

"Nothing, Girl. I'll tell all when I'm finished."

Over the next hour, Deidre endured Crolt's examination. It became more intimate and more disturbing with the passing minutes. Several times, Crolt groaned or panted as if in the throes of marital relations. Deidre kept her eyes on the wall, on the paper, on the leaf. When his fingers became too personal with her, Deidre clamped her eyes shut – a child's defense against bogeymen and other frights.

Finally, Crolt's hands left her body. "Lord," he muttered. This was followed by another of his coughing chuckles. "You get your things on and meet me and T. Roy in the parlor."

With that, Crolt hurried from the room, leaving the door open as he raced into the corridor. Deidre let out a single sob. She bit her lower lip to keep the flood of misery inside. Then she left the table and went to her clothes.

In the parlor, T. Roy sat on a plush red sofa, smoking a cigarette. He didn't look at her when she walked into the room. Deidre felt a burn of flush on her cheeks. Guilt for what Crolt had done gnawed at her, and she wanted her husband to say something so she'd know it was all okay, so she'd know she hadn't endured such a degrading ritual only to drive her husband further away.

"It's cold in here," Deidre said, because there was nothing else she could think to say.

"We'll be gone soon enough," T. Roy said, drawing on his cigarette.

Deidre took a seat on the other end of the sofa. T. Roy didn't look at her again for quite some time.

Years later, Deidre leaned close to her radio. Her hands clasped her stomach where the memory of Crolt's touch wove sickness into her anticipation.

"...only two minutes, now. You can hear the protestors chanting for a reprieve, while supporters of the sentence shout for justice. It's chaos out here."

A reprieve, Deidre thought. They wouldn't. She lifted her thumbnail to her mouth and clamped it between two teeth. They couldn't. Not now. But what if they did? What if they spared the monster, and Deidre was forced to carry this burden for the rest of her life? Oh no. Oh no. It wouldn't be fair. Not to her. Not to *Florence*. After all the agony Deidre had endured because of Sean Michael Walters, he had to die. He had to.

When Crolt entered the room, his cheeks were red as if he'd left Deidre in the study so he could run laps around the house. T. Roy uncrossed his legs and leaned forward on the sofa, watching expectantly as Crolt walked to a small desk on the other side of the room.

"The child will be a girl," Crolt said. Deidre's heart lightened with the news, but it was a short-lived joy. "But she won't be of God."

T. Roy flashed an angry glance at Deidre. It tore through her. "What do you mean?" T. Roy asked.

"She will become unnatural," Crolt said. "She will rise to a position of power, and will take a wife in place of a husband. She will lead others from God's path."

"You sure?" T. Roy asked.

"I believe my reputation speaks for itself."

"Get rid of it," T. Roy said through a clenched jaw. "Get rid of it now."

"No," Deidre cried. Her organs shriveled inside of her, turned to crumbling dust as she struggled to think of some reprieve for her little girl's life. But there was no discussion to be had. T. Roy had made his wishes clear.

"Do it," he told Crolt. Then T. Roy stood, eyed his wife with disgust and walked out. He slammed the front door, leaving the house.

Despite tears and protests the Seer Man again led Deidre down the hall.

Now, so many years later, sitting in a darkened kitchen with a hand wrapped around a cold cup of coffee, Deidre felt a fresh pang of loss for that child. She didn't think she'd ever feel that kind of loss again. She never wanted to. The next time she saw Xavier Crolt, only five months later, newly pregnant, she'd made no fuss. She refused to feel anything for the child until she knew it would actually take a breath. Cooly she entered Crolt's study and disrobed. She laid down on the table and this time she watched the Seer Man through all of his disgusting explorations.

"You have a son, and he will be strong," Crolt told them. T. Roy smiled and Deidre permitted herself a moment to care about the unborn boy.

It was perhaps the only moment she'd allowed herself to feel even the slightest affection for Sean.

Once he was born, Deidre cared for him in the manner of a hospital worker. His needs would be tended to, but he'd receive not an ounce of her love. T. Roy had let Crolt sacrifice her daughter – her precious Florence – clearing the path for this child's birth. If Florence had been born, there would be no Sean Michael Walters. Sixteen girls would not have endured his brutal company. Sixteen girls would still be alive. But no, Deidre's baby girl died, and Sean lived, growing into some kind of monster that needed anguish to feed his evil heart.

Now, T. Roy was dead and in just under a minute, Sean Michael Walters, her son, would also be dead. Then she could turn on the lights. Then she could smile. Then she could stand tall as the crushing weight fell from her back. Then she could dance.

Couldn't she?

Yes, she thought. *Of course, I can. I had no choice.*

T. Roy had made all of the decisions. Her life was nothing more than an extension of his, and she'd lived beneath that man's shadow, crushed under the weight of it for over thirty years. Then Sean was arrested and a new shadow fell over her. The reporters came and the documentary people, wanting to know how it felt being the mother of a monster, and she bore those burdens. But not anymore.

Deidre leaned close to the radio, her heart beating so quickly she could feel its pulse in the back of her throat. The coffee cup in her shaking hand rattled against the table, and Deidre let it go, again clasping the back of her neck as she waited for the news.

"It's done," the radio announcer said.

SHELTER

Absolutely grotesque, thought Randall Banks, turning his back on the sculpture to observe something else – anything else – in the black-walled gallery. Over a hundred patrons, critics and art enthusiasts mingled in the room, whispering and pointing at the bizarre collection, indicating that Bea's latest opening was a hit.

Hit or not, Randall thought his friend had finally lost her mind.

The shotgun gallery, long and sleek with twenty-foot ceilings provided the perfect setting for Bea's work. Her medium was acrylic sculpture, and a dozen of the pieces perched on pedestals lining the room. The play of brilliant light on the translucent forms, all set against a backdrop of midnight black, would have been stunning were the subjects of her sculpture not so completely unwholesome. Even the rhythms of the crowd added to the atmosphere surrounding the objects on display, seeming to give the sculptures movement, like opalescent apparitions gliding through mottled space.

From a distance, the effect was grand and ethereal. Up close, it was nauseating. He knew artists and their admirers felt chic when they challenged normal perceptions of beauty, but for God's sake...

Bea had created a menagerie of freaks, spent countless hours, sculpting and casting gorgeous faces and bodies, then accentuated them with abnormalities so profound they would have been comical were they not so finely wrought. He had seen a female torso, realized with near perfection, only to have her breasts extended in streamlined muzzles, lined with rows of canine teeth. A man's face was melded with that of a goat; a girl's hair draped back into smooth wings like those of a bat, her eyes pinpoints, her nose sheered close to the skull. Generally, he found Bea's work disturbing but his friend's latest exhibit was positively perverse.

Despite Banks' feelings about his friend's art, Bea drew a big crowd, and they brought along big checkbooks, which kept her producing what she pretentiously titled, "Modern Gods."

Randall stepped away from a sculpture of two children, who seemed to have been woven together by flayed skin and nearly knocked over a waiter, carrying a silver tray topped with champagne flutes. Randall snatched one of the glasses and sipped the wine.

Now, where the hell was that kid? he wondered.

He had brought a boy with him to keep him entertained should the exhibit prove a bore, which it had. Not that Chad was really a boy or any less of a bore than the majority of the people Randall met. But he was pretty, and he seemed like he might be adventurous.

Randall slid through a pack of "artsy" looking people, all dressed in black who stared rhapsodically at one of Bea's atrocities. Once he cleared the crowd, emerging into an open space, he saw Chad beside another of the ghostly sculptures, talking to a middle-aged gentleman with a white beard.

His approach was noticed, and Chad broke away from the man, walking quickly to meet Randall in the middle of the room.

"Who's your friend?" Randall asked.

Chad blushed and chuckled nervously. "He's just some guy who said hello."

"Just some guy, huh?" Randall asked, nodding his head slowly.

"His name's Orson Nye," Chad said in exasperation. "He owns this place. I figured you already knew him. He was telling me about the artist. She sounds like a cool freak. You said you knew her, right?"

Beatrice was exactly that, Randall thought, a cool freak. "Yes."

"Orson was telling me that she believes her sculptures are inspired by spirits that visit her. She thinks they can be brought to life or brought into our world or something. I didn't quite get it."

Randall nodded. He'd heard Bea's mystical bullshit for years. Even before this last batch of sculpted misery, back when she was working with more traditional, elegant forms, she had made it very clear that she was not responsible for her art, merely a channel for it. Having slept with a good half dozen of her models over the years, Randall knew the extent of Bea's charade.

"Mysticism is good for sales," Bea said once, giggling.

Chad looked back at the white-bearded Nye and nodded quickly.

"Maybe you two want to be alone," Randall said, hoisting the champagne flute to his lips.

"You're jealous," Chad said, his cheeks burning red. "God, that's so sweet."

"Is it?"

"Sure it is."

Randall let the kid squirm for a while, even got him to apologize a couple of times before Randall said, "Forget it. It's nothing."

In the men's room with the kid bent over the sink, Randall slammed his hips forward, leaning back on his heels to get the best angle on Chad's ass. He pounded his cock into the kid, who whimpered like a lonely puppy with each thrust. When the tingle of climax began to roll up his shaft, Randall dug his fingers into the soft flesh of the kid's hips; he grasped as tightly as he could and pulled back while he drove forward, grinding his pelvis into the firm buttock muscles and letting loose a flow of pure heat. Chad convulsed and reared back, his ass squirming on Randall's cock, his own climax bringing a shudder to his young body.

Randall peeled off the condom and tossed it in the trash before nudging past Chad so he could wash himself at the sink. The kid started kissing his neck and nuzzling him. Randall chuckled at the tickling admiration and pulled away. After he dried himself, he went to the door and said, "give me a couple of minutes before you come out."

He stepped into the hall and caught his reflection against the glass window of the gallery office. To his right, the storeroom door stood open and on his left, a sour-faced old matron who smelled of lilac and bourbon, tensed at the sight of him. "My friend isn't feeling well," Randall said simply. "He'll just be another minute."

The woman's face pinched even more severely, and she looked away.

Back in the gallery, amid the throng of art zombies, he eased to the far end of the exhibit hall and found himself facing the most disturbing of Bea's creations. Unfortunately, the artist arrived at his side the moment he saw the dreadful piece, and he knew he wouldn't be able to dismiss it as quickly as he would have liked.

"I knew you'd be drawn to this one, Randall," Bea said, slipping her arm through his, linking their elbows. "I call him Serphim, a blending of the serpent and the angelic. Isn't he magnificent?"

Randall would not have used the word magnificent. Horrible, perhaps. Disturbing, certainly. But no, probably not magnificent.

The piece was shaped like a kidney only of the size of a small boy's torso. A face pushed through the crest of the piece, as if being born from the clear acrylic. Eyes without iris or pupil bore a feral stare into Randall. The stunning face, which might truly have been angelic, were it not for the gaping mouth and curving, needle-sharp fangs, seemed too lifelike as if a beautiful youth had been drained of life, fitted with obscenely sharp teeth and crystallized in the name of art.

"This is amazing," Chad said, easing past Randall and Bea to put his nose close to the sculpture.

"He's a very smart boy," Bea said, knocking Randall's ribs with her elbow.

He forced a smile.

"What does the symbol on the crest mean?"

"You noticed," Bea said with some enthusiasm. "That's his birth sign."

"Oh yeah," Chad said a bit too eagerly. "Orson mentioned those. That's how you bring them to life."

Bea shook her head seriously and quit Randall's arm to approach Chad. "Not to life," she corrected. "To flesh. They are alive already, all around us. Like oxygen, they surround and fill us. Their signs simply admit them to our world of flesh, should you dare to enable them."

Chad cast an uncertain look at Randall. He shrugged.

"Have you ever enabled one?" Chad asked.

The artist's cheeks flushed bright red. Randall thought it a good act. Then, Bea laughed and patted Chad's shoulder before saying, "I've done all I can do for them."

Bea left them alone at the Serphim. "Cool freak, huh?" Randall said.

"At least."

Chad reached out a finger and touched a spot three inches above the Serphim's eyes, where a series of hash marks were scratched in the acrylic. When he pulled the digit away, Randall winced, noticing a pale smear on the sculpture.

Hadn't the kid washed the semen off of his hands?

Disgusted, Randall stepped forward quickly to wipe away the smudge. But he must have not been seeing clearly, because the sculpture's crest was unmarked, as clear as glass.

Randall blinked and again noticed the needle-sharp fangs and the smooth, vicious eyes. "I need a drink," he announced, stepping back. His shadow slid down the sculpted face and light twinkled along the ridges of its eyes and mouth.

Prisms of color danced behind the features. Randall ushered Chad toward the bar, feeling even more disturbed by the art. For a moment, as his shadow gave way to light on the clear surface, Randall felt certain that the fucking thing had been staring at him.

―――――――――

Pain shot through his chest but Randall woke unable to move. His first thought was that he suffered a heart attack, but the paralysis seemed more attributable to the effects of a stroke. Fear covered him in a cold mist. His eyes were open; he saw the gentle rise of his barreled chest and the black well of his distant ceiling where the blades of the fan made lazy circles. But Randall could not move his head; he couldn't move at all. His heart still beat and his lungs drew shallow breath, but he felt a great pressure on his ribcage as if he was suffocating, and his muscles were rigid, cramping and immobile.

Inexpressible panic blossomed within him. Asphyxia, a childhood terror now freshly blooming, seemed only moments away. As a child, he'd dreaded small spaces, and he'd never smoked a day in his life, fearing damage to his lungs, which might result in the slow suffocation of emphysema. And now, he could not move and felt his lungs growing rigid and unresponsive.

Maybe he could wake Chad. If he could make a noise, any noise, he might be able to wake the kid and get help. But through his panicked mind, he remembered that Chad wasn't staying with him tonight. After the gallery, the kid went home to study for his midterms.

Encased in the shell of his body, Randall began to drown in fear.

A head pushed into his line of sight. The face of a beautiful man hovered over him for a moment and then pulled away.

"If your heart doesn't burst, you'll survive," a whispered voice sang. "Believe I'm a dream and of no harm."

He caught a blur of movement, something rustled the hair on his chest, but he felt neither caress nor abuse. Maybe the intruder had simply blown breath over his body.

Still, he could feel nothing, and the absence of sensation added to his sense of losing life.

"You are in a position to help me," the melodic voice whispered. "All I ask is shelter. "

The beating of Randall's heart grew to a furious speed, and he felt certain it would give out from the exertion. His sense of suffocation became overwhelming. Bound within his flesh, Randall was pliant and vulnerable in a manner so extreme as to threaten his sanity.

He couldn't even cry.

He prayed to be allowed to close his eyes, wanting to eliminate sight so that he could accept the intruder's advice and deceive himself into believing these moments were simply dream. The stranger's beautiful face appeared above him again to block the slow stir of the ceiling fan blades. "Shelter," he said.

Randall stared into the ice gray eyes, studying their unnatural paleness and realizing that at some point he had slipped into delusion. To further this conviction, the man opened his mouth to reveal two slender sickles that curved back toward his ridged palate like the fangs of a cobra. While this face had been the model for Bea's sculpture, Bea's sculpture had been the model for Randall's current hallucination.

The face pulled away. The blades of the fan spun far above. A dull pressure built in Randall's gut. Something moved in him, throbbing like a second heart.

And finally, Randall's eyes closed.

He woke to bright morning light with every muscle in his body cramped so painfully that Randall phoned his secretary, telling her that he would not be coming into the office. He rolled slowly out of bed and tested his legs, his thighs screaming as he balanced himself on feet, which felt too small. He drew thick breaths down his throat and felt the relief of his expanding lungs. His temples pounded, and each step sent anguish from ankle to skull, but at least he could move.

In the bathroom, he turned on the shower until the scalding spray shot from the three showerheads to douse him in a massaging cascade. He worked his muscles slowly until some of the pain had been broken out of them. Stepping onto the cotton bathmat, his feet began to feel normal again.

What in the hell had happened? Randall wondered. He wasn't foolish enough to believe that the incident of the previous evening had been a dream. No. Some asshole had broken into his house and had shot him full of drugs. And while the prick had allowed Randall to live, he suspected that he'd lost some of his treasures in the bargain. Why else incapacitate him, if not to rob him blind?

He was wrong, though. Every piece of crystal remained in the deco cabinet. No one had touched the china or silver in the Biedermeier hutch in the dining room. His safe remained undisturbed. Randall returned to the bedroom and checked his wallet — not a penny gone. His jewelry, what little he had purchased over the years, lay nestled in the case on his chest of drawers. He looked around the bedroom suspiciously and ran a hand through his wet hair.

A sharp pain rolled up his shoulder blades, and amid his relief at finding his belongings untouched, he began to fear that his attacker had had a darker motive.

What if the prick had poisoned him?

Jesus Christ, Randall!

The memory of Doctor Clark's anxious voice curdled the acid in Randall's stomach. He had his back to the mirror and was looking over his shoulder to see the two red welts that marred his skin just above the right shoulder blade. Despite his doctor's distress, preliminary tests showed no trace of poison, medication or even chemical. In order to have the test results quickly, he had paid four times what a normal blood spectrum would have cost, but he didn't want to spend the next three days in a panic, wondering what bizarre compound floated in his veins. Fortunately, it seemed his blood was clear.

But he did not feel well. Randall convinced himself that the feeling was a residual sense of violation at having been attacked in his own home, in his own bed for Christ's sake. But more than that, he felt like something was wrong inside of him.

He left the bathroom and descended the stairs to stand before the vast picture window in his living room, absorbing the warmth from the last rays of sunlight. He fixed himself a whiskey and soda and returned to the window.

Uncomfortable with the silence and isolation, Randall phoned Chad but only got his answering machine. He left a quick message and then began to walk through the house. When he passed the cabinet in the living room, holding his collection of fine crystal, he looked away.

The Baccarat and Steuben reminded him of Bea's sculptures, and those damned things had done enough to stain his thoughts.

Only an hour before, when Doctor Clark called with his results, he'd woken from a long afternoon nap, soaked in sweat with a nightmare fading behind his eyes – a stunning face emerging from a pellucid womb, baring fangs that dripped venom.

All I ask is shelter, the man had said.

Now what kind of twisted shit was that? Shelter? From what? Randall sipped his cocktail, separating the man's face from Bea's insane representation of him because that connection confused him. His intruder wasn't a spirit, enabled to flesh. He was a man, with a syringe and some major juice that brought paralysis and perhaps even hallucination. And despite Bea's supernatural – *I channel the spirits* – public relations crap, he knew she used models for many, if not all of her sculptures.

He also knew that whoever had modeled for Bea's acrylic snake-angel had broken into his house.

"Well damn," Randall whispered. The model was probably at the opening, checking out the crowd for a mark. Randall hadn't noticed him amid the spaced-out art zombies, but the guy could have been observing people from the parking lot, waiting for a likely target to follow home and abuse.

He called Beatrice LaCroix.

"Tell me something beautiful," Bea said.

Why the hell couldn't she just say hello like normal people? Randall wondered. "Bea, I don't have time for your artier-than-thou shit right now."

"Randall?"

"Good guess. You win. Now, pull out your Rolodex."

Rush hour traffic slowed his drive across town. Impatient, Randall tried several alternate routes, finally realizing than none of them were going to get him to the Congress Park address any faster.

Bea had fought him for nearly ten minutes before finally buckling and giving him the address for the man who had modeled for her snake-angel monstrosity. The guy was named Ari Lockwood, and according to Bea, he was a medical student who modeled and frequently sold his ass for spending money. Randall didn't care about the guy's career or education; he just needed to see the guy's face to confirm his suspicion, and then he was calling the cops.

Full dark settled before he pulled to the curb well down the block from Lockwood's cream-colored, stucco bungalow. A cold, sharp wind cut through the collar of his jacket as he left the car and strolled casually along the sidewalk. Randall had always liked this neighborhood, even before it was regentrified by the beneficiaries of the dot com boom. The streets, lined with trees and well-maintained bushes, were quiet and the homes were quaint, if a bit small for his taste.

Randall walked up a steep slope of lawn to the side of Ari Lockwood's house and disappeared into the shadows of a densely foliated path. He had no intention of confronting the man. He only needed to see Lockwood's face. If he could manage that without alerting the asshole to his presence, all the better. Fortunately, the heavy brush covered him as he made his way to the backyard.

In the back, light from the kitchen window cut a rectangular swath over the neatly trimmed lawn. Shadows broke the illumination, sending liquid waves of light through the glass. Randall pushed close to the exterior wall, wishing he were further back in the yard and less likely to be seen by the home's occupant.

But here he was, and all he needed was to see the man's face. He could sprint for his car and lock himself in if Lockwood saw him. He'd use his cell phone to call the cops once he had a locked door between them.

First though – the face.

Randall leaned to the side and looked through the kitchen window, tensed to flee should he be spotted.

A powerful back, naked and muscular, appeared against the pane. If this were Lockwood, he had a tattoo on his neck, a stylized sun with wavy arms jutting out from a perfectly round center. The tattoo folded in half as the man's head was thrown back, his brown hair flattening against the glass.

Lockwood wasn't alone, Randall noted.

Another man's hand crept over the muscular shoulder; a second hand slid over the hips.

The palms of the tattooed man slapped the glass so hard, the pane cracked. His body went rigid, and then he dropped from view so quickly that it seemed his legs had been cut out from under him. Randall spun back against the wall and looked at the lawn, where the light from the kitchen lapped against the grass for a moment and then burned steadily.

Something heavy was being moved in the kitchen.

Feeling exposed, Randall crouched and eased to the path at the side of the yard, keeping low to take up a position in the bushes along the fence line. From here, he could see into the kitchen while camouflaged by leafy shrubs.

Through the foliage and the cracked window was a clear view of a simple suburban kitchen, with yellow walls and a chrome toaster on the counter beside a black microwave oven. The man with the tattoo now lay draped on the breakfast bar, separating the kitchen from what Randall assumed would be a small dining area. His arms and legs dangled over its edges. Between his legs, another brown-haired man, with a similarly muscled back, but no tattoo was hunched. His arm worked furiously, his shoulder flexing with the effort in what appeared to be a fierce masturbation.

If Lockwood was jacking his trick off, Randall thought, he was gonna tear the skin from the guy's dick if he didn't ease up.

As if in answer to Randall's thoughts, the man stopped his frantic strokes and stepped from between the limp legs to take up a new position, a position that was no more sexual than his last had been.

Under the cone of light, cast by the kitchen fixture, Randall saw the reality of what was transpiring in that room and threw a hand over his mouth.

Lockwood held a long serrated knife, which he was using to saw through the meat of the supine man's thigh. A ragged gash, from groin to knee, oozed an ever-expanding pool of blood over the countertop. Lockwood jammed the blade between the man's legs, impaling the limp penis and slicing through the deflated scrotum as he carved furiously at the meat of the thigh. A gout of blood shot like a geyser from the wound; the leg and body shuddered as the blade worked deeper into the flesh, drawing a wound that ultimately encircled the leg. And the victim, his head propped against the wall, stared through the glass and into the yard with paralyzed eyes.

Randall's heart thundered. His belly rolled.

The men in the kitchen were twins.

Both victim and butcher had been cast from the same mold.

The sick overpowered Randall, and he spun for the fence where he wretched as quietly as he could manage. After a minute of emptying his belly, wiping his face with a palm, Randall returned his attention to the crime unfolding beyond the kitchen window.

Lockwood had set down his knife. His fingers worked furiously in the gash he'd sliced in his victim's leg, and then he jerked back, tearing away the skin, the muscle, the entirety of the thigh. He lifted the dripping meat high and threw his head back.

And he began to eat.

Randall couldn't move. A new paralysis, an affliction of the unspeakable act he was witnessing rather than the effects of a chemical compound, forced Randall to endure the bloody spectacle. His belly ached horribly and his head spun with the images of violence, but Randall could not turn away.

A noise or some other disturbance drew Lockwood's attention toward the window, and then Randall saw the most dreadful thing in a night full of dreads.

The man was not chewing his victim's thigh, but rather engorging himself with it. His mouth, impossibly wide, enveloped the meat and his neck muscles, like the rollers on a conveyor system, coursed up his throat and then back down, pulling more of the flesh toward his gullet. Already his neck was distended in grotesque accommodation. His lips were pulled tight, smeared with the glistening fluids draining from the muscle.

When Lockwood finished consuming this first parcel of meat and turned his attention to the victim's pectoral, Randall fled.

Randall drove frantically, caring not for destination so much as distance. Thoughts and images collided in his head as he wove his way through traffic, leaving only enough attention to the vehicles on the road to keep him from colliding with the other cars. He couldn't go home; he knew that. This thing had requested shelter from him, and Randall would not take the chance of facing it again.

The face of the dying man, a twin to that of his mutilator, rushed up behind Randall's eyes. The frozen expression, part terror and part wonder, reminded Randall of his own paralysis under the being's shadow. Sickness rolled through his stomach as Randall understood that the man was still alive while Lockwood, or the new Lockwood, ripped his thigh from the bone.

A pair of red lights raced toward him, and Randall stomped the brake.

"Shit," he hissed, barely avoiding the rear bumper of a plodding SUV.

Randall pulled to the shoulder of the road and searched his jacket for the cell phone. Feeling he had gained sufficient distance from the murderous Lockwood, he took a moment to collect himself in the parked car but control was beyond him. He dialed the police and spoke so frantically, the operator made him repeat each piece of information twice.

He told the female dispatcher that he had witnessed a murder and gave her Ari Lockwood's address. She asked for his name, and he provided it. His stomach ached fiercely from the agitation of fear and the burn of adrenaline. He dug in the glove box for a roll of antacids. Chewing three, he gave the operator his address and then closed the phone, cutting off the woman's next question.

A sense of helplessness fell over him. He tossed the cell phone on the passenger seat and gazed at the cars racing down the freeway, their taillights glowing like the eyes of a battalion of retreating demons.

It was already too late, he knew.

He'd given that man, or whatever it was, enough time to dispose of Lockwood and assume his identity. It already had Lockwood's face, his body. All it needed was the man's driver's license to convince the police that the whole incident had been a hoax, and then Randall would have to answer not only to the police but to the new Lockwood as well. And as this realization assailed him, so did a squadron of new, dark-winged thoughts. They were not rational considerations but he was left with nothing logical to explain what he had seen.

Somehow, Bea's fucked up sculpture was born. The way it looked, the way it fed – a bastard union of snake and divinity. Certainly this new Lockwood was the realization of Bea's art, the flesh fulfilling the spirit of her sculpture.

Naturally, it would seek out Lockwood, to take his identity and dissolve into the humanity surrounding it.

But who the hell had brought this thing into Randall's world? Did Chad enable the spirit with his sex-slicked fingertip? Or had Bea finally taken the last step on her lunatic journey through the valley of art? And why did it seek out Randall? What shelter could he possibly provide for a being of such ominous origin?

Bea could not be trusted to give him the answers. For all he knew, she was this creature's guardian; she was certainly responsible for its facade. Already, he had fumbled in this game, alerting the police who would in turn alert Lockwood. As for Chad, if he were instrumental in enabling this spirit to flesh, he had done so unwittingly. The kid didn't have the ambition or the intelligence to do anything truly malevolent.

Which meant, Randall was alone.

It occurred to him that he must return to the gallery. Fortunately, Bea had spoken of her craft endlessly over the years, and Randall's memory produced an answer for him. The birth sign, etched in the sculpture's surface, was the key, he believed. If he could reach the effigy and scratch away the symbol, destroy the statue, then he could send the new Lockwood from this world.

Then Randall would see to it that neither Bea nor Chad was able to ever summon another like him.

The gallery closed, and Randall waited another thirty minutes, hoping to see its owner, Orson Nye, emerge from the front of the building. Finally, he dialed the gallery number. A recording told him the business hours and that the gallery was currently featuring the work of Beatrice LaCroix.

Maybe the owner had left through a back door, because Randall didn't see him leave. Even if he hadn't, Randall could make up a story to explain his presence if necessary. He could say that he was interested in purchasing one of Bea's hideous creations. In fact, this approach would serve him better, considering he didn't know the first thing about breaking into a building, and the gallery would certainly have an alarm system.

Randall left his car and crossed the street to the black glass door; it was unlocked. Through the window, he saw no movement in the exhibit space. A dull amber light cast a halo against the far wall, but the rest of the room stood in gloom. Randall pushed open the door quietly and closed it behind him. The chemical scent of Bea's acrylic beasts, crept into his nose with the scent of pine from the floorboards.

Animal noises, grunts and cries, echoed from the far end of the room, and Randall tensed himself, before realizing that the sounds were made by impassioned men. Apparently, Nye was entertaining in the back of the gallery, perhaps in the storeroom or the office.

Easing along the wall behind the row of sculptures, Randall reached the far corner and cast a glance down the corridor.

An icy fist seized his gut, and he winced.

In the storeroom, bathed in harsh lights, he saw Chad and the white bearded gallery owner, Nye. Nye was on all fours like a dog. Chad knelt before him. The old man grunted passionately, working his mouth over Chad's erection, while someone took the gallery owner from behind. Randall could not see this third man's face, but he already knew it was Lockwood, or the thing that had assumed Lockwood's face.

It had fed for the evening, and now it wanted to fuck.

Fine, Randall thought, as long as the old man and Chad kept it distracted. Agony flared in his belly like molten fire, doubling Randall over. He gritted his teeth against the cry trying to escape his throat and squeezed his eyes shut until the cramp passed.

Inhaling deeply to push away the ache in his stomach, Randall left the corridor and raced across the gallery to the acrylic effigy. Digging in his pocket he found his key ring. He pulled it loose, and using a short, sturdy key, he began to scrape at the hash marks above the sculpted face. The clear surface whitened under the brass teeth. Flakes of acrylic shredded away from the crest, snowing down on the visage captured beneath.

"That's not going to work," Chad said.

Randall looked up, startled. A row of track lights burst on above him. Chad stood across the gallery, framed by the walls of the corridor. He had put on his jeans and leaned against the corner of the wall, his arms folded over his chest. The blade of a buck knife rested against his chest.

"He's not a Golem, you moron. He's a god."

"You wouldn't find him so exalted if you'd seen him eat."

Chad shook his head as if disappointed by a difficult child. He tapped the blade against his pectoral. Over his shoulder, Randall saw the coupling continue in the storeroom, Nye writhing ecstatically before Chad's god. "Everything eats, Randall. And everything breeds. That's why we're here, honey. We're alive to feed, fuck and die; the rest is simply drama."

An excruciating cramp punched Randall low in the belly. "Is that your god's great philosophy?" he asked, gasping for breath.

"Of all people, I'd think you'd appreciate the simplicity of his design, Randall. People were always meat to you, just convenient places to keep your dick warm. At least he has purpose, and he doesn't gloss it over to supplicate his ego. The only difference between the two of you is, he's honest about his needs." Chad pointed the knife at Randall. "Don't you think it's about time we had a little honesty in our religion?"

Fighting the roiling ache in his belly, Randall realized he'd underestimated this kid. Chad had more than enough ambition and intelligence to fuel cruelty. But he was also insane if he found something magnificent in this being's gospel. "You call this religion?"

"Well, it's not really your problem is it?" Chad asked, stepping away from the wall. "We're almost done with you, so you can rush off and see if your god is waiting across the threshold with consoling psalms. I'll stay here with one whose power I can feel."

Randall shoved hard against the sculpture, sending it to the floor. He had wanted to see the dreadful effigy shatter, explode. But the acrylic hit the floor with a hard thunk, rolled on its rounded sides, then lay still.

"No!" an inhuman voice roared to fill the chamber like the commingling of a hundred winds. Chad spun in the corridor and was quickly knocked aside by the stampede of his god who bolted into the center of the gallery and reared back to bathe in the murky light.

There in the center of the room, Lockwood revealed his true self. The sight was nearly too much for Randall, who found himself bent over by yet another spasm of cramps.

Lockwood's eyes no longer possessed pupil or iris, but were smooth milky orbs, shot through with blue-gray veins as if they had been carved from marble. The angelic face, all smoothness and beauty, took on a horrific volume as the jaw unhinged to reveal two slender fangs, shaped like sickles and already wet with venom. The ridged palate of its mouth, like a bent spine, shone the color of pearl. Along the ripples of its abdomen, the color of the skin darkened by subtle degrees, until the pallor of his chest gave way to an ebony darkness. Its legs, the rich black of onyx, pulsed fluidly. From the crotch, a fleshy tube narrower than a garden hose hung limp and moist. A gelatinous fluid dangled from the slit at the end of the appendage. Captured within this fluid were half a dozen spheres the size of buckshot and colored the pink of grapefruit meat.

Randall saw the slimy trail the creature had left behind and noticed that many more of the pink spheres were glued to the floor by it.

His belly seized, and Randall crumpled to the floor.

Nye, his white hair disheveled and his pale body flushed from sex, stumbled into the gallery. His eyes ran over the creature undulating in the murky center of the room. Recognizing this thing as his recent lover, the gallery owner began to scream like a tortured child.

His piercing voice was quickly silenced.

Lockwood whipped around and shot a broad spray of venom in the old man's face. Nye clawed at his eyes, his scream returning for only a moment before Lockwood was on him, his fangs burying in the soft flesh of the man's shoulder. The gallery owner crashed to the floor, flat on his back and staring at the ceiling with eyes that would not blink.

Struggling against the misery in his gut, Randall crawled toward the acrylic piece. But Chad cut him off. The kid stood over him, pointing the knife at Randall's face.

"It's happening," Chad said happily.

Randall cast a glance into the gallery. The snake-angel slithered toward the front door, his fluid legs sweeping the floor in powerful strokes that sent the creature forward as smoothly as an eel through water. At the front of the store, he reared up and grasped a cord with his fist. He lowered the blinds over the glass door.

Chad watched his god, too enthralled to remember caution and Randall kicked out, knocking the kid's legs from under him. Chad hit the floor hard, and Randall rolled on top of him. He fought the knife from Chad's hand and buried it in the kid's throat, working the blade quickly back and forth to assure a breadth of wound that could not be plugged or mended.

"You fucking piece of shit," Randall panted, working the hilt of the knife like a pump's primer amid a gush of sticky blood. Beneath him, Chad gurgled and slapped uselessly at the boards.

Randall rolled off of the convulsing body, the knife firmly clutched in his fist. He crossed to the acrylic sculpture and drove the blade into its clear surface. Behind him, the snake-angel roared. He stabbed again and again, refusing to look over his shoulder, to lose his momentum. Bits of acrylic chipped away like ice under the point of a pick. Randall continued to hack, his mind crowded with panic. The snake-angel continued to cry out, but the voice was faltering.

Thinking of venom, Randall hacked away at the small sickle-shaped fangs until the mouth of the sculpted deity was a plain of ragged, scratched plastic. Only then did Randall turn to see the effect of his attack.

The snake-angel coiled in the center of the room, fluid shooting from numerous wounds on its sinuous body. Blood poured from the mouth, pooled and spilled over the unhinged jaw as its hands struggled to cover the most severe of the wounds.

Randall pierced and chipped away at the acrylic until it was an unidentifiable mound between his knees. Similarly, the flesh of the snake-angel rested in a coiled mound at the gallery's center.

"Ha!" Randall shouted, the remnants of his hysteria sending waves of adrenaline through his exhausted body. He planted the knife firmly in the center of the acrylic remains. The body of the snake-angel uncoiled in spasm and then dropped motionless on the planks.

Randall swept a low pile of plastic flakes aside and lay back on the floor.

"Shelter, my ass," Randall whispered, remembering the creature's request. And as the words left his lips, he remembered something else about his first encounter with Lockwood, remembered a feeling low in his gut, like the beating of a second heart.

Randall rolled his head to see the shiny trail, leading from the storeroom to the slaughtered remains in the center of the room. Tiny round objects dotted the viscous fluid.

The small orbs… colored pink… eggs… ?

Pain flared at his navel and Randall groaned. He threw a hand to his belly to console his agitated gut.

The skin beneath his sweater rippled.

Shelter, he thought, suddenly terrified.

His bowels evacuated a torrent of molten pain. Hot fluid filled his pants, pooled about his buttocks, and Randall cried out as another searing tide tore through his intestines. He panted for breath, trying to assuage the persistent cramping that pushed wave after wave of liquid fire from his body.

"Jesus," he cried.

Amid the agony and the burning excretion, he felt them moving. They crawled through the valleys on either side of his scrotum, scratched along his cock and pubis, slithered through the cleft of his ass and over his buttocks and hips. Randall frantically tried to remove his pants to clean the offspring from him, imagining a sheet of tiny snakes covering his midsection. He managed the button and zipper, but could not right himself to remove the garment, and by then it made no difference.

They pushed through the waistband of his underwear and emerged from the gash they had gnawed through his belly. Covered in blood and shit, the squirming children of the snake-angel boiled over his body, eager to discover this new world, at which Randall Banks was the center.

By the dozens, their writhing forms frothed. Appendages, no thicker than human hairs, scrabbled for purchase on Randall's neck while their tapered bodies drew lines of filth over his belly and chest.

Two of the creatures peered over the crest of Randall's chin and thin smiles cut their human lips. A horde of their brethren raced over the ridge of his jaw. Randall cried out for the final time, his body tightening with a slow paralysis as the tiny Serphim lapped at the drops of sweat on his face and tested their tiny fangs on the meat of his cheek.

Consciousness left him slowly as their bodies scurried over his immobile eyes, creating a flickering show of light and darkness. And Randall, the center of the new world, crossed the threshold, leaving his flesh behind, where for a time, it would remain a source of sustenance, warmth and shelter

.

The Good and Gone

My granny always told me as long as I could dance a jig and lift the moon on my finger, I had nothing to complain about. Well, she was a crazy old broad, I'll admit. She left me with some countrified profundity that got me plenty of trouble, but her dim-witted wisdom did little to get me out of it.

Through my time in the hospital, with the pain and the Percocet taking turns on my nerves, I relied on her memory for a bit of distraction. I played a child's game – a game she taught me – and it took me to a dark place, a set of rooms ruled by a maniac.

Picturing the filthy little man is far too easy. The thought of him still makes my stomach throb with revulsion.

I remember everything he did to that woman.

But first things go first.

What was I doing in the hospital? Like most things in my life up to that point, a man was involved. (A young man, actually, barely old enough to buy a beer.)

We hooked up at the gym. The kid was attractive in the most predictable of ways. He was a blond, muscular little piece of fluff of the sort that my friend Harry likes to call "twink." We played a match of eye hockey in the showers and struck up a bit of conversation while dressing in the locker room. He introduced himself as "Chawd," and I thought I'd heard him wrong, though it didn't seem like anything that absolutely had to be cleared up at that point in our relationship. After some perfunctory small talk and a bit of coaxing, I followed him back to his apartment, and the tonsil boxing began before the door clicked shut.

Everything was going just peachy. I tossed my jacket and shirt over the back of a chair, and in my haste, a small packet of lube – one of those blister-sealed, easy-to-carry, *for-the-man-on-the-go* packets – dropped out of my pocket and hit the floor.

You can see where this is going, right?

I, Max Evans, two steps from a really good time, stepped on a pack of *Wet* personal lubricant. It crushed, sprayed on the hardwood floor, and sent me ass-high in the air. Chawd's lovely, smooth body became a blur, as did the bed behind him, the wall beyond that and the ceiling.

The parquet flooring was not kind to me. I hit it hard. At first, I was just red about the cheeks and ears. After all, it was a terribly embarrassing moment. But the humor of my situation was not lost on me. There I was, a middle-aged man, buck naked, sprawled like a gunshot victim on the floor with a smear of glistening lube on the sole of my foot.

I laughed at my misfortune, and that's when the pain came.

Things could have been worse. Chawd's apartment building was only a few blocks from the hospital, so the ambulance appeared quickly, and the pain medication came soon after. Then, the doctors set to work on me.

I do not want to tell you that I broke my hip. To me, a broken hip is simply the entrance exam geriatrics take on their way to Heaven. But broke it was.

Two days into my hospital stay, most of the folks who were going to visit, had visited. My best friend, Harry came by every day, but he didn't stay long. Hospitals scared the hell out of him.

So what was I supposed to do? Reading was out of the question because the medication made me babble-brained. Television didn't interest me. What else was there?

I looked out the window at the clear, bright sky and then at the black screen of the television; a nurse came and went; my doctor popped in for a thorough forty-second examination; an orderly, who was obviously still upset about a joke I made earlier in the day, raced in to retrieve the tray holding the remnants of my lunch. He disappeared before I could again suggest that we swap head to pass the time. My hip hurt, and my back hurt, and my leg hurt, and everything pretty much sucked.

I did some personal reflection, thought about my family and my past, and that gave me a good ten minutes of boredom, but in thinking about my family, I thought about granny. I remembered the game she taught me:

The Good and Gone.

When I was a child, granny told me that if I ever wanted to see the world (because we were poor folks and couldn't afford real travel) all I had to do was go inside my head and cut my soul loose – just snip it free – and let it do the roaming. Then, I'd be good and gone.

I loved the game as a kid; it tickled me to no end. As I grew up and experienced life, the game was forgotten, replaced by real travel, but The Good and Gone was a fine distraction for a boy, and I certainly couldn't think of a place I wanted to be more good and gone from than that hospital.

So I looked back out the window, at the sharp blue sky, and wondered if I could remember how to play.

Turns out, it came back to me pretty fast. At first, I managed to hang above my body for a few minutes, to stare down on my inert form, but I could not remember the actions, the commands or the manipulations necessary to propel me away from my immediate surroundings.

The answer came from a memory as they often do. Not a memory of my dear, senile granny, mind you, but the memory of Lauren Bacall. In a famous movie clip, Bacall told Bogey that all he had to do was whistle. If he wanted to see her, he just had to press his lips together and blow.

Obviously, in my good and gone state there were no lungs or throat or lips at my disposal, but in my childhood, I equated the motion of my spirit with the act of whistling. I tried, and it worked. I blew right across that room and stopped dead at the wall. Whether it was my lack of imagination, or some limitation in my spirit, I could not pass through the wall, and it occurred to me that even as a child, I couldn't push myself through anything solid.

So, I redirected the whistle and sent myself into the hall. With a little more effort, I passed the nurse's station and ultimately, made my way into the elevator, which I road up and down for far too long before it finally settled at the lobby level.

And then, I was free. I burst out into the crisp bright afternoon, looked around at the parking lot and the road beyond. And was suddenly absolutely terrified.

The feeling came on me like an electric shock, startling and intense and paralyzing. I'd never felt this kind of fear before, but there it was, like lightning from skull to toe, nailing me to the sidewalk.

I needed to get back to the meat of me; that's all I knew. An internal alarm sounded. My body demanded my attention. In this realization, I found some freedom of movement, and I puffed a note to get me back inside the hospital. A round woman in blue stretch pants pushed past and sent me spiraling across the lobby, effectively breaking my Bambi-in-the-highbeam reaction to the lightning strikes of terror. Once mobile again, I whistled my way back to the elevator and was fortunate enough to catch a ride up with a handsome intern whose nametag read *Phil*.

Back in my room, I found the duty nurse, DeFrida, shaking my shoulders and calling my name in a rough fashion. With more than a little annoyance, I plopped back into the broken me and gave myself a moment to settle in. Once all of the nerves and tubes and fibers let me soak in, I snapped my eyes open and said, "Boo."

DeFrida yelped and clutched her clipboard to her chest. She threw me a look that indicated if I weren't already in a hospital bed, she'd put me in one soon enough.

"You oughta know better than to play possum around a place like this," she told me, in a stern *mama-ain't-happy* voice. "Good way to get a tube shoved down your throat if they think you gone coma."

There was a joke in and around the tube down the throat comment, but I thought better and let it go. "I'm a very deep sleeper."

"Yeah? We got toe tags for sleepers like you."

Before attempting another game of The Good and Gone, I needed a bit of rest. So, I napped for a couple of hours. I dreamed about roaming the halls of the hospital. Chawd was in those dreams, but then, so were a lot of men.

Despite what my friends might tell you, I don't have a one-track mind, but I'll admit that all the tracks run about parallel and end up at the same station. At least, they used to.

At the time I saw nothing even remotely problematic in this.

We spend our lives surrounded by all of these other people, and you have to find a way to build them into your philosophy. They can be a joy. They can be a misery. They can be a moment of warmth and distraction before you drive home to pay the phone bill. I always took great pleasure in these warm respites, but wanted little else from them. Most people wouldn't approve of my moral calibration, but I just never felt the need to get inside people in an emotional way. In the simplest terms, my romantic connections were based on attraction and friction not intimacy.

Once awake, I decided to play at being good and gone again. I might visit Chawd and see if he was good for a show. If not, I could always entertain myself with the goings on at one of the local gyms, or maybe just whistle through the streets until dawn.

I went inside myself and disconnected from the tissue holding me, drifted up and over to the window. If I'd had a stomach in that state, it would have fallen right out when the ledge of my hospital room's window gave way to forty feet of air (the only thing separating me from the grass and shrubs below). I felt unease at the idea of plummeting to the ground, though rationalized that there were no bones or organs to actually suffer from such a fall. Still, the altitude unnerved me, and I pushed myself downward until I was just above the lawn.

And then I whistled my way out into the world.

At Chawd's building, I pondered on a means of entry for quite some time, understanding that I would have to follow a neighbor or delivery man into the building and then take my chances at Chawd's door. The only other option would be an open window, but I wasn't sure I could locate his apartment from outside, and even if I could find the apartment, the idea of rising six stories into the air did not appeal to me.

So, I whistled myself back and forth, like a transparent balloon caught between alternating fans, waiting.

I was about to give up when an unfortunate looking gentleman with a slick bald head, carrying a bag of groceries and wearing sunglasses too big for his face, tromped up the sidewalk to the front of the building. His head moved slowly from side to side, like a turtle deciding on a direction, as he freed keys from the pocket of his Member's Only jacket. Behind this man was something quite odd.

A shape – human in form but nearly invisible and stained a burnt orange – hovered behind the turtle-man's shoulder, and just as I was identifying this shape, a second and a third, also tinted and ominous, soared up the walk. Adjusting his paper shopping bag in one arm, the man jabbed a key into the lock, cast another furtive glance over his shoulder and then entered.

I was so intrigued by this unfortunate, oddly reptilian gentleman and his ethereal entourage that I followed them in. Before going upstairs, the man retrieved his mail, and I noticed the name, *Gohling*, typed across a piece of paper the size of a cookie fortune on the mailbox.

So, I thought, what is so interesting about Mr. Gohling that he should have three spirits on his heels?

At the elevator, waiting for the car, the three wispy followers deepened in color and then faded. Gohling fidgeted with his shopping bag and jabbed the button again, all the while, his smooth head moving from side to side as if fearing an attack from his flanks. By this time, my interest in Chawd evaporated. Gohling was just too attractive, and not in the sense that he was sexually interesting or even remotely pleasant to look at; it was the mystery of him that I found so magnetic.

Many people will tell you that I'm a fool. Just an aging queer whose interests held no more depth or breadth than your average International Male catalogue, and I never would have denied that. Life was supposed to be fun, vividly colored and every now and again, exotic. The rest was just drama, created for a fix of adrenaline and a stroke of the ego to assure us that we're relevant.

As I stood there and the elevator doors slowly opened, I saw from the tension in Gohling's face and his endless surveillance of the surroundings that his life lacked both fun and color. His life was black and burdensome, and I was compelled to see more of it.

Up we rode, Gohling, his three foul orange shadows and myself. The elevator stopped on the eighth floor, two above Chawd's, and, once the door opened, Gohling scurried into the hall. Now, he was muttering to himself, words that I could not hear, or simply meaningless syllables that made his throat work.

At a door marked *8F*, Gohling buried his key in the lock and again scanned his surroundings. Noting that he was alone, he cranked the key and pushed open the door. I drifted over the threshold with a giddy whistle, and found myself in the center of a dismal, lightless room. The curtains were drawn and no interior light burned. Gohling closed the door, locked it and threw on a chain. He flicked a switch and a dull, twenty-watt glow seeped over the wall above the entry.

That's when I saw the second door. The silencing door.

The three shadows soared deep into the room, but Gohling remained, facing the door he had just locked, a bag of groceries in his arm. He set down the paper sack next to the jamb and then walked three paces to the left where he grabbed the edge of another door, a massive steel sheet framed in foam padding. This too he closed, but instead of locks, the steel door fastened to the jamb with thick bolts, which Gohling immediately twisted into their fittings.

I wondered, why would anyone need such security? Exactly what was the turtle-like Gohling up to?

Gohling walked through the apartment to the kitchen where a fog of weak light from another low-wattage bulb revealed immaculate surfaces and a nook with a dinette set stationed beneath a sheet of metal similar to the one covering the front door. A window shutter?

He stored his groceries and went to the metal plate. He pulled at it. I wanted him to open that shutter so that real light, even the filtered evening light, might slip into that place, but Gohling was only checking the security of the panel. Satisfied, he eased away from the dinette set, bumped into me and sent me rolling ahead of him across the kitchen.

Similar shutters were built into the walls of the living room to cover the windows there. He checked these, turning on lights as he went.

A claustrophobic panic rose in me, as I looked around Gohling's cell. Even in my fleshless state, I could not pass through the walls or the metal sheets blocking out all of the rest of the world, furthermore I didn't have the material being – the fingers, the hands – to tear through his shutters. Only then did I notice another disturbing attribute of Gohling's apartment.

Cheap area rugs lay piled three-high above a wall-to-wall Berber. They created a plateau, spanning the floor. These too were meant to insulate noise.

What was this place? What was meant to happen here?

My mind went to the familiar, a situation I could relate to (in concept if not in practice). This place was a kind of dungeon. Gohling was into some extreme form of S/M, and he was terrified that a neighbor might hear the pleas and the cries and the sounds of straps slapping skin. He built a soundproofed chamber so that he could entertain his passion at any volume without fear of exposure. On this, I was partially correct.

The sound of the shower pulled me out of my thoughts and back into the dread of being trapped. Down the hall, I whistled until I entered what should have been the master suite, but I found no bed or chest of drawers here. Against the far wall, I saw a simple closet door. Jutting from the wall beside me at the threshold was a plain wooden desk. A notebook of lined paper and a small mug filled with black Bic pens sat on top. Here lay another stack of carpets, but these were covered in a long, blue tarp.

The other phantoms gathered in this room, huddled in the shadow at the far corner. Their colors deepened and faded in rapid beats as if agitated. Next to them, the closet door – just a regular door like those in a million apartments around the country – stood, but it was not like a million other doors. The orange-stained ghosts circled, rose and dove on the air, running like shadows over that door, and I knew they wanted what was beyond.

As for myself, I wanted out. My curiosity was more than satisfied, so I whistled my way back into the hall. I searched for a vent, convincing myself that I could somehow navigate my way in and through the central air of the building, which was of course, idiotic. But I needed to get out of Gohling's rooms. I convinced myself that I couldn't breathe. I flung myself at the shutters; threw myself at the long sheet of metal covering the door, tried to wedge my good and gone self into the tight cracks running its length. I screamed and struggled, and when I did find a vent beyond the stacked area rugs in the far corner of the living room, I dove for it, only to be bounced back into the air, denied my escape.

I returned to the bedroom where my fellow discorporates were frantic, flying around the closet door like swarms of orange flies. Gohling walked out of the bathroom, naked and dripping wet. There was absolutely nothing erotic in this display; he was pale and soft about the chest and belly, with stick thin legs and arms, and his skin absorbed the dull yellow cast of the low-watt bulb, adding to his sickly appearance. What little hair he had was slicked back against his scalp, and rivulets ran down his neck to draw lines along his spine.

At the center of Gohling's back, perched just between his shoulder blades was an intricate tattoo, perfectly round and the size of a compact disk. The edge of the design buckled and then expanded as Gohling reached for the closet door. Around him, the shadows danced maniacally like hungry dogs seeing the approach of their food bowl.

Gohling waved his hand in the air as if he could see or feel the presence of his guests and cleared his immediate space before opening the door.

I couldn't tell her age, but his captive was a woman. Her body was tight and narrow with small pancake breasts. Thick, strips of duct tape – wrapped with great care – formed a mask over her entire head. Her nostrils were exposed but eyes, ears and mouth were gagged beneath the shiny binds. She resembled Claude Rains' Invisible Man, only smooth and silver-gray. Besides the tape, she was naked; her hands bound above her head with a chain; her legs secured to the floor with manacles imbedded in the carpet.

Something about her position, the tension in her arms and the trembling, told me she was not a volunteer in Gohling's home. This was no kink scene fallout; this was something criminal. Terrible.

I drifted back in the room and cried out in silent protest. Gohling turned from his captive, looked directly at me with a question on his brow, and then turned back to the bound woman.

He released her arms from the chain, and at his touch, she began to struggle. But she was weak and could not direct her blows with any accuracy. Gohling grabbed her arms and shoved her into the middle of the room, where the uneven and pliant blue tarp went out from under her feet. She fell with a crunch on the crinkling plastic. She began to crawl, slapping the crisp tarp with her palm. Gohling walked across to his desk, lifted a pen from the mug and opened his notebook, and he watched.

During this time, the other guests in Gohling's room were crazed like moths bumping off of a light bulb. They soared to the ceiling. Dropped to the floor.

"Stop it," he barked, as he watched the woman crawl blindly over the blue tarp. He made a note in his book, watched some more, made another note, scratched his crotch, watched, wrote some more. "Yes," he whispered. Then, scratching himself again, he dropped the pen and stood.

Gohling crossed to the helpless woman, locked his hands on her shoulders and held tight. Her legs kicked, and a muffled grunt thumped against the adhesive side of the tape. Gohling opened his mouth wide and leaned forward, affixing his lips to the woman's chest. She squirmed and fought against this unwelcome intimacy, but Gohling was attached like a leach to her torso.

And that is when I understood the presence of Gohling's guests. One by one they dove out of the air, piercing the emblem tattooed on the man's back, entering him through its design like smoke being sucked into the mouth of a vacuum. After the third guest vanished into the woven lines of ink, Gohling pulled away from the woman, who dropped back to the blue tarp, motionless and silent.

He returned to his desk and scribbled a few notes until low groans began to emanate from the tape-bound head of his victim. Gohling stood and crossed the tarp. He bent down and tore a strip of tape free, opening a narrow gash to reveal chapped, split lips.

The voice that oozed from that slit was not the woman's; it wasn't even female. For that matter, it wasn't male. The reedy fog of voice was sexless, lacking inflection yet full of insistence.

"We want to feel," she said. "Hit us. Hit us hard."

Gohling pulled his arm back and delivered a vicious slap against the mask of tape covering the woman's face.

"Lovely," the sexless voice said. "We felt that. Yes. Indeed we did. And again."

Gohling did as he was told and delivered another open-handed blow, this time striking so hard as to send the woman's body reeling back on the blue tarp. A sickening giggle, like wind blown through broken glass filled the room as the naked victim rolled on the plastic sheet. Gohling's response to this abuse was arousal.

He grabbed the narrow shaft of his erection, and I couldn't watch any longer. I turned away. Behind me, I heard the voice, neither male nor female, say, "Cut us. Cut us deep." Then another trill of the shattered glass laughter rose, slicing through the room.

Into the hall, I fled, convincing myself that there must be some escape from this dreadful apartment and its reptilian lord, but no amount of desperation could get me through the shutters or into the vents. Panicked by my trapped state, *I* became the moth against the light bulb, racing with all of my need at the steel plates, covering windows and door. But the rooms would not let me go.

That bolt of lightning, the fear that first struck me in front of the hospital, returned with a paralyzing flash, halting my attempt at flight. Something was happening with my flesh and bone. Its demand startled me like a klaxon at my back. I needed to escape this place and return to my skin. And if I didn't?

My desperate mind conjured the nurse's voice: *We got toe tags for sleepers like you.*

What would happen if I didn't return? What would become of the meat of me? Another electric charge burned through and another.

In the next room, the sexless voice cried, "Oh, cut us very deep."

If I'd had tears to shed they would have fallen then, but I was less than mist. How long would my body survive without me?

And in thinking of my own death, I wondered if perhaps this was the nature of all ghosts. Were houses haunted, not by the spirits of the dead, but of the living, trapped and confused and unable to return to the shells awaiting them? Or, and this struck me as even more likely, perhaps spirits separated prior to death, to avoid the traumatic moments leading to it, and then were deprived anywhere to return.

Fighting the charges of alarm from my distant body was difficult, but my only chance of escape was with Gohling, so I forced myself down the hall toward the horrible, sexless laughter. I entered as Gohling finished drawing a long cut on his victim's shoulder with a utility knife. Blood bubbled up from the clean line to spill into the woman's armpit and over the ridge of her collarbone to drip to the bright, blue tarp.

She giggled in ecstasy, gasping and rocking herself over the plastic, smearing the discharge of the wounds in thick red gobs. The poor woman's possessors took absolute glee in the sensations of damage.

She caressed her opened body with long trembling fingers. She reached for Gohling to pull him close, but the man was already walking back to his desk to make more notes. He scribbled in his notepad, smearing blood on the lined-pages as his fingers worked anxiously before another demand was made of him.

I looked over his shoulder and read:

All of the cunts sing my name. They need me and grow cruel. Blood within and without. They turn dry and rot without my juice. On the vine. Rotted on the vine. Never stop. They sing my name. A chorus of cunt, raising its voice to God.

From my side, the woman cooed, soft and rattling like the breaths of a dying child. I turned to see the tape-bound head. Slit for nose. Slit for mouth. The cracked, split lips pulled together.

"Fuck us," it said. "We're so beautiful. Fuck us. Oh. Now. Now. Fuck beautiful us."

The insane voice, spilling through the shiny gash of tape rode the lightning of another cry from my distant, unconscious body. Desperate. Perhaps slightly deranged now, I launched toward Gohling and the tattoo on his back. At first it refused me, but as I recoiled, it opened and drew me toward the awful little man, who looked around the room with panicked tosses of his head. Tendrils of energy, invisible yet blacker than anything I could ever describe wove with my being, scrabbled at the ethereal me. I screamed, dreading what would wait within the twisted owner of these rooms. I roared and cried, my desperation flowing from Gohling's mouth in blasts of madness.

"Let me out," Gohling cried. "For God's sake let me out of here." He performed a frantic jig, tripped on the carpet and nearly toppled on the vessel of his sadistic attentions, which writhed on the smeared tarp, demanding Gohling's sex.

Then, we were running. Down the hall he charged, dragging me with him toward the steel plate covering his front door.

"Out." He screamed. "Out. Out."

His fingers worked over the bolts on the door's edge, and he flung the steel sheet back to crash against the wall. By now, the black vines of his being were tearing deep into me, struggling against my commands and trying to drag me wholly into the body of Gohling. His hands slapped at the dead bolt and the lock on the doorknob, and he continued to dance from one foot to the next as if the floor was a hot metal grate. Behind us, Gohling's victim screamed for penetration.

Fuck us.

Fuck beautiful us.

Then, the door flew open. I saw my escape. Gohling charged into the corridor, still screaming *my* need for freedom.

A neighbor, a tall, heavy man, with a thick brush of mustache looked up startled. His keys dangled from his hand, and he watched our approach, jaw open and resting against his chest. I unwound myself from the black vines that knotted just behind the ink on Gohling's back and flew free of him...

Just as the shocked neighbor pulled back a ham-sized fist and landed it in the center of Gohling's face.

"Crazy fuck," the burly man said, already reaching for the cell phone on his hip.

I got back to the hospital too late, of course.

No. Not dead. A coma. They actually shoved a tube down my throat just like DeFrida warned, and even though I managed to slide back into myself, it took me a long time, three days, to get all of the connections right before I could open my eyes and say, "help."

Gohling was arrested. The news was full of his bald, turtle head and the vacancy sign hanging behind his eyes. Headlines announced his "Downtown Torture Chamber;" the accompanying articles went on to describe his rooms – the sound proofed doors and shutters, the piles of rugs, the foam padded closet – in painful detail, and more than once, reporters suggested that his latest victim was not the first to enter the dimly lit home and suffer Gohling's particular brand of hospitality.

Of this victim, I know little. Her name was Candice Morrison, and she was a bank teller with a boyfriend named Brad. He was quoted repeatedly in news articles, assuring the reporters that he would "be there" to help Candice through her recovery.

She's still under observation in the mental ward of Stratten Hospital. My guess is she'll be there for a very long time.

They all will.

You see, Gohling never had a chance to remove his monsters from her; I didn't give him that chance. Those perverse spirits with their need for sensation remained locked in that violated body. I don't know where Candice went, whether she was expelled when the depravity occurred or if she remains trapped in her skin with Gohling's ghosts.

I just know that because of me, Candice Morrison is gone. Good and gone.

When the nightly news showed a picture of Candice – her sweet smile, her eyes twinkling with mischief – I became ill. Violently ill.

Before my encounter with Gohling, I rarely thought about what went on behind people's faces. For me, they were just faces, some I wanted to kiss, some I wanted to make smile, and others I chose to avoid altogether.

Faces haunt me now. Candice's face. The faces of men with whom I shared friction, if not intimacy. The faces of strangers – an entire world of strangers. They unnerve me. Each one is a door, and I have no idea what lies beyond. Are the rooms behind nose, mouth and eyes inviting and warm? Or are they shuttered, cold and dark?

Granny told me that as long as I could dance a jig and lift the moon on my finger, I didn't have much to complain about. Last night, I sat at the window, looking at the sky. My elbow rested on the sill, and I captured the moon, balancing the silver disk on my fingernail.

But it was too heavy. I let it go.

Crazy old broad.

Appetite of the Cyber Tribes

When it came to the Internet, Walter knew that people weren't always what they seemed. The online world was, quite simply, a fantasy kingdom where any number of beings, some wonderful and some hideous, roamed about their realm wearing magical disguises. Cloaked in the woven spells of personal profiles and fabricated histories, the creatures of the web had the power to mask the truth of their being only to be exposed when they were conjured and drawn from that enchanted, digital land into the concrete domain of real life.

Walter knew this because he was one of those beings. Behind the guise of his screen handle, he was confident, funny and charming. But now on a chilly autumn afternoon as he approached the row of glass-faced buildings harboring shops and restaurants, he felt the weave of his magical persona unravel, and he wished he had stayed at home. He didn't like being exposed. He was an average guy in a world that demanded more.

All of the perfect young bodies – images that had once been relegated to porn sites – spilled onto every dating page he frequented. He couldn't compete with the well-hung twenty-somethings who'd spent their teen years using their allowances to buy steroids. They were a VIP generation, and Walter couldn't get past the doorman.

He walked with slow, precise steps along the sidewalk toward Downing Street, his gut twisting in electric knots. His friend, Gary, would have called him a wuss for being so anxious about his date, but Walter wasn't like Gary. His friend hooked up with guys as easily as he ordered pizzas, but Walter's experience was far more limited. The chat rooms and dating sites allowed him to observe and sometimes participate in the rituals of the beautiful. He could be charming, even somewhat aggressive, online, but when it came time to swap pics, his confidence withered. On those rare occasions when sending his photo didn't end the conversation, and he actually hooked up, he sensed from the moment he met his date, that he'd been summoned for his convenience and little else.

In no hurry to endure the awkward first moments with another disappointed date, he paused, looked up to check his location and saw a throng of pedestrians meandering along the shopping district. A mother gave her son an ice cream cone and brushed a lock of hair from his brow; two men with perfect smiles and matching white fleece jackets entered the video store; a straw-haired woman stood in front of a new age card and candle boutique, chewing gum and examining her fingernails; and a man in a forest green trench coat stood on the far corner. The guy seemed to be watching him, but Walter figured that was his imagination – another bit of anxiety to add to his afternoon.

Above, the sky threatened rain, and on the near corner just beyond the new age boutique and the chewing woman, who now returned to the store's interior, stood the coffee shop where his date was waiting.

He didn't know why he was so worried; Barry was great. At least he seemed great. He liked Chinese food, Grisham novels and gadget battle shows, where clumsy robots tore each other apart in a chain linked arena; he didn't much like crowds or bars, and he preferred DVDs to going to movie theaters, just like Walter did. But for all Walter knew, Barry was just another cloaked denizen of the fantasy kingdom, willing to lie to assuage his loneliness. A lot of people did that these days.

And what if... (and this was an even more uncomfortable prospect)... What if he hadn't lied? What if Barry was as great as he thought, and what if he didn't feel the same way about Walter? The questions made the anxiety in his belly roil and spit lightning through his gut.

He walked to the door of the coffee shop and rested his hand on the metal handle, letting the cold seep into his palm. Through the glass he saw Barry sitting at a table across the room.

He looked exactly like the picture he had sent him: blonde hair, the color of wheat, short and spiky and only slightly receding; large blue eyes gazed at the counter with a sparkle of anticipation dancing over the irises. His slender body rested in an overstuffed chair. He hadn't lied.

Walter stepped back on the sidewalk, away from the glass door.

Unfortunately, Walter could not make the same claim to veracity as his date. The picture he'd sent to Barry was nearly five years old, and though Walter looked almost identical to the image he had sent, he felt like a cheat and a liar for having passed the image off as recent. He looked at his reflection in the pane of the boutique window and saw round, chipmunk cheeks framed by a thinning hairline. His brown eyes were flat and uninteresting, and his lower lip looked too full. His sturdy build, when viewed in the reflective glass, appeared simply, fat.

Barry would give him a quick frisk with his eyes, find him plain in all of the least comforting ways; he'd finish his coffee; he'd explain he had another appointment; he'd leave and Walter would be sent home to entertain his disappointment.

The door of the coffee shop opened and Walter's heart skipped into his throat.

A man with a shaven head, chambray shirt and black quilted vest stepped into the gloomy afternoon. Despite the day's gray cast, he wore thick, dark shades over his eyes. Casually, he regarded Walter, then turned his back and entered the crowd of wandering pedestrians.

Simultaneously relieved and disappointed, Walter felt any confidence he might have retained escaping him as if someone had punctured a balloon to release his courage into the atmosphere. If instead of the bald man, Barry had been the one to come outside, if he had seen him standing there, then he would have been forced to speak with him; they might have shared a cup of coffee; they might have had a really good time.

But Barry had not come outside, and Walter knew he wasn't brave enough to join him inside.

In submitting to his cowardice, he turned to leave before Barry could discover him and nearly collided with a woman.

She was a blur of dark brown hair, and her hand went quickly to Walter's shoulder to stave off a collision. In the wake of her touch, he felt a piercing sting in the meat of his shoulder. A fingernail or perhaps a sharp ring gem had cut him. Walter tried to get a look at the woman, but she was already beyond the card and candle boutique, walking with a purposeful haste along the glass front of the coffee shop, the tail of her green trench coat, whipping in the breeze.

Walter rubbed his injured shoulder and as soon as he touched the epicenter of his pain, the anguish soothed, faded and died away completely.

Walter cast a last, hopeful look at the door of the coffee shop.

He turned away and walked back to his car.

GDTLP: *He was probably a total Teek.*

Walter laughed, reading Gary's assessment of his failed date. His friend's use of cyber-slang was a wonder, constant and always changing. A few weeks ago, Gary had hooked into the term "Teek," (apparently "Troll" was passé) and now used it whenever he got the chance. Walter thought to ask Gary what the word meant, but he didn't want to suffer through his friend's jeering, so he decided to look it up when he had a minute.

Situated comfortably in his home and sitting before the glow of his computer screen, Walter was feeling secure again. Of course, Walter had mentioned nothing to Gary about his earlier anxiety or the evaporation of his courage as he looked at Barry through the glass door of the coffee shop. Instead, he lied to save his ego.

WH61: *He looked like a whale in a Wal-Mart tank top ...* he wrote.

GDTLP: *LOL! Teek bitch.*

Walter winced. He didn't like Gary calling Barry a Teek. Even though he wasn't sure exactly what the word meant, he'd seen it in enough chat rooms to know that it wasn't good. And he certainly didn't think the guy deserved to be called a bitch, but Gary was just being supportive of his friend. So...

WH61: *Teek is right.*

He rubbed his shoulder, feeling the memory of pain there and looked at the screen, waiting for Gary's reply.

After returning from his failed date, Walter had gone to the bathroom and stripped off his shirt to examine his wounded shoulder, but he'd found no cut or abrasion. A small disc of skin, maybe the size of a nickel seemed to be discolored, grayish, but that could have been the light. He hadn't been bleeding and his clothing wasn't torn. The woman in the long coat had just clipped him on a nerve in passing.

GDTLP: *TTFN. Hooking up. C U ltr.*

Walter smiled, typed in *C U*, and pushed away from his desk. The phone rang, and anxiety writhed in his belly. That would be Barry; he'd want to know why Walter had missed their date.

He let the phone ring and walked into the hallway.

Walter's house was a big ranch-style job with everything he could possibly want. His furniture was sleek, efficient and well matched. The office, perfectly appointed with everything he needed for his job as a technical copywriter, had actually been the master suite of the house with a big bathroom and enough space for a sofa on the far wall. Since Walter spent most of his time in the room, he wanted it to be the most comfortable. He'd installed his bed and clothing in one of the smaller spaces across the hall. The living room was spare but nice with a flat panel LCD television he'd bought with money saved for a vacation he never took, and the leather sectional – forming an L at the room's center – could accommodate ten people, though Walter couldn't remember the last time he'd asked friends to his house.

In the kitchen, he retrieved a beer from the fridge, ran the cold bottle over his brow and closed his eyes in guilty frustration when the phone started a second round of intrusive ringing.

Not yet ready to be confronted or condemned by Barry, Walter ignored the phone's trill and returned, beer in hand, to his office. In the black manager's chair, he stared at the screen.

Walter sipped his beer and opened up Google to run a search on the word, "Teek." He couldn't visit any chat rooms for a while because Barry might catch him, and he certainly didn't feel up to getting any real work done, so instead he decided to satisfy his curiosity about the odd term.

He clicked on a couple of suggested pages from the menu, but they were all about some science fiction book by an author he'd never heard of, and he found no connection between the book's synopsis and the cyber slang his friend Gary tossed around. He scrolled down the listings, clicked on the second page, scrolled down.

Walter continued this casual scan until he came to a page listing with the title "The cyber legend Teek in today's interactive community." This sounded about right to him so Walter opened the page.

Derived from the word, Mortique and abbreviated as seems mandatory for the syllabically challenged denizens of the World Wide Web, Teek are to the Internet what the Bogeyman and Bloody Mary are to children: a myth for a wired society.

Well that's interesting, he thought. The page covering his screen was simple, with block type and few aesthetic touches; it looked like some college kid had posted a term paper on the web.

He sipped from his beer, scrolled down the page and continued to read:

The term Mortique can be traced back to 1867 and the works of Jean Claude Van Maele (1830-1878). A Belgian novelist, Van

Maele's early works, mostly short poems and prose fragments were collected in a volume entitled, L'ombre de l'Esprit. The title translates to The Shadow of the Spirit, though in researching Van Maele's history, it is suggested that his use of the word L'Esprit was intended to mean the less obvious definition (i.e. mind). The Shadow of the Mind as a title better suits this odd aggregation of experimental literature, particularly if one notes Van Maele's lifelong struggle with emotional instability.

Though Van Maele went on to become one of Belgium's most respected nineteenth-century novelists, his early works were written off by critics of the day as infantile "ghost stories" designed for the amusement of the lower classes. In L'ombre de l'Esprit, one such tale involved a young Marquis who stumbles into the courtyard of a crumbling castle and encounters a grizzled old man whom he finds squatting on a boulder. The old man puts a spell on the Marquis, causing the royal to wither and die. As his victim succumbs to the spell, the old man explains that he can only survive by ingesting the flesh of the dead. But plague and fear have driven the peasants from the neighboring countryside, and he has been left to starve in the broken keep. Once the Marquis is dead, the Mortique finds his personal papers and drafts a letter to the Marquis' beautiful young fiancée. The ghoulish man, writing as the Marquis, insists that the young woman join him in the countryside. When she appears, she too is placed under the creature's spell. Then, he writes to her loved ones – father, brothers and friends – and all come to the isolated fortress to become food for the aged monster.

The story itself might have gone completely unnoticed by historians were it not for the questionable success of Ian Harrison (1895-1948). A contemporary of Lovecraft and devotee of Poe, Harrison plagiarized Van Maele's tale of the Mortique. His story, Hungry are the Lost, was so unforgivably derivative that Harrison went so far as to call his hero Markus. Though the setting was changed to a dilapidated estate in New Hampshire, Harrison made no other efforts to hide his theft of Van Maele's work. The only concession to originality in Harrison's tale was a short passage that suggests the origin of the Mortique.

Appetite of the Cyber Tribes

In Harrison's version, the old man tells the dying hero that he is descended from a band of religious pilgrims, who upon finding themselves lost and starving in a desolate wilderness, are forced to feed upon one another. But being devout to their god, they refuse to partake in the flesh of their brothers and sisters until natural decomposition signals the end of the fallen as spiritual beings. Once certain that the souls of the deceased have fled, the Mortique of Harrison's tale consumed their dead. Despite their caution they were cursed for their unwholesome behavior – damned forever to exist on a diet of putrescence and decay.

Walter found this last line unduly grim, and he winced in disgust. He sipped his beer and an electronic voice announced that he had mail. He opened his mailbox and saw Barry's name in the sender field. Quickly, he clicked back to the description of the Teek, an action of avoidance more than curiosity at this point, though admittedly he was interested in discovering how these antiquated creatures had made their way from a nineteenth-century fairy tale to the present day:

Van Maele's Mortique make their appearance in modern culture through the dreadful film adaptation of his tale. The 1982 film The Voice on the Phone is an updated version of Van Maele's story, in which a group of teens are drawn by a series of phone calls to meet their fate in an abandoned butcher's shop. The film's first victim (named Mark this time) is carrying his "little black book" and the killer (a rather embarrassed looking Cameron Mitchell in the role of the butcher) works his way through the phone listings to draw unsuspecting young women to his lair. Unlike Van Maele's villain, Mitchell uses a drug compound, administered with a filthy hypodermic needle, to expedite the death and decay of his victims (in one of the worst stop-motion animation sequences this writer has ever seen).

Certainly it is this last example of the Mortique that has spawned the cyber slang definition of Teek. The film rose to cult status in the late 80's and was a favorite of the midnight movie crowds including university students, many of whom went on to prosper during the Internet boom.

With the advent and proliferation of the Internet, new fears arose in the form of child molesters, serial killers and more modern monsters that used technology to lure their victims. Early on, the term Teek was relegated to these digital predators, but has since evolved to include anyone who misrepresents themselves in chat room settings with fabricated profiles.

This takes us back to the wondrous element of anonymity the web provides for...

Walter spent twenty minutes reading and musing over the origin of the Teek, and he thought they were a perfect addition to the web's fantasy kingdom. They could pretend to be anybody, court and lure their prey, and if they were skilled enough, even maintain the identity of their victims for a time so as to throw off suspicion and avoid discovery – a perverse kind of identity fraud.

He thought that was kind of cool, but it also disturbed him. After all, he worked from home. With Netflix and GroceryNow, he could go days without ever stepping outside. No, he corrected, he could go weeks. But he was in contact with his bosses and clients almost every day, so that was something of a relief. Certainly they'd notice if he just vanished.

Walter's stomach rolled and a wave of exhaustion fell over him. The day's events, the beer and the reading had made him tired. He dropped his beer bottle in the wastebasket, stood and walked across the hall to his bedroom for a quick nap.

When the dream started, Walter was standing in the middle of a city; it could have been any city. Tall buildings of concrete, glass and steel towered above paved avenues and streets that teamed with vehicles and pedestrians. People brushed past him and the touch of their shoulders, their hands and their clothing on him felt almost erotic in its intensity. But he was frightened. In addition to the libidinous sensations the caress of fabric and flesh brought to him, there was also a feeling of dread.

Because within the throng of executives and tourists, someone waited to grab him and hold him, though for what purpose he could not imagine. Eyes that probed with unwanted attention ran like a dry wind over his neck, his back and his cheek. His exposed skin chapped and flaked under the assessment of those arid stares.

Terrified that he should be turned to dust, Walter held out his arms as if to take flight and wished the city and its crowding populace away...

And his will seared the color and depth from all around him until Walter stood not on a city street but beneath towering, yet sheer panes of glass. The limpid sheets rose to a sky that had darkened from sunlit blue to a grim, brain-gray. The street below him shifted and crumbled until the city avenue was reduced to a desert of grainy sand, from which the towering panes rose. On the surface of the clear sheets, two-dimensional representations of the city's buildings and populace were etched. In the nearest pane of glass, he saw Barry's face concerned and pleading, staring out at him.

Through this panel, Walter also saw three people, still whole and with full dimension. All three wore trench coats of a deep forest green. Their faces were swollen, lumpy and covered in a sickly yellow skin. Their eyes were small, black and hungry.

Frantic to escape this flat, horrible world, Walter spun on his heels to run.

A woman in green touched his shoulder, and Walter cried out.

His eyes snapped open as the echo of his cry faded. The room was filled with night's shade, the only light coming from the numbers on his alarm clock.

He had napped for over three hours and now woke with a parched throat and a bad belly that rolled and kicked painfully. Feeling achy and still tired, Walter climbed out of bed, went to the kitchen for a glass of water and ended up drinking three. But the liquid seemed to be exactly what his troublesome gut required for its revolt.

He barely made it to the bathroom in his office before his clenching stomach let loose. After struggling with the button and zipper on his chinos, he frantically lowered the toilet seat and perched on the porcelain just as a jet of hot fluid burned through his bowels and evacuated. Sweat popped up on his brow and Walter gasped for air as the molten stream left his body. Behind his eyes, a needle-sharp pain insinuated itself and blurred his vision.

Once he was certain that his body had nothing left to expel, Walter splashed water on the hot skin of his face and then leaned on the counter to support his weak legs. A moment later, his strength returned; his face and neck cooled and the pain behind his eyes receded, leaving only a vague ache.

Maybe the beer he'd had that afternoon had gone bad, or perhaps it was something else he'd eaten. Running through a brief list of his meals and snacks but identifying nothing that might have made him ill, Walter returned to his office and clicked off the screen saver.

His e-mail box had ten new messages; Barry's was the first, the rest were junk ads. Walter erased the spam, and with great hesitation he moved the arrow over the bold, subject line of the remaining message. He squinted in readiness as if Barry's accusatory words might cause the monitor to explode in his face and then clicked on the subject line.

Walter,

I'm so sorry to hear that you aren't feeling well, but it was very sweet of you to try to call the coffee shop and let me know (they really should have paged me). OF COURSE, we can reschedule when you're feeling better.

If you feel up to chatting later, I should be home after six. If not, get plenty of rest and know that I'm thinking about you.

Warm hugs and a kiss on the forehead (you are sick after all. LOL.).

Barry.

Walter read the message three times, feeling certain that he had missed something important, and yet experiencing a great sense of relief that Barry was not at home cursing him. Still, he had not written him an e-mail.

Had he?

Walter opened his "sent mail" folder and right at the top was a subject line that read – *Sorry, sorry, sorry!*

It was addressed to Barry.

He opened the note, which quite simply stated that he'd managed to get food poisoning, and it had hit just as he was leaving to meet him for their date. The note was brief, to the point and made it very clear that Walter was not a flake, just unforeseeably stricken. He'd even added to the deceit by noting that he tried to call Barry at the coffee shop but the clerk had refused to page him. In closing, he had begged, in a humorous yet sincere manner, that they reschedule.

Distressed and confused, Walter shook his head in wonderment and instantly regretted the action because it brought the needle sharp pain back to the cavern behind his eyes. His stomach flipped and a fresh dew of sweat broke out on his face. Despite his discomfort, he drafted a quick thank you, mentioning that he felt worse than he had, which was true enough, and assured Barry that he'd be in touch once the illness subsided.

The mysterious correspondence nagged at him, though. He began to think in earnest that someone might have hacked into his mail account.

Only last month, three guys had been arrested in Cleveland and the news reports said that they'd stolen data on over thirty thousand people. They'd used the stolen identities to rob bank accounts, max out credit cards and set up phony Internet businesses.

Maybe someone had pirated his account.

But his logic was not only faulty; it was just plain silly. Even if someone had been able to access his account and had read his correspondences to discover the details of Walter's date, who could have guessed that he'd back out of it at the last minute? How could they have been so accurate in identifying a sickness Walter hadn't even experienced yet? Furthermore, why would they?

The whole scenario made for a rather impractical practical joke.

Still, the paranoia was in his head, and for the next hour he checked his credit card and bank account statements online. He studied each transaction and played it against his memory but his financial records indicated no action beyond the authorized deductions for automatic bill payments and the few charges for CDs and DVDs he'd purchased online. He returned to his "sent mail" file and read the note to Barry again.

Sorry, sorry, sorry!

Throughout his exploration, a dull ache rose in his joints and the pain in his head persisted. By the time he closed the note of apology this last time, still confused by its content and origin, his face was shiny with sweat, and his back hurt.

His thirst returned. He left the office and made it halfway across the living room before his knees turned to liquid. Walter saved himself from a damaging fall only by clutching the arm of his sectional. He considered calling an ambulance as he navigated himself onto the sofa cushions, but reconsidered. He'd had food poisoning before and in the previous instance it had been much worse than this.

Walter lay down to let the cool grain of his leather sectional soothe his warm cheek and neck.

But as he grew drowsy, Walter thought about a grizzled old ghoul, killing a Marquis and penning notes to the dead man's relations. He thought about *The Voice on the Phone*, and a dark shape inviting a young girl out for "some fun" while chewing on the decomposing flesh of her boyfriend.

The soothing coolness of the leather hardened, dried and became like ashes on his skin. Walter spun in a tight arc until he again stood on an avenue of dust in a city of glass.

This time, Barry stood at his side, holding Walter's hand in a painful grip. He stepped forward and yanked, trying to get Walter to follow. He resisted. The Teek, wearing their forest green trench coats, wandered beyond the panels of glass. There were so many of them; they were everywhere. He tried to resist Barry's insistence.

But the man was strong and his efforts were supported by a gusting wind at their backs, and Walter's feet slid in the dust, kicking up filthy ephemeral wings from his heels. He struggled harder. He didn't want to get near the glass tapestries or the creatures that roamed between the panes.

Barry turned an angry face on him.

"You can't shut it all out, Walter," he called, his voice still barely audible over the desert wind. "You can't live behind the glass, because that is where they hunt. Do you understand that, Walter? Do you?"

Desperate to be free of Barry's demanding grasp, Walter yanked his arm so forcefully that the bones and cartilage in his hand snapped. Walter fell back in the dust and gazed up in wonder.

Barry no longer stood before him; a paper-thin sheet of glass the size of a common household door had replaced him. Through the glass, Barry gave him a final, mournful gaze and then turned away, leaving him alone in a settling cloud of dust.

The next morning, Walter woke on the sofa with a foul taste in his mouth and a horrible scent in his nose. He wiped his eyes and sat up on the sectional. A dull ache thudded in his belly and chest and the act of lifting himself from the cushions seemed to take all of his energy. He balanced on his feet for several moments until he felt that he could move without toppling over, and then Walter walked to the bathroom in his office.

Slowly, he brushed his teeth and covered the horrible taste in his mouth with minty paste. In the mirror, his face and eyes seemed to rest beneath a veil of dust.

... a drug compound, administered with a filthy hypodermic needle, to expedite the death and decay of his victims ...

The fragment of text flashed into his head and was followed by the image of a woman in green, racing over a crowded sidewalk as the place she'd touched Walter's shoulder flared in pain.

He shook as if a stream of ice water cascaded down his spine. He spit in the sink; the foamy white paste was veined with brown and burnt yellow streaks. Gray flecks floated on the unwholesome foam. Disgusted, he ran the faucet to clean away the ugly wad, rinsed his mouth, and felt another wave of freezing cold crash down on his neck.

... damned forever to exist on a diet of putrescence and decay ...

The terrible definition of the Teek continued to play in his head and the images of his dreams – the arid plain, the towers of glass, the etched faces of terrified onlookers and the things behind the glass illustrated the tale. He stumbled from the bathroom and clutched at the wall to keep from falling.

Already his efforts to erase the miserable, filthy taste with brush and paste began to fade as the dull flavor of rot rode over his mouth on a tide of mint. Walter closed his eyes, which were already filling with tears. Panic surged and then faded, muffled by the pain that had begun to radiate from his shoulder.

He must call help; he needed an ambulance.

He fell into his desk chair and reached for the telephone.

It rang, and with an excruciating effort he lifted the headset from the cradle.

"Help me," he said, his voice raw and breathy. His lungs hung behind his ribs like dry bags of flour, heavy and rigid. "Help."

"Walter, what's wrong?" Barry asked.

The man's familiar voice was at first welcome, but the comfort of his tone soon rose to a siren-pitched alarm in Walter's head. He remembered snippets of his dreams, remembered the man with the wheat-colored hair trying to drag him toward the towering panels of glass and the creatures prowling the dust between them. As Barry continued to speak anxiously on the distant connection, Walter felt hope slip away.

Only briefly did he consider that his convictions were irrational, but that voice was a whisper among screams.

"Walter? Are you there?"

Their date had been a trap; he saw that now. Barry had drawn him out into the dangerous world and one of his kind, the woman in the green trench coat, had injected Walter with sickness. He had to get him off the phone, had to call for...

The weight of the phone doubled with every second he held it. Already it felt like he held an iron to the side of his head – then, a bowling ball. He couldn't keep his grip much longer as the ache in his shoulder had become unbearable.

"Walter, what's your address? Give me your address so I can help you. Walter?"

No, he thought, struggling to keep his grip on the headset. He didn't want him (didn't want *them*) to know where he lived. They'd come for him; they'd find him; they'd...

He dropped the phone and leaned back in the chair, his eyes locked on the glowing screen of his computer monitor.

An instant message box blipped open.

GDTLP: *Where ya been*?

Walter fell forward. He caught himself before crashing face first on the keyboard, his head swirling with hungry faces and transparent buildings. He gasped for air and the effort shot bolts of pain throughout his body.

After a tremendous effort, he got his fingers positioned on the keyboard and wrote.

WH61: *Hel*...

From the front of his house, he heard glass breaking. His head lolled on his shoulders and a cry of panic sounded in his torso. The front door opened with a dry whoosh and a foot clicked quietly on the tile in the entryway. But he might have been imagining these sounds; he couldn't be certain. His pulse was too loud in his ears; his head hurt so badly that he couldn't be sure.

GDTLP: *Hel? LOL! Can't even write hello?*

A board groaned in the living room. This time, he heard the sound clearly, like a sheep bleating from a great distance. He struggled to look away from the screen. More footsteps joined the first.

He panted frantically trying to fill his flour-sack lungs with air and again put his fingers on the keyboard. With great effort, he managed to write a simple note:

WH61: *911 intruders here*

Walter fell back against his chair, exhausted by his exertion as the sound of footsteps whispered in the hall.

GDTLP: *I know.*

Barely able to keep his eyes open, Walter squinted to make out the message. When the words became clear, their meaning connecting in his mind like the terminals of a battery, panic shot in painful waves through his failing system.

GDTLP: *Our path led us from a man named Desmond to a man named Gary. From Gary we found a man named Walter and from Walter we will find the next.*

The lines of blurry script wormed into his head, and Walter spun in the chair, attempting a final act of flight. He made it to his feet and took one lumbering step forward, but his leg maintained its integrity for only a moment. The corrupted bone and muscle crumpled under his weight, popping and snapping as he toppled forward. He cried out as gravity took hold. A spray of filth jetted from his throat and over his lips, spattering the carpet moments before he crashed to the floor, pinning and crushing an arm beneath him.

Numb and broken, Walter scratched at the carpet with the arm that had not shattered. The nails pulled back and the tips eroded, coating the fibers in a foul porridge. Shadows fell over him, blocking out the glow of his computer monitor. The Teek gathered around him; he saw their black shoes and the hems of their green trench coats, and he felt their eyes on him.

Something was spread out next to him. Walter tried to see what it was, but couldn't turn his head. A moment later, he was being rolled onto a clear plastic tarp or shower curtain. They lifted him and carried him across the hall to the bathroom. Setting him gently in the tub. He tried to obey the panic in his mind and struggle, but his arms and legs were useless. One of the creatures carrying him leaned in to look at his eyes.

The woman's face was almost human. Thick brown hair swept back from a normal looking brow, but her eyes lacked irises, just a black dot of pupil amid a glistening lens of white. Pronounced and narrow ridges at the cheekbones gave the woman a gaunt appearance. Walter noticed her mouth was filled with short blunt teeth like those of a baby. Distantly, he wondered if she was the monster that had grabbed his shoulder, wounded him and infected him with the decaying poison.

Another Teek pushed into his view. He came at Walter with a pair of sheers. Walter's heart beat raced, bringing sharp pains to his chest.

Carefully, the Teek cut away his clothing. Walter groaned when he saw a layer of skin and hair peel away with the fabric.

Don't, he thought. Please don't.

More Teek pushed into the bathroom. Now there were five of them. Walter lay naked, looking up at them, unable to bear the sight of his rotting body. They all had the same iris-less eyes and the sharp facial bones. One male lightly licked his upper lip as he stared down at Walter.

Tears spilled over his cheeks. His struggle apparent only in the twitching of his left index finger.

His clothing, now nothing more than swatches of material, made filthy by his decaying flesh, was distributed among the tribe. The Teek lunged for their share of the fabric. They licked and chewed on the torn clothing, slurping at the foul meat clinging to the fibers.

Walter's body convulsed, but his weak muscles responded with little more than a shudder. Please help me, his panicked mind begged. Please. Please. Please. I'm so scared.

His index finger stopped twitching. The tears stopped flowing. His body could no longer manage these simple tasks.

Then the numbness spread to his mind and the faces above him blurred; they faded. And a flare of panic, like the popping of a flash bulb, ignited as he endured a final, desperate wonder:

Would anyone, anyone at all, notice he was gone?

Crack Smokin' Grandpa

Objectification is the identification of a person or group of persons as something other than human, often in an attempt to label, simplify and yes, even negate that individual or aggregation. Kierkegaard, anyone? Armies have been doing it since before God had pubes, because, quite frankly, it's easier for a teenager to kill a Jap, a Kraut or a Gook than it is to waste Toshiro, Franz or Ahn Dung. So, the human animal, in order to cope with his or her world, takes a person and gives them the same import as a beer bottle.

It's just easier that way.

I mention this not to start a discourse on sociology or, more specifically, interracial tolerance, but rather to explain something far more complicated: dating. In this context I've found objectification to be useful. After all, a guy named Phil can break my heart, but it's harder to get worked up when you've been dumped by Skippy the Spit Lizard, as he came to be known. The ameliorating effect is minimal, I'll grant you, but it's something, and it goes well enough with vodka and Oreos.

In order to properly objectify a guy, all you have to do is find one or two distinguishing traits – usually negatives, but not always – and link them together to form a snappy name. So, Greg becomes Needy Freckle Guy, and Vern becomes Water Sportin' Condo Pimp.

And Byron Kelley becomes Crack Smokin' Grandpa.

For those who call this process cruel and childish, I will point out that cops are very well known for their use of objectification, and despite certain news reports it's not always about racism. It can help them deal with the horrors of their day-to-day work. It's got to be tough for a person, regardless of profession, to look down on the bloated body of a kid that's been soaking in lake water for a day or two. So instead of thinking of the carcass as someone's son or brother or lover, they think of him as a floater.

It's easier that way.

I remember how Byron and I met as clearly as if it had just happened. You know those great old movies, where two strangers are in a crowded room or just walking down the street, and they see one another, and it's like everyone else just freezes in place and fades, becoming insubstantial? Then, a kind of light, like a golden ray from heaven, falls over their faces, and they find themselves enchanted with one another. Music swells.

Yeah, well, the way I met Byron was nothing like that. But I do love those movies.

We met over the Internet. Nothing special. We did the stat and pic exchanges. I found his restraint from using phrases like "I'll suck U dry," and "You want me to fuck the cum out of you with my big daddy cock?" refreshing.

As a side note, I like older men. Call them Daddies or Dust Queens, but I got a thing for gray hair, wizened eyes and maybe even a bit of a gut if they haven't let themselves go full-on Orson. This predilection is perplexing to my friends, who like myself are in their mid-thirties, but in truth, they're glad I'm not in competition for their gym rat idols.

When Byron answered the door, I did have one of those world-goes-away moments. He looked younger than I'd expected. Like most, I figured he'd sent an older snapshot, capturing him in particularly good light. His online profile said he was nearing sixty, but seeing him standing across the threshold from me, I would have put him in his mid-forties, fifty tops. He had a short brush of salt and pepper hair with a close-cropped beard to match, sparkling green eyes, and a charming smile. He wore a pair of black slacks and a white dress shirt, both of which hugged his burly, solid body. When he saw me on the porch, Byron arched his eyebrows in a quick dance and said, "Wow."

I did a mental high-five and walked in.

Over dinner – an awful chicken dish with a ghastly amount of cilantro – we did the occupation, recreation and location thing. Byron had retired early from his job as senior news producer for a local ABC affiliate somewhere in Oregon and had relocated to Pierce Valley to live on the lake and relax. He traveled extensively and spoke a few languages. He talked about his family, which is when I heard about the arrival of his first grandson, Joe. When he talked about the baby, he positively glowed with excitement. As for why he even had a grandchild, Byron was a late bloomer. He'd been married for nearly twenty years before coming out, His son's family lived in Northern California; his ex-wife had remarried and lived in Portland.

"She hates my guts," Byron said with a laugh, lifting his wine glass to his lips. "Fortunately, Sean is a lot more evolved. He took it pretty hard at first, but he's all PFLAG now. He's more excited about me being gay than I am. Not that I have a problem with it. I just see it as a fact of life, but he sees it as some kind of prestige society, like I got anointed or something."

"What brought you here?" I asked, doing my best to hide the fact that the meal would make an excellent dish for Bulimics.

"The lake," he said. "I visited here a long time ago, long before they started all of the development and long before The Valley became Seattle's bedroom. It stuck with me. Since the south shore is all condos and mod-arc breeder shacks, I bought up here, where you can still pretend you've got privacy."

"So you can dance around naked in the backyard?"

Byron chirped out a laugh. "Yes," he said brightly. "Exactly."

"Are you about to reveal your nudist lifestyle or your devotion to Satan? Because things like that really need to be addressed early on in a relationship."

"Well," Byron said, "Naked is good, but I wouldn't call myself a nudist."

"And yet, the whole Satan issue goes unaddressed."

"Spiritually, I don't believe in much of anything," Byron told me. "Every society defines good and evil in its own way. Ultimately, we serve our natures. Hell, in a lot of cultures I could be executed for doing what I'm thinking about right now."

"And what's that?"

"Well, naked is part of it. But I have the feeling I'd like to see you again, so maybe we could just make out for an hour or two."

Before I left that night, my face pleasantly raw from beard burn, we made a second date: dinner at a restaurant on the riverfront near my place downtown.

Later, I would tell my friends that despite the meal, which went from terrible to toxic, having been capped by some kind of disgusting baked pudding, my first date with Byron went surprisingly well. He seemed like a good-humored guy who had all the right parts in the right places and in the right proportions.

And he had the face. Boy, did he have the face.

I am of the belief that we all carry a mental snapshot that's been manipulated by the mind's equivalent of Photoshop. Bodies are easier to build as they require less attention to detail, but you have to put a lot of thought into creating the right face. We take one guy's eyes and another's mouth, and some other's nose, fiddle around with the brow and the jaw. If we're so inclined, we draw on the appropriate amount of facial hair, then save the image, thinking we've created a composite of the face we could, without the slightest doubt, wake up to every morning.

That's how I describe Byron's face. It was the face I wanted to wake up to every morning, and soon enough, I did.

The kid's name was Darrell Innis. He was twenty-three years old, a recent graduate of the University of Washington. His parents didn't report him missing because he was an adult and also because they didn't like to pry into their children's private lives. Besides, he'd gone away for long weekends before.

He washed up on the south shore of the lake, near City Park.

The autopsy showed no indication of foul play.

A midnight swim gone bad.

Case closed.

Sometimes, you meet a guy and the sex is so right, you wonder why so many men get it wrong. You know those times when you're with a guy, and he's tender and sweet, and you'll often pause to whisper to one another, prolonging the final moments, so you can lose yourself in that man's voice, his touch, the whole of him? You joke and laugh and make sweet talk? You want time to stop and feel that warm comfort for the rest of your life, because you can't imagine anything feeling more like love?

Yeah, well, sex with Byron was nothing like that.

It was raw and primal, and just plain nasty-porn hot, every fucking time. The tenderness came after, while we caught our breath or watched television as we drifted off to sleep. I could go on an on about what a great guy he was and how much we had in common, but in looking back, it's harder to remember the good things. Except for the sex, that is.

Our bodies were nothing alike, but they fit together perfectly. He was thick and brawny and I have a slender, lithe build. His chest and belly were covered with a full brush of fine short hairs, whereas, much to my disappointment, I was as smooth as a twelve year old. As to his endowment, I again resort to objectification. The words *horse* and *beer can* come immediately to mind.

On the afternoon that has come to be known as Crack Saturday, we had just finished a marathon session in bed, and I ached all over. By this time, we were spending four or five nights a week together, always at my place. Weekends were a given. He'd come over Friday night, and we'd didn't separate until I had to hit the office Monday morning.

On Crack Saturday, at about three, Byron came out of the shower. With the hair pasted to his body in an arcing pattern, his chest looked huge. Droplets dappled his face and neck and his shoulders. A rivulet ran from his beard, down his throat to the valley of his chest.

"Do you get high?" Byron asked, leaning against the doorjamb, dripping water on my floor.

The question startled me. We'd been dating for a few weeks, and it had never come up before. Over the years, I'd done more than my share of happy chems, though it had been a while. I figured Byron was talking about smoking a joint or something, and I saw no harm in it. In fact, it sounded like fun.

"Sure," I told him. "You got something?"

His eyes lit up, and Byron made his brows dance again before crossing to his jacket. He pulled a prescription bottle and a glass pipe out of his jacket pocket. Inside the bottle was what looked like a hunk of chalk wrapped in cellophane.

"You've got to be kidding," I said.

"Is this a problem?"

"You're keeping crack cocaine in a bottle that used to hold your heart medication. You see no irony here?"

Byron laughed. "I'll be fine," he said. "You in?"

"Light me up."

So, what can I say about crack? It made me feel powerful, euphoric, possibly deluded and made me say the dumbest shit I think I've ever uttered in my life. I imagine it's the closest I'll ever get to feeling like a Log Cabin Republican, and before it went bad, our afternoon tripping the white fantastic was a riot. I spoke a mile a minute about God only knows what. We danced, hit the pipe, tried to watch four different DVDs, hit the pipe, made out and hit the pipe. Byron was sucking back smoke at twice my rate, but seemed hardly fazed, whereas I was a sweating, babbling goof, though one who sincerely enjoyed the dangerous rapping in my chest and the taste at the back of my throat.

As the afternoon turned to evening, I noticed that Byron was slowing down. No matter how many draws he took from the glass tube, he seemed to be sinking lower and lower. I had never seen him frown before, but he wore a frown that night. As for me, I lay on the bed, body thrumming, mind buzzing and finding his every step and gesture erotic, despite my full awareness of his distraction.

"Every day it gets harder," he said. "So many rules now. The way you look. The way you behave. Time. So much fucking time, and it never stops. Just when I think I understand and everything is comfortable, it changes again. The rules keep changing. And it doesn't make sense. Nobody understands. All the others are gone. They're all gone, dead or trapped in the past and suffering and so damned lost."

"Hey," I said, trying to calm him down, but the tread of his pace increased.

"We have to be true to our nature," he said, ignoring me. "We have to be what we are, but nobody understands, so we bury things deep, deep down. And we smile. We fucking smile and pretend that everything's okay, but it isn't. There's no more magic in the world. Oh, there are plenty of tricks, plenty of illusions, but aspiration replaced wonderment, so nothing's good enough. Every ounce of imagination is wasted on cars and houses and television sets, and it's suffocating. Because no matter what you are, you should be better, and no matter what you have, it isn't enough. We pretend and lie and act like we're supposed to act until we don't even exist anymore, and I don't know what I'm supposed to be."

"You're exactly what you're supposed to be," I told him.

Byron stopped pacing. He ran a hand over his scalp a few times, petting himself. He let a smile, albeit a pained one, cut his lips. "You remind me of them," he said. "That's one of the reasons I love you."

I lay there trying to make sense of what he'd said. I reminded him of someone, some "them," but had no idea who he meant. Considering how much speed was in his system, it could have been anyone. But he'd said "I love you." That was the first time he'd told me that. I liked it, even though I'm not sure if it counts when someone says it while tweaking on rock.

Still, I imagine it's easier that way.

The next afternoon, when I woke up, Byron was gone. I searched the apartment, but there was no sign of him, no note. This breaking of our weekend ritual stabbed at me, and in light of the previous evening's drama, I wondered if I'd said something to upset him. I couldn't imagine what it might have been. I'd said some weird shit, but considering his own babbling and waxing melancholic, he certainly couldn't hold that against me.

After getting enough coffee in myself to make sure my tongue worked properly, I gave him a call.

"You're still talking to me?" he asked, without a hint of humor in his voice.

"Of course, I am. Why?"

"After last night, I just thought..."

Again, I ran through the details of the previous evening, wondering what I might have forgotten, might have missed, but despite the alcohol and the rock, the events were clear enough. He'd been upset, frustrated by growing older in a society that seemed intent on following the teachings of Logan's Run. Despite his rather disjointed dialogue, he'd been right. The standards were ridiculous and the superficiality had reached a new depth. Personally, I refused to get caught up in the style blender that everyone seemed to be jumping into. In the end, it chopped and whipped and liquefied everything into one bland mess. So, I understood where he was coming from, but I didn't understand why he was so disturbed by the conversation.

Unless I had completely misunderstood what he'd been talking about.

"Are you okay?" I asked.

"Yeah," he said. "I am. I just feel like an idiot."

"Do you want some company?"

"Maybe it should wait until I get back," he said.

"Back?"

"I'm going down to visit Sam and his family for a few days."

"Who's Sam?"

"My son."

"I thought your son's name was Sean."

"Yeah, Sean," Byron said quickly. "That's what I meant. I'm sorry. I'm not thinking real clear right now."

I thought about mentioning the fact that he'd never said anything about this impending trip, thought of questioning a lot of things, but instead I told him to give me a call when he got back. A little distance suddenly struck me as a good idea.

―――――――――

The man's name was Thomas Taylor. He was fifty-three years old and was the foreman of an orchard two counties over. His wife reported him missing early Monday morning when Thomas didn't return from an errand he had to run in Pierce Valley the previous evening.

He washed up on the south shore of the lake, near City Park.

The autopsy showed no indication of foul play.

Suicide was being considered because authorities were at a loss to explain what he was doing in the lake.

An investigation was pending.

―――――――――

Wednesday morning, I was in the office, e-mailing friends between meetings. One note came from my buddy Zack, who was known to drape himself in paranoia at every opportunity. Amid his usual whine-fest about the relative inequities of life, he made mention of the second body found floating in just over a month. That morning, I had not looked through the newspaper.

Zack told me that he suspected a connection between Darrell Innis and Thomas Taylor. Such an assertion was to be expected from a guy we referred to as Olivia Stone.

Zack sent me a link to the article, and I clicked through to it. The first thing I did was look at the picture, because you always want to know if someone hot has slipped away. Looking at the pleasant, square face of a man with white hair, an uneasy chill ran up my back. I knew this guy. Not knew him in any substantive way, as in his real name (because he'd told me it was something different) or any details about his life or his family, but we'd fucked a couple of times. I'd met him in a chat room, and we'd hooked up at my place. I remember thinking he was a nice enough guy, but firmly entrenched in the closet, so not a long-term prospect.

Startled by a familiar face staring back at me from beneath a headline that read, *Apple Ridge Man Found Dead*, I turned away from the computer to give myself a chance to breathe before reading the article. I drank from my coffee, and before I put the mug down, my phone was ringing.

"Hey, Handsome." It was Byron.

"Hey back at'cha," I said. "How was the trip?"

"Good. It was exactly what I needed. The grandson kept me on my toes, and I think Sean was glad I was there to pick up a bit of slack. I don't think he or his wife have slept in four months. So, I got to play grandpa, and they got to go out to dinner and a movie."

"Sounds great."

"Any chance I'm going to see you this evening?"

"I'd say there's a pretty good chance. But you might want to leave the party favors at home."

This set Byron to laughing. "Yeah, I think we've seen the last of that for a while."

I was never a big proponent of romantic gestures. The idea of showing up at a boyfriend's house unannounced, just because I wanted to see him, struck me as a remarkably bad idea. Said suitor might take it as intrusive. Or, said suitor might not be alone, thus killing any whimsical notions of impulsive romance.

A few weeks after his return from the family visit, I spoke with Byron on the phone, and he sounded down, nearly as depressed as he had on Crack Saturday. By this time, I cared a great deal for the man. We'd been seeing each other for a couple of months, and we continued to grow closer, more comfortable with one another, but it didn't dampen the heat between us as so often happens. Most days, his charm and humor – his absolute enjoyment of the world – showed through like a beacon, but it was becoming apparent that every month or so, like some kind of sad-making menstrual cycle, all of that would bleed out of him, leaving a man incapable of coming to grips with his place in the world.

It was a Tuesday.

"I'm not going to be very good company," he told me. "Tomorrow, we'll go have a nice dinner, but I think tonight is a bourbon and fireplace kind of evening."

Upon hearing that my boyfriend wanted some time to himself, my unexpected inclination was to go buy flowers, a nice bottle of wine and show up on his doorstep. Well, I bought the flowers from the florist shop next to my office, and the wine I picked up at a liquor store on Academy Boulevard about half a mile from Byron's place, but I never made it to his doorstep.

I saw the car, a beat up Mustang convertible, parked behind Byron's Audi before I had completed the turn into his driveway. Sensing that the fear that had driven me away from such romantic expressions was actually facing me, I backed out of the drive and along the street until my car was obscured by the trees at the edge of Byron's property. Then I opened my cell phone and hit the speed dial.

"Hello," Byron said, picking up after the fourth ring.

"Hey, it's me." My chest was tight. Anxiety opened in my stomach like a broken beehive, sending a thousand buzzing wings to tickle and agitate. "Just thought I'd see how you were doing."

"That's very sweet of you," he said. "I'm okay. I'm about to have some dinner and then I'm curling up with a bottle of Maker's Mark."

I listened for clues in his voice, something that might give him away. They weren't really that hard to find. He sounded restless. In fact, he sounded glass pipe coke-smoked wired.

The bees in my belly started stinging, and I figured it best to cut my losses and get off the phone. Yes, I wanted to know who owned the Mustang, and I was none too thrilled that Byron was tweaking again, but I have a policy of never asking a question unless I can accept the answer, and just then, I wasn't feeling terribly accepting. Pissed, yes. But not accepting.

I drove off and managed to navigate my way through town, basically oblivious to the buildings and the pedestrians, my only real concentration on the seething discomfort in my stomach and the disjointed phrases in my head. All of the stupid assertions came flying at me and I batted them away using equal parts denial, anger and hope.

He wouldn't fuck around. – Of course, he would.

I didn't really see anything. – You saw a car in his driveway and he didn't mention having company.

So a friend stopped by. He's allowed to have friends. – So why not tell you?

But he wouldn't do that. – And why the fuck wouldn't he?

And back and forth it went, like yarn in a loom, weaving over and under the possibilities, creating a truly unattractive tapestry.

I turned the car around and headed back to Byron's house.

I parked in the same place I had earlier. A low line of shrubs blocked most of my car from casual observation, but it gave me a clear view of the edge of Byron's porch, the lawn and the lake's edge. A stand of trees framed the scene, cutting a kidney shaped swatch from the lake. With the sun nearly set, the water twinkled with orange light. Gentle waves from a light breeze stippled its surface.

From this position, I could watch the house and with luck, pull away quickly should Byron or his guest come outside. I wasn't actually expecting to see them, and I had no intention of going to the door. So, I wasn't exactly sure what I was doing there, except driving myself nuts.

I was surprised to see that they did come outside.

Byron came out first. In the remains of the late evening light, his naked skin seemed to glow as he walked down the slope of his backyard to the lake's edge. Despite months of attraction to this man, his body had never looked quite this way. I'd considered his body perfect for me, but now it seemed even more than that. His arms and shoulders bulged, and his thighs seemed impossibly large, swollen thick with striated muscle. At the water's edge, he paused and turned, revealing his growing erection. It was then that I noticed the young man stepping off of Byron's porch, beginning his trek toward the water. The guy had removed all of his clothes except for a pair of black jockey shorts.

Byron reached out his hand, waiting for the young man.

And there I sat, motionless. The anger had receded, pushed away by my fascination with Byron. In that light, with that distance, he appeared unnaturally perfect, and I wanted to get out of the car and go to him. I wanted to be the one reaching out my hand to take his, wanted to be the one who pushed close to his chest and wrapped my arms around his neck. The compulsion to go to him was so profound that I held the door handle, certain I would pop it open and rush out. I fought this impulse with every bit of control I had. Jealousy did not feed my compulsion. In fact, I felt nothing but adoration for the man, and I wanted to share it, to be with him and feel his incredible body against mine.

When he guided the boy into the lake, the water climbing halfway up their thighs, I ground my teeth together and gripped the door handle so tightly my fingers ached. Tremors of longing ran through me like electric charge. Reason continued to slip away.

In the lake, Byron wrapped his arms around the young man, buried his face in the cradle of his shoulder, making a slow turn until the guy's back was to the expanse of the lake and Byron's back was to me. Then he dipped forward, gently leaning the boy into the water. With a kick of his leg, they moved away from the shore, farther and farther until they disappeared behind a drape of tree branches, leaving me in the car, staring at the ripples of water, the wake of their passing.

My breath came in short gasps. My fingertips stung from their vice-tight grip on the handle.

I had to get out of there.

You know those all-consuming breakups that don't give you a second of peace? You have dramatic arguments in your head, and you just can't wait to confront the asshole that broke your heart, because you want to say all of the great lines you've been practicing in between shots of vodka? You find absolutely trivial flaws in the guy to amplify and use to tell yourself he wasn't really all that great? But you also want the confrontation because you're hoping that he will say something or do something that will make it all okay?

Yeah, well, my breakup with Byron was exactly like that.

The Thursday after I'd gone all stalker, I sat at my office reading emails. Bryon hadn't called the previous day, and I certainly wasn't going to call him.

That morning, Zack had more news to report. This time, they'd found not one, but two bodies in the lake. For a second, the time it took for me to link through to the news article, I pictured Byron and his date with a mixture of dread and denial.

The authorities had found a fresh floater out by the Andrews Estates on the northwest side of the lake, but while they were performing the rescue, they discovered another body on the lake's bottom. The first floater was a young man named Nick Hoffman, a video store clerk from Snohomish. Like Thomas Taylor, the authorities could not say with any certainty why Hoffman had gone into the lake.

As for the other body, apparently it had been in the lake for quite some time, several months, perhaps as much as a year. They were certain that the body was that of a middle-aged male. Dental records would be necessary for any further identification. They also knew that the body had been weighted down with rocks and debris, in a manner that ruled out accident or suicide.

The man had been murdered.

But the man wasn't Byron, so I was allowed to remain pissed off.

When Byron called me just after lunch, that familiar hive of bees broke open in my gut. But I wanted to play it cool. I wanted him to know that I was completely indifferent to his presence in my life. He didn't deserve any further emotion from me.

"Hey, Handsome," he said.

"Fuck you," I said, perhaps too loudly, and slammed down the phone.

And of course, in its aftermath, for the briefest of moments, I felt absolutely cleansed. Those two words had purged the rage and hate and hurt, and everything felt light and right and good. That lasted until the phone rang again about three seconds later. Then, I was just pissed off again.

"What?"

"What's going on?" Byron asked, sounding upset. "What's wrong?"

"That's not a game you want to play right now."

"I don't understand."

"Big surprise. Crack Smokin' Grandpa don't get it. The world taxes his antique brain. I was such a fucking idiot."

"What is all of this about?"

"It's about a late night skinny dip to which I wasn't invited."

"You were spying on me?"

"No. No. No," I snapped. "You don't get to be outraged. You sounded terrible when I talked to you the other night, and I was worried."

"Look, we never said anything about…"

"Why do your lips keep moving? For fuck's sake, you're busted, and I'm gone."

"Hold on."

"Hold yourself, Aquaman."

I hung up the phone and again felt that perfect moment of satisfaction. Wanting to retain it for a few extra minutes, I left my desk and walked into the break room to pour myself a cup of coffee. At the time, I was convinced that it was over. I'd said what I had to say, not all that I had to say, but enough. There was nothing Byron could say or do that was going to fix this.

But, of course, being wounded, I wanted him to try.

———

So, how did I end up at Byron's house later that night? Good question and not one I have an easy answer for.

When I left the office that afternoon, he was waiting in the parking lot for me. He leaned against my car, dressed in a simple white dress shirt and khaki shorts. He looked amazing, and a voice in my head – the slow one with the pointed cap, that sounds vaguely like Forest Gump – suggested I just forgive and forget. Byron and I had a great time together, and I wasn't likely to find someone else like him, not in this white bread burg.

Oh, the brittle convictions of man.

He hadn't brought flowers and didn't greet me with supplicating tears. In fact, he looked as angry as I felt, arms crossed over his chest, mouth set in a tight frown, eyes glaring at me as if I'd been the one caught fucking around.

"We have to talk," he said.

"Go home," I said. "I'm in no mood for this shit."

"No. We're going to talk, and we're going to work this out."

"Uh… no."

He changed then. I don't mean that to suggest his expression or his posture changed, though that was part of it.

I watched him physically change. He uncrossed his arms, let them drop to his side as he leaned away from the car toward me. Standing straight, his chest pushed at the white fabric of his shirt, his arms filled the sleeves, testing the material's integrity. His thighs, already impressive, swelled before my eyes. And *his* eyes. Christ, his eyes. The green in his irises bled out, paled and filled the entirety of his sockets as if the orbs had turned from tissue to red veined marble.

"Get in the car," he said. "And drive me home. I'm going to explain some things to you, and then I'm leaving. Whether you come with me or not is your decision."

What was not my decision was getting in that car. It was done, but I'd made no conscious agreement to do it. I opened the door, climbed into the driver's seat and started the car, waiting for Byron to sit in the seat next to me.

Once we were driving, a thousand words vied for space on my tongue, but I was unable to speak. It felt like a hand was locked around my throat, applying just enough pressure to constrict my vocal cords.

"I'm sorry you saw what you did last night," he said. "I know it hurt you, and I hate that I did that to you. You mean a lot to me. I know that's difficult for you to believe right now, but it's true. If you didn't..." He let the sentence trail away. "Never mind. Just take my word for it."

Though I heard what Byron was saying and understood on some level that he was trying to be sweet, I felt an overwhelming panic. Byron was dangerous. I knew that, and as I thought about him, I thought about his rendezvous the night before, and from that came memories of newspaper articles, detailing the discovery of four different men who had died in the lake behind his home.

Back on the north shore, Byron's Audi was in the drive, and I parked behind it. He'd either taken a cab or walked into town, knowing before he left that I would be driving him back. Inside, we walked to the living room. I saw his glass pipe on the raw wood cocktail table and the prescription bottle next to it. Once there, his figure changed again, returning to the handsome and gentle looking man I'd met all of those weeks ago. His eyes again looked like normal tissue and not stone and his body returned to its burly if not muscular shape.

The muting hand at my throat vanished and I swallowed hard, sensing that I again had control over my voice and actions.

"Do you want a drink?" he asked.

"No," I said. "I want to go home and pretend you don't exist."

"Maybe later," he said. He fixed a bright smile on me and arched his eyebrows. Once I'd found the expression charming. Now it chilled me. "Maybe not."

"You think that's funny?"

"Nope," he chirped. "I can see why you might think that, though. There are a lot of things you don't understand about me"

Byron walked to the table and lifted the pipe off its surface.

"I never used to need this," he said, waving the fogged tube in the air. "I used to wake up every morning feeling the same rush this gives me, and I carried that feeling throughout the day. It was built into me. I had a euphoric nature. The older I got, the less that was true. I get so tired now, and it scares me. I sink into something I just don't understand, a kind of darkness. This gets me by for a while, a few days, maybe an extra week. But then, I need something else. I need something natural that this can't give me."

"So you fuck around?"

"Do you really think that's what you saw last night?" Byron asked. "Come on, you're not stupid. You know about the men they've found in the lake."

"I don't want to hear this."

"Hardly relevant to our conversation. You know what's going on. You just don't know why."

"Because you're sick?"

Byron let out a sparkling laugh, filled with amusement. "God, I love you," he said. "But a little less denial would be helpful here."

"Just tell me what you want to say."

"Fine," Byron said. "All coyness aside, those men died because of me, died *for* me. When they pass, an essence of them comes into me, and for awhile, I feel good again."

"So you kill people for a buzz?"

"No! I kill them to feel the way I'm supposed to feel. That's what my kind does. That's our nature."

"And what is your kind?"

"What difference does it make? Most of them are gone now. They couldn't keep up with the world; they couldn't adapt. They kept standing by streams and lakes, waiting for people to stumble across them because that's all they knew, that's what they were taught. But the world has changed and their enchanting facades meant nothing to people who only believed in what they could touch and own. They lost their influence. They sank into the same black ice that I fight against, without any hope of rescue. So they end it. They just end it because they are no longer relevant, they don't understand, and they'd rather die than suffer another minute feeling cold, alone and meaningless."

"But not you."

"No. Not me. I learned to adapt. I can wear this face and find joy in this world, but even I get lost."

"And what do you want from me?"

"I told you," he said. "I'm leaving, and I want you to come with me."

"Because you love me," I said, immediately regretting the use of such thick sarcasm in the presence of someone I now regarded as malevolent.

"You're alive aren't you?"

"I... " But I didn't know what to say.

Byron must have seen the fear his question raised in me. A moment later, his smile was back and his eyes lit. "We have fun, right? We're good together. I don't understand why that has to change."

"Are you kidding?"

"Damn it, there are only two ways this can end. You know that."

"Why?" I asked. "I either ignore what you're doing and we run off together or you're going to drown me? Why are those the only options?"

"Because, it's the only way I know," Byron said, his face tightening in pain. He let out a deep breath, ran his hand over his scalp in the petting motion I'd seen him use dozens of times before.

Then, he grasped the tail of his shirt, pulled it up over his head, revealing his hairy torso, which was already beginning to swell. He looked at me with green marbled eyes, now slicked with a sheen of tears.

"Let's go swimming," he said, reaching down to unbutton his shorts.

I followed Byron down the grassy incline, the lake stretching before us like a shadowy pit. Again, I was not in control of my actions. Though my mind raced, imagining numerous escape possibilities, my eyes were fixed on Bryon's powerful back. I needed to run, to escape, but I could not take my eyes off the wings of muscle at either side of his spine, his ass, his unnaturally thick legs.

At the water's edge, Byron stopped, and he turned to me. His marbled eyes were dry but, despite their otherworldly composition, showed warmth and concern.

"I won't let it hurt you," he said, reaching out his hand for mine.

Taking his hand, my panic intensified. This was the feeling of plummeting from a skyscraper, dropping from a plane; it was waking up in a nest of snakes; or being buried alive. It was the panic of having absolutely no control, with the terrible outcome perfectly clear and wholly inevitable.

He guided me into the lake, but I barely felt the chill water climbing over my skin. Waves lapped at my belly, but the only external sensation that concerned me was the tight grip of Byron's palm on mine. He turned to face me and leaned forward to kiss my neck. His muscular chest pressed against mine, sending waves of longing up and down my body as his hand released mine, his arms encircling me. I returned the embrace, because I had no choice. His muscles were hard as granite under my touch, but his skin was warm and soft.

I didn't want to die. Even then, feeling an odd sense of security in my killer's arms, I did not want to give up on life.

But Byron's legs kicked, and before I knew it, the north shore was far to his back. Only the lights from his living room window, now match flames in the distance, indicated the presence of civilization. At my back, the lights of the southern shores would cast a necklace of light, but in Byron's grasp, I had no chance to turn. Then his legs stopped pumping, and we glided through the water as if tethered to a boat. Water foamed and spread around us, making a pronounced wake as he ushered me to the lake's center.

When we stopped, I attempted to ask for my life, but my throat was locked, and all I could do was look at Byron and hope. His face shone bright above me as if throwing off light of its own, but his veined green eyes, only inches from mine, showed nothing.

He kissed me then. His lips crushed against mine, and his tongue entered my mouth, and I kissed him back, tightening my grip to feel as much of him against me as I could while my head grew light with his touch and his taste. Distantly at the back of my mind, I thought that if the kiss went on and on, he wouldn't have the chance to push me under the surface. If I could just keep this passion between us, I could survive another minute, another hour.

Only when I opened my eyes, did I realize we were already beneath the waves. Byron's face, still glowing with those damnable stone eyes, receded from me as if he flew up and away. But he flew nowhere. I was sinking, down and down and down, while all above me grew dark and hazed as if seen through a veil of putrid gauze.

And so I died. My lungs filled with water and my brain, having no oxygen to keep the factory open, just shut the whole works down. Byron didn't spare me, didn't come back for me. He made no grand romantic gesture to counter the cruelty of his nature.

Asshole.

And now, you're thinking that you've got a drowned guy telling you about the last few months of his life. How very Sunset Boulevard, right?

Not exactly.

Because of Crack Smokin' Grandpa's earlier activities, the sheriff had instigated shore and lake patrols. Fortunately, one of these saw my last moments of life, and they managed to find my ass at the bottom of the lake. They were kind enough to pull a Baywatch and get me breathing again, for which I rewarded them with about three gallons of lake water puked onto the deck of their boat. They wrapped me in a blanket and shoved an oxygen mask over my face.

Confused and exhausted, I kept trying to close my eyes and sleep until the ache in my body and the fear in my head were gone. But my rescuers apparently wanted more from me than a pool of slick vomit; they wanted answers.

Who was that guy?

What was his name?

Where did he go?

I pulled the mask from my face and told them that his name was Byron Kelley, and they looked at me like I had gills bellowing at my neck.

It was the next day before I found out why.

They identified the body of the older guy they'd dragged out of the lake the previous day.

His name was Byron Kelley, a senior news producer from Portland, who had disappeared the previous summer while on a road trip to

Vancouver. He'd never checked out of the Seattle hotel room where they'd found his luggage and most of his clothes. He was survived by his brother, Matt; his sister, Charlotte; and his son, Sean.

As it turned out, I'd never known Byron Kelley. I'd known a guy that had used his name and some of his history.

I'd known Crack Smokin' Grandpa.

Not a person at all. Just a thing. An object. A fiction wrapped in skin with a handsome mask. You couldn't want or need or be hurt by anything with such a ridiculous composition. The idea was silly. Preposterous. I certainly could never have loved him.

At least, that's how I figure it.

It's easier that way.

Anthem of the Estranged

The name of the show was derived from the practice of lifting a stone to see what filthy species had taken up residence in the dirt below. Though the apt title was not lost on any of the production staff of *Picking Up the Rock*, it seemed to completely elude the endless parade of poseurs, losers and has-beens that populated its installments; one of which, Michael Donnelley was about to meet.

Normally, Mike scheduled interviews at the studio or in one of half a dozen mediocre restaurants in the valley. But tonight, at the request of Tommy Gunn, he had parked in the armpit of Los Angeles, where pathetic victims of the Hollywood dream could still feed their fantasies on the scraps of tinsel town, like pilot fish at the ass end of a shark.

The cold wind lifted trash from the yards, passing litter from one dying field to the next. He scanned the buildings for house numbers and reminded himself to deny any future interviews that might require his setting foot on such tainted ground.

He groaned at his surroundings; this was not the life he had planned.

Picking Up the Rock was a digital graveyard for one-hit wonders with predominantly unsavory eulogies written to their memory. Overdoses, sex scandals and bitter rivalries got the bulk of the air time because those were the creatures the audience expected to see writhing beneath the stones of fleeting celebrity. The show would be pointless if it spotlighted a well-adjusted, successful, post-celebrity. Nobody wanted to hear that Tommy Gunn of late eighties glam-metal sensation *Lipstik* had parlayed his band's top ten single, *Power Tool*, into a successful dry cleaning chain and continued to live in the lap of luxury.

Where was the fun in that?

Fortunately for everyone – audience, producers, researchers and Mike himself – Tommy Gunn had succumbed to addiction and alcoholism. His descent into dependence had culminated in a ten-car pile-up on the four-oh-five, ending the lives of his spokesmodel wife,

Kandee Kane, and their year-old son, Ethan. By the time Tommy had come out of rehab and performed his community service, Seattle had given birth to the grunge movement, and Tommy had found himself without a record label.

These days, Tommy Gunn produced porn videos for Wet Angel Productions, (scoring all of the epics himself, of course), and occasionally making guest appearances on screen in the hopes that his fame among sleaze would sell a few extra DVDs. His six-bedroom manse in the Hollywood Hills had long ago returned to the care of the bank, which had financed it, and Tommy now resided in a beat-up shack in Silverlake; the very shack Mike noted upon taking the corner as the ugliest house on the block.

But despite the fact that the Gunn house was hideous, from its leprous brown paint to its jaundiced trim, the home had drawn a few curious passersby.

Half a dozen shadows moved silently across the lawn like monks on a sacred pilgrimage, their heads uniformly bowed. Though Mike could not make out their faces in the gloom (because Gunn's house was not only the ugliest on the block, it was the only one without a porch light burning), they all seemed to be wearing similar costumes: part rag, part robe.

Mike stopped on the sidewalk and watched this bizarre aggregation slowly herding across the overgrown lawn, cautiously avoiding the refuse and rusting garden tools at their feet as they made their way to the front of the house. Mike briefly wondered if he had made a mistake with the date or time of his appointment. Perhaps he was supposed to meet Gunn tomorrow night, and tonight was coven night at the Gunn household.

But the robed visitors did not seem to have been invited. Their destination was not the front door. Instead, they took up places on either side of the cracked cement porch and placed their hands on the flaking paint and rotten wood of the house's façade, where they remained like six delinquents told to assume the position by an arresting officer.

The display of worship put a tingle in Mike's belly. Disturbed by the sight, he considered turning around and returning to his Celica to put some distance between himself and this Silverlake freak show.

Just as he decided that retreat might be a good idea, the six shabby monks turned from the house and gathered at the center of the lawn in a single tattered huddle. One of the monks lifted his head as if to sniff the air, and his face fell under the bath of the street lamp.

The skin had been pierced dozens of times with small silver hoops, carving scale-like shadows on his face. The monk's eyes lacked irises. Dime-sized pupils, all blackness and depth, bore through orbs the color of watermelon juice. A taller pilgrim, a woman, noticed her companion's distraction and also looked up at Mike. A triangular hole gouged the space that had once held her nose, and beneath the nasal chasm an ear-to-ear grin split the woman's face in half. "He sees us," she sang lightly.

"Impossible," the male told her before dropping his head.

The troupe turned away from Mike and began to sing a low harmonized chant as they worked their way towards the sidewalk and ambled down the street like a single poorly formed beast. Despite its shabby appearance, this beast had a beautiful voice and a lilting melody on which to exercise it. The tune, seemingly without words, but rather a series of well-crafted vowels, remained in the night air even after its singers had taken the next corner and disappeared.

Their song still playing in his head, he stepped onto the lawn and realized he was being played for a goof. Gunn had set up this show as some sort of publicity stunt.

Now, Mike would probably be met at the door by some buxom dominatrix who would lead him to her "Lord and Master." He prepared himself for whatever else Tommy Gunn decided to shoot in his direction after he rang the doorbell, but was surprised when the door opened to reveal a rather small man, ten years his senior with a receding hairline and a pronounced pot belly, who wore jeans and a black tee shirt that had faded to slate gray. A pair of crimson lip prints painted the front of the shirt, and the word *Lipstik* was scrawled below. Thick pouches had formed under Gunn's bloodshot eyes and his once attractive face was now puffy and wore at least two days growth of beard.

"Hey," Gunn said in a rasping voice. "You're Mike right?"

"Yes," he said. "Mike Donnelley, and you're Tommy Gunn." The haggard man nodded his head. "That was quite a show you had going on out here," Mike said to let Gunn know that his production had been noticed, but that he wasn't getting away with anything.

Gunn looked into the street over Mike's shoulder and scanned the neighborhood. His brow was furrowed, and he looked back at Mike as if the journalist had claimed to be Marie Antoinette. "What show?" Gunn asked.

"Okay." Mike smiled and stepped over the threshold, passing the confused musician and taking in the furnishings of the man's home.

The rooms were pretty much what he had expected to find. Old furniture, once very expensive and stylish, sat crammed into a space one-tenth the size of the room the pieces had been designed for.

"Normally when we do one of these pre-interviews we go over our research to verify information," Mike said as he walked through Gunn's living room and poked his head into the small, dark dining hall. Again, furniture too big for its environment had been situated, leaving little room to pass on either side of the crystal topped dining table and the chrome and glass cabinet against the wall. "Then," he continued, "we just want to hear it from your lips. Tell us your story."

"Right," Gunn said. "And then you show a lot of pictures of twisted metal and me with a bottle in my hands."

"Good," Mike said. "Then we're on the same page."

Gunn's cheeks flushed crimson before he shoved his hands in the pockets of his jeans and made a vague shrugging motion. "So why should I tell you anything?" he asked. "You don't give a shit about anything but the accident."

"That's not true," Mike countered. "Your foray into filmmaking is also of great interest to us."

The corners of Gunn's mouth dragged into an angry frown. "We create our own salvation, buddy," he growled. "Once those vultures at Arista and Kandee's parents were done with me, what choice did I have? I was broke, and nobody was buying the music anymore."

"And yet so few of your peers went on to create classics like *Angela's Asses*, *Mary Potter's Secret Chamber* and my personal favorite, *Crouching Pussy, Hidden Snake*."

Mike had been with *Picking up the Rock* for just over two years and found himself appalled, not only at the sheer volume of fallen pop stars, but the uniformity of their indignation. He couldn't remember a single one of these men or women that would admit to being a mediocre musician with a single marketable song, nor could he remember one that seemed even remotely grateful for their fifteen minutes of fame. So he wasn't surprised by Tommy Gunn's assertion that the world had forced him into a life of low budget porn.

"We create our own salvation," Gunn said again.

"Yeah, yeah," Mike said, "What is that? Some of *Lipstik's* timeless lyrics?"

"It's from the bible," Gunn told him. The small man with the receding hairline opened a low cabinet and withdrew a bottle of scotch. He poured a few slugs into a tumbler and turned to Mike. "You want a drink?"

Mike dropped onto the sofa and shook his head. "I thought you were clean these days."

"Doesn't matter anymore," Gunn said, lifting the glass to his nose. He inhaled the fumes of the whiskey and closed his eyes.

"So is this part of the show?" Mike asked, remembering the odd monks performing their ritual against the side of Gunn's house. "The bad boy is back, complete with drugs, booze and Satan worshippers?"

Gunn again furrowed his brow and shook his head. "I'm moving on," Gunn said dreamily. He toasted the air with the tumbler and poured the whiskey into his mouth. "Shrugging off the coil and taking my act on the road."

Mike didn't have a clue what the burnout was talking about, so he took a guess. "You're going back on tour?"

"No," Gunn said. "That was a small dream, and I woke up in a bed of shit. What I'm talking about is the dream of dreams, the lord of all dreams."

Mike laughed at the performance of euphoria. "So you're completely fucked up right now?"

"Not yet," Gunn said with a smirk. "You know, this interview's kept me going for the last few weeks. Knowing people were going to see some of the videos and hear the music again really got me pumped. But then I saw the show. You make us look like clowns."

"We prefer the term, 'freaks,'" Mike said. "Now can we get down to business here?"

Gunn bowed lightly. "What do you want to know? My blood alcohol level when I drove into the back of that truck? Or are you more interested in the coke? Maybe you'd like me to tell you what it felt like to have my wife's head fall into my lap while the rest of her was pinned to the car seat by a sheet of corrugated aluminum? Or better yet, finding my son's body shredded on the side of the road? That's a good story, because I wasn't sure he was dead at first. I thought he was trying to crawl, but foolish me, that was just post-mortem muscle spasms."

"Let's start with the blood alcohol level," Mike said. "Then we'll segue into the death throes."

Gunn lit a cigarette and squinting through the smoke, pointed a finger at Mike. "You know what hurts the most, buddy?"

"Probably a piece of corrugated aluminum at about eighty miles an hour," Mike said, "Now, if you don't mind… "

Gunn slammed his palm on the makeshift bar; the concussion rumbled through the room. Gunn's face stormed with agitation. "Who the fuck do you think you are?" he roared. "You come into my home and act like you're doing me a favor by dragging me back over that road. I came out of rehab six months after losing my family and realized there was nobody waiting for me anymore: no audience waiting for a new album; no wife waiting at home; no child waiting for his daddy; no friends waiting for the next party. I woke up one morning with nothing, and I didn't even have the chemicals to make the pain stop." Gunn finished his drink and poured another, his hand still pointed at Mike to keep him silent as he pursued his intoxication. "You gotta have somebody waiting, man," Gunn told him earnestly. "That's the only thing in this fucking world that matters, knowing that somebody's waiting out there for you."

"Touching," Mike said blandly.

"Can you say pathetic?" Mike asked of the table of men. "I mean, the guy is polluted on alcohol and cocaine, drives his family into the back of a repair truck, and he's looking for sympathy. Then the asshole ups and disappears before we can get him on camera. The crew showed up last week, and the *looze* was gone. So now we have to use stills whenever we quote the dickhead or we have to run one of those cheesy ass videos on mute so people can hear Phil doing the narration."

"He's lost a lot," Jim said. "My guess is, he's done some suffering over it."

Mike sneered at his boyfriend, who could have found Hitler's good points, and took another sip from his Manhattan. "Fine," he said. "He's suffered, but who the hell hasn't? Jesus Christ, he's not a martyr; he's a spoiled little brat. No, he's worse than a spoiled little brat; he's a fame seeking, has-been with more skull than hair and a food baby the size of a bowling ball. Even worse, he can't stop whining because nobody cares about his crappy songs anymore."

"I always thought he was kind of cute," Charlie Nixon said.

"Of course you did," Mike said. Charlie thought anything male was kind of cute, but only because Charlie was a completely uninteresting looking man who had the chinless charms of a mounted bass.

"Well," Ray Thornton said, "It seems Michael is entering one of his moods. We'd better be going."

"So soon?" Mike asked. Ray and Charlie had been sucking down his alcohol for the last six hours, and Captain Brilliant needed an excuse to leave? "We'll be serving breakfast in about an hour."

"Charming... as always," Thornton said as he rose to leave.

Ray Thornton was Jim's ex-lover, and Mike had no qualms about offending the man or driving him away. He felt it was completely unnatural that the two had maintained a friendship after their break-up. This new age of tolerance was annoying; he preferred the good old days when exes were treated with loathing and spite.

He remained at the table as Jim escorted their guests to the door. He imagined that the appearance-conscious Jim would be apologizing for Mike's outbursts and toasted this image with his cocktail before draining the glass.

Jim was a sap, a very cute, very sweet sap.

The sweet sap returned to the dining room and began clearing the table.

"Leave those for morning," Mike said. "We don't have to be up early."

Jim put down the plates he had stacked and leaned on the back of a chair. Mike thought he looked remarkably cute when he got that serious look on his face, basically because Mike could never quite take Jim seriously.

"I'm staying at Ray's tonight," Jim said quietly as if announcing that the results of his latest test had been positive. "I just don't want to be here right now."

"Because I can't find the bright side of a chemically dependent burnout?"

"Because you can't find the bright side of anything," Jim said sadly. "You're so damned angry all the time. And I don't appreciate the way you've been treating our friends."

"You mean your ex-boyfriend?"

"I mean everyone, Mike. Ever since your father died, you've gotten nasty."

"That's not true. I was always nasty. You just used to have a sense of humor."

"That's because I thought you were joking around. But you're not. You're serious about the lousy things you say to people. You're serious about the lousy things you say to me, and I don't deserve that."

Mike couldn't help but notice that his boyfriend was genuinely upset, and he thought that perhaps he should take the man seriously just this once. But instinct overpowered intelligence and he said, "Ray must have broken world records giving you that spine implant at the door."

Jim gave one last, sympathetic gaze before saying, "Goodnight, Michael," and leaving the room. A moment later, Jim left the house.

Mike sat in a chair beside a sweating blob of dough named Ed whose fat fingers raced over the editing board as images flickered on six video screens before them. Behind them, a perpetually nervous young woman gnawed her thumbnail.

The editing room was barely the size of a walk-in closet but had so many dials, lighted buttons and monitors, they might have been orchestrating a moon mission rather than performing surgery on digital signals. The reek of videotape and dust filled the room. Mike's throat tightened against the plastic pungency, and he wriggled to get comfortable in his chair, growing more irritated by the moment with the editor and his mousy assistant. But then Mike's mood had been anything but "up" over the last few days.

Jim's desertion had stung, and nights of minimal rest had eroded what little patience Mike retained. His sleep had been disturbed by dreams of cloaked monks, chanting their contagious melody into the darkness; their song of oddly arranged vowels played lullaby as he slipped into drunken unconsciousness and acted as alarm throughout the night, pulling him from scenes of rock stars, car accidents and mutinous loved ones.

Even awake, that song rolled through Mike's head. But instead of reveling in the pleasing tune, his nerves grew raw at its repetitive invocation.

"They're going to make us recut this," Ed Hoeffer, said, drawing Mike's attention back into the editing chamber. "We're supposed to go to air Monday, and they are going to cut the shit out of it."

"Leave it in, Poppinfresh" Mike told him.

After six nights of sleeping alone, and not sleeping well, Mike's attitude had gone from bad to *blender*. Instead of stirring up shit, he now had himself set to frappe, and anybody that got caught in his carafe was going to find themselves liquefied. As a result, Mike wasn't going to take any shit from a lard-assed knob jockey. Besides, he wanted to make sure Tommy Gunn had a scenic trip down memory lane.

"It's powerful," he said.

"It's sick," Ed countered.

"Now I want a slow fade from the *Power Tool* video," Mike said. "Get the shot of him dancing across the stage with the bottle of Jack Daniels in his hands and dissolve it into... " Mike checked his book to find the tape and time designation he had noted that morning. "Tape three, four-oh-five."

"No way," Ed said, throwing up his hands. The big man pushed himself away from the editing board, sending his anxious assistant, Tammy, against a rack of master tapes. "Sorry, Tam," Ed said.

"It'skay," the intern lisped.

Michael took over the recently vacated chair and called up the archived news tape with its sweeping shot of the interior of Tommy Gunn's crumpled Jaguar. Mike would keep the soundtrack of *Power Tool* playing over the scene, boosting the volume for the lyric line, "if ya' make me choose, you're gonna lose," as the glare of a flood light captured the bloodied leather of the car seats and came to a jerking pause when it encountered the nest of hair surrounding Kandee Kane's severed head.

Unfortunately the head, left on the seat by Tommy after his escape from the wreckage, had been placed face down, so all the camera caught was a teased platinum cloud, resting like a toy dog amid the shards of glass and human fluid. "Fucking perfect," Mike announced as he sprung from the chair. "That's a wrap. Tack that between what we've already got, and don't touch a frame or it's your ass."

Ed, the moist hulk of geek, looked at Mike as if he had just defecated on the chair between them. Mike smiled his broadest grin and waved his fingers as if to a child before leaving the stifling air of the editing room.

He felt considerably better, almost giddy, after creating the video ode to Gunn's downfall, and once he was away from the stink of tape and back in his office he decided to call his boyfriend, if only to have someone to share his amusement with. Jim had left a message on voice mail (the third in two days), insisting that he needed to speak with Mike.

Swelled with beneficence, he dialed Jim at work, ready to talk and (if Jim was a good boy), ready to let him come home.

But Jim wasn't coming home.

"What are you talking about?" Mike asked angrily. "What has Ray been saying about me?"

Jim, ever the weak-willed diplomat, replied, "Ray doesn't have to say anything about you, Mike. I just can't take it anymore. Your anger is contagious, and I don't like feeling that way about people. Maybe you should see someone."

"I should see someone? The world is full of assholes, and I'm the one that needs therapy?"

"I'm sorry."

"Yes you are," he replied and slammed down the phone.

Mike left his office and stepped into the bright afternoon. He lowered the top of his Celica convertible and drove through the low buildings lining Sunset Boulevard, past the palm trees, standing sentinel over Brentwood and out towards the ocean. When he reached U.S. One, he turned right, and instead of heading into Santa Monica as he had planned, he drove north hoping to find a place to park the car and get his thoughts in order.

He pulled into the parking lot of a seafood joint in Malibu where Jim had taken him to celebrate some event or other about six months ago. He turned off the stereo and stared at the ocean. The waves crested low, rippling with white foam. The sky was bleached a pale blue, and silver tips capped the restless waters in the distance.

His life had been a clean slate when he'd come to Los Angeles. Few friends and an intolerable family had given him little to regret when quitting Portland to pursue a new life in Tinsel Town. In those ten years, he had put together a relatively decent living, a few more friends and a relationship with Jim: all of which now seemed as insubstantial as the foam disintegrating on the shore.

Anthem of the Estranged

Jim was as good as gone. Mike's "friends" were comprised of drinking buddies who collectively had the depth of a bottle cap, and he felt certain that his career was about to take a drastic turn for the non-existent in light of his creative contribution to the *Lipstik* segment of *Picking Up the Rock*. Ten years ago, a clean slate had seemed challenging, even exciting, but at this point in his life, Mike wondered if the independence he'd been so proud of had been little more than well-designed self destruction.

And for the span of a heartbeat, he understood why someone like Tommy Gunn might want to *shrug off the coil* and take his act on the road.

A lilt of song broke over him like warm waves, instantly extinguishing the flame of self-doubt. Mike pulled his eyes from the water's shimmering caps and scanned the parking lot for the source of the flowing chant. He looked back at the ocean to see if the song rolled from the surf as it certainly held the cadence of tide, but he could find no source for the tune.

Mike checked the rearview mirror and saw a short derelict standing behind his car. His heart leapt, and he spun in the seat; he opened his mouth to tell the bum to move on but something about the stocky form was familiar. Besides wearing the tattered robes of the monks he had seen on Tommy Gunn's lawn, the bum also wore Tommy Gunn's face.

The head and eyebrows had been shaved, leaving a smooth egg with the features of *Lipstik's* lead singer, looking remarkably serene and sympathetic. Mike was shocked to see that the whites of Gunn's eyes had been stained pink.

With barely a hint of effort, Tommy Gunn rose into the air and came down silently into a squatting position on the trunk of Mike's Celica.

"Get off'a the car," Mike roared. "You freak."

When his command was not honored, Mike uncoiled and cranked on the ignition. A low thread of red liquid passed before his eyes, swirling in the air like a tendril of smoke. Its progress enthralled Mike to paralysis as it wove around the steering wheel. The fluid encircled the handle of the car key to kill the engine and then rolled over the dashboard where it splattered against the windshield and continued to squirm.

A word, *Wait*, appeared on the glass.

Mike shot a look over his shoulder. Gunn's watermelon juice eyes stared back; the musician's index finger pointed at him not in accusation but in communication. The end of the finger had been sliced open and a thin rope of blood pulsed from the digit, but instead of succumbing to gravity, it danced in the air and made words on Mike's windshield. With a flick of his head, Gunn sent Mike's attention back to the glass.

Life and death are but two options, the crimson letters read. The note smeared and then a new message appeared in its place. *There is another way.*

"Who said anything about life or death?" Mike asked.

The question is coming.

"I don't think so," Mike said. "I'm not opening my wrists over a prick like Jim."

The teeth of loneliness gnaw slowly.

"You're going to have to do better than that," Mike said, but when he turned to face off on Gunn, the man was gone. He quickly searched the parking lot, anxious to maintain a fix on the monk's position.

A robed figure scurried up the side of the restaurant like a spider, but this wasn't Gunn. Even from the distance, Mike could tell that this was one of the other monks. His eyes drew a line from the restaurant, over U.S. One and up the road to the north.

The monks were everywhere. They stood on rooftops, their silhouettes cast against the washed out sky and the silver tipped waves. They sat on the gravel shoulder of the highway like large deer brought down by racing fenders. A group of ten stood twenty feet from the side of his car, but none of these was Gunn.

Gunn lowered out of the air and returned to his crouching position having traded the trunk of the car for its hood. The thin trail of visceral ink spun around his form like a ribbon; red splashed on the windshield, and Mike jerked back against the seat.

A token, the words read.

"Why don't you just tell me what you want?"

What do you want?

"My sanity returned in good working order," he replied.

No, the red letters challenged. *To belong.*

"Belong to what?"

Anything.

Mike laughed, and the volume of the outburst startled him. "I'm not you, Gunn. I didn't fuck up my life playing rock star. You pissed everything away and then wondered where it all went. Well, face it buddy, nobody wants you around."

A father's words, the red letters charged.

"Fuck you," Mike roared.

Why else here?

And then Mike remembered the evening that Jim had brought him to this place. Mike had received a call from his brother earlier that afternoon to relay the news that their father had died. The eversympathetic Jim had been more upset by the news than Mike, who had seen the drunk's passing as the removal of a well-pierced target and certainly nothing irreplaceable.

They were not close, not even speaking when the old man had died. The distance and dismissal had been the result of his father's final words to Mike before he'd moved to California.

Face it, kid, no one wants you around here.

His father's exact words were scrawled on the windshield before him in swirls of Gunn's blood. Mike began trembling in the car seat.

Tears slid down Tommy Gunn's face as his finger conducted circles of fluid in the air. The other monks on the rooftops remained motionless, carved from the bleached sky as wind tore at their robes. The message on the windshield blurred, and then Gunn was writing again.

A token.

"A token of what?" Mike asked. "For what?"

A token of you, the message read. *To become what you are.*

"Exactly what do you think I am?" he asked, his voice weak and shaking.

One of us.

"Who are you?"

The estranged. The disaffected remains.

"If I give you a token, what then?"

We become one.

"And what did you give, Tommy?" Mike asked, some part of his mind accepting this dementia as the only reality left for him. "What was your token?"

In reply, Tommy Gunn touched the collar of his robe and gently pulled the folds back to reveal the hairless body beneath. The flesh was smooth and pink like that of a monstrous child, only this child had been damaged. A deep wound the size of a fist had been carved in Tommy Gunn's throat; a similar injury appeared between his legs. Both wounds were raw as if fresh, still glistening like meat on a butcher's board.

The eunuch closed his robes. The tears he'd shed for Mike had dried in glistening trails on his cheeks, and his features radiated warmth and caring.

Somebody's waiting, the crimson line read.

Somebody's waiting.

Mike woke the next morning to the blaring trill of his telephone, which cut painfully through his hangover. "Yeah?" he asked.

"Why aren't you at work?" Jim asked.

Because they fired me, Mike thought.

As he had suspected, Ed Hoeffer had gone to the show's senior producers with a copy of the *Lipstik* segment, and they had agreed with Ed's assessment that the cut was not only exploitative, but also perverse. Mike's vision would no longer be required by *Picking Up the Rock*.

"Why'd you call here if you thought I'd be at work?" Mike asked, and then quickly regretted the sarcasm. "I'm sorry. I'm not feeling well this morning."

The rush of concern in Jim's voice when he asked, "Are you okay?" brought Mike close to tears.

"Fine," he lied. "Just a touch of the flu or something."

"Do you need anything? I was going to come by this morning and pick up a few things anyway. I can swing by the store on my way in."

"That's okay," Mike said and then quickly added, "Thank you. I just need to get some rest."

"Why don't I wait until tomorrow, then. I don't want to disturb you."

"No. I'd like us to talk, if that's okay."

After leaving the parking lot in Malibu the previous afternoon, before finding out he'd been fired and completely immersing himself in a clear swamp of vodka at *Mickey's*, Mike had put a lot of thought into the encounter he'd had with Tommy Gunn. The words, *somebody's waiting*, had run through his head so many times that he had put them to the monks' chant.

Once those words had vanished from his windshield, Tommy Gunn and his fellow monks had similarly vanished. They had not become dust or smoke, but had simply stepped from their places on the rooftops, risen from their seats on the roadside and faded into insubstantial blurs. Then, their forms were caught in the wind, a spiraling gale that carried each of the monks from their perches and blended their material together with a vicious swipe until a single mottled cloud blew away on the rapid current of air.

Mike had been left alone then with the words of his father and the words of Tommy Gunn, each answering the other in a repetitive loop.

Face it kid, no one wants you ... to belong ... face it kid ... somebody's waiting ... face it ... we become one ...

"Mike?" Jim asked. "Are you still there?"

"Yeah," he mumbled. "I'm sorry, what did you say?"

"I said, I'm worried about you."

"You don't have to be," Mike told him. "I'm going to be okay now."

Mike left the bed and put on a pot of coffee before stepping under the hot spray of a shower. He shaved and brushed his hair before throwing on a pair of jeans and an old white tee shirt. He sat in the living room with his coffee and stared out the window at the neat row of houses across the street.

On that night in Silverlake in Tommy Gunn's home, the musician had told Mike that the only thing that mattered was to have somebody waiting. Gunn had sought his salvation and made his sacrifice in order to be accepted – in order to belong. No longer a welcome citizen of this world, Gunn had chosen to enter another.

Mike pushed his tongue over his teeth, straining the muscle under it until he had as much of the spongy meat exposed as anatomy would allow. He clamped down carefully with his teeth.

Surely it was his tongue they would want for their token. Like Tommy Gunn's voice and manhood, it was Michael's tongue that had created his estrangement from the world and therefore it was this that he must sacrifice. He strained a little harder to get more of the pink flesh over his teeth and then bit down again as a dull ache rose in his jaw.

He didn't know why he felt compelled to practice this exercise; it was foolish.

He had no intention of joining Gunn or his disaffected remains. Unlike the lost musician, Mike felt he could make a place in this world; he need only sacrifice the use of his tongue rather than its substance.

We become one, appeared on his window in a sudden splash of red.

Mike turned to find Gunn and two other monks in the entryway. The three stood shoulder to shoulder, the rags of one's robe melding into the shreds of the other. The man with the multiple piercings like a chain-mail mask nodded his head, and the loops of steel penetrating his skin rippled over his features in agreement. The woman with no nose and the ear to ear grin, breathed deeply as if aroused. Tommy gazed at him with warm appreciation.

"The tongue," the grinning woman whispered. She crossed the room and held out her hand to Mike, helping him to his feet. A pool of blue-gray fluid swirled deep within the cavity where her nose had been. This same roiling tide covered the back of her throat and tongue when she opened her mouth to say, "Take my breath and make your offering." She dipped the expanse of her mouth towards Mike.

He pulled away. "I'm not going with you. I belong here."

"No," she told him. "You belong with us." Fire flashed behind the pale pink lenses of her eyes, and the rolling steel gray tide in her mouth foamed violently. "You belong *to* us."

Mike jerked his hand out of the woman's grasp. He backed away with quick, stumbling steps and collided with a solid wall enveloped in the folds of shredded robes. Gunn held his left shoulder and the pierced man gripped his right. Through the window, Mike saw the other monks, dozens of them, gathering to witness his conversion. They climbed to neighboring rooftops or walked somberly over his yard, their heads lowered in reverence. Each retained some vestiges of humanity but their appearances had been perverted, mangled by whatever token they had deemed substantial enough to gain entrance to the order.

The woman unhinged her jaw, and it fell open to reveal a pulsing tongue, bright red and marbled like freshly slaughtered beef against the swirling blue gray pool beyond. Her teeth, no different than Mike's own, were nonetheless frightening in their number as her spacious smile allowed him a view of their entirety. Mike drew a panicked breath and held it as her lips found his skin.

Her mouth locked over his face and her tongue pressed at his lips.

The penetration of the woman's tongue, parting his lips and prying open his clenched teeth, fueled his struggle, but the crushing weight of the robed bodies at his back kept him immobile as the woman's teeth clicked lightly against his.

Mike's chest thundered with fear and the need for oxygen, but he refused to take air from the disgusting chasm of teeth and tongue. Even as her jaws clamped together, severing a more substantial piece of tongue than Mike himself could have offered, he maintained his asphyxia. He needed to scream for the agony in his mouth, but he had forgotten how to breathe.

The woman pulled away, spitting Mike's tongue into her palm and wiping the blood from her lips with a long stroke of her forearm. The mound of spongy, pink meat pulsed in her hand and then exploded into a thousand tiny specks, which rose into the air like vapor and evaporated.

"He didn't take the breath," she sang in a minor key.

"Then he's lost," the pierced man dismissed, lowering his head as if to pray.

The world spun to a blur, and Mike was aware that the demanding hands and bodies had released him. He tried to close his eyes, but his swimming mind refused the command. Warm blood filled his mouth and ran down the back of his throat to pool in his belly. The pounding in his heart grew to an unbearable thunder, and finally he gasped sweet air.

The last sound he heard before dropping to the floor was the low chant, so musical and pleasing, coming from every corner of the world to lull him into darkness.

"Somebody's waiting," Tommy Gunn told him.

A warm hand touched his face, and Mike's eyes shot open as he struggled to remove himself from Gunn's touch.

But the hand didn't belong to Tommy Gunn or any of his order.

"Hey kid," Jim said.

Mike tried to return the greeting but agony flared in his mouth, bringing tears to his eyes and chilled sweat to his neck. The television, mounted high up on the wall of the hospital room, flickered over Jim's shoulder; it was also muted.

"You had a seizure," Jim told him warmly, returning his palm to Mike's cheek. "They're going to be running tests on you for the next couple of days, but they said you'd be okay."

Mike grasped the hand on his face tightly, squeezing it close to his cheek. Jim looked down on him with an expression of kindness that was absolute and loving.

He needed to speak to this man, but did not possess the means. Mike wanted to apologize, to find some way to mend the bridges before they fell away completely. If he could do that, if he could make one solid connection to this world, then no other world would ever matter again.

He made a motion in the air as if requesting a check from a restaurant waiter; he needed a pen and paper; he wanted to write Jim a note.

His fingertip tingled lightly before a geyser of blood shot into the space over the bed. The red tendril rolled nonsensically from the tip of his digit, creating a pattern of swirls and lines over the bed like graffiti. When Mike pulled his hand away, the crimson thread whipped back against the wall to splash the clean white surface.

"Jesus," Jim hissed. His eyes had grown wide as he stumbled away from the bed.

Mike made a gesture to placate his retreating savior, and the ribbon of blood snaked across the room, mocking gravity and nature. He screamed for Jim to stay, ignoring the pain in his mouth, but Jim had already opened the door to escape the snake of fluid writhing in the air between them.

The door slammed.

Then he was alone in the silence. He tried to recall the monks' chant in the hopes they might come for him, but he already knew he had been denied entrance to their order, just as he had been banished from Jim's.

The exile of two worlds gave up the song and lost himself in the weave of blood. He followed each curve and line before wiggling his finger to change the design, in which he lost himself again. He penned messages to the Gods in the sterile air. Eventually, he authored Gunn's slogan – *We become one* – and then decided he didn't like the sound of it. The Exile made an adjustment in the lettering and cast it against the wall for permanence. The trail of blood ran dry, and he stared at this

final message until sleep pulled him away, knowing the message would be there for him when he woke – would always be there for him.
    One.

I Know You're There

There are worse things than being watched.
What if you knew I could reach out and touch your skin?
What if I never stopped?

Lynch paused in the hall, quickly glanced over his shoulder and rubbed the nape of his neck with a dry palm. He clutched the file folder tighter, then continued down the beige-walled corridor toward his office. He greeted his assistant, Nancy; nodded when she asked if he'd like his morning coffee; entered his office and went to the window. The lacquered bookcases and black leather Courbusier chairs ate what little light bled through the metal blinds. Too dark. Bad for his current mood. He pushed the button on the wall, and the blinds opened, flooding the room with murky light. An angry foam of clouds, promising storm, covered the city, painting skyscraper windows in mottled shades of gray. He looked into the distance, but the mountain range, the view he loved, was obscured by the weather.

Nancy entered with his coffee and set the mug on his desk.

"Will you still be seeing Michael this morning?"

Lynch went to his desk, looked at the file and then to his assistant. "Yes." Nancy retreated, closing the door behind her.

Michael, he thought and waited for the cold fingers to finish their work on his spine. Opening the file, he reached for his coffee. Sipped. Looked at the photograph affixed to the folder's inside cover. The face staring back was smooth, tanned and narrow, with full lips and a black wing of hair draping the brow. Women found this face attractive, he knew. Nancy became a giddy, star-eyed child when Michael was in the room. But the kid was too attractive. Unsettling. And his eyes. Cold. Hard. A kid of twenty shouldn't have seen so much.

He's good at what he does, Lynch reminded. One of the best.

What if I never stopped?

Lynch leaned back in his chair. He faced Michael and struggled to keep eye contact. He wanted nothing more than to turn away and look at the floor, his desk, the wall, anything else. But that would show weakness, and after their last two meetings, Lynch needed to reaffirm his position as Michael's superior.

"Aren't you going to ask me about Pollard?" Michael asked.

"It's in your report," Lynch replied, trying to sound bored. In actuality, the report sickened him. "Asian girls. Nothing terribly interesting about it. It's good work, and we can certainly use the information to leverage Pollard's cooperation on the Fresco Initiative."

"Did you notice the age of those girls?"

"Irrelevant."

"So, you think it's okay for that hairy old hog to be plugging children?"

"Morality is simply a business asset, Michael. I don't need to judge what these assholes do."

"Do you like them young, Mr. Lynch?"

"Michael, this is the last time I'm going to remind you about Section Two of your agreement with this corporation."

The kid smiled coyly, curled up on the chair and tapped a sloppy syncopation on the arm with his finger. Lynch looked on, trying to exude confidence but feeling the sludge of discomfort in his veins. The room appeared to shrink, wring and tighten around Michael as if he were the source from which the walls, the shelves, the floor sprang. Lynch's gut clenched, and he finally let himself look away, at the file.

"Tell me about the Bascomb project."

"Waste of time," Michael said. "Vanilla to the bone. He doesn't even cross against the signal."

"You know how important his cooperation is."

Michael shrugged. "Can't see what isn't there." The kid unfolded his legs, and he slid lower in the chair. His expression of boredom intensified. He tapped the chair's arm. "Do they even get wet when they're that young?"

"I thought I'd made my position on those kinds of comments clear at our last meeting," Lynch said. He hoped his voice had sounded as stern to Michael as it sounded in his own head.

"Maybe he needs them that small. He's hung like a flea. I'd imagine they're pretty tight, even for him."

"Michael."

The kid looked through his lashes at Lynch. Heat rose from his gaze. Sultry. Intense. Disturbing. "A big guy like you would probably tear one of them in half."

"You can go now, Michael."

Lynch and the other five directors sat at the marble table in the boardroom. Rain pattered the wall of glass. Lightning flashed over the foothills. Garrison, a slender, neatly presented little prick with a paisley bowtie, finished his presentation with the news that Diedrich's cooperation on the Fresco Initiative had been confirmed that morning. A smarmy grin cut his face as he took his seat.

It was Lynch's turn to present. He began by stating that Pollard also could be expected to confirm on Fresco within the week, which assured that profit projections through year's end would be met. He followed with his reports on the Tolliver, Marcone and Lenks initiatives, all of which were met with the approval of his fellow directors.

"Before I turn the floor over to Barns, I'd like to address some concerns I have regarding Michael's performance."

Next to him, the tidy little asshole, Garrison, chuckled. The other directors stifled similar reactions, covering their mouths, pretending to cough, looking at the storm covering the city and biting their lips.

"While I'm glad you're amused," Lynch began, "Michael has consistently shown disregard for Section Two of his agreement. As you know, this is grounds for termination. Now, I don't want to lose good manpower, but I believe this problem needs to be addressed."

"Oh for God's sake, Lynch," Garrison said. "Michael's the strongest Bird we've got. If you don't want him in your department, give him to me."

"Unacceptable," Lynch said.

"You've known that Michael was problematic," said Pompher from across the table. "Christ, most of the Birds are. You also know they can't detach for more than a few hours a day. We've got full daily reports on Michael since he's been with us. He uses his time up on his shift. I think he's fucking with your head."

"I don't think so," Lynch said.

"Then, what do you propose?" asked Barns. "We're already down to a dozen Birds. After Leslie's hemorrhage last month, we're barely able to stick to schedule. We can't let Michael go; not until we're able to recruit new resources."

"Worst case scenario," Pompher said, long faced and serious with consideration. "He has an inappropriate infatuation with you, and he's detaching without authorization. Maybe he's catching a peak of you in the john. *Maybe*. It's disturbing and certainly against Section Two of his contract, but as a company, we have to consider bottom line impact. In this case, Michael's contributions to the organization outweigh his indiscretions. I'm sorry."

Lynch considered arguing the point, but knew it was fruitless. Next to him, Garrison maintained his humored expression. Lynch wanted to snap the prick in half. Unfortunately, directors were easier to come by than Birds, and Section Twelve clearly outlined the future of any employee using violence in the workplace. Pompher's hands-tied sympathy seemed sincere enough, and the other directors exhibited more than enough compassion to quell some of Lynch's frustration, but he still wasn't satisfied, nor would he be until Michael was released from his contract.

Something had to be done about the kid. Lynch had a family, and his wife shouldn't have to be a prop in Michael's voyeuristic perversion. For all Lynch knew, Michael was in the meeting with them right now, watching and taking note of Lynch's failure. Who knew what kind of shit the kid would pull if he discovered he was above reprimand? Sweat broke on Lynch's brow as he again took his seat, clearing the floor for Barns.

A tingle rose at the back of his neck. He turned slowly so he didn't draw attention. Nothing was there. At least, nothing he could see.

There are worse things than being watched.

A half-wall of glass separated Lynch from the four Birds, including Michael who sat on the far right. Dressed in comfortable clothes, positioned in a semi-circle around the room, the Birds reclined in their chairs. Eyes closed, breath shallow, Michael had detached and was on assignment. His current project had him researching a man named Bascomb, but Michael could be anywhere. Just because he wrote Bascomb's name on a report, didn't mean he was actually with the guy. Lynch stepped closer to the glass, put his hand on the pane. An itch sparked in his ear, and he ground it down with his fingernail.

New age gurus called the phenomenon astral projection, making it sound as if a simple act of concentration could take a man out of his body to cruise the cosmos. Lynch knew they were wrong. These Birds were not trained to do their tricks; they had been born broken. Their bodies and consciousness were not connected the way nature had intended. This severing could go unnoticed by Birds their entire lives, or it could be discovered, nurtured and utilized. The business applications were endless when applied to juried litigation, corporate mergers, finance and government policy. And Michael was one of the best in the business.

Lynch didn't care.

He felt Michael on his neck every moment of the day. Locked doors made Lynch feel no more secure than standing on a busy sidewalk. In the shower or the men's room or the bed, he could picture Michael, staring at him and getting fodder for their next meeting.

Until recently, their working relationship had been satisfactory. Michael performed his duties with excellence and enthusiasm. Two weeks ago, during their Friday update session that changed. Lynch didn't know what had brought about the mutation in Michael's character, but his emotional instability became pronounced. That day, Michael was sulking and distracted, caught up in his own thoughts. Lynch had shown an appropriate level of concern, and Michael rewarded his concern with a startling question.

Does your wife ever suck you off?

Excuse me? What did you just say? Michael? What did you just say?

I'm just wondering because it's big, you know. Can she fit it all in her mouth, or does she just lick around the top like an ice cream cone?

Michael, I'm going to remind you about Section Two of your contract with this organization.

I'll admit you got a bit of a belly on you. You're old right? What forty-five? Forty-six? But with those shoulders and that chest... woof.

Michael! Section Two of your contract clearly states that at no time are you to invade the privacy of a co-worker of this organization. This includes both watching said co-worker and requesting private information about said co-worker's life.

Oh, Mr. Lynch. There are worse things than being watched. What if you knew I could reach out and touch your skin? What if I never stopped?

This is completely inappropriate.

I'll bet I could take that cock down. All of it.

A hand fell on Lynch's shoulder, startling him out of memory. He spun around, nearly clipping Tim's jaw with his elbow. The tech stumbled back and yelped. His palm device dropped and clacked on the tiles, and the tech just about tumbled onto his ass.

"Christ, Tim," Lynch said, hurrying forward to pick up the tech's computer. "I'm sorry. You about gave me a heart attack."

"You're not supposed to be down here," Tim said defensively, yanking his shirtfront to straighten it over his round gut. He reached out and snatched the palm unit from Lynch's hand. "You know that."

"Yes, I do. My apologies. I was just checking on the Birds."

"Why? They don't do anything. They just sit there."

"I know. I thought I'd check on Michael. I understand he's progressing very well."

"Not so well," Tim said, punching a button on his palm device. "After the spike last week, he's leveled off. In fact, he's down considerably from last month's performance. We were hoping to break the five-hour mark with him, but with these readings, he's going to have to stay in the four-hour club. That's probably best. We don't want another Leslie incident."

"Of course not," Lynch said, though nothing would please him more. He wanted Michael to overextend himself, blow a gasket and have his skull fill with blood. If Michael's brain drowned, Lynch would be able to relax, sleep peacefully and make love to his wife again without the threat of unwelcome eyes.

Lynch finished his dinner, stared at the plate while his wife talked excitedly about her day. He tried to pay attention. His first wife had always said that his lights burned bright, but he was rarely home, and he didn't want to make that mistake again with Sandra, but Michael's god damned voice was in his head, and he couldn't shake the feeling that he was being watched.

Sandra continued speaking as she stood and began to clear the table. Lynch watched her move and thought that his second wife was too beautiful for him, too young.

Do you like them young, Mr. Lynch?

"You're not hearing a single thing I'm saying," Sandra said with a laugh. She rubbed his head and gave his brow a kiss. She lifted his dinner plate, gave him a mock pout for having left so much of his dinner untouched and continued on into the kitchen.

Lynch followed. Sandra deserved better; she deserved his attention. He tried to comfort himself with the knowledge that Michael had put in a full day. Any further incident of detaching could put his health at serious risk. But the rationale he followed didn't soothe him. Michael's issue was obsession, and obsession was never rational.

Still, he couldn't sacrifice the life he'd built just because he imagined Michael *might* be watching. He had to try maintaining a normal life.

He waited for Sandra to put the dishes in the sink and wrapped his arms around her waist, slid them under her silk top and cupped her breasts while burying his face in the nape of her neck.

"I'm sorry," he whispered in between kisses.

"Work?" his wife asked, pushing her butt into his crotch.

"Can we talk about it later?"

"Mmm Hmmm," she said, grinding against the lump in his slacks. "Later."

Lynch pushed his hips forward so he could get the full effect of his wife's contact. Leaving his left hand to squeeze and caress her breast, his right slid down, and he locked an arm around her middle. It had been too long. Weeks. All the time, Lynch imagining that Michael was with them, watching and waiting for a glimpse at some salacious privacy. Sandra turned around to face him and their lips met. Her fingers ran over the front of his shirt unbuttoning it and pushing the lapels back so her mouth could work into the hair on his chest. Lower now, her fingers unzipped his slacks, worked inside the opening and brushed over the cotton briefs separating his erection from her touch. Lynch combed his fingers into his wife's hair, pulled her face to his chest, where her tongue worked over the skin. She panted against him. Whimpered as she struggled to free his cock from the difficult briefs. Gently, he pulled her head back so he could kiss her.

He felt a tickle at his neck, and his head snapped around reflexively.

"Hear something?" Sandra asked, her breath ragged; her hands now at his belt.

"Nothing," he said.

His slacks dropped to the floor and his briefs followed. Sandra's hands were on his belly, rubbing over the hair and wrapping around his waist as she lowered herself to kneel.

Does your wife ever suck you off?

Lynch closed his eyes, tried to concentrate on the pleasant sensations instead of the voice in his head, but he could not help but picture Michael, sitting in the black leather office chair, looking confident and superior, disgusting comments pouring from his mouth.

I'll bet I could take that cock down.

Lynch shook his head to dislodge the distractions there. He opened his eyes and gazed over the curve of his belly at his kneeling wife. Her hand was wrapped around his shaft, her tongue darted out to lick the head.

... like an ice cream cone...

"Christ," Lynch hissed. The sensation on his neck, the tickling certainty that he was being watched, intensified. His ear began to itch. He looked in the window over the sink and saw his reflection. Michael was there, too, standing behind him, grinning. Startled, he stepped back, turned. Nothing.

"Honey?" his wife asked, looking up at him with sadness and confusion in her eyes.

"I thought I saw someone," Lynch explained. "Through the window. Maybe we should go upstairs."

Lynch walked down the beige corridor to his office. When he opened the door, Nancy looked up and stood quickly to rush around her desk. "Michael's in there," she said. "I know he doesn't have an appointment, but he insisted."

"Coffee," Lynch said, a hot flame of rage burning on his neck. He hadn't slept the night before. Upstairs after the incident in the kitchen, he'd barely been able to finish what had begun, and even at that, it hadn't been very good for him or Sandra as he'd insisted on having the covers secured around them through the entire act. Then, he'd been awake, feeling watched and embarrassed. He tossed and turned. Couldn't find comfort. By morning, his nerves were worn and ragged and pained.

Michael had made a mistake if he'd come to play games with Lynch.

He opened the door to his office. The blinds behind his desk were open, allowing entrance to another gray morning's light. Michael slumped low in the Courbusier. His eyes were ringed with dark skin, striped through with red veins. His skin was doughy and shone with an unhealthy gloss.

"Michael," Lynch said, crossing to his desk. "I don't appreciate you badgering Nancy. She keeps my calendar, and if she tells you..."

"I used to watch my father," Michael said, interrupting Lynch with a dry, weary voice. "In the shower. Once he got tired of mom... if he was between mistresses... he'd beat off in there."

"Michael, I'm done playing this fucking game with you."

"Seeing his wet skin and the intensity on his face... Christ, it was beautiful."

"Michael."

"It was the only time we ever spent together, you know? And he didn't even know I was there." Michael chuckled, a sound like sandpaper on stone. "Just like you. Except you know I'm there now."

"Did you enjoy the show?" Lynch asked through a clenched jaw.

"To a point."

"So you're admitting your violation of Section Two?"

"You can't fire me, Mr. Lynch. I know that."

"You were in the meeting yesterday?"

"I'm everywhere."

"And it's killing you. You've been detaching too long. You realize you could hemorrhage?"

"Too smart for that. I can feel when my body needs me. Your techs don't know shit about how this works."

"As your supervisor, I'm required to suggest that you seek help. The company retains a Dr. Ibsen for employee consultations, so there would be no cost to you. I suggest you make an appointment with him after your shift."

"A doctor would be good," Michael said. "I had a doctor named Klein once. He was very nice to me, and he liked to take pictures. One day, he decided to end our sessions. I don't know why. It doesn't really matter. The police found hundreds of his snapshots. Dozens of kids. Dr. Klein was murdered in prison. Stabbed in the throat so many times that his head came off when they moved him."

"You turned him in," Lynch said, sickened by the story.

"Why not? His sense of composition sucked."

Lynch observed the kid and was surprised to find he pitied him. Beneath his anger and outrage, Lynch felt a cool current of sympathy. Michael *was* sick. Probably irreversibly so. The traumas of his early life, the neglect, had taken bits of the kid's sanity. You couldn't get through to someone like that. All you could do was humor them until their sickness shifted to some other obsession. Or until it killed them.

"What do you want from me, Michael?"

"I want you to know I'm there."

At the end of the day, once Michael's shift was coming to an end, Lynch called his wife. Sandra sounded upset that he was going to be late, and he imagined it had something to do with his distance over the past few weeks and his poor performance with her the night before. She probably thought he was having an affair, or maybe she just felt like a stranger in his life. He didn't know what he might say to ease her mind, except, "I love you. I'll see you in a few hours."

Lynch left the office building; drove north of town. He rented a room at a motor lodge and draped his suit coat over the back of a chair. In the bathroom, he turned on the shower, unknotted his tie. The constant rapping of the water in the tub accompanied him as he unbuttoned his shirt and hung it on a cheap plastic hanger in the closet nook of the motel room. He removed his pants and hung those as well. Lynch removed his socks and his briefs, placed them on the seat of the chair and stood naked in the middle of the room.

"I know you're there, Michael."

A light tickling sensation rose up on the back of his neck. Lynch didn't turn to it.

"I'm doing this for you," Lynch said. His voice had lost any pretense of authority. He felt ashamed and foolish, standing naked in the room, knowing he was indulging Michael's sickness.

He reached down and began kneading the soft skin, ran his other hand over his balls and between his legs. He felt no erotic charge, wondered if he could even manage a fabrication of excitement under the circumstances. Michael's voice was in his head, distracting and disturbing. Lynch tried to imagine his wife, any other woman that had fueled his lust over the years, but none of those memories brought a spark to the friction. Lynch spit in his palm and stroked the moisture into his still soft cock.

Eventually, the contact brought a response. Not fully erect. Getting there.

"I know you're there, Michael."

I used to watch my father. In the shower.

Lynch walked through the bedroom, into the bathroom. He pulled the shower curtain aside and stepped in. The tingling sensation at his neck had taken hold as if it emanated from the vertebrae at the base of his skull. He unwrapped one of the small soaps and began lathering his chest, his belly, his crotch. He moved slowly under the water, coaxing himself to excitement, and then letting the sensation fade. It had to last. He had to keep the kid's attention. Every few minutes, he spoke – his voice low, hollow against the tile and plaster.

"I know you're there, Michael. I know you're there."

At home, Lynch lay in bed, staring at the ceiling. Next to him, Sandra breathed evenly. Asleep.

He hadn't felt the tingling sensation on his neck since stepping out of the motel's shower. It had faded and vanished moments before his climax. Lynch didn't know how long he'd stood under the spray. An hour? Two hours?

The phone rang at five minutes after midnight.

Tim, the tech from the eighth floor, was frantic.

Michael was in the hospital. Hemorrhage. Coma. The kid was vegetative. He could sleep another day, a week or years, but he would never wake up. The doctors were certain of that.

Lynch hung up the phone, feeling numb and sick. He told Sandra it was nothing. "Go back to sleep, honey." But he walked through the house, agitated.

Finally, he slipped back into bed, careful not to wake his wife. His mind and his heart raced. He could take no comfort in his accomplishment. There was no peace in what he'd done. Not yet. It had been necessary, and he could certainly make an argument for self-preservation, but in that moment, he stared at the ceiling and submitted to the guilt.

His ear began to itch and Lynch absently scraped at it with a fingernail, but instead of quenching the irritation, it seemed to set it free. The itch at his ear spread out and became a tickling on the back of his neck. Imagination, he thought. Guilt. But in truth he'd expected this. Michael's mind and body were not connected, not like normal human beings. Lynch wondered if he had freed Michael. Wondered if even death would stop him watching.

There are worse things than being watched.

He checked his wife. Still sleeping. Then, Lynch looked back to the ceiling. "I know you're there," he whispered to the darkness.

And felt the palm of a small hand run up his leg.

Down to Sleep

You met him on the Internet, because you're tired of standing in bars, doing the mating dance with the usual suspects. Chat rooms are little better. Flakes. Games. Lies. The web is a masquerade ball; everyone shielding their faces with facades crafted in Photoshop, identifying themselves with profiles of greater fiction than anything Stephen King could create. But the Internet is convenient. Fast. You don't have to leave the comfort of your home; don't even have to turn off the television set. You don't have to stand in a smoky room until your feet ache, comparing yourself to a hundred other guys, only to find yourself lacking.

He told you his name was Vernon and that he had a lover.

So, you wrote– Is he home?

–Not tonight.

–Cool.

You don't care. It's not your relationship. You're not lying to anyone. You haven't had anyone to lie to in a very long time.

His neighborhood is familiar. Beautiful old houses actually have space between them, not the alleys most of the modern developments call side lawns. The first snow of the year is falling, dusting the street and the sidewalk and the roofs of the Victorians, the Colonials and the Spanish-style houses. It's simple. Beautiful.

It's cold.

So, you walk faster, running the house number over in your head.

The man who opens the door looks like his picture. He is on the short side, maybe five foot six, with a fireplug body and thick arms. He wears a forest green t-shirt. Chest hair, much of it silver, crests over the collar. His beard is steel gray and neatly combed over his jaw. A shadow of close-cropped stubble runs over his head. He wears shorts, and his legs are deeply tanned. He is handsome. That's good.

He's a top.

That's what matters.

But what does he think of you?

You search his face for disappointment, fully expecting it to show in his eyes or the edges of his mouth. You are not ugly, but you think only of your flaws. Too pale. Too smooth. Too young. The opposite of the men you want to love. How many hours have you wasted wondering on that particular irony? What it says about your self-worth?

–Hello, he says, stepping back so you can enter the house.

You've identified no visible regret on Vernon's face, so you cross the threshold.

The place smells like old flowers. Dead and dried. It smells vaguely of dust. It smells of weathered wood and lemon polish.

The hallway ahead is dark. A light burns from the room at its end, casting slivers of illumination over a dozen framed photographs hung in the hall. To your right is a staircase with a crimson runner, intricately woven with gold and black thread. On the left through a tall doorway, you see the living room, notice the fire burning on the hearth.

Vernon closes the door. He steps forward and wraps his arms around you in an affectionate embrace. You lean forward a bit and put your chin on his shoulder. –Welcome to the Den, he says.

His voice is gruff. Pleasant. Hearing it and holding the man sends a spark of longing through your body. You feel the muscles on his back and his arms as you return the hug. He releases you and steps back.

–Let me take you coat.

You hand him the parka, and Vernon places it gently on the hook of the mahogany rack standing next to you in the foyer.

–Can I get you a beer, Handsome?

Handsome is a lie, and you know it, but you smile anyway.

–Thank you.

–Make yourself comfortable, Vernon says, indicating he wants you to sit by the fire. Then, he is walking down the hallway, past the framed photographs, toward the crack of light.

The living room is what you expect. A place of nostalgia. Antique furniture. Aged knick-knacks. Leather-bound books. Photographs. So many photographs. You prefer modern décor, but this place is comfortable. And what difference do such aesthetics make? You won't be here long anyway.

A photograph on an old cherry wood table catches your eye, and you lift the silver frame. The image startles you.

In it, two men (one of them Vernon) are in the middle of the woods. Sunlight cuts like rain between the lace of pine branches. Both men are wearing thin flannel shirts, open in front. You see the weight in Vernon's chest. It summons your lust, but only for a moment. Your eyes can't stay with Vernon. The man next to him is too compelling.

He is tall and broad. A thick pelt of hair covers a muscular chest and streams down a gently rounded belly. He too wears a beard, and though he is likely the same age as Vernon, his facial hair is chestnut brown, like the hair on his stunning body. You look into the eyes of the photograph. Heat creeps through vein and artery, sending flush to your cheeks and desire to your cock.

You know this man. His name is Tom. Though you haven't seen him in over a year, though he was with you for only one afternoon, you remember every moment you spent with him.

His smile from across the bar.

The intensity on his face as he fucked you.

And the shower after…

You fight to breathe. Your memory is working too well.

He stands under the spray, not moving at first, not noticing you've entered the room at all. The light through the glass brick window is faded, but more than sufficient. Water streams over his face, caught in his beard. His round shoulders and full chest seem tensed, flexing for a moment. Water flattens the hair on his chest and runs in sensual sheets over his belly. His cock, still swollen post climax is caressed by the cascade, which rolls in a steady stream from the thick head.

You couldn't breathe then, either. The sight was just too overwhelming, and with it came a deep sadness. A mourning. You knew he would leave. You knew he would never come back. Giving him your phone number was a reflex. A ritual. A pointless exercise, designed to strengthen your already well-defined sense of inadequacy.

That sadness returns and you place the picture back on the cherry wood table. Your hands are shaking.

—Oh, have a seat, Vernon announces, entering the room with a bottle of beer in each hand.

You meet him on the sofa, before the fire. You thank him for the beer and again gaze at his attractive face, wishing it were another. You hate him just then. You envy this stranger. After only a few minutes, he has managed to show you everything you will not be, all that the world has carefully plotted to deny you.

—Are you in a hurry? He asks, and you tell him —No.

—Good, he says with a warm smile. —A lot of guys just want to show up and get off. I mean, that's fine every now and then, but sometimes it's nice to just relax a little. Get to know one another.

You agree with him.

—Did you have any trouble finding the place?

You tell him, —Not at all.

Vernon nods happily at that. He lifts his beer and clinks its neck against yours. You both take a sip.

Then, you decide to play a little game. You ask him about himself, but you really want to know about Tom. He tells you all about the house, why they bought it. Where they lived before, and you catalogue these details, attributing them to the man who isn't in the room.

You finish your first beer, and Vernon offers to get you another, which you accept. He stands, leaving you alone for a time to imagine what living in this place, with Tom, might be like. It hurts too much to imagine, so you stop and wait for Vernon to return.

—Have you guys always had an open relationship? you ask. You drink your beer. Act casually. You're just making small talk. But you really want to know.

—Yeah well, the spice of life and all that. Simply put, we both like to fuck, a lot. And not always with the same person.

Vernon laughs.

A board creaks from upstairs and you feel your heart beat faster. The sound comes again. Footsteps?

—Is someone else here?

The older man shakes his head and says, —No, it's just an old house. You'd think it was haunted from all the weird noises it makes. Vernon winks at you. He takes a sip from his beer, pushing the mouth of the bottle into the nest of steel gray hair sprouting like a bush from his lips. You notice a single hair of his mustache, longer than the others, curling out over the bottle.

—Do you and your partner ever play together?

—Sometimes.

Vernon leans away from the back of the sofa and puts his bottle on the coffee table. He scoots closer to you, very close. His hand reaches out and cups the back of your head, and he draws your face near his.

—But some things are too good to share.

He kisses you then. For a moment, it's awkward because you're holding the beer bottle, and it's pressing into your chest. You free it and move into the kiss. He tastes of beer and mint. His lips are firm and insistent. His beard brushes your skin, caressing it. The whiskers are so smooth. His tongue slides over yours, and your pulse pounds in your ears. You hear the fire crackling and find the pleasant scent of smoke.

A board creaks from above.

You think Tom is up there. You want Tom to be up there. The thought arouses you faster until your sex strains against constraining fabric.

Vernon pulls away. He takes your beer bottle and places it on the table. In a slow practiced motion, he lifts the t-shirt over his head. You see the fullness of his stomach, covered in a thick brush of hair. You gaze at his nipples, brown and firm, jutting between the salt and pepper thatch on his chest. He is muscled, but a soft layer of extra weight covers his torso. The kind you like. Full and strong, but pliant. Comforting. Warm.

Your host drapes his shirt over the back of the sofa and leans in for another kiss.

You accept it and run your hands down his body, pausing with your thumbs to trace the arc of his chest, the firmness of his tits. Then you stroke your palm over the rise of his stomach, over the cotton fabric of his shorts and feel the ridge of hardness beneath.

–Let's go upstairs, Vernon says quietly, sounding out of breath.

You look into his eyes and for a moment you see adoration. It has been too long since you've witnessed such an expression. And you kiss him again before letting him take your hand and lead you from the couch.

You reach the base of the staircase when another board lows its complaint. Above you is darkness. Shadows on shadows.

–Are you sure we're alone? you ask.

–My partner won't be back until tomorrow.

You notice that doesn't answer the question. Perhaps it's your eyes playing tricks but you think one of the shadows above is moving. Fear trickles, cold and writhing, into your system when your foot comes down on the first step. Vernon is ahead of you. He turns back with his charming smile and holds your hand tighter.

–The bed's a lot more comfortable than the floor, he says.

You chuckle, humoring him. But the sense of unease grows. Each step upward takes you into greater darkness. You feel it enveloping you, swallowing you. The excitement of lust is joined by dread making you tremble and resist the strong hand guiding you.

–What's wrong? Vernon asks. His voice is kind. He sounds concerned. –Would you rather go back downstairs? We have a guest room.

You tell him you're just nervous. Still, you consider his offer. You're halfway up the staircase. When you look over your shoulder, you see firelight dancing over the foyer floor. Above, beyond Vernon's smooth tanned back and his handsome face, is nothing but a sheet of night.

But you climb the stairs, and on the landing, Vernon turns to you. He presses his body against yours and kisses you. His embrace is so tight, you think he might break you in half, but his enthusiasm is passionate, not violent.

As you walk down the hall, you're aware of the doors. Three on the right and one on the left. You want to walk faster, to get past them. You're reminded of Halloween and the haunted houses you visited with friends. You remember college kids, boys and girls, wearing tacky rubber masks, jumping through doorways or grabbing your legs to frighten you. The icy streams of fear run faster, from your neck to your belly.

You tell yourself to calm down. It's not like you're in an isolated cabin in the woods. You're in a nice home in an affluent suburb of a major city. You might as well be tricking with Mr. Rogers or Ward Cleaver.

Vernon leads you into the bedroom. He turns on the light and you quickly search the room. It too is what you expect: four-poster bed; an elegant hand knitted quilt laid over a pricey designer duvet; more antiques. There are two other doors in this room. The one on the left you imagine is a closet; the one on the right, a bathroom.

–Let's get you comfortable, Vernon says.

He reaches out and begins to unbutton your shirt. The fear of the unknown is replaced by a fear of your own body. You're too pale. What little hair you have on your chest is centered in a ragged oval between your pecs. Ugly. Vernon doesn't seem to mind. In fact, he is already kissing your chest, running his tongue through the odd patch of hair. A low growl emanates from his throat.

And what follows is – initially – familiar. Kissing and caressing give way to more intimate explorations. His cock is not overly long, but it is fat and the head flares like a mushroom cap. You take it in your mouth and work the head with your tongue, then slide up his body, wetting his stomach hair and chest hair with your saliva. You kiss him, lay on top of him, let him cup your ass. A finger works its way inside of you and you moan, kissing him harder.

Tom is in your mind. You remember his strength and his scent, a scent he shares with his lover and you lose yourself in it. He rolls over on top of you and works his way down your body, nibbling the flesh, licking it. He sucks you, and you look down at the way your cock disappears into his beard.

When he turns you over, you hug the pillow and think you can smell Tom there too. He reaches over you to the nightstand, retrieving a condom and a bottle of lube and you relax into the pillow, waiting.

The sex is at first slow and gentle, Tom (no *Vernon*) growling and cooing into your ear, his weight pinning you to the mattress. His hair and the heat from his body blanket you. He rears back and pulls you with him, until you're on all fours, and his thrusts become more insistent. Harsher. Hotter.

Something crashes beyond the door to your right and all motion stops.

—It's nothing, Vernon whispers.

But before he can resume, a thunderous booming fills the room. Strong fists pound at the closed door. Your mind is in turmoil as you throw yourself across the bed. You roll searching for something to cover yourself so you don't feel so exposed.

The pounding on the door grows louder. Another sound, a low wail, joins it.

Vernon collapses on the bed and rolls onto his back. —Son of a BITCH! he roars at the ceiling.

—What the hell is going on?

The battering of the door ceases for a moment, but the rhythm of it is with you. Your heart has never beat this fast before. It feels like something *other*, something with a panicked life of its own is trying to escape through your ribs.

—Can't I get one fucking moment of peace? Vernon cries.

You know he isn't talking to you. This is confirmed when he slides off the bed and walks toward the closed door.

—One hour? Would it have killed you to wait one fucking hour? But no, it's all about Tom. It's all about what Tom wants, and when *he* wants it. Son of a BITCH!

You don't understand what is happening but you want out of the room. You cross to where your clothes are piled and lift your jeans from the floor. You nearly stumble sliding them on, but you right yourself and get them fastened.

The pounding returns. This time, you see the wood of the door and the jamb shake under the attack. You gather up your clothes. You'll dress downstairs. You'll dress outside in the snow. You'll freeze to death. Anything is preferable to this nightmare.

—Just calm down, Vernon says.

And this time, he is talking to you.

But you aren't listening to him. You reach for the doorknob and find it locked.

—Let me out of here.

—Relax, Vernon tells you. —Just calm down.

The next blow to the door is so forceful the jamb cries out.

—Alright! Vernon yells, spinning to face the door. —I'll do it. Just let me find…

The older man, the one you thought was handsome and kind, leaves his place at the door. He is naked but there is nothing erotic in it. What you once thought so comforting, now appears powerful and dangerous. His eyes fall on the chest of drawers standing against the wall by the door you cannot open. You follow his gaze. On top of the chest is a doily, another silver picture frame, three small ceramic figurines. A large steel mallet.

—Is it so fucking much to ask? Vernon says, stomping across the room. —Christ, I like him. He's cute. We were having a good time. And then you had to throw a fit. Jesus fucking Christ! This isn't over, Mister, he shouts. —When you're done, we are having a serious talk.

You watch all of this, Vernon's voice playing against the terrible rhythm being beaten on the door. You know he's going to the chest of drawers, and he isn't likely to be headed there to admire his figurines.

You leap forward, race to the dresser and snatch the mallet out from under Vernon's hand, which comes down on top of your own.

—Don't try it, Kid, Vernon says.

His grip is strong, but panic feeds you adrenaline. You pull out of his grasp and back away, lifting the mallet high above your head.

–Look, I'm sorry, Vernon says, walking toward you. –You seem like a nice guy, and damn if we weren't having some fun there, but the relationship comes first. You know? We're committed to each other, and that always requires some level of compromise.

–You're out of your fucking mind. Where's the key? Let me out of here.

You let Vernon get too close, and he swings out with his fist. The blow would have sent you on your ass if he were only a couple of inches closer. As it happens, the knuckles graze your chin painfully, but you keep your balance. Without knowing you're doing it, you kick out. Your ankle hits him in the sack. Vernon doubles over. Gasping.

The thunder of fists on the closed door increases. Wood splinters. The frame creaks.

You don't know what you're doing. You don't know what you can do.

Vernon's exposed head is bent down in front of you as he clutches at his wounded testicles. With all of the force you can muster, you bring the mallet down on the back of his head. It hits with a dull clack. Vernon rocks forward. You hit him again. His scalp breaks open. Blood flows. The skull beneath is dented. Crushed.

Vernon topples. A wet gargling sound escapes his throat. His leg kicks spastically against the carpeted floor.

You back away, not able to understand exactly what has happened. For a moment, you don't remember hitting the man. You remember meeting him at the chest of drawers, but all memories of the mallet and what you have done with it are gone. One moment, Vernon was coming at you. The next, he is dying, curling slowly into a fetal position as his leg continues its twitching jig. You see the weapon in your hand. See the blood on its head and drop it to the floor.

The bathroom door comes apart then. Fists break through wood and pull with tremendous force. Beyond the door is a tiled room. Clean and shimmering white behind the man standing on its threshold.

It is Tom. You knew it would be Tom, but he is different than you remember him. His eyes are wild, his head pans from side to side, and then lifts as if testing the scent of the air. His body is no longer defined. It is bloated, covered in thick layers of fat. His chest juts out, lays over the top of his ample belly. When he steps forward his entire body rocks to the side as if his hips have locked.

You cry out and Tom throws a curious look at you. He lumbers into the room, eyeing you suspiciously.

He's still beautiful, you think. The wayward thought strikes you as perverse, but once it has surfaced you can't drown it. Still, you fear this man and you back away to the far corner of the room. You're trapped here, with him, a man who seems devolved into a beast.

Tom reaches the body of his partner and pauses. He casts another look at you. He seems to rear back and grow another three inches, but it is just your mind playing tricks. Again, his head pans, his nose lifts. He bends down and grasps Vernon by the throat, his fingernails digging in deep beneath the unconscious man's jaw.

A moment later, Tom is dragging Vernon toward the tiled room. He manages his lover's body as if it were weightless, a scarecrow of straw and fabric. You watch this, thinking your life has been spared, but only by a matter of minutes. It is not relief you feel. It is an even greater sense of dread.

In the tiled room, Tom lifts his lover by the throat. He wraps an arm around the unconscious form. You see them clearly. Tom holds Vernon against his chest. To you it looks like a tender moment between lunatics. Then Tom drops his head and bites into Vernon's shoulder. He jerks his head back, tearing away a thick chunk of flesh. Blood sprays from the wound. It splashes and stipples the white tile. Tom chews with him mouth open, skin and muscle drop from his lips as his teeth crush the tissue. A dew of blood dapples his beard. He swallows. Takes another bite. A long strip of flesh peels away from the wound, draws a finger-width line down Vernon's back, and then snaps free, to be drawn into Tom's snapping jaws.

Repulsed by the sight before you, your mind unwinds, and you think you will faint, or at the very least vomit. But you look away, breathe deeply. Still, your mind no longer functions quite as it should. It feels as if your thoughts are melting, becoming indistinct and fluid. This same liquid sensation enters your muscles. When you turn your head its as if a water-filled sack pivots on your neck.

Tom lowers his head and gnaws on Vernon's exposed shoulder joint. His teeth crush through the muscle and the gristle. The joint pops and the arm falls to the tiled floor. You follow the limb's motion. It drops so fast. Then the palm slaps the tile, and the sound frees you.

A weapon. The keys. Escape. These thoughts cut through the flowing indistinct contents of your mind. You physically shake your head to bring them clarity. Then you break from your place in the corner and retrieve the heavy steel mallet from the floor. You hold it tightly, and check on Tom to make certain he isn't yet finished with Vernon.

In the tiled room, Vernon's body is sinking to the floor and Tom is following it, his teeth gripping the collarbone as he guides the descent. A wet snuffling echoes against the white ceramic grid.

Next to the bed, you see Vernon's shorts by one of the post legs. Quickly you cross to them and search the pockets. When your fingers find the keys, elation floods you with cool sparks.

You look up to check on Tom.

He is staring at you. His face and beard are awash in scarlet. Bits of skin hang from his lips and teeth. In his eyes, you see concern. He lifts his head and growls. Then buries his face in the hole he's chewed through Vernon's chest.

Now is the moment you escape. Without shirt or shoes, you throw open the bedroom door and flee down the hall. Even your jacket, still hung by the front door is forgotten as you run headlong into the night. The snow.

The cold.

You call the police from a pay phone. You have reasons not to involve yourself. Mostly it is seeing Tom. The police won't need you anyway. It's been less than an hour since you left that nightmare house behind. The den. Tom's den. If they take you seriously, they will walk in on Tom's predation. Vernon's destruction.

You remain anonymous and return to your home. You prepare to sleep but know it will not come. Not tonight.

Maybe never again.

Tom has called you three times before you finally decide to speak with him. The police did nothing. Found nothing. You don't know why. You don't call to ask them.

—You've made things very complicated for me, Tom says.

—How did you get my number?

—You gave me your number.

—That was over a year ago, you tell him. —That was before...

Tom yawns loudly over the phone line and you are taken aback. Not only does the mundane nature of the act disgust you, but you feel oddly insulted.

—The police will find something, you say. —You won't get away with what you did.

—I've been getting away with it for years, Tom says. —I'm not proud of it, and I'm not ashamed. It's just the way it is, and I've learned to adapt.

—The way *what* is? What are you?

—Something you'd rather not tangle with.

The threat silences you. You look over the familiar terrain of your apartment, and you don't feel safe here.

—The police are done with me, Tom says. —They didn't find anything, because there was nothing left to find. So, I'm going to ask you to let this go. I would prefer no one else gets hurt.

—Until you get hungry again, you mean?

—It's the only thing that sustains me through the winter.

—Sustains you? You're talking about human beings.

—I'm going to ask you to let this go, Tom says again.

You hang up the phone.

You met him on the Internet, because you were tired of standing in bars, doing the mating dance with the usual suspects. His name was Vernon, and he told you he had a lover. You didn't care. It wasn't your relationship. You hadn't had anyone to lie to in a very long time.

Now, you stand in front of that house again. You hold Vernon's keys in your hand and stare at the black windows. Your father's gun weighs heavy in the pocket of your new coat.

You ring the doorbell and wait. You gird yourself for what is to come. You try to think of the feral Tom, the beast that devoured his partner without so much as a tear shed. But you can't conjure that image. Instead, you see him in a shower. Muscular. Beautiful. A god statue brought to life, bathing under the spray of a magical fountain.

He will be alone in the house. With Vernon gone, he will be completely alone.

Tom does not answer the door. Not after the first ring. Not after the second. You use Vernon's keys to enter. Once inside, you make sure the lock is secured.

The coat rack beside you is naked. The fireplace in the next room is cold and dark. The pictures that cluttered the surfaces and decorated the walls are gone.

Those were Vernon's souvenirs. Not Tom's.

You walk up the stairs. The trepidation of your first visit does not return. Instead, you feel a soothing numbness in your chest. The darkness above does not frighten you. The doors you pass offer no threat.

In the bedroom you pause. You expected to find Tom here. You expected to find him asleep. He told you the flesh of men sustained him through the winter and you assumed some form of hibernation. Seeing the bed, neat and empty, unease seeps through the resonant numb.

It would be so much easier if he were asleep.

You look at the tiled room and shudder. Briefly, you are able to remember the atrocity that happened there. Tom's face, smeared and littered with human refuse, gazes out at you. But you blink, and he's gone.

A rattling breath startles you, and you spin toward the left wall, your hand digging in the jacket pocket for your father's gun. It snags on the fabric as you pull it free, but soon you have it gripped in your palm.

You take the knob of the closet door and the rattling breath comes again. So, you open it and find what you expected.

Nestled on a pile of clothing nearly two feet thick, Tom lies curled. His bulk fills much of the space. His face is serene in sleep. Your eyes run over his swollen body. The dense hair covering his chest and belly.

And you think of warmth.

Right then, you want to lie down with him. You want to feel the concentration of heat you know he provides. He won't push you away. Someone has to protect him while he sleeps. Someone has to manage the house during his slumber. You know what being his requires.

Being his.

Tom opens his eyes. He looks neither shocked nor disturbed. The serenity of his sleep carries over into waking. He rolls ever so slightly on the bed of clothing and lifts his arm away from his belly. It is an invitation.

Right then, you want to lie down with him.

So, that's what you do.

I'm Your Violence

The victim's name was Charles Clarke. He was fifty-eight years old and apparently in good health – prior to death. Clarke had plans with friends to try a new trendy restaurant downtown before catching the premiere of *Hole*, a somber little play at the Wilkes Repertory Theatre on Jackson Street. He never showed for dinner, and he didn't answer calls. These behaviors were unlike Clarke, or so his friends claimed when they called the police station just after 9:00 pm. A patrol car was dispatched and finding the back door ajar the officers entered and announced themselves before investigating the scene. Clarke was found in his bedroom.

The officers who found the body reported the victim looked as if he'd been run through a food processor.

Detective Dean Kaiser rolled this information around in his head as he ground his cigarette into the car's ashtray and exhaled a cloud of blue-gray smoke over the dashboard. He stepped from the car. Icy wind sliced along the collar of his overcoat and caressed his cheeks like frigid palms. He pulled the coat tight over his chest and hurried toward the house.

Two patrol cars had joined the first in the street outside of the house for a total of three. Four officers wrangled the dozen or so neighbors who'd been drawn into the cold night by flashing lights and the prospect of a glimpse at some intriguing misfortune. A waist-high wrought iron fence ran across the front of the property, beyond it a low rise of lawn, beyond this a circular drive, beyond this a three-story Edwardian home, which in any other part of the city might have been considered a mansion, but amid the opulent domiciles in the Country Club neighborhood seemed simply typical.

An unattractive officer with skin like a bleached pumpkin rind met Dean at the door. The officer nodded. Despite the cold, sweat clung to the young man's brow. Dean pegged him as a rookie who'd just seen too much, trying desperately to keep from losing his dinner to the bushes.

That bad? he wondered. *Food processor*, he remembered.

Inside he found another young officer, this one built heavier with a soft pudgy face and cool blue eyes. He approached the kid.

"Where's he at?" Dean asked.

"Upstairs. Third door on the left."

"Has Detective Harper arrived?"

A nod of the round head sent Dean up the stairs. He followed a red Persian runner along the corridor. A shape broke the light coming from an open doorway ahead, casting a shadow in the dimly lighted hall.

Dean stepped into the room and saw Reg Harper on the far side of the bed. The man was looking down at the remains of Charles Clarke, which covered the bed in a crimson paste. His skin had been ripped away. Fluids still leaked from the body. The skull and sternum appeared to float in a puddle of blood and viscera. Bits of bone, yellow fat and pale skin showed like vegetables in a shiny stew. Blood pasted similar tissues to the headboard and wall in a ragged fan pattern.

"Watch your step," Harper said, his voice low and gritty. He pointed his index finger, which was gloved in latex. "He's all over the place."

"Jesus," Dean whispered, casting his eyes downward. His stomach rolled. He pulled a pair of protective gloves from the pocket of his jacket and snapped them on, before picking his way across the bedroom to join Harper. This vantage was worse.

The victim's right hand had avoided the kind of damage the rest of his body had endured. Slathered in blood, it hung over the side of the bed, dripping. Dean made out the shape of a ring with a large stone on the pinkie.

"You ever seen anything like this before?" Harper asked.

"No," Dean replied. "Any idea what did it?"

"I'm guessing it wasn't a butterfly."

"I meant the weapon."

Harper stepped toward the bed and reached out with a latex-covered hand to grab the dangling arm. Coagulating blood acted like a poor adhesive; the sheet lifted with the arm then peeled away.

"Look at the wrist," he said.

Dean leaned forward and immediately saw what Harper meant. The marks punched through the skin. Darker blood filled them.

I'm Your Violence

They were made with human teeth.

Dean stood on the porch smoking while the forensic teams worked over the house. The medical examiner had already confirmed Harper's supposition regarding the cause of death.

You're telling us he was eaten alive?

Not eaten. There's too much tissue here. Yes, his attacker removed the flesh with his teeth, possibly even masticated the tissue to some degree, but he spit much of it out. You can see it all around the body and on the floor. Clarke wasn't cannibalized, at least not completely. On the up side, your boys can make some good dental casts, and saliva samples are a given. You catch this guy and you'll have no trouble confirming the ID.

How long would it take to do that to a body?

As long as the killer wanted, the ME said. *On the short end it wouldn't take long. Fifteen minutes. Twenty. I'd only be guessing. I've never run into anything like this before.*

Neither had Dean, and he didn't know what to make of it. He took another drag off his smoke and surveyed the sidewalk and the crowd milling there. Concerned faces hovered above the low wrought iron fence. Many of the aggregated gawkers hadn't dressed for the cold. A woman in a terry cloth robe trembled. Next to her a man built like a linebacker, wearing nothing but cargo shorts and an olive green t-shirt at least one size too small for his stocky build hugged himself against the cold. The guy laid a hard stare on Dean, an expression of unapologetic lust.

Maybe some other time, Dean thought. The guy was attractive, no question, but his timing sucked.

Harper appeared in the doorway, his face screwed into an uncomfortable grimace. "You need to see this."

"There's more?"

"Yeah," Harper said. He sighed. "We just hit a whole new level of fucked up."

Dean dropped his cigarette on the porch and ground it out, then he bent down to retrieve the butt. He dropped it in the front pocket of his chinos and followed Harper into the house.

Harper led him back up the stairs but instead of returning to the bedroom and its grisly content they continued down the hall and entered a home office, where he found sleek furniture and multiple flat screen monitors on a broad glass and iron desk. Harper crossed the room to a laser printer. With a pair of tweezers he lifted a sheet from the tray and held it by the corner, dangling it in Dean's face.

A photograph had been printed on the paper. Though the image was clear his mind took several moments to process it:

A middle-aged man in ecstasy…

An adolescent boy in pain…

Both unclothed…

"Shit," Dean hissed. His blood grew thin and hot, racing through his veins like acid. His heartbeat turned to thunder in his ears. He jerked his head toward the photograph and asked, "The older guy our victim?"

"Looks that way."

Good, he thought.

"I'll bet his computer is choking on these things. The men with candy like their glossies."

"Could be," Dean replied. "It certainly gives us a hell of a motive if that kid's not a pro."

His pulse continued to race and his face burned. Dean's head grew light for a moment, and he drew in a deep breath to quiet his ragged nerves. He gave the disgusting picture a final glance then turned away.

The monitor on the glass desk before him swirled with colors. He reached out and jabbed the space bar on the keyboard with his index finger. The screen saver disappeared to reveal the computer's desktop.

Amid the folders and application icons displayed on the screen, a window was open in the center of the screen. Dean found himself looking at the crimson fluid pooling on Charles Clarke's bed. Men and women wearing masks and gloves – the forensic team – worked over the surfaces of the room.

"What the hell?" Harper asked.

"Video cam," Dean replied. "The sick fuck has one hidden in the bedroom."

"Remember, 'the sick fuck' happens to be the victim in this case."

Dean disregarded the statement. He stared at the monitor, the bed, the room, the people moving there unaware of his watching.

"If this thing was recording our job just got a hell of a lot easier," Harper said.

I'm Your Violence

"Yeah," Dean said. "Maybe."

Lifeless stifling air poured into the office. Already uncomfortable, the stale atmosphere felt suffocating. Through the window on his door, Dean looked over the expanse of the station. Half of the desk lights were off, and the floor was deserted. His colleague's on the Clarke case were off in different departments, checking on forensics, running phone numbers, grabbing cups of coffee for the long night ahead. The scene gave him the creeps, and he turned away. Dean opened the window and stuck his head into the wintry night.

For now, Dean waited. Charles Clarke's computer was in the hands of the techs downstairs. Departmental procedures were in place to assure data wasn't corrupted. Plus, if the family of the victim came forward to claim defamation of character once Clarke's crimes hit the press, the department could cover its ass with reams of detailed paperwork.

Currently, this last point was likely far more important to the Barnard Police Department than the investigation.

After word of Clarke's twisted pastime had made its way through the crime scene, the attitudes of the on-scene investigators had immediately changed. The eagerness to find the murderer seemed to drain from his colleagues' eyes, making room for disgust. Dean understood the reaction; he'd felt it himself. Did Clarke deserve to die for molesting children? The law said no, but Dean certainly wouldn't lose any sleep over his passing. No, his slumber would be sacrificed to anger. In the aftermath of this crime, Clarke wouldn't be seen as a hebephile or pederast, he'd be seen as a homo deviant, emphasis on the *homo*.

Likely Dean's colleagues were already growling about it in the locker room, volleying misguided opinions through the sweat-thick air, liberally peppering their dialogue with words like "queer," "cocksucker," and "fag." Fortunately, they knew better than to get in his face with that shit.

It was infuriating; being painted with a brush frayed by the behaviors of a monster like Charles Clarke. Were all straight men rapists? Were all straight men responsible for JonBenet or Megan

Kanka? No. But some fuck like Clarke gets exposed and the idiot faction processes it as another example of the predatory queer.

Harper entered the office carrying a cup of coffee and a thick folder. "We got the most recent pictures," he said, crossing to the desk and setting his mug down. "They cover the last two years. The techies are transferring the video clips to DVD now. They're starting with tonight and working their way back. Should have the disk in a few minutes."

"Why didn't they start with the vids? That's our best chance of catching this guy."

"You just answered your own question. My guess is they'd erase the things if they could. Hell, they'd probably buy the guy dinner and put him on a plane to Rio if they had the chance." Harper chuckled and placed the folder on the desk.

"Glad you're so amused," Dean said, still fuming.

"Don't play that shit with me," Harper said. "I know what's going through your head, and I get it. I do. We can discuss it all over breakfast or a beer, but right now we have the job. So save the rage; sit your ass down; and let's get to work."

Dean accepted Harper's direction and sat; his partner was right. He pulled the folder toward him and lifted the manila flap. "Sorry," he muttered, gazing at a photograph similar to the one he'd seen in Clarke's home office.

Dean shook his head, flipping through the two-dozen photographs. He identified seven different boys. At least one of them was from the streets; Dean could tell by the shabby jeans and tattered tennis shoes he wore, but this was the only kid that was dressed in the pictures. Others might have been runaways, hustlers or kids from Clarke's neighborhood. It was hard to tell. The very rich and the very poor had the same hairstyles these days.

As for Clarke, he was a bland looking man with a dark suntan. His white hair lay back against his scalp in a perfect wave, looking as properly coiffed as a banker, a real estate agent or a political candidate.

"I don't get it," Dean said.

"What do you mean?"

"The attraction to youth." That wasn't exactly what he meant. Dean knew the psychology. Clarke's crimes weren't about sexual attraction so much as they were about control and loathing, but every goddamn television commercial and magazine ad pushed this youth shit down his throat. Ten year olds dolled up to look like whores. Nineteen-year-old pop star has-beens. According to those advertising fucks, people were supposed to desire children. But if one of their neighbors actually acted on it and went all bad touch on one of their kids, they'd be the first ones to form an action group. The first ones to ask 'why my child?' It's a wonder the whole fucking country hadn't gone pedophile. "I just don't get it."

"What's to get? You have youth on the left and old age and death on the right. You keep looking to the left because what's on the right scares the hell out of you."

"I've never dated a guy under thirty." Truth was, he rarely dated men under forty. Younger men all looked somehow unfinished to Dean. He found a few of them pretty, but found none of them attractive. Only when youth was shed for a more distinct masculinity did men appeal to Dean. He knew it was uncommon. Some of his friends even considered his preference a pathology, but he didn't care if his friends got hard for his dates or not; they didn't have to fuck the guys.

"You're not afraid of death," Harper said.

"Come again?"

"Never mind. Look, we need to run these pics through juvy and social services and see if we can get a match."

"Did any names appear in Clarke's files?" Dean asked.

"Nope. He numbered them. Kept them all in a folder labeled 'Puppies.'"

"Charming," Dean said.

Dean rewound the digital movie until the moment before the man entered Charles Clarke's bedroom. Clarke lay naked on his bed. Freshly showered, he looked relaxed and comfortable. No shades of remorse or shame colored the man's face in the aftermath of his abuse. The prick even waved at the camera and grinned. His unrepentant satisfaction infuriated Dean, disturbing him deeply and far too personally.

At fifteen, Dean had experienced his first sexual encounter, with a man three times his age. For Dean, it had been consensual. The man, Rick, had done nothing but present the opportunity, he hadn't gotten Dean drunk, hadn't drugged him or enticed him with porn. Rick asked if Dean wanted to get sucked off and Dean had said, "Yes." All of his friends at school talked about having sex, and Dean was determined to have it, though not precisely as his friends would have; his peers' tastes ran towards actresses, cheerleaders, and swimsuit models.

A month later, Rick was arrested for forcing sex on a nine-year-old boy. He committed suicide in a jail cell three floors down from where Dean currently sat.

The man's arrest, highly publicized in the local paper because of his position as a teacher, had terrified Dean. He listened, ashamed, as kids at school talked about the "fag teacher," emphasizing that suicide was too good for the pervert. For weeks Dean had lived in fear, convinced his friends already knew what he'd done or would soon know. The fear had filled Dean's chest like shards of glass. It would be ten years before he was again intimate with a man.

As an adult, looking back on that time in his life, the shame of that encounter rekindled, but not for the reasons some might imagine. His fear had changed over the years to guilt. He understood the teacher's aberrant behavior. Dean knew that he wasn't to blame for Rick's sickness, but he couldn't help but think his acquiescence had encouraged the teacher's crimes. Ridiculous, he knew. Rick had been a molester long before Dean had ever entered the man's life, but if Dean had known enough to deny the man, to stop him, a nine-year-old boy – an innocent who couldn't fathom let alone consent to the teacher's demands – wouldn't carry the lifelong scars of Rick's touch.

On the screen, Charles Clarke rolled from his bed startled and clutching at the duvet to cover himself as he scurried across the mattress. He shouted for someone to get out of his house.

Then another man entered the shot, standing in partial profile, head turned as if aware of the camera. He wore loose-fitting blue jeans and a black t-shirt. Dean noted the bulk of muscle beneath the garments. He estimated the man stood six-feet tall and weighed 240-250 pounds. He appeared to be younger than Clarke, but not young. His hair was thick, with salty strands lightening the near black hue.

"I have an alarm. The police are coming," Clarke claimed.

"The alarm isn't set," his killer said evenly. "You didn't set it. You never do after your crimes. You never lock your doors. When you're done with them and send them on their way, your deepest wish is for their return, their subservience, their adoration. You want them to misinterpret what you did to them as love."

"I'll pay you," Clarke cried. "I'll..."

Before he could finish the next sentence, the killer crossed the room in four quick strides, revealing nothing of his face. He landed a ferocious punch to Clarke's jaw. Even with poor sound, Dean heard Clarke's bones crack beneath the blow. The abuser dropped to the carpet unconscious. His killer bent low and lifted the man and tossed him onto the bed as easily as discarding a robe before dressing. Then the killer pulled his shirt over his head, revealing a powerful back and thick shoulders. He folded the shirt and removed his pants and shoes. He stacked the clothing tidily and carried it off camera, perhaps into the hall. Then he returned.

Clarke's murderer walked to the edge of the bed, head canted away from the observing lens. He leaned over Clarke and bit into the man's thigh. Skin ripped and gouts of blood poured over the leg. It happened quickly. No hesitation or clumsiness. Then it happened again. The killer didn't chew the flesh, but rather spat it out in the rapidly forming pool of blood. Clarke came to then. Frantic eyes as wide and white as golf balls dominated his features. He opened his mouth to scream but all that emerged from his throat was a shrill hiss.

The killer changed his position, moving closer to the headboard. His palm went to Clarke's brow. He shoved the abuser's head back into the pillow, and then he leaned forward and ripped Clarke's throat out with his teeth.

Dean stopped the clip and rewound to the point just before the killer dipped his head to take out Clarke's throat. In this action he revealed more of his face – a full cheek, a strong jaw smeared with Clarke's blood, the crescent pool of an eye socket. The blood acted as a mask, making clear identification impossible, but Dean would know this man if he met him.

The killer reminded Dean of a teacher named Rick.

Interviews with Charles Clarke's neighbors yielded nothing of value. Like all good neighbors, they minded their own business. The time counter on Clarke's computer put the time of death at 5:33 pm, which meant there was still some light in the sky when the murderer let himself into Clarke's house, but of the neighbors who were home at that time of the evening none could "recall" seeing anything of interest.

The techs went through Clarke's computer several times, looking for the names or addresses of victims. They scanned his Internet browser history, trying to ascertain if he'd met his victims (perhaps his killer) in a chat room. They combed his emails, seeking evidence of pornography trafficking, possibly the names of other men who shared his disease. After twenty-four hours, they'd found nothing. Apparently, Clarke was a rarity: insular in his perversion.

The video itself was of little help. Though the murderer was distinct in appearance – muscular, middle-aged – there wasn't enough of the man's face to capture a functional image. They couldn't put the back of his head on the departmental website or the six o'clock news and hope to field accurate leads.

No, despite having captured their killer on tape, the break in the case required a little more effort. Clarke's cell phone records showed a call to Capital Taxi at 4:48 on the afternoon of his death. Based on the video clock, this would have been shortly after his abuse of the boy Clarke had labeled "Puppy Number 16a."

The boy was featured in several of Clarke's photographs and at least one video. He was the frightened boy with the grimace of pain in the photo Harper had lifted from Clarke's printer.

Following up with the cab company, Dean got an address for a home on Arnold Street in a rundown residential district called Four Points – about as far from Clarke's Country Club address as was possible while remaining within the city limits. The home was owned by a property management group and leased to Mr. Jesse Bolton and his wife Janis. The couple had been under lease on the property for just over nine months. They were currently two months behind on the rent. Both had records with the Barnard Police Department – drunk and disorderlies and a DUI for Mr. Bolton – and both were on file with social services, stemming from an incident involving their son, Matthew.

With the address plugged into the GPS system, Dean drove across town. Harper occupied the passenger seat.

"So how are we going to handle this?" Harper asked. "I mean if this is the Puppy's address."

"Could you not call him that?" It had been bad enough seeing the demeaning term listed among Clarke's documentation; he saw no point in encouraging its use from his partner.

"Fine. Regardless. We check the place out, meet Jesse Bolton and realize he isn't our guy, cross everyone off the suspect list, then what?"

"Then we inform the parents their son has been abused and suggest they get him therapy so he doesn't end up as fucked up as Clarke."

"You think a family in Four Points can afford to send their kid to a shrink?"

"There are services available."

"If they'll use them."

"That's their decision to make."

"I hate this shit."

"We all hate this shit," Dean replied.

He drove out of downtown and over a viaduct, spanning a broad ditch filled with litter, scrub grass and the cardboard homes of those who found even Four Points out of their price range. The houses on the far side of the bridge were single and double story wrecks with peeling paint and sagging porches. Shingles draped loose on rooftops like scabs displaced by eczema. Most of the vehicles – pickup trucks, cheap sedans, bloated mini-vans – offered transportation if not style. Grass browned by early frost and grown wild from indifference ran from property to property, the yards differentiated only by the junk littering them. Four Points was the colon of the city; a dismal and diseased organ processing a constant flow of waste and toxicity.

An exception to the decaying appearance of the district caught Dean's eye as he turned down Arnold Street. One house wore a fresh coat of white paint; it's roof looked healthy and the yard was, if not lush, well maintained and free of trash. It looked like a single healthy tooth amid a rotted mouth. At the corner of this house, Dean saw a man, wearing a red ski parka and blue jeans. His dark hair was brushed back neatly. White threads lightened the field of near-black strands.

A frisson of recognition ran through his chest.

Is that him? Dean wondered. He played back Clarke's video in his mind. The man beside the house on his left was certainly the right size, and the hair was similar if not identical. *Jesus, that could be him.*

"You missed it," Harper said.

"Missed what?"

"The house," his partner said. "The GPS chick said we arrived at our destination. Don't you listen?"

"Yeah, right," Dean said. He pulled to the curb, turning his head to keep the man in his field of vision. The front tire rolled up on the sidewalk, jolting the car to a stop.

"Watch the rubber," Harper said.

But Dean was watching the man across the street and two doors back. He stared in the mirror, refocusing his eyes as if the act might magnify the man's image or produce a clear identification.

"You see that guy?" Dean asked.

"Where?"

"Two houses back. Other side of the road?"

"No. Why? He and old boyfriend of yours?"

"Fuck off Harper," Dean said. "He could be our guy."

The man stepped back into the alley beside the house. Dean kept his eyes on the mirror, hoping he would reappear.

"Are you serious?" Harper asked, turning to look over the seat and through the back window.

"I don't know," Dean said. "Probably not. There have to be a hundred guys in Four Points that fit the description. I'm probably just overreacting. On edge or something."

"Should we check him out?" Harper asked.

"I'll do it," Dean replied. He opened the car door and stepped out. Speaking to Harper over the roof of the vehicle, he said, "You check on the Bolton's. More than likely this isn't our guy, but if it is and he thinks we're close he might bolt."

"Or he might blow your head off. I'm going with you."

"And what if the perp *is* Jesse Bolton? He sees us out here and tears out the backdoor because we went chasing geese? You handle the family, I'll go talk to this guy."

Harper wasn't satisfied with the arrangement – it wasn't procedure – but he nodded his head.

Dean turned to face the house across the street. The man in the red parka was there again, crossing to the front door. His head turned slightly as he attempted to unsnag a key ring from one of the jacket's pockets. Seeing the man in partial profile set off a web of chill at the back of Dean's head.

Shit, that's him.

He stopped at the mailbox on the curb and read the name *Baker* on its side. Dean jogged over the man's lawn and paused on the front doorstep. He breathed deeply and released the strap that secured his sidearm in its holster. Then he knocked on the door.

When the man opened the door, Dean saw he had shed his parka. The bulk of frequently worked muscles pressed at Baker's white button down shirt. Thickly veined forearms grew from rolled up sleeves. The face was chiseled and striking; the eyes as clear and blue as the winter sky. The man's appearance unnerved Dean, caused a thick and inappropriate lust to settle low in his belly.

Watching the killer on the video, Dean had been reminded of a teacher named Rick, but Baker looked nothing like that man. There wasn't even a passing resemblance to the soft-faced teacher who abused boys and finally killed himself. Dean couldn't be certain what random connection he'd made equating the two.

"Hello," the man said.

"Hello, Mr. *Baker is it?*"

"I'm Paul Baker."

"Mr. Baker, I'm Detective Dean Kaiser with the Barnard Police Department."

"Yes detective," Baker said. "Do you want to come in? It's colder than shit out here."

"Yes, thank you." Dean stepped inside, his hand close to the gun on his hip.

The inside of the house was as impeccable as the exterior. The furniture, while not expensive, was clean and modern and fit the space well. White high-gloss paint covered the moldings at the ceiling and floor, framing walls painted a soft fawn color. Anywhere else in the city, the house would have struck Dean as pleasant, but it didn't fit the Four Points model. He found the neatness of the home wholly wrong.

"Mr. Baker, I'd like to ask you a couple of questions," Dean said, watching as Baker crossed the room.

"I assume this is in connection with the deviant?"

The statement was close enough to a confession for Dean's taste. He took a step back and removed his sidearm, which he aimed at Baker's torso.

"I'm going to ask you to lie down on the floor with your hands behind your head."

"That isn't necessary."

"My gun disagrees with you."

"So shoot," Baker said. "This body has already lived its time. Your bullets won't change the shape of things."

The serenity in the man's tone disturbed him. No one should sound that calm with a gun pointing at him.

"I said get on the floor."

Baker ignored the request and walked along the far wall, brushing his hands across the vertical blinds, making them clack and whisper. He paused and licked a thumb, which he pressed to one of the white plastic panels. He rubbed lightly as if to remove a stain.

"The boy would have damned himself without me," said Baker, seemingly lost in his massage of the blind.

"You're quite the guardian angel, now lie the fuck down!"

"That won't happen," Baker noted with amusement. "You'll find that Clarke wrote a check to Matthew Bolton's father; it wasn't a very large check. People pay more for a mediocre television set."

"Excuse me?"

"That's why Matthew couldn't go to his parents. Surely, you must have been wondering that. Clarke bought the boy's services and his parents' silence. Matthew really had no choice."

"But *you* did."

"Not so."

"Down on the floor!"

"You'll find Clarke wrote a lot of checks to a lot of people."

"I'm only going to tell you one more time."

"That's true," Baker agreed.

A blur of motion startled Dean. He nearly fired his weapon, but the target was gone; Baker no longer stood at the window. A thick arm slid around Dean's neck, clamping across his throat like a boa constrictor. Baker's other arm shot out and grasped the gun. With a painful twist, he freed the weapon from Dean's hand.

"You don't need this," Baker whispered, rocking the gun in Dean's field of vision. "I'm not going to hurt you, and you can't hurt me." Baker inhaled loudly, air rasping through his nose and throat. He let the breath out cold and dry on Dean's neck. "Now, I could snap your neck, or if I was feeling particularly cruel, I could suffocate you slowly. You know that, don't you?"

"Yes."

With the uttering of the word, Baker released Dean's throat and stepped away.

"Sorry, but guns have a way of making people deaf to the important things. Now, as I was saying, Clarke wrote a number of checks, to procure company and to keep things quiet. You'll find ample evidence of these transactions."

"If you know so much about this, you should have turned him in."

"That's not the shape of things."

"Because you'd rather kill."

"I have no choice."

"Bullshit."

"I was created with a purpose. I'm a fabric, a weave of needs, created from man's effluent."

"You're a fucking psychopath."

"No," Baker said, evenly. "I'm your violence."

Baker walked in front of him and pressed his face close to Dean's. He cocked his head slightly to the left, peering into Dean's eyes.

What is he looking for? Understanding? Fear? Fuck that.

Dean drove a fist toward Baker's throat. The man didn't flinch. His eyes remained locked on Dean's as he caught Dean's wrist in his hand.

"How frustrating," Baker said. "You so badly want to hurt me, but you can't. Not because you don't possess the determination but because you're helpless against me. Imagine a small boy with no place to turn, backed into a corner, betrayed by the only people in the world he thought he could trust. Imagine that. Imagine what that must be like for the boy. Just think what he might do."

"But the boy didn't do anything. *You* did."

"If I hadn't destroyed Clarke, Matthew would have. His thoughts were already leading him to it; he might have even succeeded, but then his soul would carry that soil, and I couldn't let that happen. So I intervened on his behalf. That is the shape of things."

"He told you to kill Clarke?"

"Of course not. If he had asked, he would have been complicit in the act."

"But he told you Clarke was abusing him?"

"His desperation summoned me."

"Let go of my hand, Paul. Come with me. I can get you help."

"This is a carousel," Baker said in frustration. "Perhaps another approach?"

Baker tossed the gun to the floor, and his hands shot to either side of Dean's head. He pulled their faces close. Remembering Charles Clarke's death at the teeth of this madman, Dean struggled against the grip, fearing his skin would soon be pinched and torn away, but his efforts against the sturdy hold were futile. Baker's lips crushed against his in a violent kiss. The skin of Dean's upper lip split with the impact. His head grew light, his struggles intensified.

A flash of blue light blinded him, and Dean fell back and down, his body shaking in spasm as if he'd just been struck by a taser. He hit the floor hard, and pain flared at his elbow, his hip, and his leg. Baker also collapsed on the floor, but unlike Dean the suspect was motionless.

Once the seizure-like tremors released him Dean crawled away from Baker's body. "Shit," he hissed. "Shit. Shit."

He stood and looked about the room frantically as if expecting another attacker to emerge from one of the archways. Dean's eyes fell on his sidearm laying on the floor less than a foot from Baker's clawed fingers. He scrambled across the room and retrieved his gun. From this angle Baker appeared dead. Glazed eyes stared blankly at the ceiling. His mouth, stained with Dean's blood, was open and slack. Dean thought to check the man's pulse, but feared his host was playing possum, waiting for a clean opportunity to strike.

Instead of touching the suspect, Dean fished his cell phone from his pocket and flipped it open, intending to call for back up.

His finger refused his command to dial. Dean tried again, thinking he must be in shock. He took several deep breaths, steadied himself and tried again. Still he could not force his finger to press the buttons.

Don't, a voice shouted.

Dean looked around, seeking the direction of the voice, but he shared the room with no one but Baker, and the man hadn't moved.

The walls about him began to melt, blurs and smears replacing hard edges and angles. This odd shifting forced Dean off balance. A moment later, he stood in a different room – a bedroom – and Charles Clarke was alive and offering him money in exchange for his life; he tore the man's throat out. The room spun, and Dean dropped to his knees. Strange faces appeared like memories behind his eyes. A slender, cruel-faced woman knelt before him as he brought a hammer down on her skull. A handsome young man in an expensive business suit flopped on the floor – a length of bailing wire tightly wrapped around his throat. A blubbery man with few teeth, dirt-splotched cheeks and watery eyes howled. He lay crucified on a floor of raw wooden planks. Dean gouged at the man's genitals with a broken whiskey bottle.

The ghastly show played behind Dean's eyes. He couldn't push it away, couldn't hide behind his own thoughts. His head swam with the grotesque images.

Then Dean was walking away from Baker's body. His mind cleared momentarily, but foreign thoughts surged over the moment of relief. Paul Baker's life and death surfaced in the wake of the blood-soaked montage.

Baker had pumped his body full of muscle enhancing drugs, had spent hours at the gym to reshape a body that had earned him the nickname "Porkster" in high school. Baker had been so obsessed with his personal beautification he'd drawn away from people. He'd slaved and struggled and sacrificed for a body considered perfect, but in the process had totally removed himself from the society he'd meant to impress with his newfound physique. The information came to Dean like a memory, like a fragment of his own life clearly remembered.

Recently. Late one night, Baker answered his front door. On the stoop stood a young boy with blond hair and an innocent but sorrowful face. (*Matthew Bolton?* Dean wondered) The boy showed Baker his palm, where a long cut ran from index finger to wrist. Baker took the boy's hand amid a flare of blue light.

And then this other – this Violence – moved into Baker's skin, the way it now resided in Dean.

Yes, a gentle voice whispered in his head. *The dead and dying... the weak. They give me shelter. Baker died only minutes after I joined him. The drugs he used to manufacture his physique destroyed his heart.*

Am I dying? Dean thought. *Am I dead?*

No, the other voice replied. *Your arrival interrupted my final duty to Matthew. You are simply being borrowed.*

Dean felt his body move, but he'd made no command for it to do so. He walked across the room to the front door and pulled it open. Dean tried to exert his will, struggled to make even a single finger move of his own volition, but his attempt failed. Inside his head, his own body, he was an impotent prisoner.

His thoughts twisted and tangled, knotted by an extreme and manic claustrophobia, but his body produced none of the phobia's physical manifestations. The sick gut. The sweaty palms. The clenched muscles. His mind struggled but his body was untouched by the fear.

Dean's body walked across Baker's lawn, his sidearm gripped in the hand at his side. A new collage of grisly images erupted in his thoughts. Blood. Bands of shredded flesh. Organs, glistening and twinkling wetly, but no longer serving the human machine.

Christ, Dean screamed within his head. *What are you?*

You already know, the voice replied.

My violence.

Man's violence. Emotional energy, like all energy, unbreakable and eternal. I'm woven of it. I'm the sum of it. But for you, violence comes with guilt and fear. I lack these obstacles, and I absolve you of them.

You're a creature of revenge, Dean asserted.

I'm a being of justice, unhampered by the viscous fluid of shifting moralities. This is my purpose. Others of my kind were woven of different emotions, with dissimilar purposes. Some are pure hate and others pure joy. Some have gone mad because they were woven of so many disparate threads.

And you're not mad? Dean asked. *You ripped Clarke apart with your teeth.*

With Baker's teeth, the voice corrected. *And the method is prescribed by the one I serve. Lacking a viable weapon, Matthew was led by tortured thoughts to a resolution not wholly common.*

Dean's foot stepped up on the far sidewalk. A gunshot echoed. It rang in his ears, but his body was otherwise unmoved by the sound.

Matthew's house, Dean thought, suddenly panicked. *Harper?*

He willed his legs to move faster, to run. Concern for his partner flared like static charges all around him, but his body was not his own, and it continued to stroll along the sidewalk at an aggravatingly measured pace.

Maybe that will make what follows easier for you.

Make it easier? What happened?

You'll see.

Harper? Dean asked.

Yes, the Violence replied, *Harper.*

They reached the house far too slowly. Dean's imagination played cruel games up to the second his hand wrapped around the front door's knob. He imagined Harper lying dead on the Bolton's floor. He clearly saw a hole punched between his partner's eyes. Then the door opened, and his body moved inside to find his teasing imagination hadn't been completely inaccurate.

Harper lay against a cheap and tattered brown sofa. A shimmering crimson stain blossomed across the left lapel of his coat. He struggled for breath, chest rising and falling in ragged gasps.

Across the room, in the archway separating the dismal room from another stood an emaciated couple. Their faces were tight and pale like latex masks pulled too tightly. Through these masks wild eyes scurried in their sockets like insects fleeing sudden light. Janis Bolton bit a fingernail furiously. She wore only a bra and a pair of blue sweat pants frayed at the cuffs. Her ribs showed through the thin membrane of sickly skin on her chest. Pale blue shadows accentuated the protruding bones.

Jesse Bolton wore blue jeans and a gray t-shirt with a beer company's logo printed on the chest. He held a narrow, cheap rifle at his side.

"We found him that way!" Janis Bolton shrieked, suddenly, pointing a bony finger at Harper. "He was like that when we got here."

The grossly ridiculous claim would have been humorous if its subject hadn't been Dean's partner. He felt the urge to shoot the woman on the spot. Perhaps fortunately, his body was not his to control.

"Yeah," Jesse blurted. "Yeah, this isn't mine. It was here."

He threw the rifle on the floor, where it clacked on the rotted wooden planks.

"You lying sacks of shit," Harper said weakly from his place against the sofa.

Dean's arm lifted. He took a moment to aim down the barrel. Then, he pulled the trigger. The bullet hit Jesse Bolton in the chest and threw him back to the floor amid a spray of blood.

Janis Bolton screamed. She started a silly jig, stomping back and forth in frantic steps, bent low as if trying to hide behind currents of air until her gaze fell on the rifle. Dean watched as she lowered herself to snatch up the weapon. Once her hands were on it, his finger tightened. A bullet entered through Janis Bolton's left temple. Her head was cocked toward him so the bullet traveled through her jaw, sending a spray of teeth flying from her mouth. She crumpled to the side, arms splayed, landing on the corpse of her husband. Again, the rifle clattered on the floor.

Dean lowered his weapon and holstered it. He crossed to Harper and put a hand behind his partner's head.

"You okay?" he asked. "Hey, Reg, can you hear me?"

"I'm not deaf," Harper muttered. "Shoulder wound. Broken collarbone. Blood loss. Get something to apply pressure. Thank god the asshole only had a twenty-two."

Dean stood from his partner's side. Only then did he realize he was again controlling his actions.

The Violence had released him.

He took no time to entertain his relief. Instead he spun away, searching for a suitable bandage for his partner's wounds.

A boy stood in the home's entryway. His eyes were soft, filled with tears, but Dean could see the boy's struggle, and it sickened him.

Matthew Bolton fought to keep a smile from pushing up the corners of his mouth. His lips trembled with the effort. Soon enough, the boy gave up the fight, and Matthew grinned happily as tears streamed down his cheeks.

Dean walked into Harper's hospital room and presented him with a bag of barbecue flavored Ruffles potato chips. He sat in the gray chair beside the bed and looked at the floor. Two sleepless nights and days had passed. Moments of recent brutality mingled with incidents of long ago bloodshed to make a disconcerting loop in his mind, playing endlessly, showing him faces – familiar and strange – all in some pose drawn from the spectrum of anguish. The Violence had left him, but the visions it had brought remained, hardly discernible from Dean's own memories.

More disconcerting was the idea that this thing existed at all. It had violated him, used him. It called itself Violence, but what *was* it? This mystery haunted him. Naturally phases of disbelief punctuated his thoughts about the entity; it couldn't have been real. But Dean wiped away the skepticism whenever it arose; he wanted the thing to exist. He needed to believe in it.

"You're golden," Harper said, obviously trying to ease Dean's mind, though he was miles away from understanding the source of that unease. "As far as I'm concerned it was a clean shooting. I've already made my statement."

"Thanks," Dean replied.

Dean knew Harper was right. He didn't feel guilty for what had happened to those people. Though his finger had squeezed the trigger it was the Violence that had killed the Bolton's. Dean had merely been a witness as the creature used his body to fulfill a duty, to complete the shape of things.

"Weird about that Baker guy, though," Harper commented.

"You heard about that?"

"Dumb ass M.E. Sometimes I think he makes all this shit up as he goes."

Initially, Paul Baker's time of death was placed at sometime on the evening *before* Charles Clarke's murder. Naturally, when forensics confirmed Baker's ID as Clarke's killer, the medical examiner adjusted his original report, adding twenty-four hours to his estimate. But even with this modification Dean's accounting of events was fucked; it seemed he had left his partner alone with the Bolton's to go question a dead man.

Still, his superiors weren't making an issue of it. Harper had backed up Dean's statement every step of the way, going so far as to positively ID Baker as the man standing beside the house across the street from the Bolton's, when Dean knew damn well his partner hadn't even seen the guy. Grudgingly, the medical examiner was forced to change his report a second time.

"You need to snap out it," Harper said. "In a couple days you'll have your hearing. I was there. Matthew was there. Neither of us are going to change our stories. You'll be back at your desk by Friday."

Matthew, Dean thought. *Jesus, that kid was going to be a wreck.*

Maybe the Violence had intervened on behalf of the kid's soul, but the boy still had to live with what had happened to him, would always live with the fact his meth-head parents had rented him out to a diseased freak like Clarke for a few blasts of crystal. Matthew's smile returned to Dean, and he tried to push it out of his head. It too had haunted him these last two days.

The kid was now in the custody of social services. Dean didn't know if that was a good thing or not.

"I saw some weird shit that afternoon," Harper said, "but I also saw both Bolton's holding that rifle."

But Bolton dropped the gun before he was shot. Panic drove his wife to it. They didn't have to die.

"I will, of course, leave out all mention of hallucinations."

"Hallucinations?" Dean asked.

Harper smiled and shook his head. "Weirdest thing. Probably a result of trauma, but I could swear that someone was standing next to you when you fired on Bolton. I mean I couldn't see the guy's face or anything. It was like this blue-white smear. This shape. I thought I was seeing ghosts."

Dean's pulse quickened as the blood drained from his face. "You said you saw this thing *when* I shot Bolton?"

"Sure, I guess."

"Not *after*?"

"I don't know, Dean. Jesus, I wasn't exactly in the most focused of mental states at the time, what with the pain and the bleeding. I'm not even going to mention it at the hearing, so just relax."

"Was it before or after?" Dean insisted.

"What fucking difference does it make?"

All the difference in the world, Dean thought. The only thing that had made the last two days bearable was the idea that he hadn't been responsible for the Bolton's deaths. He hadn't followed procedure in the shooting, not even close. He'd walked into the house and gunned the couple down. Clean. Cold. *Unhampered by the viscous fluid of shifting moralities*. He'd believed the Violence was responsible, but now he couldn't be sure.

Had he used the entity as an excuse to execute that family because they disgusted him? Was he capable of that?

Harper wanted to know what difference it made. It was the difference between harboring a mystery and being one.

"Please," Dean said. "I have to know. Was it before or after?"

Tears to Rust

You never remember it right.

In the street below the market, Tom climbed out of the taxi. Before him, the shops, boutiques and restaurants were quieting for the night as patrons finished their meals or paid for last-minute purchases before returning home to escape the foul weather. Rain pelted in sheets over the twelve-story façade, and lights played against the mesh of the persistent downpour, encircling the great structure in a halo of static amber. Tom walked through the storm, drawn by the comforting glow.

In the window of the Kirkland Trattoria, a family of artificials – mother, father and two beautiful children – laughed, hugged and chatted over a platter of pasta. The mother of the faux family noticed him and waved.

Tom smiled as he often did when he saw a pleasant face and waved back. Then, he left the window and crossed the cement walk on the market's ground floor, moving away from the mechanical family and their never-ending platter of spaghetti Bolognese. He stepped into the elevator, punched the button, and the capsule car rose six flights and slid three retail blocks to the left. The door opened in front of Bellevue Menswear, and Tom stepped out to face his reflection playing on a fashion screen. The sign above the panel told him: *Fall Fashions Cry Elegance*. Amused to see himself on the full-length screen, Tom stood very still and watched his attire change.

A variety of outfits appeared to replace the rain-soaked sweater and jeans he wore. Casual, business and formal attire materialized over his reflection. When a black suit with narrow lapels appeared on his form, Tom turned to the side to get an impression of the fabric's drape. He turned to the other side and appreciated the way the suit fit over his heavy frame, but his attention was quickly drawn to a mark on the rise of his cheekbone, just below his eye. He stepped closer and found a small red cut nested in a purple blotch.

Tom traced the wound lightly; it hurt to the touch. But for the life of him, he couldn't remember when he had hurt himself.

He walked away from his confusing reflection and passed the entrance to the store. Farther down the walk he stopped at a vending machine that dispensed coffees, teas and soups. At the panel beside the beverage display, he punched in his selection so he could have something warm in his stomach, but the machine asked for his credit code or home phone number to make the charge.

Tom stared at the digital panel in confusion.

He couldn't remember the simple combination of digits. Frustrated, he felt along his pockets for the bulge of his wallet or the outline of a credit card, but found nothing. It was then, looking down at the legs of his wet trousers, watching his hands pat empty pockets that he noticed something odd: He had lost his shoes.

Now numbers, like his credit code or his phone number for that matter, came and went, and Tom accepted that as a residual effect of his accident; hell, he couldn't remember his address half of the time, but to lose his shoes and not remember doing so, now that was something uncommon.

Why would I take them off? he wondered. On the tail of this thought, a disturbing parade of words marched through his head:

... shoe fly by night, night honey comb your hair ...

These odd mental ramblings were another souvenir of his accident, and he found them far more disturbing than the scallops in his short-term memory. As a journalist, he needed clarity of thought, and though these spells were infrequent, they often had the ability to frighten him into a panic. Anxious and uncomfortable in his drenched clothes, Tom looked along the walk for his misplaced loafers but saw only rain-soaked concrete and the few remaining shoppers on level six, scurrying past the lighted window boxes of the retail establishments.

He walked back to the elevator platform and called the car. An alarm sounded overhead and Tom froze, thinking he had done something wrong, but the fault of the alarm was not his.

Before the window of a toyshop farther down the walk, a little girl hopped up and down, watching two small artificials playing with a laser plane under the bright lights of the display booth. Excited to share in the fun, the little girl slapped on the glass to get the attention of the mechanical boys inside.

The alarm peeled across the corridor of the Market, but the girl was not distracted. She eagerly danced and slapped at the glass, while her mother looked on in amusement.

Tourists, Tom thought. The mother should have known better...

... or worse case scenic drive by shooting fish in a barrel chested ...

Shoeless and without a phone number, Tom rode the elevator to the ground floor, searched the promenade for his lost shoes, then wandered into the shadows skirting the market. He stepped on a pebble and hopped a few steps, hoping he hadn't cut himself. At the street lamp on the corner, he stopped and observed the sole of his foot. No blood stained his socks, so he hadn't done any real damage.

He had to find a hospitality café. There was one just outside of the market. He could find his phone number there and his address, and while he couldn't find his shoes, at least he could call George to come pick him up so he could get home and take a nice hot shower. Once he made it to the cafe, all he had to do was remember his name, and nobody ever forgot their name.

His name was Tom... Tom...?

Tom *thumb tack toe truck*...

He tried to smile, but as he walked away from the market toward the café three blocks down, he felt the spell getting worse.

By the time Tom reached the hospitality café, he was a wreck. His drenched clothes weighed heavy on his shoulders and hips, and though the pain on his face and in his stomach had diminished, so had his memory.

He clung to his name. He repeated it in his head as he worked his way through the crowd, many of whom were watching the WWW Smack Down on the holo-field above the stage at the far end of the room. Angry-faced men circled one another. Sweat slathered their bodies. They mouthed violence. Tom had to look away, down at his wet, shoeless feet.

He found an empty terminal in the corner and sat down, his heart racing as if he had stepped off of a cliff and would at any moment collide with the rocks below. The patrons of the hospitality café mingled and chatted noisily behind him, occasionally bursting into cheers when one of the wrestlers performed a particularly flashy move or flew over their heads to vanish beyond the reach of the holo-field. The Celebri-servers carried trays loaded down with drinks and plates of food. Next to him, Katharine Hepburn flipped her hair and unloaded a plate of hotwings and a pitcher of beer for a table of four enthusiastic young men, and though the café thrived with energy, movement and sound, Tom felt alone, absolutely alone. He was a stranger, dropped into the middle of a ritual he didn't understand. Every noise and motion felt like threat.

George could help; he had to help.

Tom placed his hand in the identification mold to the right of the monitor; he spoke his name, and the screen filled. Following his identification statistics – brown hair (now mostly gray), blue eyes, six foot tall, two hundred-thirty pounds – he found historical data. August 1st was his birthday, but he'd known that. There was the year he graduated from high school, then college, and below that was the date of his marriage to a man named George Marshall.

"You want a toddy?" Kate Hepburn asked, her voice a stern vibrato in his ears.

"No thanks," he said. He returned his attention to the information that should have been so familiar, yet had somehow slipped away.

He squished his sock on the tile and again looked down at his shoeless feet.

Already senile, George always said, laughing at Tom. *Without me, you'd walk around the streets with your Yo-Yo hanging out.*

A shiver ran down Tom's spine, and he focused on the screen. Finally he found his phone number and touched it. The screen told him the number was dialing.

"Yes?" George answered.

"I'm sorry," Tom said. He didn't know why he was sorry, but he was, and he wanted nothing more than to be with George by the fireplace in their house, where he could warm his feet.

"So come home," George said.

"I don't know the way," Tom whispered in shame.

"That's right," George said. "You don't know anything without me, do you?"

Of course, his husband was right. Tom always had his spells when he left the house. Ever since the accident, his memory was a questionable companion at best. This time, he'd lost his wallet and his shoes. Who could say what he might lose the next time?

"George, please. Just come get me."

"Why should I let you come back?" George asked. "You'll just run off again."

"I won't," Tom said. "I love you."

"Well, I don't want you here," George said. "I'm busy."

Electric fingers wrapped around his heart and coaxed panic through his system. "Please," he whispered.

"Goodbye," George said. The screen flickered before being eaten by a field of blue.

Twenty minutes passed before George pulled up in front of the café and honked the horn. Tom, who stood by the door, knew the sound and spun quickly. He wiped panic-born tears from his cheeks and straightened his damp hair before racing through the glass doors and into the downpour.

His mind cleared quickly; the word parades halted; the forgotten digits of his phone number returned; and he felt that he'd come through the dark tunnel of his spell into the lights of George's car. He reached for the door handle of the Mercedes, and George gunned the engine, rolling the car several yards down the street. Tom rushed after the vehicle. Just as he was about to touch the handle again, George punched the gas.

"Knock it off," Tom called. "I'm sorry."

The next time he reached for the handle, the car waited. He hurried into the passenger seat and turned to find George scowling.

"This is the last time," George said. "Every time we have a disagreement you run off, and I won't have it. If you're going to desert me every time you don't get your way…"

"I won't," Tom said quickly.

"Shut your Goddamned mouth!" George roared. "I'm sick of hearing it. I'm not coming after you the next time. Do you understand that? Can your feeble mind get around that? You can't use your accident as an excuse for everything. The doctors say you're fine, so all of this drama is… where the hell are your Goddamned shoes?"

Tom looked down sheepishly. His moist socks, like a billboard for his idiocy, filled his eyes. He shrugged and waited for what would come next.

The fist caught him on the ear. The world blurred for a moment and a shrill humming, like the sound the vacuum made, filled Tom's head. His hand went to side of his head, a new wound to join the cut on his cheek.

Cradling his face, Tom remembered that George got angry sometimes. In fact, Tom remembered a lot of things now.

Tom woke and looked around the bedroom before climbing out of bed. In the bathroom he dragged a brush through his hair, carefully avoiding the tender spot over his left ear. A long cut from George's ring underlined his right eye; a bruise, like a small plum, stained the corner of his mouth. He ran his fingers over his chest and belly, combing through the thick hairs, checking to see if any other wounds marred his skin.

Tom pulled his robe from the back of the bathroom door and secured the belt around his waist. George's voice startled him when he opened the bedroom door.

"No, Goddamn it; this is not what I asked for...Yes the recall governor is working. That's not the point..."

Again knotted with tension, Tom quietly stepped across the black carpet, looking through the glass balcony at George who paced angrily in the room below.

"That's none of your fucking business," George yelled. "I'll do whatever the hell I please with it. I paid for the fucking thing." And with that, he threw the phone against the sofa cushion and stomped into the kitchen.

After downloading the newspaper in the den, Tom walked into the kitchen and poured himself a cup of coffee, which he carried to the far end of the chrome counter. George sat in the nook across the room, staring through the glass at the expanse of lawn behind their home. Outside, Napoleon and Naomi, George's prized Basset Hounds, lumbered after one another with flapping ears.

"Everything okay?" Tom asked.

"Martha's on the fritz," George said.

Tom nodded his head. He'd thought it was something like that. Martha, the domesticon that kept their house, was an old model that suffered from mild logic spasms. "Where is she?" Tom asked.

"In the shed," George said.

"Did she wander off again?" Tom asked.

"No," George told him, "that's your specialty."

The words cut sufficiently to silence Tom.

"If I weren't still paying off the bills from your accident, I could buy a new model and send Martha to the dump where she belongs."

Agitated, Tom turned his attention back to his coffee and considered the day ahead. He had an article to start on the Picasso exhibit at the Skyye Museum of Art and wanted to watch a special on the Cuban Renaissance, which was airing on PBS. The last thing he needed was another all-night brawl with his husband. He remained silent, sipping his coffee, glancing over the plastic reader and thinking about the museum before rising from the barstool.

Tom left the kitchen. In the shower he let the spray massage the tender spot over his ear and then rolled his shoulders and neck under the hot beads. He tried to convince himself that George was angry with Martha. After all, he had been yelling at the manufacturer on the phone, but as was always the case, Tom absorbed George's anger to fertilize his own anxiety.

Fortunately, Martha's recall governor was still working. Even if it hadn't been, she wouldn't have gotten far. Like all of the artificials, she was dependent on a localized power source, an electrical impulse device the manufacturers had whimsically marketed as "The Leash."

While drying his hair, he accidentally bumped the wound above his ear. Tom winced with pain and leaned on the sink to stare at his reflection in the mirror.

At least Martha had a good excuse for staying. After so many years, Tom wasn't sure what kept him from packing a case and going. And not just to the market for a few hours to clear his head, but really getting his ass off this carousel and onto something else.

They'd been married for twenty-two years, but to Tom it seemed like a handful of weeks, played over and over again. Fight and reconcile. Fight and reconcile. Round and round.

Flashes of memory climbed into his thoughts: George smiling and kissing him; George giving Tom a new virtual projector for their twentieth anniversary; George — fists raised, face red, eyes madly distant — screaming and backing Tom toward the balcony. The night of the accident that had scrambled his mind came back in a dull blur of motion, and Tom shook his head quickly to dislodge the gnawing images.

You never remember it right, he told himself. *You always think the worst. George would never do that. Never.*

Tom was taking a virtual tour of the museum when the doorbell rang. The sound surprised him. Usually they didn't get visitors, and Tom couldn't remember the last time a friend had stopped by. Most of his friends had not liked George, and Tom had seen them fall away over the years, leaving only a handful of buddies from school who lived in different parts of the world.

He closed out of the tour and hurried from his office. He said "good morning" to Martha, who was busy watering a fern in the living room and proceeded to the front door.

The delivery boy, a kid of about twenty with bad skin and oily hair, looked up at him, bored, and held out an envelope.

"You Gotham Randall?" the kid asked.

"Call me Tom," he replied with a smile.

"I don't have to call you shit," the kid said. "Just take the envelope and sign."

Tom did as he was told and managed to maintain his smile, despite the delivery boy's rudeness. He turned the envelope over and found that the package had been sent from the Yellow Cab Company.

After closing the door, Tom opened the envelope with a quick swipe of his fingernail. Inside he found a note and a credit card. He looked at the card, surprised to realize it was one of his.

Now, where the hell did I lose this?

The note read: *Thank you for patronizing YCC. We thought you might like this back. We have taken the liberty of charging a nominal fee to the card for delivery. Have a splendid day.*

Well that was nice of them, Tom thought. When he looked up from the note, he found Martha, looking worried and somewhat confused, at his side.

"I'm sorry, Mr. Tom," she said. "I was watering. I should have gotten the door."

"I don't mind. You have enough to do."

"It's my job," the housekeeper said, her voice cracking as if with impending tears.

She's just like a person, Tom thought. He wouldn't be surprised if she broke into tears right there and then, but of course, he *would* be surprised, because utility models didn't cry.

Whatever the case, she was obviously upset, and Tom didn't see any reason for it. "It's just fine, Martha."

"Mr. George is mad at me again."

"He's under a lot of pressure, right now."

"He won't erase me, will he?"

"Martha, George would never do that to you," he said, thinking on the peculiarity of the fear. "I wouldn't let him."

"I don't want to be a puppet, Mr. Tom. That's what happens if you get erased. They make you a puppet, and you have to perform at the Market. Don't let him do that to me, Mr. Tom. Don't let him erase me."

"I promise."

"Thank you, Mr. Tom."

"Are you okay now?"

Martha nodded and wiped at her cheeks as if she had been shedding tears. Tom patted the housekeeper on her shoulder, and gave her a comforting squeeze before turning away. He climbed the stairs to his office and dropped the note from the cab company in his waste chute.

Then, he walked to the closet, opened the door and slid the credit card under a low pile of boxes.

"Do you remember that night we were in Vancouver?" George asked.

They sat on the sofa, drinking wine. They'd made love on the floor, passionate and intimate, George whispering sweet words in Tom's ear. After, George ran upstairs for their robes and then into the kitchen to pour more wine. *Here, Baby*, he'd said, handing Tom the refilled glass.

Now, relaxed and exhausted they sprawled. Naomi the hound nestled in George's lap; her ears like soft wings spread over his thigh. Before them the fire worked through a stack of eco-logs. George absently stroked the dog's head, and Tom did the same thing to George, running his fingers through the thick gray strands.

George nudged Tom with his shoulder. "Vancouver? Eh? Hello? Anyone home?"

Tom smiled when he thought about Vancouver; it had been one of the few vacations they'd taken that hadn't ended in an argument. "I remember you dancing naked on the hotel balcony."

"You would," George said.

"Hey, you were the one who had to try love dolls," Tom reminded. "You bought the capsules from that guy in the bar because you thought we needed a little 'pick me up' in the bedroom."

"Well they picked me up," George said with a chuckle. He rolled his head over the back of the sofa and cast a warm look at Tom. "Why don't we fly back there? I've got some connections, and Diva is playing at the Dome. I'll get us some tickets, and maybe I'll even dance naked on the balcony again."

Tom rubbed the back of George's neck a little harder and nodded. "Just give me a couple of weeks to clear up these articles." He stared into the fire, watching the contained destruction as he might a hypnotist's watch.

The truth was, he didn't want to see Diva. As a kid, he had loved her music and had danced to her songs more times than he could count, but after she had been downloaded into an artificial form, he just didn't feel the same passion for her work. Most fans were satisfied to worship the handful of tech-enhanced stars, but Tom found their performances insincere and not particularly interesting.

More importantly, he didn't want to be trapped in a strange city with George. Not now. Not when his spells were so bad. If they had a fight, and that seemed a given these days despite these moments of caring, George could desert him and leave Tom wandering for hours, for days or forever.

He pulled away from George and patted Naomi on the rump before nestling into the crook of the sofa arm.

The artist's fascination with an array of mythological abductions and rapes position the male figure – often a centaur or minotaur – as a symbol of dominance, leaving the female subjects to act as receptive, sometimes grateful...

Tom had been working on the Picasso article for nearly a week. That afternoon, only two hours into his work session, the words started slipping away from him. Naomi's tail swept the carpet rapidly, and she whined for attention. Her excitable presence usually didn't bother Tom, but now that the words were harder to hold on to, he put the dog in the hall and closed the door so he could concentrate on the article.

...female subjects to act as receptive, sometimes grateful...

Panic settled on him like a fever.

...as receptive, sometimes grateful dead head strong as an ox bow incidentally...

Tom quit the article and walked downstairs to get some coffee, hoping the caffeine would help his ailing synapses. When he returned to the desk, he stared at the words he had already written on the computer screen, and they made no sense to him. He sipped the coffee, put his head down on the desk, closed his eyes and fell into a deep sleep.

The front door slammed; the crash woke him. George was home.

Tom sat up and looked at the jumble of words he had written in his attempt to capture meaning in the exhibit of Picasso's erotic art. He erased the last line and pushed away from the desk.

Tom went to the door of his office and turned the lock on the knob before returning to the desk. Things had been so good over the last few days. They hadn't had a fight in over a week, not since the night he had run off to the Market, and Tom saw no need to tempt the fates. He'd stay behind the closed door, pretending to work, and maybe George's mood would improve with a cocktail and a pill.

Maybe.

Two anxious minutes passed before George started beating on the office door. "Hey!" he called. "Open the fucking door."

"I'm working," Tom said.

"*I'm working,*" George mocked. "I didn't *ask* what you were doing; I *said*, open the fucking door."

"Just a minute," Tom said, unable to move from the desk. Shaking hands clutched the metal frame. Memories roared behind his eyes, and he felt himself near the point of tears. In each recollection, a virulent argument battered him. George's words and fists took turns bashing Tom.

"You've got one second to open the Goddamned door," George bellowed.

He stood. Resignation drove him forward, and he opened the door to George's scowling face. His husband's eyes were veined red and slightly swollen – a bad day at the office. George rested his forearms on either side of the jamb, blocking Tom from the hall.

The scene was so familiar that Tom leaned on the doorjamb, trapped and sickened, drained of energy.

Amid George's bellowed complaint, a different memory, one that had eluded Tom for far too long, for years – the years since his accident – tore through Tom's system to settle like frost in his mind.

Something about the balcony. Something about George's angry face.

The sight of his husband, so near the office door, so near the glass balcony...

"You can't even meet me at the fucking door. Would it kill you to fix me...

They were fighting outside of Tom's office on the second floor of the house. Then, George's hands were at his chest, shoving, hurting. The world, and George at its center, spun out of control. Glass shattered and the dislocating rush of descent froze his heart. Tom lay on his back on the tiles, unable to breathe, motionless, staring twenty feet up at the balcony, where George looked down at him, his face suddenly stained with fear.

The memory, like a shudder, raced through him in less than a second. When it passed, George had not ceased his complaint:

"...a drink and maybe pretend that you gave a shit about me?"

He still saw the angry mask looking down on him. For a moment, it was three years ago; he was lying injured on the tiles in the foyer amid a spray of glass, staring up at George who babbled in terror before screaming for help.

You never remember it right, Tom told himself. *You always think the worst. George would never do that. Never.*

But like a warm breath on cold glass, an apparition of the past remained behind his eyes. George. The balcony. Falling. Broken.

Tears to Rust

George left the dinner table, announcing his meal's completion by throwing his napkin in the center of the plate. Tom hated it when he did that. It stained the cloth but he knew better than to say anything. George had taken one of his sedatives just before dinner, and it seemed to be working, but Tom knew it took very little to cancel the calming effect of the pills.

Once George left the room, Tom stood and went back to his office. He closed the door.

The early evening argument had not grown to violence but it had come far too close, and the memory of his accident played over in his mind like a commercial for a movie, looped endlessly in his mind. George screaming. Then, hands on his chest, a cruel push and glass shattering as Tom escorted the cascading shards to the tiles below.

Tom needed to walk, to get some air, to get out of the house. He threw on his jacket before searching for his wallet. Normally, he left it in his office, on the desk next to his computer screen, but once again he had misplaced it, or...

George hid it, a small voice told him. It had happened before, a hundred times. Without identification or credit, Tom was trapped in the house, a fish in a barrel, easily shot.

He went to the closet and removed a stack of boxes. Underneath the third box, he retrieved the credit card and slid it into his shoe. At the desk, he wrote his phone number on the back of his hand. Then, Tom bolstered himself for the trip downstairs. He found George lounging in the den.

Cautiously, Tom asked, "Have you seen my wallet?"

George sat on the sofa with Naomi nestled in his lap. He stroked the hound's neck and stared into the fire. "No. You lose it again?"

"I guess."

"Well you don't need it right now anyway," George told him.

"I was going to go out," Tom said evenly.

"Maybe later," George said. "I bought a few love dolls this afternoon, and I wanted to have some fun."

"Not tonight," Tom said.

A lightning bolt of anger flashed over George's face. The thunder rolled from his mouth. "Yes. Tonight."

Naomi leapt from the warm lap and raced with clicking toenails into the kitchen to avoid her rapidly rising master.

Tom winced and backed up a step. "George, calm down. I just need to get some air."

"Why is it always about what *you* want? We're going to do what I want."

"No," Tom said in a tiny voice.

George crossed the room in three quick strides. His pretense of bravery challenged, Tom shrank at the man's approach. He backed to the wall and held out his hands, but George slapped them away.

"Stop it," Tom barked. Loud. Angry. "Knock this shit off."

"Why don't I just knock your head off? It's certainly not doing you any good."

"And whose fault is that?" Tom asked. "Who threw me off the fucking balcony?"

The parade of emotions crossing George's face went from humor, through confusion and on into a very dark quarter of rage. "You never remember it right. You always think the worst. I would never do that. Never."

"But you did. You shoved me through the glass and watched me fall. You could have killed me, but no, lucky me, I survived so I could come back to you and start the ride all over again. As it is, my head's a mess. I can't even think anymore. Do you know what that's like? Do you know how it feels to forget your own fucking phone number?"

George shook his head like a dog with a tic in its ear. "You are not going to pin your stupidity on me. The doctors said you were fine."

"Well they're wrong."

"If you'd stay home where you're supposed to be, your memory would be fine."

"Bullshit," Tom said. "I couldn't put a sentence together this afternoon. I just looked at the page and all I saw were a bunch of meaningless letters."

"I had a meeting," George told him. "I went a little further out of town than usual."

"What in the hell does that have to do with anything?"

"You were out of range, that's all."

The odd terminology tangled in Tom's head, a rope puzzle that he lacked the dexterity to solve. Out of range? Of what? Had George actually deluded himself to the point that he believed Tom was incapable of a life without his proximate influence?

George began to play with the band of his watch. Finally, he got the clasp open, and he pulled the instrument from his wrist. "You know what this is, right?" he asked, dangling the watch between them.

"I'm not that stupid," Tom said, exhausted by the rapidly changing direction of the conversation. "I'm getting out of here."

George grabbed Tom by the lapels of his jacket and pulled him close. "You walk out that door, and you can forget everything. I took you out of the system, sweetheart. Erased. You leave and you've got no way back. And I promise you," George said, "if you walk out that door, I'm smashing your leash." He backed up two steps and set his watch on the table. "It's right here buddy. You walk. I smash the fucker to bits. No more signal. No more Tom. You can just haul your ass back to the Market, and suck up some residual juice from the transmitter until they use your useless ass for a window display."

Tom shook his head slowly. "You're sick."

"Am I?" George spat. "I felt guilty for your accident. Fine, you pissed me off, and maybe I overreacted. I was upset. I admit, it was partially my fault, but I saved your life, and I spent a fucking fortune doing it. But do you appreciate that?"

Tom turned to leave.

But George wasn't finished with him yet. "I should have let you die," George said. "I should have turned off the respirator and buried your ass, but no, I thought a download would give us a second chance. I thought we might finally be happy, but you keep running. Nothing I ever do is good enough for you. It never was."

Tom opened the door and stepped into the night.

"You'll never find your way back," George roared. "I'm not coming to get you this time."

Tom closed the door.

Round and round.

At the Market, the cab pulled to the far side of the street and sat idling as Tom searched for his wallet. Where the hell had he put it? He checked his pants and his jacket. Had George hidden his wallet again? Probably. That's why he kept a spare card...

Tom remembered the card in his shoe.

He removed his right shoe and tipped it up but the credit card was not inside. He set the shoe next to him on the seat and reached for the left one.

There was the card.

He handed it over the seat to the driver and felt the pull of the Market.

Confused and eager to be near the shops, Tom left the cab carrying one of his shoes at his side. The driver called after him, something about a card, but he kept walking toward the warm glow of the building.

His mind began to clear as he stepped into the light cast from the hundreds of windows of the Market. Happy artificials performed behind glass panels, selling products and services to the late-evening shoppers. A non-specific anxiety rode on his shoulders, a heavy shawl, the fabric of which, he couldn't identify.

Something about a fight.

Then, a tickle rose up the back of his neck; it quickly turned to a lightning bolt and beneath the falling light of the market, Tom felt his mind jolt, stutter and begin to slip away.

He looked at the shoe in his hand and dropped it on the promenade. Forgot about it a second later.

Where was he? Where was George?

He needed to find the café.

"Gotham Randall."

The screen in the hospitality café remained blank. Where was his picture? He looked over his shoulder at the mob of patrons, and the waitress noticed him. He'd lost his phone number and his shoes, and now he couldn't find his profile on the system. Something wasn't right. "It's broken," Tom said, pointing at the screen.

Kate Hepburn looked at him and turned her head to the side, just like Naomi did when she … well when she …

Naomi?

"It's broken," Tom repeated, his finger still jabbed at the screen.

"I'll..." Kate began and then paused. She scanned the café suspiciously and then came around the counter to kneel beside Tom. "You been erased?"

"What do you mean?" Tom asked. "It's broken."

"What's your name, kiddo?"

"It's...It's Tom..."

"Tom what?"

"Tom... Tomorrow..." But that wasn't right. That wasn't his name. His name was Tom *Thumb Tack Toe Truck Tires*. He leapt to his feet and spun quickly. Where was he? Where was George? He needed George. Ever since the accident...

"You've been erased," Kate said miserably. "God, that's a tough break."

"What?"

"Your leash. They shut it down. Took you out of the system. Tough, tough break."

Tough break dance on air conditioning cream rinse cycle cell anemia. Where was George, Tom thought. Oh God *deity father son holy ghost story time to go to bed.* Where was he? He couldn't think. He didn't want to be alone. He didn't want to be...

I'm sorry, he thought. Please come get me. I'm sorry *wrong number one son also rises like the phoenix arizona iced tea leaves falling down to the sea with shipping included for a limited time only one per customer is always right where you want to be all you can be...*

or not to be...

That is the question.

In one hand, he held a long forked utensil, which he jabbed into a well-cooked steak. His other arm looped over the shoulder of a pretty woman, who tickled his ribs and waved away the grill's smoke, so that it could be drawn up into the vent in the display case's ceiling. Under their feet, shiny green blades of plastic grass carpeted the booth.

Poke the steak with the fork, he thought. Turn it over.

He looked through the glass and saw an old man standing in the rain under the black dome of an umbrella. The man looked sad, his face a crumpled sheet of aging skin; he looked at his watch and then back.

Tom waved as his program dictated and smiled as he often did when he saw a pleasant face.

The Tattered Boy

We learn from failure and not success.

I've offered those sage words more times than can be counted on the scarred fingers of a legion. I always believed it to be a brave statement, an optimistic tonic for the disease of fear, with which all men are chronically afflicted. Like the rough handle of the axe, failure is the wounding that summons the ameliorating callus, and this callus reminds us of and protects us from insidious and redundant missteps. Perhaps lust is the exception proving my rule, or perhaps I am simply weak; few would doubt – particularly those of God's church – that I am of sin.

But speculating on the path of my soul illuminates nothing, as all that is to come is blackness, blinding and cold. Only in the examination of my skin and bone and damnable heart, can any light be found, and in using the word "light" I define this not by an airy, gay pleasantry, but rather a stark bath in keeping with the harsh cast of the surgeon's lamp, which is to say that much can be revealed, but for most, the grotesquerie cannot be borne.

The boy entered my life as I strolled through the walled city of Maastricht. I was in my forty-first year and had brought my wife and child to summer in the stone house that had once served as home to a favored uncle, but which I now used for reflection, study, the writing of books and to some smaller degree, respite from my heart's home, Amsterdam.

To compare these cities is to compare shades of blue, for both are beautiful, warm of heart and exciting to the intellect. A framed map of Amsterdam, drawn by the skilled mapmaker Johann Murray hangs on the wall of my study. My first impression upon seeing this artful rendering was that the outline of Amsterdam looked much like a bat, striking prey. Maastricht, to compare, more resembles a butterfly, with grand, blunt wings spreading out from the river Maas, as if taking fresh flight. Walls had been built over the centuries to protect this fragile butterfly-city, shielding her from the shifting aggressions and authorities of the ever-changing European theatre.

Within these walls I strolled, enjoying a morning of crisp sun-brightened atmosphere as I passed the brick and whitewashed homes and shops, making my way to the grand gate, the Helpoort. Though many of the residences remained shuttered, the streets were busy as merchants prepared for the day, stacking loaves in fabric-draped windows and putting flame to wick so that their lamps burned in greeting.

As I approached the Helpoort, I paused to admire the fortress of stone that protected this small kingdom. The Helpoort gate, with its high arc and a depth of fifteen men, stands as one of the earliest city walls. For centuries it stood in wait and service, only relinquishing its guardianship when the Nieuwstad, was itself walled in, sometime at the birth of the 16th century.

And there he stood, this tattered boy, his face pressed to the mortared stones, his black hair ragged and slicing the plane of his neck into a jagged ridge. From his clothing, I assumed him to be an apprentice, perhaps to one of the many potters or bead makers in the city, but as I approached this odd young man, I saw the looseness of his shirt's weave, worn holes and stains, which led me to believe he had no vocational standing in the least. The boy mumbled into the stones at his face, a prayer or jest I could not discern. A breath of wind rustled the serration of hair at his nape, and he craned his neck in its direction, at which time he noted my presence at his back.

Upon turning his full face to me, I discovered that while young and slight, he was not truly a boy. Though youthful, he was surely of University age, or nearly so. His eyes were of a unique blue, not quite sky but shimmering and rich like the surface of the river Maas. His face, spotted with smudges and (I saw with some distress) streaked by tears, was of cream and ivory.

This was not the type of face that I had grown accustomed to as a professor; my students wore a variety of masks, painted by the confidence of their social positions, their fathers' wealth and experiences, though limited, with matters of the world. No. This striking face was free of guile, and I felt an instant paternity with its wearer. Seeking to ingratiate myself with a lightness of word, I asked, "And what does the gate tell you?"

I nodded my head toward the chipped surface of the Helpoort to indicate my meaning, and he looked at me then as if I wore a bonnet of tulips on my head. Certainly, he was unaccustomed to answering the rhetorical questionings of strangers. His river-rich eyes turned hard and judging-cold, and then broke and thawed.

No two men could have looked more opposite then, I'm certain. Me in my proper jacket and pressed trousers, and he attired in little more than rags; I, wearing a wave of wisdom-bleached hair, while he remained coiffed in the deep hues of youth. I assured and content. He stricken and weighted.

"A gate is the most wonderful part of a wall," I told him. "Stone is unmoving and segregates without bias, while a gate can be locked or opened, depending on the needs of its keeper."

"Locked is safer," he told me.

"Indeed and without question. Perhaps you'll tell me what it is that you have locked out?"

"Who are you, sir?"

"Willem."

"And where do these questions take us, Willem?"

"As with all questions," I said, "they take us forward."

"And if I choose to go backward?"

"If any of us had that magic, God would certainly shrug his shoulders and depart."

"I think, Sir, he already has."

Confounded by what I took to be no more than an innocent blasphemy, I found myself drawn deeper in my interest of this tattered boy. His proposition that perhaps God had left us behind intrigued me, as it suggested a clinical mind and not one wholly reliant on the rigid foundation of religion, further appealing to my sense that all can be questioned and little should be taken at its face.

I asked if he would join me, and we walked then, to the banks of the Maas, where we continued discussions and watched the current run from past to future. He told me that his name was Bastiaan, and in the course of our conversation he described the particular pain that drove him to the gate where we met.

Bastiaan's beloved sister had taken ill, acutely so. In the last week, she had not left her bed and seemed to wither before his eyes. They were alone in the world, their parents and a younger sister dead from the flu – victims of the epidemic that had swept Maastricht five years before. As a student of disease, I pushed for details of her decline, but Bastiaan told me little beyond his sister's shortness of breath, a general lethargy and lack of appetite, resulting in a rapid wasting.

Naturally, I offered my services to the boy; I would gladly visit his sister and render a diagnosis, but he declined my offer vehemently. Though I pressed and assured him of my expertise in such matters, going so far as to make list of my many studies, he remained resolute in his refusal.

"She's beyond nature, now."

"Nothing is beyond nature," I told him.

"I should go," he said, abrupt and anxious. "Adda will be waking soon."

"Then I propose we meet again. Tomorrow at the gate?"

"No," he mumbled. "Too many have already been stained."

Such a curious word that was to use. *Stained*. I questioned it.

"The actions of a child's weakness and stupidity," he told me. "Unspeakable."

Sensing that I might never understand the mystery of this boy and might indeed be denied the company of one with whom I had made such quick kinship, I said, "I'll be at the gate tomorrow. You come see me if I can help."

But he didn't seem to consider this possibility. He repeated his concern that "Adda will be waking," and hurried up the slope to vanish beyond its ridge.

I returned home in time for lunch with my wife and Wouten, our twelve-year-old son. The sight of him warmed me, as it always did. Annetje doted on the boy; her motherly concerns fierce and consuming. I'm sure that all parents feel that their children are fragile, fine pieces of blown crystal, irreplaceable and delicate, but Annetje, perhaps more than others, felt the particular burden of possessing such a treasure.

Together, we had conceived four children that never saw birth: all taken by God or nature. Wouten succeeded where his siblings failed in the simple act of coming into existence, and Annetje pained herself with his every movement.

Candles lit the table and a fire roared on the hearth. Annetje fussed and served, while Wouten bounced in his chair like an anxious babe, but my mind was with the solemn young man, who seemed convinced that God had forsaken his family in punishment for some undisclosed misdeed.

"Stew. Stew. Stew," Wouten exclaimed when a bowl of that very dish was placed before him.

I smiled at the boy, wishing he could have become more, but loving the presence of him. It is my supposition that Wouten suffered from a trauma while in the womb, something that occupied or damaged his mind and kept his focus on things, not around him, but within. Few distractions of the world bore the power to draw him out, and of those, only the simplest – a rainbow, a sweating icicle, a stew – were cause to rejoice.

"And how was your walk?" Annetje asked, finally taking her own chair after serving her family. At her elbow, Wouten slurped loudly, devouring his lunch.

I looked at his round, simple face, and a terrible thought occurred to me: what if Bastiaan was our son and Wouten had emerged into that other family? What would it have been like to have a handsome, strong and intelligent boy, who might come to facilitate tremendous events sitting at my table, instead of a boy whose body would grow into manhood while his mind had brimmed to full at the age of five?

"Willem?"

"Exhilarating," I told her. "I should think tomorrow, I'll have another."

"And what about your book?"

"Stew," Wouten shouted, spraying a good amount of broth and bits of carrot to the table. Annetje leaned across the table and dabbed at his mouth and chin with her napkin.

"The book is much like a stalk of corn," I said in answer to her question. "It needs nourishment and light, and though you watch it, and think it does not grow, it does indeed rise and spread with every passing moment, though imperceptible in its maturation. Yes?"

Annetje smiled and nodded her head at me as she often did when I spoke to the nature of a thing. Next to her, Wouten coughed, giggled and then spit up a barely chewed wad of lamb, which hit the table like a dead bird.

———

I returned to the Helpoort the following morning, earlier than I had that first day. At the wall, I waited and recalled the various ailments I had researched the night before and their respective symptomologies so that if Bastiaan returned, as I so hoped he would, we might find solution to his sister's degenerative condition. After an hour at the gate, however, I told myself that it was time to abandon this folly. Bastiaan would not return.

And, so convinced, I stood from the rock on which I sat and straightened my coat. My legs had taken me no farther than five steps when I heard my name called from a great distance. There, behind me far outside the city gate, Bastiaan raced; his weathered shirt whipped behind him as he made haste toward the shadowed arch, separating Maastricht from the greater world.

"She's so sick," he said upon reaching me, his breath coming in harsh gasps. His hand went to my shoulder for support as he doubled at the middle, clutching his stomach. "Adda... She can't breathe... She's... You understand medicine and science... Please."

"Of course."

He led me through the Helpoort and along the river to the south. Bastiaan said little as we left behind the neatly packed city, trading it for the tall grasses and marshes of the farmsteads. He looked very young to me then, truly a boy who was frightened and alone. Again paternal notions unfurled in my mind and heart, like the wings of a guardian hawk, and I urged to wrap my arms around this boy but understood the impropriety of such action. Instead, I made attempt at words of comfort and strength, but they did little to assuage his overwhelming despair.

After much walking, we paused near a squat, stone shed. The exterior walls wore bands of mud to insulate from the wind, and lichens, bright green and white, peered through the unwholesome coat. Beyond this small shed, I looked for a house of some sort, but saw only long fields of waist-high grasses and weeds. At the horizon, clouds foamed like frozen surf, and I knew that if we didn't get to Bastiaan's home soon, we would lose considerable light.

But of course, we were already at Bastiaan's home. The dismal stone shelter, hardly acceptable for the keeping of livestock, served as manor to the tattered boy and his ailing sister.

At the door to the hut, I grew cold. Something awful, trapped in the stone walls, exhaled and covered me in foul breath.

Long I had read of the existence of evil, but never had I actually believed it to be a tangible entity, and yet there on the threshold of that unwelcoming hovel, I became certain that evil was as real as the sky, the air. Even if I could not touch it, evil did exist; its breath was covering my face and neck and burrowing into my skin to take root on my bones like the lichens feeding on the house's foundation.

Bastiaan felt my disquiet but it did not stop him from opening the door.

Evil exhaled again, and I took a step back, away from the viscous, pungent atmosphere that emerged from the opening. My skin by this time was ice cold, and I trembled.

Even from the threshold, I saw that Bastiaan's beloved Adda was taken on to her Lord. Her skin was so white it seemed to glow in the shadowed recess; eyes stared at me without fear or gratitude; her arm draped over the side of the small cot on which she lay; her primary finger pointed at the corner of the room as if trying to send attention away from her tragic state.

Next to me Bastiaan gasped and turned from the door. Sobbing, he stumbled into the grass at the side of the shelter and collapsed to his knees. I went inside to the cot and grasped Adda's hand, which met my skin like an icicle. Touching her then, kneeling on the stone floor, I felt a presence in the gloomy chamber, as if her soul had not quite moved on. I felt her gaze on me, or more accurately, I felt *her* on me, since the observation I sensed came from the shadowed air and not the flat, faded lenses of her eyes. Of the dozens, perhaps hundreds, of corpses that had greeted me over the years, Adda's was the first to alight me with fear. She showed no overt signs of disease, no lesions or blisters to indicate advanced fevers or pox. If anything she appeared remarkably lovely and content in her quietus, and this fact, if no other, chilled me.

Upon finishing my examination of Adda, I went to Bastiaan. He clutched at me as if drowning, throwing his arms over my shoulders and burying his head in my chest where he sobbed violently for several minutes. I accepted his grief and harbored some pride in knowing that I might still tend on him, if not with a physicians' skills, then simply with my presence. He mumbled incoherent passages into my shirt, again making reference to a stain he had brought to his family, stating that Adda's was only the most recent life it had ruined.

I did not question him then. Instead, I lent him my support and sincere regret. After a time, we sat on the ground and watched the clouds approach. I invited him to come stay at my home for any length of time he wished, but he declined, again declaring himself guilty and in some way deviant.

The severity of Bastiaan's emotion faded with the morning, and his thoughts moved to more practical matters.

"She'll need burying," he said with a dry, spent voice.

"I can summon the church, if you like."

Bastiaan shook his head. "God won't have her now."

"That is a matter for God to decide. Her soul deserves prayer."

"She is unholy," Bastiaan told me, and he uttered a word I hadn't heard in years, not since my University days. "*Uitzuiger.*"

I must admit that I laughed then. I meant no disrespect to Bastiaan or the memory of his sister, but to hear that antiquated term of folklore and fairy tale spoken aloud broke apart my solemn considerations.

"Have you no respect, Willem?"

"Do you think that I am not sad, though I laugh?" I asked.

"You're mocking me."

"Bastiaan, I assure you, I'm not. But why this belief in monstrous mythology?"

"I saw it," Bastiaan said. "I saw the thing come for her at night, but I couldn't stop it."

"You're distraught."

"It came through the fields on the backs of rats," Bastiaan whispered. "It rose from their matted hides in a blood-tinged cloud and poured into the room. I'd try to stop it, but I couldn't move. When it stepped out of the shadows, it was a woman, all black and white, except for her horrible burning eyes. Every night, I'd tremble and scream, but my legs and my arms wouldn't move. She made me watch it. She made me watch it all."

"You must come with me," I told him. "You're overwrought, and it plays with your memory. We'll speak with the ministers and have the groundskeeper come out to collect Adda, but for now you need to be away from here. You'll come to my home… "

And with that suggestion, Bastiaan leapt to his feet like the ground beneath him had suddenly grown hot. "You have to leave here."

I stood then and approached the tattered boy. Again, I wrapped my arms around him in a gesture of comfort and though he tried to shake off the embrace, I continued to hold him until he calmed.

Eventually he accepted my wisdom and agreed to allow his sister a proper burial. I made the arrangements with the church and gave them more than enough money for her care. Bastiaan would take no money from me directly, so I paid for tea, bread, meats and cheeses at the market in Maastricht and left instructions to have the foods delivered to Bastiaan's modest home.

He refused my invitation of hospitality outright, however. He would not even entertain the possibility of visiting, let alone staying in my home.

Though I could not know it, Bastiaan's refusal of my roof and hearth would one day change, and everything I had thought as solid as the walls of the Helpoort changed with it.

As I had promised Annetje, I spent my afternoons in the study working on my book, or at least occupying time at my desk. Occasionally I observed the map of Amsterdam, framed on my wall. I still found Johann Murray's map to be of exceptional rendering, but more and more, I was stricken by the unwholesome resemblance this chart of my heart's home had to a feeding bat. On those afternoons, I considered Bastiaan's claim of *uitzuiger* and recalled bits and pieces of the stories told me at University, stories that made mention of vermin and magic and blood. In the evenings when light waned, I joined my family for supper. Annetje questioned me on the book's progress, spoke eagerly of our impending return to Amsterdam, and related the stories she had heard in town while shopping. I listened, or perhaps it is better to say that I heard her words so that I knew where to reply and when to make the proper gesture with my head. Through these meals, Wouten splashed gravies and sauces with his spoon, giggled and every now and again, interrupted his mother with an excited noun that seemed important in his world, but held no great bearing on our own.

More and more, I looked forward to morning, when my strolls took me through the Helpoort and into the marsh and grasslands to the south. Though solemn, Bastiaan greeted and welcomed me to his stone hovel with an embrace and an offer of tea from the supply I had paid the market to deliver. We sat inside, on the cot where I first met his sister, now covered in clean linen, another gift, and crowned by a down pillow. The exhilaration of being in this place with him brought back sensations of youth and vitality, feelings that I once cultivated from the eager faces of my students before the soil of that field was over sown and sapped of nutrient. Here the ground for such emotional and intellectual fruit was fertile and nourished further by the crudeness of setting.

"I envy your fortunes," Bastiaan said on the fourth day as he held a stein of tea and gazed through the open door of the shack. "Your family and students. My past and future are this cell of rocks and a field of weeds."

Can I tell you now that Bastiaan's complaint wounded me? Though why, I could not be certain. I thought much of this young man, and believed he felt the same of me. Though our time together had been brief, our words were often intimate and caring, and yet, there I sat on his cot, feeling the warmth of him at my side with his declaration of emptiness contesting all that I supposed.

More than ever, I felt a need to express the kinship I felt for him, if only to assure us both that my presence was valuable.

"The future is a black place," I said. "It is lit only as we approach it, never knowing what our candle's flame will reveal until our next steps bring it within the viewing cast. Do you think that I cannot help you? Do you think my coming here is a whim, a curiosity?"

"It is the action of a kind gentleman, but it stretches no further than these walls. Soon, you will return to Amsterdam, to your hospital and your students. For me, there is rock, weed and crosses in a cemetery to visit and mourn."

I reached out and took his hand in mine, patting it as if obliging a patient with comfort, only sensing far more in myself than obligation. "You'll take my house in town when I leave. You'll make it your home and be so comfortable there that before I return with my family, we will be your guests, and then in time, we will be your family."

Bastiaan's hand went rigid in mine, and in his eyes, I saw a concoction of gratitude and defiance, boiling like a potion. He wanted to accept my offer, for surely it presented him with a far more satisfying future than any he had yet imagined, but something within him struggled to deny this offered happiness.

Sensing his refusal, I took a different tack. "Perhaps you would consider Amsterdam. I could assist in your studies. A lady friend of mine has rooms for let very near the hospital, and I could tutor you mornings until you're prepared for University."

"You're being cruel, Willem."

"Only if you think me disingenuous."

The Tattered Boy

I was resolute in my determination to free Bastiaan of his cell and his field of dead grasses, but this boy, this tattered child, had known little sympathy and less generosity in his life, so who could find blame in his doubts of me? "You'll think about it," I said. "You'll find an answer for me in your own time."

He startled me then with an act of intimacy. Looking back, I see that it was this act, or a sin of similar composition that had stained Bastiaan in God's eyes, and in gratitude, ignorant and damnable gratitude, he drew close to me for its sharing.

His face filled my eyes, and then his lips were on mine in the way that only Annetje lips had ever been on mine. My body pulsed as if nothing but heartbeat, except this thunder paled the organ behind my ribs as a cannon pales a rifle shot. The taste of him on me, and the roar of my heart's quickened efforts, were, for a moment, the stuff of wizard's work.

But soon I considered the open door of Bastiaan's home, and I imagined, with more than minute clarity, a passerby witnessing this uncommon embrace. Fortunately, it was as these thoughts took on the distress of panicked phobia that Bastiaan released me.

He gazed on me with worried eyes, but any legible response was absent from my face, just as it was most assuredly absent from my mind.

"Thank you," I said.

Still cautious, he reached out his palm and touched my cheek, and I let the touch rest there, but this gesture of acceptance was as much a lie as it was truth. Beneath his touch, I wrapped myself in logic's armor for the sake of my soul, but its thick plating was brittle and could not long repel. My body and blood wanted nothing but for more. I was in a moment of such profound intimacy, his taste lingering and sweet with promise, that logic seemed a scratchy, burdensome attire to be removed and cast aside without regard for my soul's protection.

The discord of thought and of blood deconstructed me. His face drew me. His intent repelled. Of all I wanted I could have, said his river-rich eyes, but whether this was a gift or a snare, I could not determine.

I removed his hand with mine and held it for a moment.

Now, it was I that played the lost child. Though aware of all that I felt, I was in no way able to identify these feelings. With distance I might better categorize the specifics of this oh-so unfamiliar land's topography. So, I said my goodbye with a promise to return.

I have damned myself every day since for keeping that promise.

The tangle of thoughts that knotted my mind as I returned to the gate of my butterfly-city was perhaps the greatest I ever endured. I thought of sociology and science and poetry and theology, and none of these disciplines provided a clear and concise philosophy to which I could attach my emotions. I imagine that is the very nature of emotions; though they can be examined, dissected and studied, it remains my belief that they exist as a pathology that defies understanding.

Once back within the walls of Maastricht, I felt compelled to buy a box of chocolates for Annetje and a sweet candy for Wouten, both of whom accepted these gifts with bright glee and much fanfare. I spent the rest of that afternoon entertaining Wouten, who slurped at his candy with slobbering tongue and lips and complete joy on his face, while I read to him from the stories of Hans Christian Andersen, a man I had met some years before and who had graciously sent me a bound volume of his works. Wouten paid me little mind, though I imagine he took great pleasure in the sound of my voice. After supper, once Wouten had been put to bed, I sat before the fire with Annetje. I held her hand and threw my tangle of mental knots at the flames, hoping to burn them away and leave me with some little comfort.

This was not to be.

Science teaches us to explore, while religion teaches us to accept boundary. If these two disciplines can find a balance, it must certainly be in the heart of a stronger man. For me, they war.

The next morning, instead of passing through the Helpoort and wandering across fields to Bastiaan's home, I remained in my study and buried my face in books, taking notes and thinking of many things in an attempt to rid my thoughts of the tattered boy who had granted me some dreadful wish, and in so doing condemned me to tortured dissonance. But the great thoughts of greater men proved insubstantial distractions, easily torn away by gusts of embattled logic. For every argument I made on my soul's behalf, another argued for the nourishment of my flesh.

The Tattered Boy

    Disturbed, I remained in my study through supper and late into the night. The following day, the same.

    But after so much time of consideration and exploration, I found myself no more learned, no less confused. All I knew with any certainty was that I had to see the tattered boy. Perhaps in so doing, I would find revelation.

    The so common rain of this region was falling that morning in a light mist from rot-black clouds, which suppurated above in promise of greater, perhaps even torrential, downpour. I rose and left the house before Annetje or Wouten woke and paused many times along the city streets, standing for an inordinate time under the arc of the Helpoort, fancying that a step through the stone arch would remove me, wholly and forever, from the familiar resonance of family and self. In fact, my first step into the diseased light on the far end of the arch brought a bolt of shudder that quaked in my veins and nearly paralyzed me. But being determined, I took another step and another, and while the thrumming disquiet remained with me on the road and in the fields and right up to Bastiaan's door, I never again faltered.

    Yet when my knock of introduction on that door was met with a low call of "Yes?" I was truly halted, because with that word came the exhalation I had felt on my first visit to this place, that breath of evil that clutched for purchase on my skin. I looked to the fields running from this stone box to the cloud-bruised horizons and was instantly struck with a child's fear of being lost, or worse, trapped. The rain was indeed coming down in greater sheets, and I stood in the drench of it, the urge to flee this terrible place not unlike that which had sent me away days before.

    "Willem?" Bastiaan called.

    And so I was discovered, but this was of no surprise. Who else would it be at his door? What other visitors might he have had?

    "Willem?"

    I reached out and pushed on the door, bracing myself for the grasp of the tainted atmosphere within. Oh, it was worse, so much worse than my imagination could have conjured. The air that fell over me not only clung, but it pulled, dragged at my coat and hat and legs, fighting to usher me over that threshold, and I would have run then, would have hastened myself back to the walled city, were it not for what I saw within.

Bastiaan lay unclothed, his skin luminous in the cave of stone, and the beauty of him there replaced the blood in my veins with opiate. I stepped into the room, assisted by the vaporous fingers, and Bastiaan sat up in the bed.

"You came back," he said, exhaustion adding a drugged sensuality to his voice. "She said you wouldn't but you did."

My gaze followed his form, rolling from his weary face to the nest of his sex and back to the river-rich eyes, the examination of him bringing lightness to my head as if the motion of my eyes were the rocking of a cradle. He had taken ill, I could see this, but his malady played beneath a costume of ornate and exotic stitching that made the pallor of flesh and protuberance of bone inviting.

"She said that I disgusted you, but you came back to me."

The ill quality of his voice was not lost on me, but it played so well into the daze filling my head that it was not initially disturbing. Indeed, the sin of my thoughts unnerved and unhinged my medical judgment as the thundering pulse conquered my body like it had with his kiss. What did skin that white feel like, I wondered. Would it be cold like sculpted ice or warm like fresh milk? How would it taste on my mouth?

"I told her you'd save me," Bastiaan said. "I knew I wasn't alone in love, but she just laughed."

And it was in those words that my sense found purchase and struggled back into the current of my mind. The love of which he spoke, I could not fathom, but that it had been mocked by a woman, I understood.

"Who laughed?"

"Adda."

"You dreamed of Adda?"

"Not a dream," Bastiaan whispered. "She's an angel, and she comes to me. She said you couldn't love me, but you came back."

Why did I not leave then? Why was I not chased from Bastiaan's terrible shack by his lunatic ramblings? Excuse I can make, but explanation is beyond me. I know that I was looking on something exquisitely beautiful, and this simple superficiality conquered logic.

"I came to see... " But no words followed to finish that lie.

"To take me away?" he asked.

"Perhaps when you are recovered," I told him. "First, we have to make you well."

He smiled then, and again, my gaze was drawn over the length of him.

"She said you'd not sacrifice your position or family. She said you'd use me as a toy and cast me aside in time, but she lied."

"Bastiaan? What is this you're saying?" Because surely, I did not know, or perhaps it is better to say, I would not let myself know. "What intent have you read into me?"

A shadow flickered over his brow as if a swallow had flown between his face and the source of that which gave it light.

"You said you'd take me from this place. Have you lied to me?"

"I hoped to better your circumstance, but I said nothing of sacrifice, not of family or of soul."

"Soul," he whispered and again the sparrow flitted across his brow. "Adda was right, then."

"You're very sick, Bastiaan. Your thoughts are fevered, uncontrolled. You're in no state to understand."

With this statement, he rose from the bed. The bird's shadow now permanently affixed to his brow, cheek and chin. "Lies," he spat.

"I should go," I said, and by way of excuse, I added, "My family."

"Now you're leaving me alone with rocks and weeds and lies." He stepped forward, a lithe rippling of leg and hip that brought further agitation to my distress. "Your family doesn't know you, Willem. They can't make you feel what I can. They can't show you what I can make you see."

I backed away from the fever-dazed boy, and I would have made to run back into storm and mud had he not leapt forward and grasped me by my jacket's lapels. He kissed me again, harsh and angry. His hands grasped the side of my head and held me tight as he pressed his body to mine and began a slow rhythmic dance against me.

My physical reaction to this embrace was immediate and humiliating, but before I understood the fluid warmth on my skin, I threw Bastiaan away from me, toward the corner of the stone box. He crumpled there, again a broken and lost child.

"Your family doesn't know you," he muttered. "They can never know you."

But his nonsense had no effect on me. Shamed and angered by the brutality of what I can only describe as sexual violation, I backed to the door. Feeling the clean, wet freedom to my back I gave what I had hoped was my final look at Bastiaan and fled.

I stumbled home through the pepper and chill of storm in search of the secure walls of my uncle's house. Once there, once I had again put myself within the resonance of my family, I brought them to me with tight embraces and adoring kisses. Even still, the nightmare of Bastiaan and his perverse adoration proved unwelcome companions in the days to come. Sleeping or awake, I felt his breath on my cheek, his taste on my lips, and his body against mine, with the sinew of youth writhing against my trembling, anxious skin.

Bastiaan had found and manipulated something dark within me, and I hated him for it. I hated his youth and his stupidity and his contagious lust, which infected and spread and sickened me.

But how, after so many years of knowledge and experience, had I been weakened and made such a victim?

The answer came to me one afternoon, three days after I left Bastiaan with his rocks and weeds. I examined all I knew of myself and of Bastiaan, and found myself wanting for explanation. But then, in my study, looking at the sketched map of my heart's home, the answer emerged from the shape of a bat.

Adda, Bastiaan's sister, had indeed succumbed to the dark intentions of *uitzuiger*, then took her place among the undead. I had, after all, felt her presence in that stone house, though her body was truly deceased. Naturally, she would seek to influence the brother she'd left behind. Wanting sole possession of Bastiaan and fearing my interference, she forced us to actions that would upon unhindered evaluation repel me, thus leaving him to her manipulation.

And so I found the purifying bath of logic that cleansed both the tattered boy and myself; we were under a cursed influence, brought from the devil on the lips of the damned Adda.

Such thoughts occupied my mind as night fell. Annetje knocked to alert me to supper, but I declined in favor of pursuing my study of this matter. None of my texts offered insights, but never before had I reason to collect volumes with such content. I made note on paper of what I experienced and the general series of events that led me to my final visit to Bastiaan's house.

The Tattered Boy

Did an hour pass since Annetje's interruption? Two hours? So lost in my thoughts, I could not be sure, but it was while noting my last moments with Bastiaan that I felt the breath on my neck. The evil atmosphere descended on me as it never had before; it did not cling or grasp, but rather it pushed with palpable force, and I found myself unable to rise from my chair.

Annetje screamed from the room below, and my heart shot through with lightning. I doubled my efforts and struggled to my feet. Though able to move, walking across my study and into the hall was akin to pushing against a river's current. On the stairs, I waded against the evil exhalations as tides of sick desperation crashed in my stomach.

The stair and hall below were dark, but light from the stoked hearth spilled from the mouth of the living room. Annetje shrieked a prayer. I threw myself against the thick atmosphere, toward the light.

And the sight awaiting me in that once comfortable room, which had to my knowledge never known anything but contentment and normalcy...

Annetje hugged herself and cowered against the wall beside the fireplace, her body looking to have bloated and shrunk. This trick of the dancing flames taunted my eyes as I attempted to find my wife in the dwarfed body of the screaming woman. What met my eyes in the opposite corner was an abomination so profound that it stole the planks beneath me, leaving only vast descent before I crashed to the floor of Hell.

Bastiaan held Wouten in his arms; my son's startled eyes, made bright by firelight, saw nothing; his mouth lolled open to reveal the innocent pink tongue within. Where Wouten's throat had been was a ghastly crater with a ridge of stained skin. My son's blood poured over the bib of his shirt in a horrible cascade, and the fire's light revealed similar wounds on his exposed arms and his hands. Bits of my son lay on the floor in abattoir scraps, spat from Bastiaan's horrible, painted mouth. Across the room from this atrocity, Annetje cried for her God, not understanding, as I certainly did, that it was my offense of this God that had brought such misery to her home.

"Welcome home, Love," Bastiaan said, in a voice so high and child-like that it settled in my stomach like glass shards.

"Bastiaan," I whispered, trying to keep my tears in my eyes, praying that their sting might cleanse me. "What have you done?"

He released my tragic son's body, and it crashed to the floor. "I've come for you, Willem."

Amid the flickering light, I looked for signs of the undead on this boy, but was further sickened to find that his brutal insanity was wholly human. Adda had been at him. Of this I was certain. But while her taint was in him, it was not the entirety of him, and this made his actions all the more horrible.

"We'll finish these," Bastiaan said, stepping forward. "And then we're free."

"Willem!" Annetje cried from the corner.

I backed toward the hearth with heavy feet, shaking my head in protestation of Bastiaan's presence. He moved quickly, as he had that last day in his hovel; his face filled mine and his lips pushed forward, their red stain reeking of my son's ended life and Bastiaan's lunatic need. Those lips settled on mine, and I tasted Wouten's death, felt it run through me in a lightning bolt of grief.

As to what happened next, I'm sure I managed to strike Bastiaan or somehow cause him pain, as the next thing I remember was him kneeling before me on the carpet, sobbing, begging, clutching at the hem of my jacket with insane desperation. I kicked him then. My knee landed squarely against his nose, and he collapsed on his back. I snatched the tongs from beside the fireplace and cracked him across the brow with the weight of the iron rods until he wore a crown of blood. When his eyes closed I used the tool to lift a narrow, burning log from the hearth; this I dropped on the murderous boy's belly. The flames leapt to his shirt and his trousers in a flash, the burns reviving him. His screams filled my house, joining Annetje's prayers as I looked on.

Bastiaan squirmed and flailed as the fire devoured his body; his voice reached a shrill pitch that I thought would ring in my ears for the rest of my earthbound life.

Only when his struggles ended did I allow myself to move. I went to the sofa and retrieved the heavy blanket from its back and attempted to suffocate the flames, while shouting at Annetje to fetch water from the kitchen. But my wife did not move from her place in the corner.

I consider our salvation the only miracle I have ever witnessed. Already the quilt in my hands was catching fire and surely the house would burn down around us in minutes if it continued unchecked. But instead of licking outward and continuing over the carpet to the furniture, the floor, the walls, the ceiling, the flames crept inward, toward Bastiaan's charred body. The fire rolled into him as if pulled in the wake of a great wind.

It flickered.

It died.

Staring at this impossible consumption, I allowed myself a moment of peace, my arrogance assuring me that God meant for my punishment to end in the immolation of this tattered boy and with him, the sins we had sewn to us.

And perhaps God did forgive me, or he simply shrugged and turned away.

In the corner, Annetje squatted close to the ground, her bosom resting on her knees. The fisted knuckles of her left hand were jammed between her teeth and her right hand pointed at our murdered son, and she cried and giggled with shattered sanity.

Over the years since those terrible days with Bastiaan, I continued to tell my students, colleagues and friends that each failure brings with it a lesson.

I hope this is true, but I'm not as certain as I once was. What lesson have I learned?

Upon returning to Amsterdam, I took sabbatical as professor and returned to the role of student. I studied the dark inhabitants of what I once believed a fairyland. My philosophy had failed me once, proving all that I knew was not all that there was to know.

I lost much in my failure, but I pray that some good might still come from it. I have faith. I have knowledge but still have so much to learn. I can only pray to prove myself a devoted and attentive student. For Annetje. For Wouten.

Afterword

Michael Rowe

Hello fellow reader. I'm surprised to see you're still here. At the same time, I'm very pleased for the company. It's less lonely in here with the two of us to keep each other company as the shadows leak out of the pages of this book we've both just read, lengthening and coming alive around us.

Pull up a chair and collect yourself, and I will too.

When I finished the stories from *In the Closet, Under the Bed*, there was no warm shoulder to lean on, no embrace, not even a hand to hold, much less someone to tell me that the stories I'd just allowed into my nightmares were just stories, not a possession. What I was left with, simply, was whatever trap door in my mind Lee Thomas had opened, and the darkness that squirmed and pulsed with tenebrous life beyond it.

And there's a reason for that, a reason for why these particular stories touched the nerve of fear that most of us, as gay men, don't know is even exposed—the stories are about *us*.

The history of gay horror fiction is, by and large, a history of transposition. While this may be true of gay literature in general, unlike mainstream gay literature gay horror fiction is still in its infancy as a genre. In spite of its long and illustrious history of bending landscapes, horror fiction has traditionally been a conservative genre. Stephen King once famously compared horror writers to Rotarians, and even at the time of writing this, I'm not sure that the field doesn't remain largely a white straight boy's club. Women horror writers have often commented that they feel almost like an afterthought in the field, in spite of some of the truly stellar literature by female writers within the genre. And gay writers, well, it's not unusual to be approached at a horror writer's convention, for instance, by a well-meaning midlist straight male paperback writer who guilelessly asks if you're still writing that gay horror stuff, and if you ever think of writing something that a mainstream reader might enjoy.

An optional retort would be to point out that any sane writer would love to attract "mainstream readers" (as though the thought had never occurred to the gay horror writer to whom the question was put) and, even more honestly, that if more straight writers were tackling gay characters then maybe there wouldn't be a need for us to write them. The question is so seamlessly homophobic that most of us wouldn't even notice it. What makes gay horror "gay horror?" The sexual orientation of the author? The fact that some of the characters are gay? Is there a minimum number required to make it "gay horror," and if that number isn't met, is it "straight horror?" Why is it that when horror stories are about the lives of heterosexuals (presumably that elusive tribe of "mainstream readers") it's just horror fiction, but when a gay writer writes from his own life experience, it suddenly needs a classification that serves as a caveat for readers that it's "gay horror fiction."

In the long run, however, perhaps the most honest answer for any gay horror writers is this one—"I write what occurs to me, and I'd love it if 'mainstream readers' wanted to read it too, but I'm a writer and this is what I write. And I think it's pretty scary."

After decades—centuries, really—of having to take the stories written for a heterosexual reading audience and insert ourselves into them like an awkward, barely tolerated poor relation at a wedding to whom he was invited reluctantly, readers of gay horror fiction are beginning to have our own stories, told by our own writers. Among the advance guard of this new breed of queer horror writers is Lee Thomas, the author of this fine collection.

In the interest of full disclosure, I'll say that I don't know Lee Thomas well, but what I do know I like immensely. We've met on numerous occasions in a professional context, usually at conventions and other gatherings where horror writers are assembled to do business, meet fans, and, of course, drink the hotel bar dry. Lee's good company—very matey, yet simultaneously immaculately gracious—what the French would call *bon chic, bon genre*.

Lee and I were introduced at the World Horror Convention in New York 2005. Several people had told me that I should meet this fabulous horror writer who seemed to know everyone and seemed remarkably free of detractors. By the time Lee introduced himself to me in the hotel

Afterword

lobby, I had already recognized him on sight based on numerous enthusiastic descriptions. He was warm and affable—and yes, as strikingly tall and handsome as his numerous admirers along the full Kinsey spectrum had warned. A New Yorker by adoption at the time (though he struck me as somehow southern) he was a generous and welcoming force of nature for those of us who had come to the city from elsewhere.

Over the course of the weekend, however, those qualities were eclipsed by two things: his complete seriousness about the craft of writing, and his lack of "persona." By that time he had already been awarded the President's Medal by the Horror Writer's Association the previous year, and he was quickly developing a small but devoted and growing readership for his short fiction. At that time, his Bram Stoker Award for his first novel, the southern gothic horror tale, *Stained*, was several months away, but there was already the beginning of the undeniable buzz about his work that would culminate in the various books of Lee's that are currently in print in various editions, spanning various genres, and even pseudonyms. That first weekend will be etched in my memory as the time I met my friend, the novelist David Thomas Lord (who wrote the fine Foreword to this book) with whom I would later collaborate on the literary triad *Triptych of Terror*. That being said, when we signed the contracts for Triptych, I remember distinctly wishing that the third writer working with us had been Lee Thomas.

That weekend, Lee told me he had enjoyed the two *Queer Fear* anthologies of gay horror fiction I had edited. I in turn wondered aloud where he had been when I was putting the second volume together. I don't think that he even answered me. In my recollection, he just smiled, his brilliant ice-blue eyes twinkling like a frozen pond seen through a window in a cozy room on the coldest, brightest day in winter.

The answer was self-evident: he was where he had always been, writing. If I hadn't known who he was at the time I put the anthology together, I would soon.

Life is circuitous, and rarely more so than in the case of the lives of writers and books.

In late autumn of 2006, I received an invitation to write the Afterword to Lee's collection of short stories, *In The Closet, Under The Bed*, which is how I came to find myself in Palm Springs over Christmas reading, in manuscript form, the very book you have just finished reading. In the time between our first conversation in New York and my opening of the manila envelope containing the book, Lee's output was such that he had become a little bit famous.

I would be very surprised if your response to it wasn't similar to mine, though every reader of horror fiction brings some of their own darkness to bear when they open a book like this. As someone who has watched the evolution of what *Rue Morgue* magazine calls "the queer horror sub-genre," I was struck by the borderline-campy title of the book, and I was very interested, on various levels, to see what horrors Lee Thomas would tuck in between those covers.

In record time, and through no conscious act of will, I stopped reading these stories as a critic or anthologist, and started reading them as a reader. There is a needle-sharp ice-pick of dawning dread and recognition in these stories that disturbed me, and it took me a long time to understand why they disturbed me yet riveted me just as declaratively.

You've read the stories, so I don't need to write a review, or a precis. I'm sure you have your own favorites, moments that struck you, chilled you, for your own reasons. Maybe they're as universal as I feel mine are, maybe they aren't. That's the magic of reading in private. As a horror reader, however, let alone as a *gay* horror reader living in an epoch where my personal *Grand Guignol* (nudged into the 21st century by the daily reality of war for profit, torture, savage religion, and the daily destruction of our planet) isn't restricted to the horror of AIDS and social alienation anymore. It makes odd sense, then, that the cold dawn of gay horror fiction as a legitimate literary territory should be ushered in by authors like Lee Thomas, and books like *In The Closet, Under The Bed*.

I've already stated the reason, but here it is again: they're about our lives. Well, if not our lives, then certainly about the lives of people we know, or have known, or will know. Lives suddenly cut off from light, from sound, from anything as exotic as hope. Supernaturally nudged, directed, and manipulated by some horrible eldritch intelligence that isn't afraid of inflicting unimaginable pain, and terror beyond anything sane.

The best horror fiction takes place in a milieu, and with people, to which and whom the reader can relate. Our lives, in so many ways driven by sexual desire at the expense of emotional connection ("friction if not intimacy," as the narrator of "The Good and Gone" wryly notes) are made to pay for it, whether it means calling to horrible life

Afterword

the true shape of those desires with our own bodily fluids in "Shelter," or having the safest haven of contemporary cruising—our computer room—become a doorway to the unspeakable in "Appetite of the Cyber Tribes." And my personal favorite, "All the Faces Change," when Tim comes face to face with the demonic revenants conjured by his scorned first love, we are reminded by the author that although there was a time when faggots' "first loves" were shameful, write-off glitches in an adolescence that was already perverted, that time is long past, and there is a horrible price to pay. As we acknowledge the legitimacy of our lives and our desires, so do we acknowledge the legitimacy of our own demons. The closet doesn't hold them anymore.

For once, there is no transposition, no wondering what it would be like if the stories were in any way encompassing or acknowledging our realities as gay men. The sound of screaming in these stories is horribly familiar—the voices are our own.

Hallelujah. It's about bloody time.

MCR/09

About the Author:

Lee Thomas is the Lambda Literary Award and Bram Stoker Award-winning author of *Stained*, *Parish Damned*, *Damage*, and *The Dust of Wonderland*. In addition to numerous magazines, his short fiction has appeared in the anthologies *A Walk on the Darkside* (Roc), *Unspeakable Horror: From the Shadows of the Closet* (Dark Scribe Press), *Wilde Stories 2008: The Best of the Year's Gay Speculative Fiction* (Lethe Press), *Darkness on the Edge* (PS Publishing), and *Inferno* (Tor), among others.

Under various pseudonyms he is the author of a number of suspense and horror titles for young adult readers.

Lee currently lives in Austin, TX, where he's working on several projects, including the forthcoming titles *The Black Sun Set*, *Focus* (co-written with Nate Southard), and *Torn*. You can find him on the web at www.leethomasauthor.com.